TWISTED THIEVES

Elizabeth Rose Archer

Ebook ASIN: B0CNL66SKB
Paperback ISBN: 978-1-3999-7375-5

Cover design by: Christina Roberts
Edited by: Jodie Keegan

For my dad,
who always believed in me when I didn't
believe in myself

And for Will,
who carries on that legacy

Author's note:

Twisted Thieves contains themes of grief, loss, mentions of sexual/physical assault, descriptions of violence, blood, and gore/bodily harm, descriptions of anxiety, and foul language.

Part One

The Rules of Thievery

1

Vera

There were very few things Vera liked about her life. She did not like heights, she did not like the cold, she did not like that godsforsaken city, yet there she was on a miserably cold night in Ytavosk, clinging to the fourth-floor window ledge of a townhouse in Gambit Square.

She often wondered how she found herself scaling buildings and hunting down whispers. The answer, annoyingly, was very simple. For all her misery and complaining, there was one thing Vera did like: *magic*. She had never been one for admiring the view or seeing things in a way that was not strictly practical, but Vera could see the beauty in her magic, her power. She liked the way magic coursed through her blood and she liked being able to feel it, no matter how weak, pulsing at her fingertips.

Her night had begun with a scruffy note on the back of a shop receipt, a short train journey, and an inelegant ascent up a well-manicured pergola.

Now, Vera resisted the urge to shiver. The cold air was stiffening her limbs and drilling straight through her clothes, making her eyes and nose run uncontrollably. The Sikveyan winters made her long for the summers she'd spent on the Isles of Lattiere, for the gentle breeze and the almost sickening smell of wildflowers. Memories like those did not serve her well and she'd quickly learnt to keep her eyes on the present. She was there in Ytavosk. The city was the heart of Sikveya beating stubbornly in spite of its decaying body. It was a dreary place when you looked beyond the Palace and Gambit Square; it was a place of poverty, a den of vice and theft.

Turning away, Vera risked another glance through the window. The glass in this part of the city was crystal clear. The air was still thick with dust and smoke but tenants this side of the Ytavosk were rich enough for them to be cleaned regularly so that they could see the lights bouncing off the harbour and the ships sailing down the river.

Inside the house, Karina Vitov was sitting at a glass vanity table watching herself in the mirror. The woman was beautiful and – Vera couldn't help but notice – very young. She couldn't have been much older than Vera's twenty-one years. As she sat in her green gown, Karina began draping herself in strings of emeralds, her sure fingers used to the motion and the weight of expensive jewellery. Vera considered lifting the emeralds instead – they'd fetch a far better price – but the art was less subtle and, while Lev had tried his best to teach her, she didn't have his talent for petty theft.

Instead, Vera stretched out her frozen fingers and reached towards Karina.

Looking through a victim's mind was complex art. Each part became a tangible thing as the glowing strings all tangled together in a ball. Memories were blue, feelings were red, dreams were a hazy white, and secrets were gold.

Vera Datsyuk could steal secrets, and she did not have to steal trust first.

When she was younger, she had doubted the value of her ability. She'd thought stealing secrets was useless when she could earn them instead. It was only after she had moved to the city that she realised just what her power meant. It was true, rumours could be whispered into ears; they could catch the wind, spread like a plague through the streets and devour those in close proximity. They were not effective at proving someone's innocence or guilt, at starting or ending a scandal. Their origins were often too ambiguous, and they were written off as idle gossip or bitter whisperings. By stealing secrets, Vera's power could expose the truth in those whisperings. She acquired proof. She turned hearsay into gospel.

She was no fool; she knew there were powers out there that were stronger than hers, that her grasp on the art was flimsy at best, but it was enough to survive.

A cold breeze pressed Vera against the wall and sent a shock of fear to her heart. She was determined not to look down, so she shut her eyes for a moment and took three deep breaths. As she regained her balance, she opened her eyes and reached out once more for the wires of Karina's mind.

Lev had left her the note the night before, tucked in the door jam, so she knew vaguely what she was looking for. He often picked up bits of information from the restaurant and left them for her. There were no pure acts of kindness in the city, so she gave him a small percentage of her profits in return.

As she worked to detangle the golden threads in Karina's mind and picked each one apart with delicate fingers, Vera saw Karina's secrets as if they were her own: a handful of pennies stolen as a child, the hatred she harboured for her husband, the guilt she felt as she refused to be walked down the aisle by her father. And then there it was. The rumour Lev had heard materialised before her, transformed into truth.

Vera watched the face of a young man dance across her vision. He was closer in age to Karina than her husband was. She kissed him and he brushed the hair back from her face, the gesture delicate, soft in its execution. Karina's eyes fluttered shut.

Vera had no doubt of this woman's situation: her family had needed money, so they'd traded their daughter, handed her to the old man and taken the money in exchange. She was young and beautiful and could give her husband an heir for his trade empire. Vera was almost sorry for what she was about to do, but as her stomach rumbled and she remembered the backlog of rent due and the feeling disappeared as quickly as it had come. Ytavosk did not let people feel sorry – it barely let them survive.

Reaching into her satchel, her fingers frustratingly slow, Vera pulled out a glass vial. She removed the cork stopper then reached back towards Karina's mind. She curled her fingers and tugged softly at the gold thread, feeling it come loose like a pulled tooth. Karina reached up towards her temple and winced. Vera held her breath and wished, not for the first time, that her magic could be stronger, seamless, *better*.

She waited a beat and then another, until Karina went back to adjusting the bodice of her dress. The string of light danced in the palm of Vera's hand before she guided it into the vial and replaced the stopper.

She'd left her conscience in a gutter long ago, concerned more with the emptiness in her stomach and the lack of roof over her head than people who hoarded jewels and could smile their way out of any scrape.

Vera did not have strings of emeralds and she did not have a pretty, forgivable smile. The cold air and dry summers had made her smile coarse and tightened the skin around her eyes. Years of bordering on starvation had made her skull jut out beneath her skin. There was nothing lovely or charming about her. Sometimes she mourned the girl she had been, the girl with a youthful face and a voice in her head telling her right from wrong, but each night she had to remove her glass eye and she remembered how weak she had been, how vulnerable she had felt. That feeling tended to put things into perspective. Vera did not need to be beautiful or delicate, she needed to stay alive.

She needed to get out of that godsdamned city.

Bidding Karina a silent goodbye, Vera began her descent from the window ledge. She had what she needed and there was no need to linger on the edge of a life she'd never have.

Vera's descent was about as graceful as the climb up – that was to say, not graceful at all. Her feet missed the stone rests a few times and she almost plummeted to her death.

She was relieved when she finally hit the ground in the front garden, narrowly avoiding a row of shrubbery. The grass crunched beneath her feet, frozen by the night air. Her limbs were shaking, though she could not tell if that was from the cold or the height from which she'd just come down. It was undoubtedly the most bitter winter Vera had seen in Sikveya and it needled her skin.

It was Vera's sixth winter in the city. She had quickly learnt that the winters here were more brutal than they had been back home on the Isles. There, she had been able to weather the cold in a hat and coat, with her hands tucked into her pockets and sometimes an extra blanket at night. But those winters were mild in comparison to the icy rage Sikveya threw at her each year.

Vera tucked her face into her collar and pulled her fur hat further down over her eyes in a desperate attempt to cover every sliver of exposed skin. Now that her feet were firmly on the ground and the threat of imminent death was no more, she was able to truly take in her surroundings.

Gambit Square was a beautiful place full of clean town houses. They were painted in pastel colours to match the flowers in the window boxes and were set out in neat rows. Each one had its own stable, a manicured garden, and a private boathouse down by the river. The streets were wider in the square than they were in the rest of the city, the cobbled roads more even and filled with flower markets and stalls selling pastries. Gambit Square was accustomed to the more seemly, pretty trades. From where Vera was standing, she could see it all. She watched the civilised folk make their way home from their jobs to settle in for the night beside warm fires.

Across the street from the Vitov house, two children played in the centre of the square. A woman in a long black dress with her hair pinned back in a tight bun stood watching the children. She was too old to be their mother, but her eyes were too full of love to just be a governess. Perhaps, Vera thought, she was their grandmother or an aunt. Her eyes were trained on the children as they laughed and chased each other. Their cheeks were full, their smiles broad, and their hair was not thinned by malnourishment.

Avoiding attention, Vera stuck to the shadows and snuck out of the garden. She held her bag close to her chest, hugging the leather to stop the vials from clinking together. Vera hated that to steal from the rich meant travelling to the outskirts of the city. It meant she had to take the train.

Gambit Square was beautiful because it was so separate from the rest of Ytavosk. The coal smoke still blackened the cream walls of the houses, but it was far enough away from the squalor that the beggars did not find homes on their front stoops. Vera knew that the intention was to keep a strong divide between Ivenko's Cauldron and Gambit Square, to create two versions of one city. One version was built on wealth and prosperity and one, well, *wasn't.* It served as a reminder too. The wealthy could see what would become of them should they fail to keep their eyes on commerce or lack loyalty to the crown and the poor had something to reach for, an unattainable dream to keep them from rioting or killing themselves. Vera liked the defiance she felt whenever she breached that divide, when she brought the darkness of Ivenko's Cauldron to their polished doorsteps.

The walk to the railway station was brief, and soon Vera found herself shoving her way through the crowd lining the track. That was the one part of Gambit Square they never tried to clean up. It was disgusting and dingy and the station was little more than a platform and a small waiting room which leaked but provided a shelter for those with nowhere else to go. It was by no means pretty, but it was practical. Things in Ytavosk could not be both.

The railway ran along the river's edge from Gambit Square to Ivenko's Cauldron, stopping along the way to pick up cargo from the dockyards. It was a good way to get from one end of Ytavosk to the other for those without money for carriages. The trains were not designed for passengers, but each time they stopped to pick up crates of imported goods people crammed themselves into the small cars and soon it became the norm – people pressed together between crates of cloth and fruits grown in hotter countries.

There were no train times; the trains came and went as the conductors chose, annoying in their irregularity. But when the passengers had no money, they had no say in the matter.

Vera forced her way onto the eastbound platform, squeezing herself between an elderly man with a shabby briefcase and a woman with three children crowded around her ankles. The man held tight to his briefcase, the woman held tight to the collars of her children's coats, and Vera held tight to her satchel full of secrets. They all waited impatiently, keeping their heads down and their possessions close as the train approached, the tracks screaming like a wounded animal. Vera, along with the crowd on the platform, pulled her collar up to cover her mouth as the air filled with soot and smoke so thick it was almost opaque.

The train drew to a stop and Vera was pushed forward with the surge of the crowd. It would have been polite to wait and let the exiting passengers off first, but the train did not wait for manners. Vera shoved her way into the stuffy car, one hand holding her collar, the other pinning her satchel to her stomach. She felt the glass through the worn leather and pinched the top of the bottle. She hoped it would be enough to buy a hot meal, something to ease the hunger that bore through her.

The trip to Ivenko's Cauldron was not a long one and after a short while she was shoving her way out of the confines of the train to be met with the sticky, damp air of the Cauldron.

The Ruined District.

The Cauldron was named after a reformer who had come to the slums of Ytavosk to bring them back to life. As the story went, he had stayed too long and had fallen victim to the chaos that seemed to thrive there like vines on an uninhabited building. It was described as the melting pot of people. In Ivenko's Cauldron, it didn't matter who you were or where you had come from, once you entered its streets of vice and villainy, your name and connections were forgotten. Or in poor Artyom Ivenko's case, your name was put on the map of Ytavosk for tourists to laugh at.

Ivenko's Cauldron, despite its dirt and disgrace, was Vera's favourite part of the city. The rest of the Ytavosk was boring, too organised, too restricted by propriety. The Cauldron was different. She liked the confused equality that came from sitting together at the bottom of the food chain. It really was a place of ruin, a hub of criminal activity and evil outgoings, smuggling and dirty trade. It was a huddle of streets rammed with people trying to survive.

It may have been loud and utterly disorganised, but it was the place that had welcomed Vera when she'd first come to the city.

Now, Vera made her way home, winding through the streets of Ivenko's Cauldron. The streets got tighter there, almost suffocating her. Wooden panels made makeshift bridges across wide, uncovered drains and laundry lines were strung across alleyways so low that anyone taller than Vera would struggle not to get tangled up in them. She'd walked that way with Lev more times than she could count.

Once, he'd forgotten to pay attention and had got his neck caught in a line. "One day," he muttered in an irritated voice, "I'm going to accidentally hang myself from one of these."

Vera looked at him as she slipped easily beneath a line. "I don't have that problem."

"I think you were made for this city, Vera," Lev grumbled.

She wondered if that was true, that perhaps she *had* been made for Ytavosk. She had no trouble wandering those streets, slipping through the cracks in the walls, sifting through the minds of drunkards and addicts. She knew she had to take something back from the city, that she needed to use it to her advantage.

No, she'd thought bitterly, *this city was made for me*.

Now, she arrived at the boarding house. She'd moved into the decrepit house six years ago almost immediately after she'd stumbled onto Ytavosk's ports. The exterior was not impressive; the sign was hanging at an angle, the curtains inside were moth-eaten and barely covered the grimy windows, and the steps were dangerously crooked. The reason she loved it so much was because it ran like a house with a family living in it, though she had only met one of the other residents. There was a kitchen which she had access to, a shared bathroom, a living area, and she had a small shoebox of a bedroom upstairs. It was just big enough for a bed, a set of drawers, and a small desk tucked away in the corner. The owner of the house, Mrs Hanovich, meandered around the place, constantly carrying a basket full of rags which she never seemed to do anything with, and she always called out to her tenants when she heard the door open. The fire was always lit, though the house remained quite dark, and there was always a sense that you were not alone. Having been deprived of it for so long, Vera liked that feeling.

Vera tried to enter the house quietly, but her key got jammed in the door and she had to wrestle it back out again. The second she stepped over the threshold, she heard Mrs Hanovich calling out to her.

"Good evening," Vera replied with considerably less enthusiasm.

She had been avoiding Mrs Hanovich for the past week. Her rent was due and, while she had it, she was holding out just a little while longer so that the dent in her pocket didn't feel quite so deep. She wanted some new gloves, though that dream seemed far off.

She was not lucky enough this time and Mrs Hanovich met her at the bottom of the stairs with her hand held out.

Mrs Hanovich was a stocky woman, with long grey hair pinned up on top of her head in big looping curls. She was always a bit red in the face as if she'd been running, and her hands always flapped as she spoke. She was not a mean woman, but she was firm. She took exactly what she was owed and a little more for the trouble.

Vera stared at Mrs Hanovich for a long moment before the woman said in a tone that made her feel like a child, "Vera, you know what I'm waiting for."

"I don't have any money on me," Vera lied. She did have the money. She kept it with her in the safest place she knew – the bodice of her dress – at all times. There was no better protector than Vera herself with a knife in her hand and the proof of a scandal at her fingertips.

Mrs Hanovich frowned. "Then you can leave."

Vera sighed and rolled her eyes, removing a fold of cash from her clothes.

"You know," the landlady said, "Lev is always on time with his payments."

"He's better paid than I am." Vera counted out the money.

"Then get a proper job," Mrs Hanovich snapped, taking the money from Vera.

Vera sighed and muttered under her breath, "Or you could be a bit more lenient."

As it happened, Vera couldn't get a proper job. She was not in the country legally and she had no paperwork. Her name was not her real name. She would not reveal herself to a world that had very strict and very cruel laws against people like her.

"You have to pay your way through the world, and the quicker you learn that the better," Mrs Hanovich replied, shifting the basket on her hip. "Lev knows that. You spend enough time with him, his attitude should have rubbed off on you."

"Well, it hasn't," Vera hissed, turning away from the woman before she said something that would get her kicked out of the house for good.

Mrs Hanovich had always made her preference for Lev very clear. She called him a sweet boy and was constantly muttering that Lev was too good for the city, that it had never given back what he was owed. It was true – Lev was kinder than Vera, more patient and thoughtful, and she knew that he was more worthy of Mrs Hanovich's praise than she was. He was easier to love, and Vera found that people only wanted to love you if it was easy.

The older woman let out an irritated sigh and tucked the money into her apron pocket. "Don't be late next month, Vera. You're on probation."

Vera felt the urge to take Mrs Hanovich's apron strings and strangle her with them, but she thought she'd better not. She didn't want to risk her place at the house. Instead, she looked down at the remainder of her money – a few pitiful notes and coins – and stomped upstairs to her room.

2

SOFIYA

"Sofiya, come quick, I'd like you to meet someone!"

Sofiya, at twenty-three, was still taking orders from her mother. *Sofiya, come here! Sofiya, head up. Sofiya, do not look so miserable, you're not being sent to the slaughterhouse.* Sofiya found it very unfair that *she* had to look desirable when most of the men she was being introduced to were three times her age and seemed to find it impossible to keep their mouths closed while chewing. She also did liken the art of matchmaking to being sent to the slaughterhouse, though she thought it best to keep that to herself. Sofiya had no choice but to obey, smile, and hold her head up high as her mother, Queen Ruslana Meskov of Sikveya, paraded her around like a show pony.

The ballroom was absurdly extravagant even by royal standards. When Sofiya had made her entrance at the beginning of the evening she'd tripped over a real swan sauntering past and had almost tumbled headfirst down the stairs. She watched the room now with her head up and the corners of her mouth pinned in a tight smile. The ballroom was made up of three separate rooms joined by broad marble arches. Each room was decorated in the same fashion with gilded mirrors stacked from floor to ceiling and dozens of rubies and emeralds embedded in each golden frame, and the floor was a perfectly smooth checkerboard of cream and sage tiles. In the centre of each room hung a crystal chandelier. Her mother gasped every time she entered one the candlelit rooms as though it was her first time seeing them. Sofiya thought they were garish.

She glanced towards her mother now. The Queen was waving her hand wildly in her direction, gesturing towards a man with thinning hair standing beside her. Her mother was about as subtle as a Vorian moose ploughing through the snow. Embarrassment seared Sofiya's stomach. Queen Ruslana Meskov of Sikveya was an avid drinker, though she was not good at *holding* her drink. Her eyes were wild, her tiara was slipping from her head, and at some point throughout the evening, the straps of her dress had slipped from her shoulders.

Sofiya's mother was not a responsible queen. The old, well-trodden thought slipped through Sofiya's head. *This woman is running a country. And I'm doing nothing about it.*

Moving towards her mother, Sofiya took a deep breath. Her corset felt too tight and the orchestra currently gracing them with a waltz wasn't quite loud enough to cover the sound of blood pulsing in her ears. She wanted to just sit down for a moment. She wanted to go to bed and sleep for three days.

She wanted to find a girl she didn't know and hide somewhere dark, with nothing to think about but the nameless lover.

She did none of those things. Instead, she straightened her spine and held her hand out for a kiss. The suitor's lips were wet, and she could feel the thin hairs of his moustache against the back of her hand.

"A pleasure to meet you, Your Highness."

"Please, Princess Sofiya will do just fine."

The Queen cut her a sharp glare. Ever the obedient princess, Sofiya smiled graciously.

The man took his hand back and dragged it though his hair, moving a few strands to cover the baldness at his crown. He nodded and stammered, "I–Oh, yes of course, Princess Sofiya."

"If you don't mind my asking," Sofiya began. "Who are you?"

"Sofiya," Ruslana hissed. She opened her mouth and closed it again and Sofiya realised that her mother didn't know who she was talking to either.

"Lord Oleg Tresovich." He turned back to Sofiya. "I knew your father."

Join the queue, Lord Oleg, my father was somewhat of a public menace. "Oh?"

"We used to discuss matters of… business together. Yes, business."

Sofiya got the distinct feeling that they discussed something a lot more crude than business. In fact, she had heard the rumours herself. They were never exposed as truths, but rumours were enough to complete the miserable image she had of her father. Like the string of kings and queens before him, he was frivolous, self-serving, and utterly irresponsible.

"Oh," she muttered, forcing the disgust from her face.

Oleg took her hand in his. It was slick with sweat. "May I–"

"Sofiya!"

Saying a silent prayer, Sofiya turned towards the bright voice. Before her stood a man around her age with hair the colour of honey. He was lean, objectively beautiful, and by far Sofiya's favourite person in the room at that moment because he reached his hand towards her and asked for a dance. From the outside, the pull of his lips looked like a smile, but Sofiya knew better than that. She knew Stas very well, in fact.

Returning Stas' smirk and releasing a very unladylike sound of disgust, Sofiya followed Stas away from her mother and the old man.

Stas looped his arm around Sofiya's shoulder. "You resisted the urge to wipe your hand on your dress. You're my hero."

"It's still wet," Sofiya said as she turned towards Stas sharply and, like the mature lady she was, wiped her hand down the sleeve of his immaculate dinner jacket. He shoved her away as a bright laugh lit his face and Sofiya felt the tension in her shoulders ease.

Once upon a time, Sofiya had been betrothed to Stas. Their fathers had arranged it and they were to be wed the following year. Her dress had been sewn by hand; each bead, each thread of lace had been secured with a tiny stitch by a seamstress in Gambit Square. Her father had died suddenly, and the plans had fallen apart as quickly as they had come together. She was glad for it now – she liked having Stas as a friend, though she often considered him to be more than that. He was her ally too, and she was his.

Stas pulled Sofiya towards him as the music drew to a close and the orchestra readied itself for another song. Sofiya watched as the violinists stretched out the cricks in their necks and the brass section gathered their breath. She'd always liked to hear orchestras play, but their talent was wasted in a room like that, where most of the guests were too drunk to take in the beauty of their instruments or the skill with which they were played.

They were too drunk or too self-important to take in anything at all. At the back of the room sat three large tables brimming with imported foods – quiches, cakes, golden pastries, and tiered platters of berries and crackers. The guests were shovelling bite after bite into their mouths with little to no regard for the time or effort taken to prepare such a feast. The entire court seemed to follow the Queen's lead. They drained their glasses and filled their stomachs.

Stas pulled Sofiya out of her angry reverie and into a gloriously slow dance. They had both been raised for those kinds of scenes – the ballrooms, the dances, the relentlessly straight spines and bright faces – and yet they seemed to be the only ones in the room keeping up with the etiquette.

"So," Stas began. "He looked fun."

"Incredibly," Sofiya replied, looking up at his amused face. "Though her vision escapes me."

"Marry you off like cattle, have some grandchildren–"

"Watch those grandchildren go bald at twenty," Sofiya grumbled. "Ah, yes, I see it now."

Stas bit back a laugh. "Oh, he wasn't terrible looking."

"He was three times my age, Stas."

"That's three times closer to death. You'd still have time to get a new husband."

"I don't want a husband," Sofiya snapped.

Stas fell silent. He adjusted his hand on her shoulder, took a step towards her then one back, carrying her with him. Something moved across his face, carving its way across his features. It was a kind of soft melancholy, an understanding. She did not want a husband any more than Stas wanted a wife.

"And anyway," Sofiya continued. "If I *did* have to take a husband, I would at least take one with some kind of political gain or monetary value – not some beat up old man who has spent more time in the parlour of a gentleman's club than behind a desk."

"He–"

"I'm not done."

Stas laughed.

Sofiya continued. "*And* I would make sure he wasn't a further embarrassment to the throne. How are we ever going to bring respect back to the family name if we keep breeding with irresponsible, selfish, spoiled, rats?"

Stas cleared his throat and Sofiya looked up to see that he was smirking. "Can I speak now, please?" he asked.

Sofiya nodded reluctantly.

"I have money," he said. "And a good name. And, even if I do say so myself, dazzling good looks."

Sofiya couldn't hold back the soft bubble of laughter rising in her throat. "And I have a drunk mother, a dead father, two spoiled, selfish little siblings, and a ballroom full of people who would rather stuff themselves until they are sick than give anything to the people who genuinely need it," she said. "Why would *you* want to marry *me*?"

"Because together we could have freedom. We could

perform our duties as we must and keep the company we truly wanted." Stas wasn't laughing now.

That much was true and Sofiya couldn't deny it, but deep down a part of her longed to live a bolder life. She wanted to be able to stand before her country and say *this is who I have chosen — this person is right for me and for Sikveya.* As much as she loved him and appreciated his company, Stas would never be that person. Together they would live a life that held too many secrets in a world like theirs.

Sofiya had to be pragmatic; she could not be selfish. She was not the most important thing in her life.

"You're also the heir to the throne. Who doesn't want to be a king?"

"Prince consort."

"Same difference."

Stas spun Sofiya again then bowed, never once letting go of her hand. Sofiya curtsied. She looked around the room and steadied herself before Stas pulled her in for another dance.

Sofiya listened to the echoes of laughter and the rise and fall of the music.

The ballroom was often shrouded in whispers. She sometimes wondered if that was why the music was always played so loud, if the musicians were under strict instructions to cover the sound of gossip spreading from one guest to the other. The mind was a strange thing. Its elements were so often stolen and sold that the memories, the feelings, the dreams, and the secrets were no longer sacred.

A secret without proof was little more than a rumour, but rumours still spread and dragged her family through the dirt. Dragged *her* through the dirt.

Something was stirring in the room now. Sofiya could feel it.

Breaking her from her reverie, an unfamiliar hand landed on Sofiya's arm. She pulled away instinctively, turning sharply towards the man; he was barely able to stand as he bowed to her. "Your Highness."

Sofiya could practically feel her mother glaring at her, so she smiled and curtseyed and bit down the bile rising in her throat. She could smell the alcohol on his breath. She bid him good evening, though really, she wanted to tell him to never lay eyes on her again. She could see his gaze drifting up and down her figure to her hips, her full bust, her thick waist. He shot her a watery smile, his eyes leery.

"No," Sofiya said sharply. "I'm sorry – actually, I am not sorry. I am not doing this." She turned on her heel and stalked towards the balcony doors. She could hear the whispers as she moved through the stationary crowds. They were talking about something, their eyes darting shiftily around the room. Sofiya knew there was a high chance that they were whispering about her family.

That was the problem with their world. The inner workings of the mind were not secret, they were not sacred, they were things to be stolen and manipulated. Nothing could be safely tucked into the back of your mind. Every time a rumour rose in the ballroom Sofiya felt her heart stutter, felt her dread rise and flood her body like somewhere deep down inside her, a dam had broken. *What do you know?* She wanted to shout at them, bombard them with questions, lay her worry to rest.

She tried to push down the anger she felt towards her mother, towards the woman who threw men at her as she drank herself senseless. It was as though Sofiya's future were a game to her but she was too lazy to explain the rules. She tried to blame her mother for all their secrets, but she knew that wasn't strictly fair. Sofiya had plenty of her own.

As she approached the vast glass doors, gilded in gold and various jewels to match the mirror frames, the guards pushed them open. She was immediately hit by a cool breeze. She lifted her face to the wind, feeling it lift the sweat-soaked hairs off the nape of her neck. She heard the doors slam shut behind her.

Sofiya knew she was being ridiculous. She knew she was overacting, but she was so tired of standing straight and having her godsdamned hand kissed. She could imagine the whispers coursing through the ballroom like an airborne disease, but at least with the doors shut she could no longer hear them.

From this vantage point, she could see the entire city, from the soft glow of Gambit Square to the shrill light of Ivenko's Cauldron. She could even see stars far above the smoke of Ytavosk – she doubted many people within the city saw them. She looked down into the streets. Though she could not see them, she gave a silent apology to her subjects. She was one of the vultures slowly bringing decay to Sikveya.

Sofiya wanted so badly to change it, but she couldn't seem to find her way in. She had been trying for so long and yet her feet were stuck to the ground, her progress non-existent. She was to find a husband and then what? Was she expected to hand her country over to him, to let someone else lead Sikveya? In what world would that be practical? There were no signs that her mother had any intention of raising her into any position of power, of letting her be a better queen. She had not been welcome in any political discussions, her voice had never been listened to.

They know something. The thought came to her unbidden, the worry seizing her every thought. *A storm is brewing, and they know something.* Whispers were never good. They were something to be exploited. They were fragile things, like the little glass trinkets her father had hoarded.

She had stolen one of those trinkets once, kept it for a month before he'd noticed, then he'd taken it back after one too many drinks and dropped it. It had smashed into a thousand tiny glass pieces and as Sofiya cried, her father had hit her hard across the face.

Even now, amongst the muffled voices behind the balcony doors, she could almost hear her father's voice droning on about the power the Meskovs held, the right they had to wield it, and most importantly, the line of succession. *Our heir is unstoppable*, he'd say, *our heir will hold this country together as we have done.* She was certain he had never been speaking about her. She was also certain that her predecessors had never held the country together. But he was gone now, and all that stood between Sofiya and her throne, her freedom, and her *right* was her mother. Her mother and whatever secrets she held.

Princess Sofiya Meskov of Sikveya, heir to the Sikveyan throne and sure saviour of their country, pushed that thought to the back of her mind. She needed to be stronger than those rumours, she needed to hold her head higher than those who spoke of them. She took a deep breath and marched back towards the party.

3

LEV

Lev was running late. He was always running late. In fact, Lev's life seemed to be a continuous string of missed appointments and disappointed sighs.

And now he was manically searching his room for his waistcoat which he was sure he'd thrown onto his desk chair the night before. It had mysteriously disappeared. He found himself in this position – frantically searching for things he hadn't put in a sensible place – most days, but he was yet to learn his lesson.

Lost in his search, the sound of a door slamming shut startled him. He felt it reverberate around his room as though it made the earth shake. Vera was home; she had a way of crashing through the world. And as though confirming it, the slammed door was followed by the sound of glass clattering through the thin walls and her voice cursing in the soft swoops and dives of her home language. He recognised a few of the words; after hearing them so often, he'd asked her to teach him what they meant. He found it difficult to remember her language, but he remembered her curses. They were a regular part of her vocabulary.

Lev turned back to his search, picking up his clothes and tossing them onto his bed.

"Where are you?" he muttered to himself, trying to coax the clothes out of their hiding place. One of these days, he promised, he was going to be organised. Then his gaze landed on a strip of black velvet tucked beneath his desk chair and he decided that being tidy was for the uninteresting. He grabbed it as he left and locked the door behind him.

As Lev bounded down the stairs, he caught sight of the clock in the entryway. He was almost an hour late which for him was almost on time. The only constant in Lev's life was his tardiness. It was as though his own personal clock was an hour out from everyone else's, like he'd been set wrong in the first place, and he was constantly trying to catch up.

"Good evening, Lev!" Mrs Hanovich called from behind her desk. She was counting out a stack of money, setting the notes into piles of ten ykas, and humming a disjointed melody under her breath.

Lev smiled at her and retrieved a small leather pouch from his pocket. He dropped it on the counter. "It should be all there."

"I'm sure it's fine," she replied.

You wouldn't tell me if it wasn't, Lev thought, but he knew better than to say it aloud for fear that she might start charging him properly.

Lev had lived in the boarding house for almost ten years. Mrs Hanovich's love for him was shown clearly in the leftovers she gave him and the money she docked off his rent. He wasn't sure what he'd done to be on the receiving end of her selective good nature, but he was hardly going to discourage it.

When he'd first arrived at the boarding house, the place had been all but deserted. There was no sign, the front porch had half caved in, and the windows were smashed and covered with sheets of newspaper.

Lev had knocked on the door which had half come off its hinges and when no one answered, he pushed it open and went inside anyway. He heard someone cluttering around and he knew he should have run but he was so desperate for somewhere to go that didn't cost the entirety of his wages that he ventured further in. When he got to the kitchen, he saw a woman in her forties throwing various odd-looking items into a stew pot.

He watched her for a moment, scared to be seen, before she turned around and said, "Can I help you?"

"Uh," Lev stuttered. He'd been a nervous boy at twelve. "Are there rooms vacant? There's a sign out front–"

"You're too young to be looking for a place to stay. Where are your parents?"

Lev opened his mouth to speak. The words were too fresh, too raw to speak.

When he said nothing, the woman tutted and said, "Dead, huh?"

Lev nodded. It was partially true.

She grabbed a bowl from the cupboard beneath the sink and spooned some of the lumpy liquid into it. When she handed it to him, Lev took it awkwardly, not wanting to tell her that it smelt odd and he'd actually rather go hungry. "Eat up," she said. "You're all bones. This place kills the weak for sport."

As Lev reluctantly ate the stew, the woman introduced herself as Mrs Hanovich.

"Take any room you want," she said. "The business is new. You're the only one here."

Lev had taken the room directly at the top of the stairs.

Over time, the place had filled out and now all of the rooms were occupied. It was rare for Lev to encounter anyone but Vera, who seemed to storm in and out of his life like a stray cat treading mud into the carpet. The house was full to the brim of crooks and criminals all operating at different times of day. Eventually, the door was fixed, they'd all been given official keys, the windows were replaced, and a self-explanatory sign reading 'BOARDING HOUSE' was hung above the porch. The first time he referred to the place as home, a melancholic guilt had coursed through his chest.

Now, Lev tied his cloak around his shoulders and smiled at Mrs Hanovich. "I have to run," he said, tapping his fingers once on the counter.

She waved him off with a wash rag muttering sweet boy in his wake.

Despite his words, Lev had enough dignity and self-respect to keep him from running to catch the train.

For once it seemed time was on his side and the train pulled up as he got to the station. As it approached, Lev pulled his cloak up to cover his mouth and shoved his waistcoat into his pocket to protect it from the coal smoke.

He pushed his way onto the train and almost gagged as air thick with human sweat filled his lungs.

Vera always liked to keep her head down when she took the train. They had ridden it a handful of times together and she always ducked her head into her collar and stared at her feet. Lev preferred to watch other people, to see how they behaved. He liked to watch as a man slipped a handful of berries from one of the crates into his pocket or as a cat peeped out from the top of a woman's bag. He liked those moments the most: the ones trapped between the unmarked pages in a journal. He liked the commutes, the spontaneous conversations, the small scenes no one else paid attention to. He liked interesting people; he liked it when people confused him.

Lev was very good at picking up pieces of other people's conversations and when he heard a man beside him whisper "Did you hear?" in a conspicuous voice, Lev couldn't help but think, *no, I did not.*

He was not like Vera, he didn't have magic at his disposal, but that didn't stop him from catching rumours. He was a thief nevertheless, and a good one at that.

As the man spoke, Lev pulled out a small scrap of paper and a pencil and wrote: *Emil Ossman. Affair with older woman. In it for money.* He tucked the note into his trouser pocket ready to slip it under Vera's door when he got back to the boarding house.

Lev glanced around the carriage now and his eyes landed on a woman standing by the door. She was not particularly interesting upon first glance, but the more he watched her, the more out of place she appeared, as though his eyes were adjusting, and the finer details of her character were slowly coming into focus. He was sure that she was not meant to be in this scene, that she had crawled from The Royal Theatre onto the set of a gaudy, undercooked play you'd find in Ivenko's Cauldron. The copper hair poking out from beneath her hood was too bright, the velvet of her cloak too fine. The strangest – or the most interesting – thing about her, however, was that she was not covering her mouth. It was customary to shield your mouth and nose on the train. All travellers were regularly exposed to the thick smoke and were all too aware of how much it clogged their lungs. She was either new to that part of the city or making a quick visit. Lev could hardly imagine why.

The girl seemed to notice his gaze, tilting her head slightly to the side and raising one eyebrow. Beneath the shadow of her hood, he could just make out her features – the rounded cheeks and bright eyes of a girl who had never known an uncomfortable life. She looked clean, wealthy, and entirely out of place.

Lev resisted the urge to straighten his own collar in a vain attempt to make himself look less scruffy.

He was grateful when his stop arrived.

The horn sounded above their heads and the doors to the carriage rattled open to Lev's right. Immediately, the crowd on the outside surged inwards and the passengers inside forced their way out. Lev, having taken that same train every day since he'd landed his job at The Eva, was used to the mad rush. The girl with the copper hair seemed less accustomed to it. She stumbled and her eyes widened. Instinctively, Lev reached out and grabbed her arm, dragging her with him as he shoved his way off the train and holding fast to her wrist as the doors shut and the crowd dissipated.

She glanced at him. "Thank you." She was well spoken, her voice crisp.

Lev smiled and squeezed her hand once before turning away from her. Without looking at it, Lev slipped the girl's ring into his breast pocket for safe keeping. He knew better than to examine his findings whilst he could still be caught. As he strode across the platform, he slipped his hands into his pocket to feel for the scrap of paper, but it was gone. He looked around to see if had landed on the pavement, but he couldn't find it.

With a shrug, Lev paused for a moment and breathed in the fresh air. While the station itself was not pretty, the district beyond it was. Lev loved Gambit Square. He loved the way it seemed to glow in spite of the dirt and grime that covered the rest of the city. It was the sea gleaming beneath the sun despite the oncoming storm. He even liked the people. They felt like an abnormal species to him, the kind he learned about at school. They were completely unaware of the rest of the city, the poverty, the lack of food and jobs and education. Lev was never quite sure if they were turning a blind eye or whether they were genuinely just naive, and it amazed him. He could also admit that he liked the people because they were incredibly, unapologetically rich. Lev knew very well that rich, ignorant people were the easiest to steal from.

He had started out with a bit of spontaneous pickpocketing and swiping food from the carts as he passed them. As his need for money grew, he gave up stealing pocket watches and other easy things and started lifting cash. Lev was very good at that. He'd tried many times to teach

Vera, but she'd always preferred the more magical approach to theft. She didn't have his sleight of hand or easy charm.

"How are you still so poor when you steal so much?" Vera had asked him once.

They'd been out together, scavenging for something to eat. Lev had a wad of money stowed away in his room back at the boarding house, but he couldn't spend it.

He plucked an apple off a cart and handed it to her. She took a bite and curled up her nose, bored by the powdery texture and lack of flavour.

"They're better back in the Isles," she said, taking another reluctant bite. "We have orchards there. They don't spend months on ships."

Vera rarely spoke of her home on the Isles of Lattiere. All Lev really knew was that, for whatever reason, she'd been forced to leave and she hadn't been back since.

He didn't answer her question and she didn't push it.

That night Lev had felt a heavy weight settle on his heart, chafing against his empty stomach and the bone-deep coldness he felt. He'd lain awake and watched the sun rise, listening as Vera's door shut behind her as she left.

Despite the cold and the hunger, Lev had fees to pay. When he was asked, he took the money from beneath the floorboards and handed it over.

Now, Lev looped past private boutiques and bakeries, all painted in the pale colours of Gambit Square. He didn't take anything from passersby. Instead, he soaked in the rich scents as he passed the bakery and the florist, the colours unnaturaly bright in the dull winter evening. He wondered, not for the first time, how they managed to keep this part of the city looking so fresh and alive despite the cold winter air and lingering dampness.

Past the riverside markets sat a small square of restaurants and coffee houses, all lined with beautiful entryways and perfectly manicured hanging baskets. Each shopfront was illuminated with the soft glow of the paraffin streetlamps dangling above their heads, the cobblestones reflecting the buttery yellow light.

That was where The Eva was situated. The exterior of the restaurant was a grand white stone building decorated with gold and bronze railings over the windows, kitted out to look like a gilded cage with purple wisteria crawling over the walls in controlled bursts. Somehow both regal and quaint, the building fit the landscape. From the windows, you could just about make out the river and on the opposite bank, the Palace came into view.

Lev crossed the square, darting between two horse drawn carriages, his feet slipping on the rain-slicked cobblestones. He pulled his crinkled waistcoat from his pocket.

As he drew nearer to The Eva, Fillip, the restaurant valet, opened the door for him. He was a tall and thin man who somewhat resembled one of those flimsy clothing lines hanging from the rooftops with his coattails fluttering in the wind. "Good evening, Valensky," Fillip said as Lev strode towards him.

Lev stopped half inside the opened door and turned back towards Fillip. "You're being polite," he said, shucking off his cloak and pulling on his waistcoat. "You're never polite to me, Fillip." He straightened the rest of his uniform and tried unsuccessfully to press out some of the wrinkles with his fingers.

Peering through the door, Lev examined the restaurant beyond. It was a cavernous place with high ceilings and white walls, softened by the glow of the golden candlelight. The floor was made up of well-polished black and white tiles laid out in a checkerboard pattern and the walls were draped in velvet curtains. There was a bar in the back corner, stocked high with the most expensive liquor and aged wine. It was a beautiful place. Lev had once asked who had built it and he'd been told that the architect had worked for the palace for a long while and had redesigned the ballroom. Each time Lev came into work, his breath caught a little at the sight.

Lev turned back towards Fillip, who smiled wryly and said, "I'm leading you to your last supper."

As if on cue, Lev's boss – an angry, balding man in his late forties whom they all referred to as Ol – called out to him. He was angry. Lev was very late.

Fillip let the door fall shut, trapping Lev inside the restaurant. *Well,* Lev thought. *There are uglier places to die.*

"Where the hell have you been?" Ol spat, his face turning red.

Lev shrugged and pulled his watch from his pocket. He'd taken it from a lawyer as an eighteenth birthday present to himself four years ago. He checked the time as though it had only just occurred to him that he might be late. "The train wasn't on time."

"Watch it, Valensky, or you'll be out on your arse."

Lev nodded in feigned remorse, keeping his head low.

"You're more trouble than you're worth."

Lev looked up then and shot Ol a smile. "I don't think that's quite true, is it?"

Ol scowled at him, but all he said was, "Private parlour. Now." He chucked Lev a clean apron and Lev tied it around his waist.

The old man was mean and surly, but he wasn't stupid.

Lev made his way through the restaurant throwing broad smiles and quick greetings at the customers as they called out to him or clapped him on the shoulder. They were all regulars who splashed out on private parlours for their poker games or business meetings, and they treated Lev like an old friend. They were blissfully unaware of the money he stole from their jacket pockets or the jewels he unclasped from around their necks.

As he approached the bar, Lev saw Irina polishing glasses and stacking them neatly onto a shelf. She waved her towel at him, and he smiled at her. Irina was a barmaid at The Eva. She worked constantly, though Lev suspected she could afford not to. Irina was from Gambit Square and as far as Lev knew, she still lived there in the comfort of her family home. The long hours and poor pay never seemed to take a toll on her; her face was smooth, and her hair still shone a dark, glossy ebony. She was tall and thin, her features sharp but not starved like Vera's.

"That was disappointing," Irina said.

Lev leaned his elbows on the marble countertop. "What was?"

"We all thought Ol was going to hand it to you."

Lev grinned at Irina, and she turned away from him.

The truth of the matter was that Ol would never fire Lev; he couldn't afford to and they all knew it. Lev was a pretty good waiter – he was well liked and generally looked happy whilst he was doing the job – but he was an excellent pickpocket. Vera had told him once that he had an innocent face and it served him well. He couldn't disagree.

Lev took a bottle of champagne from an ice bucket and wiped the water away with his tea towel as Irina set out a tray of champagne flutes. "Do we know who's in there?"

Irina shrugged. "Probably some pompous idiots," she said, as though she was not raised alongside the pompous idiots.

Lev nodded, lifted the tray onto his palm, and made for the thick red velvet curtain at the back of the room.

The private parlour was always unruly and easily the worst table to wait on. There were two reasons Ol gave Lev the parlour: one, as a form of punishment, and two, because those who splashed out on the parlour usually had cash to spare, and all good thieves and pickpockets knew that cash to spare was cash to steal. Lev didn't feel bad about stealing from those in the parlours. They assumed that as they paid so much to be there, they could do as they wished and while that was true, they were annoying and the mess they left behind was backbreaking to clean up. He thought of it as more of a tip than an act of thievery.

The parlour was a smaller version of the main room with its gold and red furnishings, black and white tiles, and a round glass table in the centre. Unlike the main room, however, it was shrouded in a layer of cigar smoke so thick it rivalled the railway. The scent had wormed its way into the upholstery and never left. Lev hated that smell; it reminded him too much of home.

He quickly assessed the guests – a group of men, all large and greasy, no doubt husbands to young wives, each with a cigar or pipe hanging from his mouth. And, Lev heard with dismay, they were incredibly loud.

Their voices boomed, carried by the high ceiling and tiled floor.

Lev knew it would not be an easy night. He wanted to turn around and leave, but it was time to get to work.

The guests were not yet seated, so one by one Lev removed their jackets and hung them over his arm. Their eagerness to be waited on only made Lev's job easier. Thievery of that kind could only be done to the upper class; the art was reliant on the delusional belief that they were respected, and of course, Lev painted that picture for them, fed their egos, and slipped petty cash from their pockets.

Draping their coats over a rack in the corner of the room, Lev picked up the bottle of champagne, popping the cork as he approached the table. They hadn't asked for champagne, but they all put their glasses down to accept some. He filled each flute.

When he was done, he gave a curt bow and left the room. They would no doubt call him back in mere minutes, but he wanted to dispose of his earnings before they grew wise.

He had made a deal with Ol when he first transferred from The Red Dumpling to The Eva. It was a big leap for Lev, going from pub service in Ivenko's Cauldron to a restaurant in Gambit Square. He was allowed to steal as much or as little as he could get away with, but all the money had to be split evenly throughout the restaurant. Given the wealth of those he was stealing from and the access working at The Eva gave him, Lev supposed it was a fair deal. He also enjoyed the irony of such a fine establishment deliberately hiring minor criminals. The people of the upper city thought they were so far from the crowds and squalor of the rest of Ytavosk; Lev had to laugh at how wrong they were.

He smiled to himself now and flicked the cash between his slender fingers.

Irina was waiting at the bar, scrubbing down service trays. "How much?"

"About three hundred ykas." He never took enough to be noticed, though what they would consider loose change would make a month's rent for Lev.

She laughed. "Fools."

Lev somewhat resented any of the stolen money being given to Irina. He knew she had a rich family and a very comfortable roof over her head. He didn't think she needed any more money going towards whatever grand tour or sparkling future she had ahead of her. She did not need the money to survive the way most workers at The Eva did. Lev tried to not feel angry about it – he saw the way Vera nursed her anger towards the world and he didn't want to burn with it the way she did – but it was hard not to feel a soft, bubbling irritation in his chest.

As Lev stuffed the cash into a tin box, a bell rang behind the bar.

Irina glanced up at it, the metal plaque beneath it reading *parlour*, then moved her gaze back to Lev, who sighed and looped a clean towel over his arm.

He was about to brush aside the curtain and re-enter the room when he heard a booming voice exclaim, "The whole situation is a mess!"

Silently, Lev moved closer. He didn't want to disturb them. He could just about see through the crack in the curtain to where the men were lounging in their chairs. The man talking was broad and had a thick moustache that took up a large portion of his face. From the way the other men around the table seemed to lean forward in their chairs when he spoke, Lev guessed he was the ringleader.

The man rubbed his moustache. Lev often found that most rich old men only grew moustaches so they could say cryptic things and rub them. Irina was right. These men were fools.

"So, you've heard about their most recent… problem?" Another man said as he lowered his glass.

Lev desperately wanted to shout *who* and bash their heads together until they gave him all the answers he needed, but he knew his place and it wasn't in that conversation.

The man with the moustache nodded, a sly smirk spreading across his face, just peeking out from beneath his facial hair. "Ah, yes."

The men around the table sat up eagerly. Lev rolled his eyes. He had to applaud the man and his gift for storytelling.

"The royals have lost a secret," he said at last.

Lev almost laughed. Vera would love that. A part of him wondered if Vera was the one who had stolen it, but he knew she would never go that far. They were opposites in almost every way – where he was soft, her edges were sharp, when he smiled, her frown only deepened – but they had the same logic when it came to thievery: to steal little and often, and never enough to get caught. She was never one to put herself in any kind of real danger or to draw light to her power. She was a threat that the royal family would dispose of at their earliest opportunity.

The men around the table seemed gleeful at the idea of a secret and Lev theorised that they were an extension of the Pravinya. The Pravinya was a supposedly democratic government organisation poised to eliminate the royal family. They'd emerged in the last decade, though no one was quite sure where they had come from or at what point they'd become a true threat. They just seemed to row with no one taking any notice of them until they were seven feet tall and had their teeth bared. Lev was sceptical of the Pravinya. He was sceptical of the Mescov dynasty too, but they were familiar at the very least, and while he was by no means living a life of luxury, he was surviving.

"What is it?" another voice asked. He was just outside of Lev's sight but from the softness of his voice, he sounded young and unsure.

"It hasn't quite hit the city yet," the man with the moustache said.

"So, you don't know what it is?"

"I never said that." He was being irritatingly cryptic. "Where the hell is that waiter? My drink is empty." And then he was being irritatingly rude.

Lev waited a beat before he brushed the red curtain aside and made his way into the room with a fresh bottle of champagne. "I'm sorry for the wait," he said with a flash of a smile.

"You should be."

He didn't much mind their rudeness when the money he stole from beneath their noses paid for his dinner each night.

The men continued to talk despite Lev's presence. He wasn't surprised. Their disregard of Lev's ability to hear and retain information was half the reason he even had a job. None of the men or women welcomed into the parlour ever took note of the waitstaff coming in and out, dropping off their food or taking their drinks. It made stealing both their money and their words easy. It made Lev wonder whether he really was talented or whether the job just wasn't as difficult as his boss thought it was. He didn't like that idea; he wanted to be good at something.

Lev topped up each of their glasses, using the cloth on his arm to wipe away the drops of condensation running over his fingers. No one thanked him, though he hadn't really expected anyone to. The conversation didn't turn back to the royal secret, and Lev hadn't expected that to happen either.

A rumour was beginning. Lev could feel it in the air like a sudden storm on a humid day in the summer. A rumour could be a dangerous thing.

4

ANYA

For the third time that day, Anya had lost her sister.

She looked around for her, hoping she would appear from beneath one of the canvas awnings or from behind a stall, but the girl did not. Anya's heart started to beat a little faster as she whipped her head around at every squeal of young laughter. She was gone, Daria was just *gone*. She felt an uncomfortable mixture of panic and irritation flood her stomach. Anya's little sister was under strict instructions not to leave her side, and yet she had disappeared. She'd vanished. *She's been taken*, the catastrophic voice whispered in the back of her mind. *She's been taken and she's being tortured and she's dead and it's your fault.*

She couldn't seem to turn that voice off.

Anya was tall but she was not tall enough to see over the

crowd swarming the market. Her chest spiked every time she caught a glimpse of dark curls. She knew she should stay at the stall and wait for Daria to return — the little girl knew the market better than Anya did herself — but she desperately wanted to go out and find her. She tried to breathe deeply, to calm herself down. This was not the first time Daria had disappeared, and she was sure it wouldn't be the last time the eight-year-old's attention would be whisked away.

The market had been quiet when Anya had arrived that morning, the buzz of the day before dulled down to scraps of loose fabric and discarded bills scattered across the dusty floor. A few sellers had been there early like Anya and Daria had been, too unsettled by hunger and the cold to allow themselves a slow morning. They had all grunted to each other in greeting over their tin cups of lukewarm tea.

Now, the market was alive. It was a maze of close stalls and torn canopies with wares hung from every possible point, and hordes of people weaving between the narrow passageways like fish at a shipwreck. It was a dim place, lit only by the occasional paraffin lamp hanging from the frames of the stalls or from metal bars sticking out of walls.

The market had been born in the disused railway burrowed beneath the city. It was supposed to be a hub for travellers, but it had fallen into disrepair when those rich enough to travel decided they didn't want to do so in a railway with no ventilation, and those poor enough to tolerate the smoke couldn't afford to leave the city anyway. It was a waste of money and was soon taken over by the criminally inclined. It was the centre point in Ivenko's Cauldron, though Anya refrained from calling the market a beating heart; to Anya its rhythm was closer to that of someone dying from a long-term illness, unsteady and fragile. The Cauldron's heart was little more than a stubborn but diminishing thud.

Glancing around the market, Anya's gaze snagged on a woman trying to sell a silk scarf whilst a small boy screamed ceaselessly in her arms. The infant wanted to run around, to play, unable to understand the dangers of a place full of criminals and crooks. Anya could sympathise with the woman; it was a difficult task keeping a child close when they had the attention span of a magpie. The voice appeared again, though this time it was more irritated than anxious. *Where are you, Daria, you little shit?* She moved her eyes onward to a seller polishing fingerprints from silver lockets and a young boy picking up coppers from the floor.

Anya thought of her little sister and the night she'd spent awake with her as she coughed and sent blood splattering across a torn cloth. She thought of the ragdoll Daria refused to put down and the way she insisted on coming to the market with her today despite the sleepless night.

Anya had taken Daria to the doctor once, though he had not been able to identify the problem. Instead of helping, he had charged Anya a week's wages and sent them both on their way. Since then, Anya had been scraping pennies together and forging prescriptions to take to the apothecary for anything that could alleviate some of her little sister's pain. The coughing never stopped, though her energy returned in fits and bursts. *She's got enough energy to run away from me,* Anya thought bitterly before an overwhelming sense of guilt overtook her.

Closing her eyes, Anya took three steadying breaths. She'd spent her years fighting to steel herself against the constant influx of worry. She found that the best way forward was to close her eyes, breathe through her nose and pretend for a moment that her life was easy.

Her momentary peace was disturbed by a familiar accent.

"I found your child."

Anya opened her eyes to see Vera Datsyuk shoving Daria forward. The foul mixture of emotions forgotten, Anya smacked Daria on the shoulder and gave her little sister her best *you-should-know-better* look she'd learnt from their mother. Daria smiled and Anya could practically feel her anger and worry seep out from beneath her skin to make way for her usual good nature. She pulled the girl into a quick hug and planted her down behind the counter once more. "You move out of my sight again and I'm not bringing you here anymore, okay?"

"Fine," the girl said, pulling a stolen apple out of her pocket.

"I mean it, Daria. I'll lock you up in that flat all day on your own."

"I said *fine*."

Turning back to Vera, Anya let out a sigh of relief and said, "Thank you. She's a menace, I—"

"I don't care," Vera replied, digging around in her satchel and placing three bottles on the counter. "What can I get for these?"

Anya had known Vera for many years but every time she encountered her, she was taken aback by her bluntness. She was never sure if it was a barrier between languages or whether she really was just rude. It was likely the latter. She looked at the scrawny girl. Vera was shorter than Anya by a few inches, her face was narrow and sickly, and her hair hung in frizzy curls so blonde they almost looked white. Her eyes were hollow and sunken in bruise-like circles, her pale skin stuck to her bones like wet cloth, and her mouth was pressed into a permanent frown.

Vera adjusted the strap of her satchel and crossed her arms over her chest impatiently.

Anya sighed as she said sarcastically, "Hello, Vera. It's lovely to see you again. How are you?"

"Hungry." Vera pushed the bottles closer.

The substance within the glass glowed like liquid gold, swirling and glittering in the dim light of the lantern hanging over Anya's head. "Whose are they?" She asked, retrieving three notecards beneath the desk and the pencil from behind her ear.

Vera reached into her pocket and pulled out a scrap of worn paper, flattening it on the countertop. It took her a moment to read from her note before she pointed to each bottle. Anya saw that her fingertips looked bruised from the cold and her gloves were threadbare, reaching only to her knuckles. "Karina Vitov, Hektor Kasya, Lora Savan."

Anya had heard of Karina and Hektor. Karina was a decorated wife and Hektor was a rich old man who had descended from a long line of rich old men. "Lora Savan?" Anya asked.

"Works for the Pravinya."

"That's bold for you."

"She doesn't have much to do with it."

Anya had guessed as much. She knew Vera's tactics: to steal from people consequential enough to get a half decent price, but who would not have the means to come after her. She needed the money in her pocket not hanging over her head.

Humming beneath her breath, Anya labelled the bottles and picked out some coins from the tray beneath the countertop. She handed them to Vera. The value of a secret was entirely dependent on who it had come from. The more important the person, the further they had to fall, the more their darkest secrets were worth. There was always someone with a thirst for vengeance and enough ykas to make it happen. The three secrets Vera had given Anya sat somewhere in the middle; they were valuable to *someone*, but they were not in demand.

Vera didn't argue with Anya's prices, though Anya could see a darkness settling over her features. The pale girl tucked the coins into the bodice of her dress and left without saying a word.

In all the years Anya had known her, Vera's exits had always confused her. There were no goodbyes, no indication that she was done with the conversation. It unnerved her that she seemed to just go.

Anya felt a tug on her sleeve, and she shoved Daria back behind the counter.

"*Look*," Daria hissed impatiently, jabbing Anya's side with her sharp elbow.

Anya followed Daria's gaze to a figure in the corner of the market. They were being watched. The figure's features were completely hidden, the hood of their cloak pulled up over their head despite the stuffy heat of the subterranean market. The cloak was a rich fabric and even from that distance, Anya could see that it was not poked by moth bites or torn from too much wear. It ran like a river of ink from the hood to the hem of the forest green dress beneath it. The figure seemed to notice Anya and Daria staring back, because they moved with startling speed towards their stall.

"Go," Anya hissed. "Go home, Daria. Lock the doors and don't leave until I come back, okay?"

"But you said—"

"Stop arguing with me," Anya said. "Just go."

Anya had been responsible for Daria since she had been born. She had never been able to just be Daria's sister. She was her mother, her protector, her provider, and it showed in moments like that when Daria gave in to Anya's authority.

Daria cast Anya a swift glance before hopping down from her stool and disappearing into the crowds. She was gone again. Anya ignored the spike of fear in her throat.

The cloaked figure stopped before the stall. For a long moment, delicate fingers browsed the bottles of threads glowing blue, red, gold, and white, flipping over labels and reading them.

"Can I help you?" Anya asked, placing her hands firmly on her hips and swallowing the hard lump of panic rising in her throat.

"Perhaps." The voice was smooth, as though the accent had been polished and refined, and sounded feminine.

Anya noticed when the figure reached towards another bottle that her fingernails were clean and perfectly shaped, and her skin was soft and smooth. This was not someone born or battered in the Cauldron. She was too pristine, too serene in nature. She was not raised being scrubbed raw in a communal bathtub or having her hair cut short with a rusty knife to avoid lice. She was someone who had maids to help her dress in the morning, who brought her trays of tea and broke her silk slippers in for her. She must have crawled out of Gambit Square or perhaps had been raised outside of the city entirely.

Anya perched on Daria's stool and tried to look casual. She had never been raided before. The royal family generally let the thugs and thieves go so long as they stayed within their bounds, but she knew if they were going to make an example of anyone, it would be Anya and her stall. Magic was strictly illegal in Sikveya. She would be hanged for trading in it.

Anya had inherited the stall after her mother had died. They'd had a neighbour living above them – Lilja Hohlt – an elderly Vorian woman who stomped across her floor when she felt Anya and her mother Iskra were making too much noise. It was only after Daria had been born and the coroner's men had come for Iskra that Lilja, having watched the scene from the slats in the stair bannister, introduced herself to Anya.

Anya was cradling Daria as the men draped a dark cloth over her mother's body and put her on a stretcher. Daria was screaming murder and Anya, with tears streaming down her face, was trying desperately to quiet her down.

"Gods," one of the men said with a sigh as he lifted the stretcher. "She's been left with a handful."

"*Fuck you*," Anya spat through her tears.

The men shrugged and took Iskra away. Anya stood there numb even after the door closed firmly behind the men and she heard the rattle of horse's hooves on the cobblestones. She heard a creak on the stairs and looked up to see the old woman peering through the wooden rungs. She was crouching on the stairs, her torn, dirty skirts billowing out around her and her scraggly grey hair hanging around her waist. The woman wore a lot of necklaces, and they rattled as she moved to stand and make her descent towards Anya.

The woman stopped before Anya, pulled a tissue from the pocket of her waistcoat, and dabbed at the tears on the young girl's face. Though the movement was stilted and awkward, it felt so familiar and maternal that it only made Anya cry harder. She realised then that she would not be mothered anymore. She *was* a mother, she had to care for her little sister in the way Iskra would have, and she would not be on the receiving end of any care herself. That was her life now.

When she finally managed to quell her tears, Anya turned to the woman and asked, "Are you the lady living above us?"

"I think so," the woman said, her Vorian accent peeking through in the soft curves of her words. "I'm Lilja."

"Anya."

"And her?" Lilja pointed at the small baby in Anya's arms.

"Daria," Anya said over the baby's screams.

Lilja reached out towards Daria. "May I?"

For a moment, Anya hesitated. Daria had been in the world mere hours and already she was protective of her. She was Anya's family now; Daria was all she had. She glanced up at Lilja, at her sunken eyes and wrinkled hands reaching towards the baby. She took a deep breath and handed Daria to her carefully. Lilja smiled and shushed the baby.

Daria quieted in Lilja's arms.

Anya wanted to scream in frustration. "I don't think she likes me," she said, feeling the heavy ache of tears press against her throat. She wanted her mother back. She wanted some help. Most of all, she wanted to just be fifteen and she wanted to be Daria's sister, not her carer. She scolded herself for being selfish and a fresh wave of tears flooded her face.

"She can sense that you're stressed," Lilja said softly. "Take a deep breath, girl."

Anya did as she was told, desperate for *anyone* to tell her what to do next.

"And another."

Anya did.

"Do you feel better?"

"No."

Lilja passed Daria back to Anya, who tried to push back her grief, her anger, the burning need for comfort that was slowly flooding her veins. "Breathe."

Anya closed her eyes, focusing on the small, defenceless girl in her arms and took three deep breaths. Daria settled into her and Lilja chuckled softly under her breath. "I don't know what to do now," Anya whispered.

"I can strike a deal with you," the older woman said, brushing her hair back from her shoulder.

Anya's chest turned cold. "What deal?" she asked cautiously.

"You have a job?"

"It doesn't pay well. And I don't think I will be able to take Daria there with me."

"I'll care for her," Lilja said.

Anya squeezed Daria closer to her chest defensively and took a small step back towards her door, ready to slam it in the woman's face. "She's mine. I'm not giving her up."

Lilja scoffed and threw one wrinkled hand up in the air. "Not all the time. Just when you're at work."

"What are the conditions?" Nothing was free in Ytavosk. People did not help people for no reason.

"You run my stall down in the market."

"What do you trade in?"

"Magic."

Anya felt her heart swoop and dive like a bird shot out of the sky. "You couldn't pay me to do that. I'll be killed."

"Do you have any other options?"

Anya opened her mouth to answer but shut it quickly. The answer was very simple, though she didn't want to admit it – she did not have a choice. She hadn't had a choice in any of it. She had a stable job at a theatre, swinging from a trapeze or hanging high above the stage floor on a sheet of pink silk, but she would not be able to continue it with Daria needing her. The joy and exhilaration that filled her nights would quickly be replaced by feeds and changes if she didn't take this woman's offer. Lilja was right. "You look after Daria while I'm at the market and at the theatre."

Lilja smiled. "You give me fifty percent of the profits."

Fifty percent of the profits was better than nothing at all, but Anya couldn't deny the sharp irritation that darted through her stomach – she had to take on the danger of the market and the pay didn't even make it worth it. *For me*, she thought bitterly. *It doesn't make it worth it for me.*

Anya hesitated for a moment as she weighed up her options, then said, "Deal."

She was about to take Daria back into their flat and bolt the door so she could finally put the baby down and clean up her mother's blood when she turned back to Lilja. "Why? Why are you helping me?"

"I don't want to do it anymore, Anya. I don't want to risk

however many years I have left. I want to die naturally, not by hanging," Lilja had said. "And besides, I always liked children. I just never got the chance to have my own."

Now, Anya watched the girl standing at her stall and wondered what her life might have been like had she not taken that opportunity. *No*, she thought, *the market stall was not an opportunity. It was a poorly considered risk.* "What are you looking for?"

"Not what," the girl said. "Who were you just trading with?"

Anya considered for a moment. There was a code in the Cauldron that if you fell, you fell alone. She would not drag Vera down with her. "I don't know who you are talking about."

"She was just here."

"I trade with a lot of people. I didn't catch her name." Anya knew her name, she knew where she lived and what she traded in, but she would not tell this girl. In a world full of crime and trickery, Anya tried her best to be loyal.

"You spoke with her for a long while. She had that kid with her."

Anya smiled casually. At least the girl hadn't clocked that Daria was *her* kid. "I was being polite. You know, friendly. She wasn't very chatty though, actually I'd say she was quite rude—"

"You know who she was." It was not a question.

Anya dropped her cheer, flattening her features into a look that would have rivalled Vera's. "If you're not going to buy anything, you can move on."

The girl lifted her head slightly and Anya could just make out her features from beneath the shadow of her hood. Her cheeks were round, her eyes wide and a shade of blue Anya couldn't quite describe. She was trying to get a closer look when the girl's hand reached out suddenly. Anya flinched, but she only plucked up a bottle containing a blue that was bright like illustrations of water she'd seen in her fairy tale books growing up. The girl tipped it one way and then the other, watching as the memory spun and swirled within its confines. She put it back down and the colour settled at the bottom of the bottle.

Anya noticed the crumpled-up piece of paper in the girl's hand, though she had missed the moment she'd retrieved it. The girl said nothing more as she turned on her heel and marched back into the crowd. This time she disappeared completely.

Heaving a sigh of relief, Anya readjusted the bottles on her countertop, neatening them in their rows and making sure each little label was visible. She still felt unnerved, the image of the hooded girl burnt across her mind. What had she wanted? What had Vera done? No, there was no question as to what Vera had done – she had been living a criminal life as long as Anya had, and it was no real surprise that she was being caught out. The real question was *why now?* They had been working together for a long while and as far as Anya knew they had never been picked up for it. She worried for Vera. It was strange to worry about her when Anya knew the other girl would not spare her a second thought. Since Iskra had died and Anya had taken on Daria as her own daughter of sorts, worrying had become second nature. She worried about their money, she worried about Daria's coughing fits, she worried about her friends – or those she would consider to be her friends.

Anya hoped Daria had made it home.

Lilja had died when Daria was seven. Anya had gone to pick Daria up from the woman's flat when she noticed the woman had dropped dead on the third-floor landing. She found Daria curled up in a ball in an unlocked cupboard beneath the stairs. They never found out what had killed Lilja, though the coroner suspected it had been a heart attack.

"I can confirm it," the coroner said as Anya and Daria stood behind the counter waiting. "But it'll cost you."

"I don't really need to know," Anya had replied, dragging a crying Daria towards the door of the coroner's office. "She'll still be dead."

Anya hoped now that Daria was on her way to bed to rest after a fitful night's sleep. She wouldn't have time to visit her sister before she went to the theatre that evening.

Her job at the theatre was the one thing she didn't worry about. She loved walking tightropes in glittering costumes or standing tall on a magician's box. She spent her days dealing in magic, but it was at night in the theatre when she really *felt* magical. She wanted smoke and mirrors, she wanted a beautiful, sparkling kind of magic that didn't ruin people's lives.

But she could think about that later once she'd donned her pink costume and the matching feathers. For now, she had no choice but to resign herself to destruction.

5

SOFIYA

Sofiya had waited until the sun had fully set and the workers had all gone home for the girl to leave the market. She'd watched from the shadows as she tucked the folds of cash into the coin purse hidden beneath her cloak and locked away the glowing glass bottles. Then she'd followed her from the market to a rundown theatre on Tretr Lane.

She had only ever ventured that deeply into the Cauldron once with her father. Mikhail had insisted that Sofiya see the city in all its misery.

"You see," he'd said, gesturing to a woman in a low-cut dress leaning off her balcony with a cigar hanging from her mouth. "This is exactly what we are trying to save ourselves from."

Sofiya wasn't quite sure what her father had hoped to prove in bringing her out into the city proper, away from the pretty cobbled streets of Gambit Square or the walk that led from the Square up to the palace. If he had wanted to convince her that the rest of the city wasn't worth saving, he'd be severely disappointed. When Sofiya looked around at the starved faces of their people, all she felt was angry – angry that their family cared so little for those who struggled to care for themselves, angry that she had to fight so hard to change it and that in all her years trying, she had achieved nothing.

"You can't beat corruption out of people, Sofiya. It's like a plague," her father said. "You have to contain it."

They turned onto a street and were hit with a wall of sound. The noise seemed to echo off the stones and the crooked houses, blaring from the entryways of each of the shopfronts. Men and women were flooding the streets, some in gaudy costumes handing out leaflets, others enjoying the view, their hands wandering, their clothes slipping from their shoulders. On the corner of the street a sign hung in two parts, cracked straight down the middle. The splintered fragments read *Tretr Lane.*

To their left, a man sat playing an accordion. His face was wrinkled, weathered from years of exposure to the brutal cold that engulfed Sikveya. His hands were cracked and bleeding as they played the instrument delicately, lovingly. As her father turned the other way, Sofiya slipped a handful of coins from her pocket and tossed them into the upturned hat in front of the man. He smiled at her, and the song flowed from a hearty theatre tune to the national anthem. Sofiya stared at him a moment longer until her father realised she had stopped walking and turned to call her back.

Sofiya left the man, but she couldn't stop thinking about him, the way he held the instrument so lovingly, or the way he had managed to smile at her despite the blood seeping from the cracks in his skin.

She fell a little bit in love with Ivenko's Cauldron then, with the chaos of it all, though she could never tell anyone.

As Sofiya caught up with her father, he grabbed the hood of her cloak and pulled her to his side. "Stay close to me. They'll infect you too," he snapped.

A scream echoed through the street, ricocheting off the cobblestones. It cut through the buzz and Sofiya turned towards the noise. A woman carrying a baby in her arms was sprinting down the street. She had a shawl across her shoulders that fluttered in the wind as she desperately clasped her baby to her chest. Her face was stained with dirt, and she had a bruise blossoming across her cheek.

"They're going to take him," she screamed at Mikhail, falling to his feet. "Please help me."

The King turned away, holding his chin high in the air and the woman grabbed the hem of his cloak. Sofiya knew instantly that the woman had made a mistake. The King whipped around and, pulling the coat from the woman's balled up first, kicked her shoulder. She fell backwards, her body fighting to shield the baby in her arms. A shot sounded and the woman slumped forward. Her baby screamed, trapped beneath her limp body. The guard accompanying Sofiya and her father put his gun down.

Sofiya felt a sour taste in her mouth. Her eyes filled with tears as the crowds on Tretr Lane formed a circle around the commotion. A man stepped forward and pulled the baby from beneath the woman's crumpled body. Someone else untied the leather pouch from the woman's waist. The coppers inside gave a metallic rattle as they disappeared back into the crowd.

"Come on, Sofiya," Mikhail said. "We need to be back in time for dinner."

Sofiya couldn't quite believe that he could so easily move on from the murder of that woman. She was determined to commit her face to memory, to never forget what she'd seen that day, but when she turned back towards the crumpled body, the woman was already gone, thrown onto the top of a cart full of other bodies. That image was worth remembering – the bodies piled up, their faces bruised and rotted, their identities forgotten. Sofiya wanted to be sick, but she forced it down, forced herself to keep her eyes on the image of the bodies, to remember the gunshot, to promise that she would fix this.

Mikhail shoved his way through the crowd. "Animals," he muttered to himself.

Sofiya had snapped then. "They're not animals. They're survivors." *They're surviving the storm you brought on.*

Now, Sofiya turned back towards Tretr Lane as the market girl shoved her way through the crowd. She was careful not to lose sight of her red hat bobbing through the onslaught of people. She felt for the revolver in the leather belt at her waist. It was safely hidden beneath her cloak and Sofiya liked the weight of it even if she had no intention of actually using it. She wasn't sure she even knew *how* to use it.

The girl arrived at a theatre painted a shade of green so offensively bright it almost glowed in the dim evening light. She waved to the bouncer before making her way to a small alleyway that ran down the side of the house. Sofiya followed, keeping a good enough distance back that the bouncer didn't see her. The alleyway was cluttered with crates full of rotting food and empty barrels. The girl manoeuvred herself through and over them with ease, but it took Sofiya a little more time to navigate the maze and by the time she was over them, the stage door was already falling shut. Sofiya shoved her foot into the door to stop it from closing and when it slammed against her toes she cursed under her breath, squeezing her eyes shut as a sharp pain ricocheted up her shin.

"Evening, ladies!" she heard the girl shout, her voice high pitched and overly cheery.

Sofiya waited. She heard the girls break into a chorus of chatter, asking each other to borrow their makeup or to lace them into their costumes. She paused for a moment, listening to the chaos inside the room, to the women jumping to help each other and telling each other that they looked lovely and were going to be great. Sofiya had missed that part of growing up, of being told that she was doing well, that she was going to be okay. She'd never known the solidarity that grew between women as they were shoved down and cut up and she couldn't help but miss that thing she'd never had.

Eventually, the noise fizzled out. She heard something clatter to the floor. When it rattled someone swore loudly and Sofiya recognised the voice of the girl from the market.

"What's wrong with you?" the girl hissed.

Another voice cleared her throat and said in a whisper, "Sorry, I thought it would be heavier."

"It's a secret. It's a jar of light, Elmira. How heavy were you expecting it to be?"

"Well, it's heavy to *me*," Elmira replied sharply. "And this is Hektor?"

Sofiya listened to the clink of bracelets rattling together and then the girl from the market said, "Yes."

Hektor. The name sounded familiar to Sofiya. She pulled the scrap of paper out of her pocket. She'd picked it up from the market after the white-haired girl had disappeared, leaving it on the counter. And there it was, scribbled in jagged handwriting. *Hektor Kasya.*

"What about Jia?"

"I can get you it, but it might take a while."

"Anya, you promised me both of them. I'm not paying you for just one."

Anya sighed. "Vera will be back tomorrow. She comes every day. I'll ask her to get it and I'll have it for you by the week's end."

"Elmira! Hurry the fuck up!" a hoarse voice called from somewhere outside of the dressing room.

Elmira replied, "Coming!" in a voice that was considerably more chipper than the one she'd used when talking to Anya. "I'm serious. If I don't have it by the end of the week, we're going to have a problem."

Sofiya heard the click of heeled shoes against hardwood flooring before the dressing room door banged shut.

It was only after a still silence had settled in the dressed room that Sofiya booted the stage door open and stepped inside, letting it slam shut behind her.

Sitting at an oak dressing table lit by a handful of candles around the room, the girl sat carefully painting her face with gold glitter. She had dark skin, and her hair was cropped close to her head. She jumped out of her chair when the door slammed shut and was now standing in the centre of the room in only her white shirt. The rest of her clothes were strung over the back of her chair, though her red hat had fallen onto the floor. On a hanger beside her mirror sat a pink costume complete with a short silk skirt, a corset, and a pink wig.

"What in Yarisich's name do you think you're doing?" Anya said, one hand held in front of her and the other clinging to the back of her chair.

"You lied to me," Sofiya said, pulling the pistol from its sheath on her waist and aiming it at the girl opposite her.

"Excuse me?" The girl sputtered a laugh and pulled herself up straight. The initial shock of Sofiya's presence had clearly worn off and Anya was putting her mask back on. She smoothed out her voice, stepped into the line of the gun, and said, "I lie quite often. You can't expect me to remember what you're talking about."

"I just spoke with you at the market. You said you didn't know that girl."

"Which one?" Anya asked as she rolled up the cuffs of her shirtsleeves.

"The blonde girl. She sold you some secrets," Sofiya replied. "And I think you just sold one of them on."

Anya eyed the gun in Sofiya's hands and looked back up at her face. She had a slow, feline way of moving that made Sofiya's body tense. Each movement was deliberate, each small glance felt like a hard glare. "Please put the gun down," Anya said with a sigh. "You look ridiculous. Do you even know how to use it?"

Sofiya adjusted her grip on the gun. She *didn't* know how to use it. She was more used to swords and knives, the weapons which required a bit of artistry as well as aim. She didn't like the instant damage of firearms, she liked the slow, measured dance of blades clanging together; she liked to have a moment to think before she delivered the killing blow.

Regardless, she had a point to prove and she cocked the gun. It made a satisfying click. Sofiya fought to keep her hands steady as they clutched the pearl handle of the pistol, aiming the gun just above Anya's head, though she hoped the girl didn't realise. She needed her to believe she'd shoot.

Anya scoffed and gestured to the thin fabric covering her body. "I'm half dressed in an enclosed room," she said. "What do you think I'm going to do?"

"I'm not taking any chances."

Ignoring her, Anya's soft smirk broke out into a grin. "Well," she said. "There are things we *could* do if you want to lock the door, honey."

Sofiya could feel the heat rising on her cheeks as she fought to avert her gaze from the smooth, dark skin of Anya's exposed thighs. "Tell me what I want to know, or I'll shoot you."

"That's a tall order. I don't *know* anything."

Sofiya raised the gun slightly and shot once, taking out the mirror behind Anya. Anya flinched and jumped away from the mirror, glancing back at the fractured shards now scattered across the wood floor.

"Oh, seriously? Do you know how difficult it is to get glass out of the cracks in the floorboards? And I'll have to pay for the replacement. Marina is going to kill me." Anya bent down to pick a postcard up off the floor. It had been trapped between the mirror and its frame and had fluttered to the ground along with the glass. "Fine. *Fine*. Her name is

Vera Datsyuk. She lives in the boarding house opposite The Red Dumpling."

"The what?" Sofiya questioned.

"Oh," Anya replied, still focusing on picking up the largest splinters of the mirror. She was completely unconcerned by the gun still aimed at her head. "So, you're not from around here, huh?"

"No," Sofiya said. The gun in her hands felt like overkill against Anya's casual chatter.

"It's a pub in Ivenko's Cauldron. You'll know it when you see it."

Sofiya had never heard of the place, though it sounded like food poisoning with four walls and a barmaid.

She couldn't help but think about how easily Anya had given up the information. Sofiya remembered how quick people were to rob that woman's body of her money pouch and to take her child away. They were like flies on a carcass. They were suffering and they were just trying to survive; that was what Sofiya chanted in her head each time she saw a part of the city she didn't like. *It's because of you*, the voice said sharply. *Because you do nothing.* When she heard it, the shame shoved away any other part of her that was scared, that wanted to shut these hapless criminals out of her life the way her father had, the way her mother continued to.

Straightening her spine and tucking the pistol back into the strap hanging around her waist, Sofiya nodded at Anya, who was now moving her things to a different mirror. "Thank you," Sofiya said.

Anya snorted a laugh. "You're *polite*? You're definitely new here. Don't worry, it'll be beaten out of you."

Her voice was amused, but Sofiya could hear a level of sadness beneath it, like Anya truly didn't believe there was anything good left in the Cauldron.

Sofiya moved towards the stage door, but Anya caught her arm. Sofiya froze, her fingers itching for the smooth handle of her pistol, for the security it gave her. But Anya only said, "You're not going to tell her I sold her out?"

Sofiya looked at the girl's face. They were closer now and she could make out the sprinkle of freckles across her nose and the way the gold glitter on her cheeks sparked something in her eyes. "No," Sofiya said.

Anya released her tight grip on Sofiya's arm and said, "Then good luck. You'll need it."

6

Vera

Vera liked to disappear into the crowded streets of Ivenko's Cauldron. She felt safe there, buried beneath people more interesting than her or more recognisable. She'd worked hard in the years spent in the city to limit her notoriety. She could have become a public enemy or perhaps the villain of a bedtime story, but she had refrained from doing anything terrible enough. She kept to the strict rules of thievery that Lev had outlined for her all those years ago.

They'd been walking down that very street – Vera had a hard time translating the street signs, but she thought Lev had called it Bekar Street – winding their way between the crowds of people and the sellers leaning out of shop doorways. Lev had been showing her the different types of people she would encounter in the Cauldron, gesturing wildly with his arms.

"It's a melting pot," Lev explained. "It doesn't matter who you are or where you came from. The Cauldron is an equaliser. If you look close enough, you'll see everyone here." He pointed to a woman in a ragged cloak.

"What about her?" Vera asked.

Lev leaned in conspiratorially. "Look at what she's wearing. She's a good target."

Vera looked closer. She was about to give up when the woman took a step and from beneath her threadbare cloak emerged a polished beige boot and the hem of a perfectly sewn dress. The image the woman was trying to portray melted away and from it emerged someone clearly raised in the better part of the city. Her hair was glossy, her skin was smooth, and her eyes were glowing.

Lev steered them closer, but his hands stayed by his side. Vera knew to watch his hands. That was how she learned from him. She watched his graceful movements carefully, from the charming smile he plastered across his face to the swift and almost unnoticeable movement of his hands as they lifted things from people's pockets. But he wasn't moving now.

Vera prodded Lev in the side. "Aren't you going to–"

"No." Lev pulled Vera to a stop at the side of the street. Passersby grunted and shoved them out of the way. Nothing could stop the tide of hungry workers trying to get home. Vera stood firm. "There are three golden rules of thievery."

"Right," Vera muttered, sure he was about to pluck *three golden rules* out of thin air.

"Don't get caught," Lev proclaimed, counting on his fingers. He tilted his head towards her and smiled. "Obviously, that's a very important one."

"Obviously."

"Steal little and often."

That was the only one Vera really kept in her mind.

"And lastly," Lev said. "Never keep the things you take. That way it can't be traced back to you."

"Got it."

They'd started walking again when Lev stopped short with a startled, "Oh!"

Vera almost crashed straight into his back as he spun around to face her, his hands gripping her shoulders tightly. When they stood like this, Vera was very aware of how much taller he was than her. He wasn't a big person – his physique was slender, boarding on scrawny – but he had a personality that felt larger than anyone she had ever known. "I forgot a rule. So, there are four rules. It doesn't quite have the same ring, does it? *The four golden rules of thievery.* No, I don't like it–"

"Lev," she snapped. "Get to the point." She'd come to realise that Lev talked a lot and that he was very easily distracted.

"Sorry." He didn't sound sorry at all. Clearing his throat, he continued, "Don't make an enemy of yourself." He enunciated each word clearly.

"Surely stealing anything makes you an enemy."

"Keep quiet," he clarified. "Don't make yourself a villain. Don't make a name for yourself. The Meskovs don't like being made fools of, and they don't like their friends being made fools of."

The country was a financial wreck, tearing at the seams and rotting away. The royal family did not need *her* to make them look like fools; they were doing a very good job of that themselves.

"That is to say, don't steal from anyone with any true power," Lev said. "That's a sure way to get yourself killed."

"Thank you for the lesson," Vera said, though the lesson felt very self-explanatory. *How to steal things: take them and don't get yourself hanged.*

"You're very welcome." Lev smiled and grabbed the top of Vera's arm, guiding them back into the busy street.

They were silent for a moment until Lev piped up suddenly and said, "Five rules." They didn't stop walking this time. "I think there should be five rules."

Vera wasn't paying attention anymore. She'd smelt the rich syrup from a restaurant across the street and now her mouth watered. She hadn't eaten a proper hot meal since Lev had given her one at the pub she'd found herself in. She didn't have any money and had been leeching off the scraps Lev could spare. That was why he was teaching her to steal, though her thievery wasn't limited to material objects. She pulled her cloak tighter around her and hoped if she just held her stomach tight enough, she could keep all the hunger in, squash it down until it disappeared completely.

"One, don't get caught. Two, steal little and often. Three, never keep anything. Four, don't be an enemy. Five– Are you still listening to me?" Lev asked, tilting his head so he was looking down at Vera.

She hummed under her breath and looked up to meet his gaze. She could admit he had a pretty face. His skin was pale and smooth, a stark contrast against his black hair that fell in pin straight strands. His eyes were dark grey, set in an angular face and she realised then that, unlike most people in the Cauldron, Lev looked very much alive. Vera looked away, back towards the smoke being funnelled out of the roof of an old factory. She could practically feel the grime coating the bare skin on her face.

"Five, don't be a victim."

Vera's head snapped back towards the boy beside her. He was smiling wickedly. That was the first time she'd seen that part of him, the part that might actually be a danger to her.

"What?" Vera snapped. She felt that familiar feeling bubbling up in her stomach, sitting beside her hunger and her anger, two things she'd been nursing for a long while.

Lev held his hand up and opened his palm. In its centre sat a small glass bottle with a cork stopper. It glowed golden in his hand, the thread swirling around and hitting the edges like a caged animal. He'd lifted the secret from her satchel.

Vera snatched the bottle back and shoved Lev hard in the chest.

"What the fuck is wrong with you?" Vera spat, tucking the bottle back into her bag. "You said don't get caught. Are you trying to get me killed?"

She hated the feeling that came next. Fear didn't sit in her stomach with the others, it coated her heart. She had been scared since she'd come to Sikveya, to Ytavosk, to the Cauldron, the feeling constant, weighing her down like lead. That was what her power did – it made her fearful. Every breath she took was illegal, every step broke the law. Her very existence went against their world's codes. She was a threat to their longing for a magicless society.

She didn't know Lev well enough then to know what he'd do with that fragile information.

"Keep your guard up, Vera. Remember the rules."

"Fuck your rules."

Vera had turned away from him then and stormed back towards the boarding house.

She looked around at the now familiar street. At the time the whole place had seemed so confusing. She'd been in the city a couple of months and was desperate to understand it. Now she *did* understand it, she was desperate for her blissful ignorance to return. She'd learnt the streets well. She no longer tripped on drain covers or hesitated before walking over makeshift bridges. The city hadn't become hers; she'd become a part of the city.

She tilted her head back slightly and let herself breathe. She missed the fresh, crisp air of the Isles, the way it felt to inhale something so pure and clean. The coal smoke from the factories or the second-hand cigarette smoke from the pubs didn't quite cut it, but she'd have to make do. When she let herself dream of her home, she let her guard down. She was a fool.

Someone grabbed Vera's arm and yanked her sideways. Her first thought was of Lev, that he had something he needed to say to her, but the hand was too tight on her arm and didn't feel familiar at all. A surge of panic rushed into Vera's head, and it felt like her mind was being stuffed full of wool. It took her a moment to adjust, to fully understand that this was an attack.

Vera just about had time to register her surroundings – she was just outside of The Red Dumpling, the woman in front of her had bright copper hair which was slipping out from beneath her hood, and it was starting to rain – before she was slammed back against the wall. She cursed loudly but she didn't cry for help.

An arm pressed against Vera's throat, holding her shoulders against the brick. When the air finally returned to her lungs, she let out a sigh and levelled her gaze on her captor.

The figure's hood slipped off to reveal a woman around Vera's age with plump cheeks and bright eyes staring back at her. Her whole face was dusted with light freckles and her hair glowed as it cascaded down over her broad shoulders in thick curls. She was taller than Vera and managed to lift her completely off her feet.

"What do you want?" Vera asked through gritted teeth.

The woman's grip tightened.

Vera felt her throat close as the pressure built up in her head. "Put me down and we can talk." She'd been confused before, but now she was just annoyed. She kicked out with her leg and kneed her attacker in the stomach. Surprised, the woman's arm loosened, and Vera dropped to the floor. Her landing was inelegant, but she managed to stay on her feet. She rubbed the skin on her neck and rolled her shoulders. She had a knife in her hand in moments, slipped out from beneath her cloak.

The woman stepped back when she saw the silver blade in Vera's hand, and Vera saw she had the stance of a fighter – not the scrappy kind she was accustomed to, but the kind who had been trained professionally. Her feet were set, her shoulders pushed back, and her hands looked deceptively casual as they hung at her side.

"What do you want?" Vera asked again, straightening her

clothes and brushing her hair out of her face. She shoved down her anger and smoothed out her voice.

"To be allies," the woman said.

Vera held back her laughter. "You could have just asked me. You didn't need to throw me against a wall."

"You're a threat, I know that. I'm not stupid." She brushed her hair over one shoulder and raised her chin.

"So, you want my help?"

"No, I want to strike a deal with you."

Vera ignored her. "I don't help people. It gives me a rash."

The woman sighed in irritation and wrung her cloak in her hands. Her mouth was set in a straight line that wrinkled the skin on her cheeks and there was something oddly familiar about the determination sparking to life behind her eyes. "I'm not asking for help. It's an exchange – you do something for me, and I'll do something for you."

"There is nothing I want," Vera said firmly. That was a lie. There were many things Vera wanted – a late start to her morning, regular hot meals, to finally leave the city and go where her mother had wanted to send her. They were not things she could afford. She would never feel warm again and she would never see Vor.

"I can give you freedom."

A voice scratched at the back of Vera's mind. *What does she know about you? Does she think you're the enemy?* But she shoved it away. There was a high chance that this woman knew Vera's power and she couldn't change that. At least if she was offering Vera freedom, she wouldn't kill her right now. The girl needed her.

"And how exactly do you intend to give me that?"

There was a pause. For the first time, she looked hesitant, as though she was debating how much of herself she wanted to reveal. "I have means," she said at last.

Vera laughed then; a quiet, bitter noise that echoed from somewhere deep in her chest. Lev had once said she laughed like a prisoner seeing the sun for the first time. She hadn't really understood what he'd meant, but the longer she was trapped in the dark, the more Lev's analogy made sense to her. She was not used to laughing and when she finally did the sound came out like a puff of dust. "You have means?" Vera straightened her shoulders and started to turn away. "Very convincing. My answer is no."

"I know what you are. I could have you killed."

"Then do it," Vera spat. She was tired; perhaps death wouldn't be the worst thing. "Run along and tell that dead-beat family. My hanging could be their evening entertainment."

"They don't kill for the fun of it."

Vera sensed a defensiveness in the woman's voice and smirked, raising her eyebrow and giving her a hard glare. "They hunt magicians like animals. They're the ones who should be slaughtered."

Vera turned just as the girl's fist connected with her face and she was thrown back against the wall once more. Too stunned to move, she waited there for a moment, her body pressed against the bricks as hot blood ran down her face. She opened her mouth to speak and the blood oozed in. She tasted metal. Cursing violently under her breath, Vera pressed her hand to her nose.

One of the bouncers for The Red Dumpling called out to Vera, "You of all people know the rules – no fighting!"

Vera gestured wildly to the blood now smeared across her face and neck, soaking into the collar of her cloak. "Yes," she hissed back. "*I* know that." When she turned back towards her attacker, she realised the girl with the copper hair was gone. She spat on the ground and wiped her hand across her nose, hissing at the stinging sensation.

Tired, angry, and now in a lot of pain, Vera stomped across the street back to the boarding house. She was usually at her best when she was angry – her mind seemed to focus more, her actions grew bolder, braver – but this time when the feeling rolled around in her chest, she just felt confused.

As Vera unlocked the front door to the house, her key jammed in the door, and she wrestled it out with an untamed fury. When Mrs Hanovich called out to her in her usual voice (somehow both chirpy and gruff) Vera ignored it, instead trudging up the stairs. She enjoyed the angry protests of the wooden steps beneath her feet, the way they shrieked with every hard thud of her boots.

Vera almost crashed straight into Lev as he rounded the dark corner in a hurry, his cloak slung over one his arm and his untied tie thrown across his shoulder. He was late as he always was, his hair dishevelled, his clothes wrinkled, and yet he stopped short at the sight of her.

"Are you okay?" Lev asked, grabbing Vera's shoulder to stop her from tumbling back down the stairs.

"No," Vera said sharply, tilting her face towards the dim light.

Lev choked back a startled laugh.

"Oh, fuck off," Vera snapped, her anger firing up inside her. She shoved past him and made her way towards the bathroom on their floor. It was at the end of the corridor and held no light but for a small candle on the windowsill. The walls were painted a muddy green and the copper taps had long since rusted.

"I'm sorry," he called after her, failing to suppress the amusement in his voice. "I just wasn't expecting that!"

Late and surely fired, Lev followed her down the corridor to the bathroom, closing the door with a soft click behind them. He tossed his cloak and tie over the chair in the corner and turned the tap on at the sink. As the basin filled with water, he took out a rag from beneath the porcelain bowl.

Vera sat on the edge of the bath and looked up at him as he dipped the rag into the water and pressed it to her face. She flinched at the pain and the shock cold water – they weren't so lucky as to have it running hot – and Lev hid his laugh.

"Shall I even ask what happened?" He rested one hand on the top of her head and tilted her face towards the pitiful candlelight.

Vera huffed a sigh. She could feel bruises forming beneath her eyes. "I got offered a job."

"Doing what?"

"I'm assuming it was to steal something. But she didn't get to that part."

"Did you recognise her?"

"No."

Lev hummed beneath his breath and dabbed Vera's face once more with the washrag. He wrung it in the sink and the water turned pink with her blood. "She's got quite a punch on her."

Vera swatted Lev's hand away and stood so she could see herself in the dirty mirror. "I liked my nose." She tried not to be vain, but it was difficult for people like her who looked like death incarnate.

"It could have been worse," Lev said. "You could have lost some teeth."

Vera glared at him.

He winked at her.

"Don't you need to go to work?" Vera asked him with a meaningful glance at his discarded clothes.

Lev shrugged. "Probably."

She was used to Lev's complete lack of organisational skills and the subsequent lateness, but he wasn't her employee. She wondered what his boss thought of him, his manic energy, and his inability to be punctual. She doubted that Lev's boss was all that impressed by it, but it wasn't her place to judge. He'd been working as a waiter since she'd known him and the only time he ever left a job was because he'd made a choice to, not because he'd been fired.

"What did she look like?" Lev asked, drawing her back to the conversation.

Vera thought back to the girl in the alleyway when her hood had slipped back. "Average height, copper hair, looks a lot less like a dead person than all the other people in Ivenko's Cauldron."

"That's a pretty identifiable factor."

"She looked wealthy," Vera clarified.

Lev laughed. "I bet she did." There was a clink as Lev placed something on the edge of the sink. Vera looked down to see a large silver ring with a flat green stone embedded in it. On its surface were two connecting circles with a large 'M' set in the centre. Vera reached out and picked it up.

She looked up at Lev. "Care to explain?"

"I was on the train the other day. I came across someone very interesting."

"Was she average height with copper hair and looking very much alive?"

Lev smiled as brightly as he always did. "You bet."

"You know something." Vera smiled back at him.

Lev pulled the plug on the bloody water. "I *overheard* something. The royals have lost a secret."

"And then a girl wearing the royal crest appears in the Cauldron," Vera finished. "She wants me to help her get it back." She couldn't stop the cogs whirring in her head. She wanted to maintain her usual stance that this was not her country, this was not her problem to fix, but the girl had been right — she wanted her freedom, and this could be it. The 'means' by which she had intended to pay Vera were clear now. She at least had links to the royals, to the money they bled the country for. She could pay Vera and pay her well. She could finally get the money together to move on from the city, to leave its coal-streaked sky and slick cobblestones far behind her. Vera could finally learn to use her power properly, to become more, to be *better*.

Vera looked up at Lev then. "Do you think you could get a message to Her Royal Highness?"

"I think so."

"And a meeting place?"

Lev's smile turned to a conspiratorial grin that Vera returned with her own smirk. "Of course, my dear, sweet Vera."

7

SOFIYA

Most of the meetings Sofiya attended seemed to go on forever and achieve nothing.

She sat there now in the boardroom, her eyelids heavy. The small of her back had gone numb right around the third time they'd looped back to the question of Haver's Bridge.

Haver's Bridge was a crumbling ruin in the centre of the city which had been named a landmark during her great-grandfather's reign. At the time, it had been royal and regal, a beautiful centrepiece in Gambit Square, but as the perimeters of the city had shifted with various gang wars and grapples with wealth, it had slowly fallen into the Cauldron and was now little more than a safety hazard. They wanted to repair it, though there was a perfectly functional bridge mere minutes up the river. It would cost millions to fix, millions the family did not have due to generations of irresponsible spending and frivolous luxury.

"I just don't think—" Sofiya started with a sigh.

"That," one advisor snapped, "is because you never saw it in its prime."

She found that most matters deemed worthy of discussion were before her time. It didn't stop her from attempting to join the conversation. Someone had to be there in her mother's absence, and she very much doubted either of her siblings would be advocates for productive change. As the heir to the throne, Sofiya tried her very best to be a part of the conversation, though she often found this to be a futile mission. She was not just ignored; she was actively disregarded.

Sofiya swirled the remainders of her tea in the bottom of her cup. She watched the leaves clump together, a sludgy green mass, then looked up at Petyr — a man who clearly felt embarrassed to be shorter than Sofiya by quite a few inches and shouted at her to make up for it. He was one of the most vocal advisors, though he was far from the most intelligent. He also happened to be the biggest supporter of repairing Haver's Bridge. "There are children not learning to read and write because they can't afford it, and you care more about an irreparable bridge?" Sofiya questioned, appalled.

"The bridge is a staple of this city."

"And so are the people."

"The bridge will outlive the people."

Sofiya couldn't help but laugh, loudly, brashly. "Are you being serious?" She was beyond irritated. In fact, she was downright furious. She knew it was a big ask for them to finally take note of the things she was saying, but it still made her seethe every time they didn't. Clenching her fists in her lap to stop them from shaking, Sofiya fought to hold her tongue. She wanted nothing more than to scream at them in frustration but that would only set her back and she hadn't made any progress to lose. She nodded tightly. They continued their discussion of the bridge.

When the meeting finished, Sofiya was just about ready to find a dark room and scream until her throat was raw. She was sick of being ignored, tired of being treated like a child sitting at the table with all the *real* men and the *real* diplomats having their *real* conversations. She wondered if that was why her mother had stopped attending meetings, if being routinely ignored had pushed her pride to its limits and it was easier for her to just give up.

She thought of her father then in his last moments, how even then as she'd crouched beside his body, he had made her feel so small and inconsequential.

Sofiya had decided resolutely at that moment that she would not give up.

On her way to the hall for dinner, she stopped before a mirror and straightened her spine. She looked worn down by the day; her hair had half fallen out, the laces of her bodice had loosened, and her eyes looked tired. She ran her fingers across her eyelids and forced brightness into her smile as she re-pinned her curls atop her head and did her best job at tightening her dress. She would look presentable, she would be a princess in the face of their discouragement, and she would not look as tired as she felt.

The dining room was on the ground floor. It was a tall room with dark oak panelling imported from Quipjin, decked out with rich red furnishings. The seats were covered in red velvet and studded with gold pins. The curtains matched the seats, drawn back by glittering strips of gold rope to reveal a broad view of the grounds beyond, lit by stars and small hanging lanterns. Sofiya could admit the view of the garden was by far the most beautiful part of the palace. It was quietly pretty and the least gaudily decorated part of their home.

Sofiya took her seat at the centre of the table next to Stas, who knocked her knee with his as he poured her a glass of wine.

Opposite Sofiya sat her siblings. Olga and Miron were the epitome of spoilt and selfish and the line connecting them to their parents was so bold it almost hurt to look at. They were whispering to each other and giggling, already drunk on red wine.

Olga, Sofiya's sister, was four years younger than her. Her hair was a deeper copper than Sofiya's and was always worn slicked back to show her sharp, feline features. She had a way of holding her chin up so her nose stuck in the air. Miron was the youngest of the siblings. He had deep brown hair and grey eyes that set him apart from both Sofiya and Olga. He had spent most of his life battling the rumours that he had been the result of her mother's affair with a merchant down at the docks.

Sofiya watched as Olga turned to Miron. Though Miron was sixteen, he had already inherited the bad habits of Olga and their mother. His hand rested casually on the base of his wine glass. Olga leaned closer and whispered to Miron, who snickered into his drink and glanced sideways at one of their advisors. Sofiya rolled her eyes.

"How was it?" Stas asked. He knew the exact level at which he should pitch his voice. They had to find that fine line between shouting along with the rest of the revellers but not so loudly that they could actually be heard.

Sofiya sat up straighter in her chair and tried to stretch out the pain beaming at the small of her back. She needed to go for a long and preferably endless walk. "If you wake up tomorrow and the entire palace has been massacred, you'll find me on Lattiere's most remote island," she grumbled, sipping her drink.

"You're not going to kill me too?"

"Someone has to stay behind to clean up this mess."

Stas laughed into his wine before leaning to the side to allow for a waiter to place a plate of potatoes down in front of them. Sofiya looked to the waiter to thank him and stopped short. She knew that man – she'd met him on the train. He had the same dark, straight hair, the same wicked smile she'd seen before. There was a certain brightness about him too, an amused look that seemed to rest across his features like a favoured cloak. He smiled at her. She stared back at him. Stas raised his eyebrow but said nothing.

The man took a step back towards the edge of the room before disappearing completely.

Sofiya turned towards Stas and said sharply, "That bastard stole my ring." She held her hand up to show a line where the ring had once been.

"When?" Stas asked.

Avoiding his gaze, Sofiya began spearing potatoes and slipping them onto her plate.

"Sofiya," Stas pressed. "When?"

"When I was in the Cauldron last. I was on the train, and

he stole it from me."

"What the hell were you doing in the Cauldron? You're lucky you weren't killed."

Sofiya didn't believe it was luck that kept her alive but her nature and skill set; she also didn't believe that now was the time to mention that. Instead, she set her mind to the question at hand, but it was surprisingly difficult to answer. *Why was she in Ivenko's Cauldron?* It wasn't as simple as, *because I felt like it*, or, *because I was bored*. The real answer was embedded a lot deeper than that, right down in the dark caves of Sofiya's soul.

It had started with an overheard conversation and was followed by the awful realisation that to get the secret back would mean to traipse over the entire city in search of something as visible as air. It was a ridiculous idea, but one Sofiya hadn't been able to shake.

She'd spent the following days doing exactly that: stomping through puddles, across makeshift drain covers, dirtying her favourite cloak all in the hopes that she would find what she was looking for, catch it fleeing someone's tongue. She hadn't found it. She had, however, lost her ring, shot out a mirror, and punched a magician. The secret was still as far away now as it had been when she had embarked on her journey.

Sofiya sipped her wine and watched the guests at the table, avidly avoiding Stas' hard gaze. While she'd been neglected in her childhood, she had taught herself all the things she thought she might need – combat, politics, how to hold a conversation with someone she didn't like – and she hated having to admit it, but none of those things had prepared her to chase a secret round the city. Besides, she was not capable of doing anything about it even if she did find the secret.

She frowned at Stas and said, "I fancied something fun to

do."

Stas scoffed and turned back to his dinner. "Then cut your hair off or actually let yourself enjoy one of these parties. You don't have to go to a part of the city that actively hates us."

"Well, I know that now," Sofiya said, running a finger over the smooth skin where her ring once sat.

She looked up again, to where the man with the sharp face had been standing. He was gone. She watched the other waiters bustle around the table, come in and out of the room with plates carrying oil slick beans and platters of golden bread. The boy with the wicked smile did not come back.

Petyr stood then, about as smart and regal as a chicken strung up in the palace kitchens, and said, "Little Sofiya here wants to let the bridge go! Can you believe it?"

After the dinner, Sofiya felt sufficiently exhausted. She'd spent most of the dinner being criticised for having the wrong opinion on the bridge and for wanting to push education. For a while, she'd tried to defend her choices, to argue the benefits of country-wide education, but she had quickly given up when she realised they were no longer listening to her. When Stas had given her a pitiful look she'd shrugged her shoulders and turned her attention fully to her meal. If she couldn't argue her point, she could at least have a good dinner.

Now she was walking back to her rooms. When she was fourteen, she'd moved to these rooms, though now she couldn't quite remember why. She guessed she'd felt sad and lonely and, fuelled by her teenage angst, had sought isolation. She was glad for it now. The rooms at the back of the palace were quiet and secluded, looking out over the gardens. The rest of her family filled the front of the palace so they could see the horses and the revellers leaving in the early hours of the morning, but Sofiya did not care for any of that. She wanted to find peace in the soft glow of the lanterns, in the quiet comfort of her rooms.

She bid the guards goodnight, though they didn't respond to her. She was never quite sure whether the guards did their job out of patriotism and pride or because it paid well and jobs in the city were scarce. Sofiya suspected that for a large percentage of the guards, the latter was true. It was only the older generation – those who had worked their way up the ranks – that still held some kind of misguided pride in their hearts.

Sofiya pushed open her door and the pressure that had been building in her chest melted away. She closed the door behind her and basked in the sweet solitude. Her rooms were decorated simply with blue banners above her bed and green curtains covering her windows. She had one mirror in her room which was beautifully void of anything gold; she did not need her cage to be gilded.

Loosening the laces of her corset, Sofiya took a deep breath. It was the first time since that morning she had been able to get a full lung of air. It didn't take her long to shed her dress, remove the pins from her hair, and throw herself onto her bed. She wanted to scream into her pillow, but she was not a teenager any longer, she had long since learnt to contain her anger and irritation, to save it for a fight. She reached over to her bedside table, lit the lamp, and grabbed her book.

Sofiya had become an avid reader when her life had become boring. Eventually, her mother had stopped her from playing with practice swords wearing men's trousers and it had been ingrained in her to become a proper lady, to wear tightly laced dresses and shoes that blistered her feet.

Sofiya still remembered the first time she'd ventured out in a gown and her father had laughed at her.

Standing in the throne room, she'd wanted to curl up in a dark corner and cry. Her pins were aching her scalp, the corset was crushing her ribs, and the cuffs of the sleeves were cutting off the circulation to her hands. She tried to hold her head up despite the weight of her new tiara, but she could feel her eyes starting to water and wanted nothing more than to lower her gaze to the floor to hide the fat droplets pooling in her eyelashes.

"Are you in a play?" King Mikhail asked, leaning back in his seat to reach for his drink. "Is that a costume? I'm not sure it suits you, Sofiya, darling."

Sofiya looked up at her father then. He was a squat man with a scrappy beard and wide, yellowish eyes like that of a toad. He was hardly one to be commenting on her appearance, especially as she'd been very carefully dressed by their country's finest designers, and he looked as though he'd just crawled back in after a night of debauchery. His comment was supposed to make her feel small, she knew him well enough to hear the venom in his voice, but his words only made her angry and she felt a flame light in her chest. She felt her tears evaporate and in their place a ball of fury settled in her throat. She was not sure the costume suited her either, but if there was one thing that fuelled Sofiya it was spite. She would make it suit her; she would become the part.

Sofiya steeled herself against his words. "Are you in a play, father?" she echoed, raising her head to meet the King's gaze.

"Excuse me?" Mikhail asked.

She'd spent so long in the shadows, longing for her father's approval, for him to turn to her and admit that he believed in her. She knew it would never happen, but the childish hope had always had its place in the back of her mind. Sofiya's childhood had been ended when she'd shed her old clothes and been pushed and pulled into the corseted dress – each second spent running around the palace grounds, every crumb of food dabbed from her plate with her finger, the sweets stolen from the kitchen maid gone with the last pin stuck into her hair. If she could lose her childhood memories so easily, she could lose her childhood hopes too.

And she did.

Sofiya took a deep breath, facing the King with her strongest self. "You're playing the king, though you don't seem to understand the duties of your role. You have a country out there, Your Majesty, but you're ignoring it."

She knew she hit the mark when something flared to life in her father's face, a short fuse that Sofiya had ignited. He rarely showed emotion, too intoxicated to care, but he didn't like to be challenged. "How dare you–"

Having said what she'd needed to, Sofiya lifted the skirts of her new dress and headed out of the throne room before he could respond to her. She had a new resolution then, made after just one line from her father. She would be better than him. She would become a good queen if it killed her, she would save her country and she would find her way onto the throne.

That was the first time Sofiya had gone to the library.

The Royal Library was a white stone building in the centre of Gambit Square. Outside, a water fountain sat in the centre of a courtyard, surrounded by students reading and tourists throwing pennies into the pool, their eyes squeezed shut as they made their wishes. It was a beautiful, tranquil place, as most places in Gambit Square seemed to be, far enough away from the rest of the city that you could even hear birds in the manicured trees overhead.

Sofiya pulled her cloak tighter around her shoulders and headed towards the large doors which sat between two stone statues carved into variations of Henygast, the god of sight. She gave a respectful nod to the statues as she passed, catching the door as a professor exited the library in his billowing cloak, purple to match the colours of the royal family.

As she entered the library and the doors slammed shut behind her, Sofiya fell hopelessly in love.

She stood there for a moment, taking in the dark oak shelves and spiral staircases as the scent of age-old pages and ink filled her senses. It was a busy place, but a silent one, the students, professors, and librarians taking books off shelves and flicking through the pages wordlessly. Sofiya realised then that she loved the sound of book pages fluttering like the wings of a moth; she loved the way even the smallest sounds echoed in the silent chamber.

"Can I help you?"

Sofiya looked up to see a woman dressed in a dark grey cloak facing her, a hood pushed back to hang around her shoulders. She was carrying a bundle of books tied with string and pushing a trolley piled high with dusty papers.

"I–" Sofiya grappled for the right words. She had never been anywhere so beautiful, and she wanted to look around, to browse the leather tomes piled high on the shelves. "No, thank you. Can I just look?"

The woman smiled at her softly in understanding, like she knew Sofiya felt utterly overwhelmed by the tranquillity of the room. She almost laughed at the thought. Since when was tranquillity overwhelming? The woman nodded once and turned back towards the shelves, leaving Sofiya to venture further into the library, her footsteps quietened by the plush carpet.

At first, she lacked direction completely, too wrapped up in the spiralling shelves to really know what she was looking for. Then she stumbled upon a shelf full of books on botanicals. She ran her fingers softly over the edge of the first book marvelling at the smoothness of the cover before pulling it off the shelf. She flicked through the first couple of pages watching as the carefully painted pictures of plants both pretty and poisonous fluttered past. She tucked the book under her arm and headed towards the counter to check it out.

"Just this one?" the man behind the counter asked. "You can take more."

"No, thank you. I like this one."

The man smiled and stamped a ticket before tucking it into the front cover. "What could a princess want with this?"

"I might want to be a healer," Sofiya replied, taking the book from his hands. "What's so wrong with that?"

"I don't think you were born to be a healer."

Sofiya tucked the book under her cloak and reached back for her hood. "Well, I think I can be both."

That wasn't strictly true. She knew she could master botanicals. It was the thought of a crown atop her head that filled her with doubt.

Unable to stay away from the beautiful calm that fell over

her, Sofiya had gone back to the library at least once a week since that first visit, gathering books of both fiction and fact, beginning her studies on botanicals, literature, science, and politics.

Now, as Sofiya reached for her latest book to soothe the headache building behind her eyes, something fluttered to the ground. She leaned over the side of her bed and retrieved the note that had been tucked into the worn pages. It wasn't a library slip.

Her heart started to thud. Someone had been in her room. A cold sweat broke out over her body as she unfolded the note and read it. *The Eva. 3am.* She knew that handwriting. It matched the two notes tucked into the pocket of her cloak, written carefully by the same hand which had stolen her ring. The same man who had something to do with the magician, who had something to do with the girl at the market. It was an infuriating web that Sofiya was yet to untangle, a world she was yet to understand.

Reluctantly, Sofiya crawled out of bed. She was tired and cold and wanted to go to sleep. She was also stubborn and determined to be better than her family before her. She would not be like them; she would not be lazy.

Sofiya planted her feet firmly on the floor, ran her fingers through the tangles of her hair and redressed.

She had an appointment to keep.

8

Vera

Vera usually avoided Tretr Lane. It was a street on the edges of the Cauldron that housed the theatres and gambling halls and was relentlessly loud. She could see the street from her bedroom window at the boarding house. Each night she would shut her moth-eaten blind and catch sight of men and women in gaudy pink and purple costumes parading up and down the cobblestones. They'd brush their hands across the arms of passersby, slipping papers and cards into their pockets advertising their houses' discounts.

But she was there now. It looked like fun beneath the evening light, once the sun had come down and the entire place was lit by a soft yellow glow, but in the daytime, it was a depressing scene – the lines on the performers' faces showed, their hunger no longer hidden by the shadows of the night, and the glitter on their costumes lost its sparkle. Seeing Tretr Lane in the daytime was like seeing the trick explained; the magic evaporated and left behind nothing but a sense of foolishness.

Irritated, Vera shoved her way through the thick crowd. She could feel the breath of every person she pushed aside clinging to her skin like the air on a humid day, sticky and uncomfortable. It smelled foul too – the smell of too many bodies in too narrow of a space, of cheap fried food, cigarette smoke, and room temperature lager. She fought the urge to cover her nose with the back of her hand.

Vera looked up as a hand caught her arm and a girl appeared in a thin blue dress. The cheap cloth stuck to her skin, the fabric charged with a static energy. She must have been freezing but it didn't show. "Hello, beautiful lady," she whispered, pressing a card into Vera's hand.

Vera settled the girl with a stern glare as she crumpled the card into a ball and gave it back. The girl was startled for a moment, then gathered herself enough to plaster on a passive smile as she threw the ball of card onto the ground.

Ignoring her, Vera pressed on through the street. With every trip, her list of reasons to avoid Tretr Lane grew. *Too busy, too chaotic, too demeaning, too uncomfortable.* She was not a sociable person in any sense of the phrase – she didn't like small talk, or pleasant smiles, and she certainly didn't like being grabbed. Every time she found herself settling in Ytavosk she thought about the times she had to walk Tretr Lane and suddenly she couldn't wait to leave.

At her sides, Vera flexed her fingers and reached into the nearest mind. Her unlucky victim was a street performer, dressed head to toe in a red striped suit. When she was in crowded spaces, she liked to search through minds. She liked to test her powers on hapless strangers, see their worst fears or their most embarrassing moments. She never kept them. It was as an exercise, a way of testing the strength of her power, and it always ended in Vera's disappointment.

She flexed her hands now and focused on the performer's mind. She saw the threads and examined them like she was flicking through files in an old cabinet. She could feel the strain as sweat beaded on the back of her neck. She saw the man in a dimly lit room get down on one knee before a woman in a feather hat. She saw the woman's cheeks flush the same crimson as her dress, saw her take one step back and then another as her head shook back and forth. The man rose from his knee, chasing the woman as she fled. Vera curled the secret around her finger and tugged. The man touched his temple and she let it go.

Her power should have been seamless. She should be able to flick her fingers and remove the secret without the victim knowing, but she was not strong enough for that. She hoped it was a lack of training, that when she finally scraped together enough pennies to get to Vor, she would be able to strengthen it.

With an ache, Vera remembered her mother, the way Agathe had taught Vera to hide her power, the way she had taught her to have her very own secret.

"You have a gift, Valerie," Agathe had whispered. "But the world isn't ready for it."

Even in her memory Vera cringed at the old name, at the meek girl she'd been, and the way that with each of her mother's soft words, Vera had shoved her power down. She had never learnt to use it properly and she regretted that.

The thought set a pressure in the back of her head.

"One day, we will travel to Vor," her mother had promised. That plan had fallen through when her mother had been shot dead the day Vera fled the Isles.

They had never gotten to Vor – it was still a far-off place in Vera's mind, a fairy tale land. It was thought that somewhere deep in the Vorian mountains, a city existed just for magicians, though it was little more than a fable. Her mother had believed in it deeply, but Vera was never sure whether it was true belief that had driven her mother or the hope of safety for her daughter. The rumours had never become a truth and so the story of those sacred mountains remained just that – a story.

The furthest Vera had gotten to safety was Sikveya after her mother had given her life to put Vera on that ship. Vera had never been able to scrounge together enough money to get to Vor, but she held the memory of her mother's voice in her head. There, she could keep her mother alive, and with her, the promise of the secret city.

Vera looked up at Tretr Lane and wondered how she must look in a place like that, where colour and light pushed their aggressive agenda. She exclusively wore dark clothes to blend into the bleak background of Ytavosk, but when she came to these parts of the city – the parts that seemed determined to defy the decay – she seemed more like a plague personified travelling through a circus.

Plague she may be, but Vera was efficient, and it wasn't long before she had made it to the theatre at the end of the street.

St Polya's Theatre did not stand out despite being painted an almost luminous shade of green. It looked pretty dull in comparison to the rest of the buildings which had broad windows giving onlookers a peak at what they were missing. St Polya's was a solid building with little to decorate it bar two hoops hanging from what Vera assumed were disused balconies. A man and a woman hung from the hoops, their faces plastered in bright smiles as they spun in slow circles and contorted their bodies in a way that made Vera's cold, seized limbs cry.

Vera forced her way towards a green canopy with a bouncer standing at the edge of it. He was a large man and would probably have been intimidating had Vera not looked through his mind and seen that he was secretly afraid of the holes in sponges.

"Six ykas," the man grunted, holding out his hand.

Vera shoved her hood back and looked up at him. "Are you serious, Larin?" she asked. "Move."

Larin, who was twice Vera's height, three times her width, and could definitely pick her up and throw her with minimal effort, coughed and shuffled awkwardly out of Vera's way. She smiled at him and entered the theatre.

The interior of the theatre was just as offensively green as the exterior, though it was harder to see through cigarette smoke and the sweaty haze radiating from the stage. Through the thick fog, Vera could just about make out the figure on the stage – a girl with dark brown skin and a mane of pink hair. Her costume was little more than a bodice and a silk skirt that barely reached her thighs, and her face was set in a serene kind of smile. She was objectively beautiful, hanging from a sheet of pink silk that cascaded from the ceiling.

Vera watched as Anya loosened her grip on the silk and spun, her arms outstretched, her body tumbling to the ground. She caught herself at the last moment and untangled herself from the silk. She strode to the front of the stage and bowed deeply, spreading her toned arms wide. The applause was pitiful, the men and women in the parlour too engrossed in their card games and excessive drinking, but Anya stood for a moment like an actor observing her standing ovation before she left the stage.

Vera manoeuvred through the rows of round tables, narrowly avoiding the uncontrolled limbs of drunk men high on a winning streak.

A hand caught her, and she was jerked back by a man in a grey suit clutching the already fragile fabric of her cloak. A piece tore off in his hands as Vera pulled away from him. "Come on, honey!" he called after her, holding the shred of her cloak to his chest as though it were a piece of her. "Come celebrate with me."

Vera turned back towards him and smiled her only smile – a wicked mask for her ill-temper. "Oh, okay," she said smoothly, resting a hand on his shoulder. She ran her fingers down his arm and entwined them with his.

He giggled like a spoiled schoolboy and gestured to his friends at the table. They all smirked and spluttered, sipping their drinks and whistling.

Vera clutched his hand tighter and suddenly he didn't find it quite so funny. She revelled in the way his face contorted in pain as his smirk turned to an open mouthed *oh* and his eyes widened in surprise. She yanked his fingers back and they cracked and popped as the bones broke. She threw his hand back against the table. The man shrieked in pain and Vera laughed as the waiters rushed towards the sound, determined to quash it before it disturbed the other tables.

Vera glanced up to the corner of the room to where a woman in her fifties stood flicking through cash. Marina managed the theatre and was known for the pearls she wore in her hair like a halo. She was a brutal woman, but only to those she didn't like. She was a fair boss and stood tall as one of the most inspiring people in Vera's life – relentless, mean, unapologetic. Marina smiled and nodded at Vera, laughing quietly to herself as she glanced towards the chaos. Vera couldn't force back the satisfaction bubbling in her chest.

Slipping back into the crowd, Vera moved away from the shrill cries rising from the table. She made her way towards the dressing rooms behind the stage. As she brushed a curtain aside and slipped into the room, she saw Anya unpinning the wig from her head to reveal her cropped black hair. Anya met Vera's eyes in the mirror.

"Good evening," Anya chirped with a smile.

Anya was a tall woman with dark eyes and short black hair which she usually kept under a ragged red hat. But now, she was dressed head to toe in a sharp tone of pink which stood out against her dark skin. Her eyes were painted the same gold dusted on her cheeks and collar bones. She'd painted her nails gold to match.

Vera nodded, lingering in the doorway. "Do you want a job?" Vera asked bluntly, cutting straight to business. She had never been a fan of small talk.

"I have two."

"Interesting," Vera replied. "Do they pay well?"

Anya paused.

Vera already knew the answer – *no*.

"And how's little Daria?" Vera asked. It was cruel to press Anya's one weakness – her sick sister – but she did it anyway.

Anya glared at Vera in the mirror. "Fuck you."

"So?"

Anya took out a cloth and ran it over her face to remove the makeup. She scrubbed at her left eye for a long moment before stopping and looking back towards Vera. She had gold and black makeup smeared across her face. "What would I be doing?"

"I'm not sure yet."

"And how much would I be paid?"

"Again, I don't know. I imagine quite a lot."

Anya laughed and pressed the cloth to her face again. Vera could see the tension in her shoulders, in the pin straightness of her spine. She found Anya difficult to read. On the surface the girl was bright like Lev, but in the lines of her body she held a kind of darkness, a stress you could only see once she removed her cloak. Vera liked Anya. She thought she was interesting, a puzzle that itched the back of Vera's mind. She thought she understood Anya's motives – her sister was sick and in need of expensive medications – but Vera always wondered if there was something else there too, buried beneath the rubble.

"You can contact me when you know," Anya said.

"You come to the meeting tonight or you're out. I won't ask again."

Anya seemed to weigh this up. She stood and pulled on an old, torn dress that had been slung over a closet door. It was ill fitting on the girl's muscular frame, tight across the shoulders, but loose at the hips. Lastly, she pulled her cap out of a bag hanging on the back of her chair and shoved it down over her shorn head. "Where is it?"

"The Eva."

"Time?"

"Three."

Anya sighed and slumped back into her chair. "There best be wine."

9

LEV

After his brief expedition to the palace, Lev made his way back to the boarding house to where he'd left the blood-soaked rags in the corner of the bathroom.

Vera had left promptly after their plan was put in place, catching sight of herself in the mirror briefly before she went and sighing at what she saw.

Now, Lev looked down at her blood in the sink. It was not the first time they had found themselves in that position – her sitting on the edge of the bathtub, him blotting the blood from her face with a cloth. The first time he'd met her, he'd spent an evening cleaning the blood from her eye, though he'd been more delicate then as her body had curled in on itself, the tension in her shoulders that of a wounded animal.

It was very hard to connect the Vera he knew now to the girl she had been then. She did not look scared anymore. She was not waiting for attack; she was the snake striking first. She held her shoulders straight, her chin high, an aggressive glint in her eye. She was the threat, not the victim.

Lev rinsed the sink out and watched as the last tendrils of blood drained down the plughole.

She'd asked him to reserve a private room after The Eva closed for the evening. It wasn't a difficult task, but Lev wondered whether he should kick up a fight every once in a while to make his job look a little more challenging. She asked for things, and he gave them to her and that was how it had always been. She was selfish. He knew that. She had been remorselessly showing that side of herself since he'd met her.

Once, an elderly man had been struggling on the stairs that led down to the river's edge. The rail had been partially broken in the middle and the man asked Vera for assistance. Vera stormed straight past him, ignoring him entirely. After Lev had helped the man and he'd graciously given him a few pennies for the trouble, he caught up to Vera and asked her why she hadn't helped.

Vera looked him dead in the eye and said, "Would I help you?"

Lev thought about it for a moment, desperate to believe she *would* help him, but he shook his head in defeat.

"Exactly." She continued down the street. "I don't even help my friends, Lev, why would I help a stranger?"

It's nice to know she considers me a friend, Lev had thought drearily.

Heaving a sigh, Lev unlocked his bedroom door and entered. His room was just as messy as it had been that morning, the week before, and the many years before that. Should anyone break in, they'd have a difficult time finding anything of value to steal.

Once upon a time, he'd kept his money in his bedside cabinet. That was until Vera had stolen it and he'd started keeping it beneath the floorboards. He shoved his bed aside and crouched down next to the wooden panel he'd pulled loose. He hitched his nail up under the board and pulled. For a moment it stuck, and panic spiked in his chest, but then it released and beneath it sat a neat roll of cash. He stuffed it into his breast pocket and replaced the floorboard and then the bed.

Throwing his cloak over his shoulders, Lev headed out.

He liked to take any opportunity to leave the Cauldron, but he did not want to go to the home. He could have gotten the train, but he wanted fresh air, even though 'fresh' meant thick smoke and other fumes Lev tried not to think about. It was a short walk through the Cauldron, past the market, and across the river to the Veleer District.

Lev took a moment to steel himself. He leaned against the railing of Second Bridge, the smell of seaweed and damp sand assaulting his senses. He looked at the crumbling wreck of Haver's Bridge, watching the boats hesitate as they passed beneath it. He wondered how many of those boats carried people trying to start new lives in the city. He knew Vera had done just that and Anya had too, though he knew relatively little about their stories. Beyond the water, the dock workers called to each other as they unloaded and reloaded cargo, their layers of clothing heavy to ward off the brittle evening cold. It wasn't too late in the evening, but the night had started to set in, turning the sky dark and the air bitter.

He'd spent many winter nights playing cards with Vera beside the fire, both of them trying to keep their hands from seizing in the cold.

Lev closed his eyes for a moment and took a deep breath before continuing on his way.

The Veleer District had raised Lev. It was the part of the city designed for those with enough money to get by, but not so much that their lives were comfortable. As a child, he'd had to wear his shoes long after he'd outgrown them but there had always been a meal on the table to warm his stomach. Veleer was not pretty like Gambit Square, but it held a kind of charm for Lev with its gabled roofs and terraced houses. Each house was granted a small plot of land most used to dry their clothes in the summer. The houses were skinny and tall, but they were not pressed together as tightly as they were in Ivenko's Cauldron, the bricks less loose, the alleyways less dangerous.

Lev glanced at his pocket watch. He was late as he always was, and he picked up his pace. They were expecting his payment and he knew he couldn't sweet-talk them the way he could with Mrs Hanovich.

When he arrived at the home, he took a moment to remind himself why he worked so hard to pay so much. It was gloriously clean. The outside of the building was soot-stained but when he stepped through the door, the interior was pristine. The floors were swept and polished, the wallpaper was perfectly flat against the walls with no hint of damp or mould, and the staff wore clean and crisp uniforms. A clean, hygienic environment was such a small thing to be grateful for, but it was so rare in Ytavosk unless you could afford to live in Gambit Square.

He approached the front desk to where a boy was sitting in his doctor's apron. He couldn't have been older than sixteen.

"Good evening, Mister Valensky," he said as he rose from his stool.

Lev hated being referred to as mister. It made him sound a lot older than he felt and in that moment, beneath the bright lights of the home and the weight of the meeting ahead of him, he felt like a child again.

Taking the money from his pocket, Lev rolled out the right amount of cash, counted it quickly and placed it upon the counter before the boy.

As the boy swept it up and recounted each note, he looked up at Lev. "Our fees are going up next month."

Lev tried to ignore the spike in his pulse and the sudden sweltering heat in his chest. "How much?" He could hardly afford to pay them now.

"By a third," the boy said. "You know how things are. Costs are going up everywhere."

His heart sank. He would have to move his father to a different home, though he would not be able to find one as good for less money. Franchesko Valensky had always called the Veleer District home and Lev had worked hard to keep him there. He dreaded the thought of moving his father to the Cauldron. He knew he would not survive in the city's underworld.

Lev didn't argue with the boy, only nodded once to show that he had heard and made his way upstairs.

When he pushed the door to his father's room open, an almost complete darkness welcomed him. It was broken only by a beam of moonlight which lit Franchesko as he sat in a worn armchair looking out over the city. Lev couldn't help but wonder how much of the city he remembered, or whether he was trying to keep him in that part of town for no reason at all.

Beside his father's bed sat a tray of untouched food. Lev gathered the tray and perched on the small footstool beside his father's chair, the tray balanced precariously on his lap. It wasn't until Lev was sitting beside him that his father looked up.

"You brought food," he said softly, pointing to the tray. He made no move towards it.

Lev swallowed the lump in his throat, the same ache that rose every time he saw his father. "Yes, I did. Do you want to eat it?"

His father stared at him for a long moment, blinking slowly before nodding.

"Okay," Lev said, picking up the spoon.

The man sitting before him did not look like his father at all. His skin was sallow, and his eyes were dull. His head had been shaved to stave off lice and his chin was shaven too. Lev knew he had long since lost his father and sitting in that chair was a lingering shadow of the man who had held Lev's hand in the street to stop him from running off, who had clapped him proudly on the back when he'd got a mediocre score in a school test.

Lev held the bowl close to his father's chest and scooped up a small spoonful of broth. His father opened his mouth to eat, but some of the broth still dripped onto his night clothes. He chewed slowly as Lev wiped the food from his shirt but seemed to hold the food in his mouth.

Tapping his own throat gently, Lev mimed swallowing.

His father hesitated before swallowing the food. He rested

his hands in his lap and said, "You must be new staff. I haven't seen you before."

Lev no longer clung to the idea that his father would remember him. When his father's memory had begun its steady decline, Lev had taken each of his memories and locked them away for safekeeping. They were sweet, fragile things that he could keep forever, but he had to let his father go. There was no point trying to cling to the man who could not remember picking Lev up from school – it would only hurt them both.

"I started last week," Lev lied.

"Oh, will you be here for long?"

"As long as you need me."

"Okay," his father whispered. "Thank you."

The sadness Lev felt was a melancholy set deep in his chest. The break wasn't clean and each time it started to heal, he'd jolt it and the ache would start up again. He didn't need his father anymore, not the way he had when he was a boy. He didn't need him to teach him to catch the train or to make sure he left the house with a coat, but it still hurt to know that this man, who was once so prideful, was meeting such a bitter end. He did not die quickly; he was fading away.

"You know, I have a son," his father said.

Hope struck Lev's heart. He couldn't help it.

"He's a lot younger than you. Just a boy. You look a lot like him actually, but no, he is a lot younger than you."

"Oh," Lev said, the sound hitching in his throat.

Perhaps he did remember teaching Lev to tie his shoelaces.

"I've got a wife too. Her name is Mei," Franchesko mumbled softly. "She was travelling here from Quipjin. She was supposed to be passing through, but she stayed. Her family were furious."

Lev smiled.

He'd heard the story of how his parents met a thousand times. It became like a fable to him, a tale about the importance of love and faith. He was not religious, but their story made him believe in powers beyond those he saw in Sikveya. His mother had been the daughter of a trader selling bolts of silk and they'd come to trade in the ports of Ytavosk. She'd been visiting the factory where his father had worked, and their eyes had met across the dusty, oil-slick floor. The rest was history.

Lev's story was less romantic than that, though he guessed it could still be called fate. He was obsessed with the girl he'd found in an alleyway. He'd thought she was dead and had gone to rob her body when she'd stirred. It had been his mother's voice in the back of his head that had told him to help her, to make up for what he'd almost done.

His father smiled as he finished up the last of the broth. "She'll be there when I go home."

There it was again, the lump in his throat, that same withered sadness bursting deep within his heart. His mother had been dead for fifteen years.

Lev stayed with his father until the intense heat from the fire made Franchesko's eyelids droop and Lev helped him into bed. It was an odd thing to put to bed the man who had once kissed him goodnight and turned out the lights.

"Wait," his father called as Lev put his cloak on. His voice was weary, slurred as he drifted off to sleep. "Can you tell Mei and Lev I won't be home tonight? They'll be waiting for me."

"Of course," Lev said, closing the door behind him.

10

Anya

Anya was the first to arrive at The Eva. She was sure Lev wouldn't be there yet – his timekeeping skills were notoriously poor – but she thought Vera would have been waiting for her at the table like the phantom she was. At least Anya could choose a seat with her back to the wall.

She sat down at the table and began folding and unfolding the napkin in front of her. This was not the first time they had gathered in the private parlour surrounded by red and gold, colours that were too rich for the likes of them. Anya felt extraordinarily out of place in her scruffy clothes and boots. She had almost definitely trodden dirt into the carpet.

Having come straight from the theatre, Anya hadn't had time to check on Daria. She hadn't seen the girl since she had told her to go home, and her mind was spiralling through all the ways Daria could have gotten distracted on her way back. She hadn't been able to tell Daria that she would be home late, and she hoped the girl was tired enough to sleep through until the morning.

She could not miss the meeting.

The curtain was shoved aside, and a cloaked figure entered the room. She looked around for a moment before her gaze landed on Anya. She pulled off her fine cloak to reveal a dress of deep blue, the colour of which exaggerated her pale skin and bright hair. She was beautiful and looked healthier than anyone in the Cauldron; her waist and hips were broad, and her shoulders were set in a line. Her face, made up of soft curves, was stern.

When the girl reached out her hand to pull out the chair beside Anya, she noticed her knuckles were shiny with a purplish bruise. She sat up straight, her forearms resting against the table. She was born to exist in a room that grand.

"You owe me for the mirror," Anya snapped at her.

"There," she said sharply, as she reached into her pocket and threw a handful of coins onto the table.

Before Anya had time to respond, Vera shoved her way into the room. She stopped short when she saw Anya and her companion. She smiled her tight, wicked smile and sat down opposite them without removing her cloak.

When Vera pulled her scarf down to hang it around her neck, Anya said with a little more concern than she'd intended, "Gods, Vera, what happened to you? You look terrible."

Vera had a glossy bruise that sat across her nose and flooded the space beneath her eyes. She was sporting an eyepatch over her left eye which was secured with two straps tied around her head.

The girl held up her bruised hand and Vera glared at her.

"Ah," Anya said.

"You ratted me out," Vera snapped, untangling the wool scarf from her neck.

Anya sat up straighter in her seat and narrowed her eyes at Vera. "She had a gun to my head."

"Oh please," Lev said as he entered the private parlour carrying three half-drunk bottles of wine tucked under one arm and a platter of mismatched foods in his hands. "Don't act like you wouldn't have done the same, Vera."

Anya looked towards Lev who winked back at her. She'd always liked Lev. He was kind and loyal and no matter how much she puzzled it out in her head, she couldn't quite seem to understand how he'd grown attached to someone as cold and bitter as Vera.

They'd first met at the pub where he had been a waiter and Anya's mother, Iskra, had been a waitress. She remembered her mother coming home each night and telling her about the boy at the pub who deserved more, who was too kind and would be crushed underfoot like daisies in the spring. He was the only person who'd visited her after her mother had died. He'd brought wilting flowers and some bread and had wrapped his arms around Anya as she'd wept into his shoulder.

Now, turning to direct her glare to the girl beside her, Anya muttered, "So much for not telling her."

"She didn't. You just did." Vera huffed out a laugh and picked up a chunk of bread.

Anya poured herself a glass of wine, filling the glass almost to the brim. She sat back in her chair with a sigh, resisting the urge to roll her eyes skyward. She was getting a bit tired of these people and yet for some reason she couldn't help but come running when they called.

Lev took up the seat beside Vera. He always seemed to gravitate towards her.

"Shall we make some introductions?" Lev asked, his face aglow with a bright smile.

"Anya, I'd like you to meet Princess Sofiya," Vera said.

Anya looked at the girl beside her as the realisation hit. She looked born to riches because she was. *The Princess.* Anya laughed. "We keep company with royals now?"

Sofiya straightened her spine as though she was now preparing for a fight.

Anya swiped some cheese and a cracker from the plate but Princess Sofiya Meskov of Sikveya did not touch the food or the wine. Anya suspected the girl had a lovely hot meal waiting for her when she got home, a fire already set, a warm bed, a hot bath, and a solid door to lock out the demons that prowled the street at night.

Anya was expecting some kind of confrontation. She was expecting an explanation. But Sofiya just leaned across the table, pointed her finger at Lev and snapped, "Give me my ring back."

Lev swallowed his mouthful of wine and said innocently, "What?" He was very good at playing the fool.

"You stole my ring. I want it back." Sofiya did not try to cover the anger on her face. It was a different kind to the fury Vera wore; it was more righteous, better suited for a dignified battle than street fights and vengeance. Her anger was bolder and well rounded.

Lev did what he always did in tense situations – he laughed. "I don't have it anymore, I'm afraid."

Vera leaned forward then, resting her chin on her hand as her fingers curled up the side of her starved face. On her middle finger sat what Anya assumed was *the* signet ring. "If you don't offer us enough, I'll have to use *this* to pay my bills."

Sofiya scoffed, her fingers moving to the patch of pale skin where the ring must once have sat. It was comforting to know that even princesses had nervous habits. She seemed to catch herself and tucked her hands into her lap. "This is an alliance, not a job."

Vera ignored her. "You said you could offer me freedom?"

Sofiya said nothing.

"I want immunity from your laws."

The girl beside Anya paused then and considered. It seemed to pain her to speak again. "Just you?"

"Just me."

A spark of irritation lit in Anya's chest. It was not unusual for Vera to be selfish but some part of her had hoped the reach of Vera's bargaining would be a little broader than just herself.

"Fine," Sofiya conceded.

"You'll give me access to your royal doctor," Anya said suddenly, her words surprising even to her own ears. "They'll help my sister."

"What's wrong with your sister?" Sofiya asked.

"I'll speak with your doctor, and they will help. If not, I'm out."

Anya knew she was playing a risky game. She knew the money was better than nothing at all and if Sofiya said no, she would just be replaced, not bargained for. But she thought of Daria, the blood, the sticky sweat that covered her feverish skin, and she knew she had to at least try.

"Fine," Sofiya conceded.

Anya ignored the questioning look from Lev.

Vera slipped the ring from her finger and tapped it twice against the table as if testing its strength. "And fifty thousand ykas," she said. "Each."

"Absolutely not."

Vera sat back in her seat as Lev leaned forward and poured himself more wine. Anya noticed the way his shoulders straightened, as if he was just now entering the conversation. He seemed determined to maintain his relaxed posture, to scream his carelessness as loudly as possible, but Anya saw the tension flooding his body.

Lev's hand brushed past Vera's; the movement was so subtle Anya doubted Sofiya would notice the two thieves making an exchange.

"You're rich and we're hungry," Vera said. "And if you say no, I'll dig through your head and sell something from there instead." She raised her fingers and curled them slightly.

Sofiya grabbed her hand in mid-air and turned it over. "Where is the ring?"

Lev held the ring out, but in a single flick of his wrist, it disappeared once more.

Pressing her fingers to her temple, Sofiya took a deep breath.

Anya knew Vera was lying. She cared more about survival than stealing from Sofiya's family. As far as Anya knew, Vera had no personal thirst for vengeance. *Well,* she thought, *other than them wanting her and all magicians dead.* Anya almost felt sorry for Sofiya, who had clearly not been expecting the task to be quite so difficult. Then she saw the impeccable fit of her dress and the way the candlelight reflected off her hair and the feeling vanished.

"If you go through my head, I'll have you arrested and killed." In the Cauldron, defeat had its own language carved out of jagged letters. Sofiya had found herself in a pit of snakes and Anya could tell from the defensive note in her voice that she was resigned to the high price.

Lev sat back in his chair once more and smiled.

"Thirty thousand ykas and you give me my ring back."

"Forty thousand *each*, you grant me legally binding immunity, you let Anya have access to the doctor, and I give you your ring back." She glanced at Lev beside her. "Did you want anything?"

"No," Lev replied cheerily. "I think I'm good with the money."

Sofiya sighed.

The thieves cut each other satisfied glances.

"Who am I paying for?" The Princess frowned.

Anya waited for Vera to calculate the numbers in her head. They all knew she didn't need any of them for the alliance, that she would find a way to do it on her own. She would barter with the right people, pull in the right favours, and blackmail the rest. But there was a protocol in the Cauldron that meant more than any blood pact or prayer. It was the thugs' and thieves' way of helping a neighbour when they had nothing else to spare. In Ivenko's Cauldron, poverty was not scarce. It ran thick in the gutters of the city and if one had the fortune of falling upon wealth, it became their responsibility to drag a team up with them.

"Anya is good at forgeries. I will capture the secret, and Lev–"

"I'm just here for a good time," Lev said, tipping his drink towards Sofiya who rolled her eyes.

"Lev is broke and needs the money," Vera clarified.

"That too."

"I'm not paying for whatever gambling habits or drinking problems you've acquired," Sofiya replied.

"Lev knows the city better than any of us," Anya cut in, her defences rising. "He's the only one of us who is actually from here."

It was true. Lev had the best knowledge of the city. Vera was from the Isles of Lattiere, her thick accent giving her away, and Anya was from the opposite end of the country. She had lived in the city since she was fourteen, but it was a place you had to grow up in. Lev had been living in the city since he'd opened his eyes and he knew its heart.

"*I'm* from here," Sofiya snapped.

Lev just smiled. "You grew up in the palace. You'd have better luck finding your way through a maze drunk."

Anya could see Sofiya fighting the urge to argue with him, but all she said was, "Anyone else?"

"Aleks," Vera replied.

"What does Aleks do?"

"Depends on what we need him to do."

Aleks stole memories – Anya had recurrent business with him – but Vera would not reveal that before Aleks revealed himself. She hadn't bartered immunity for him.

Aleks had come onto the scene when Anya was fifteen and had taken over the market stall. She wasn't sure where he had come from or what had driven him to steal and sell memories. At the time he'd felt so much older than her, but now she realised he must have only been four or five years her senior. He'd been fresh-faced and clean when he arrived, his accent so crisp it was obvious he was from one of the nicer parts of the city. Eventually, he'd married the apothecary's daughter, though Anya hadn't seen her in a long while. Anya was sceptical that the man would want to get involved with Vera's antics, but there was also a high chance that Vera knew something no one else did.

"So, four people. That's one hundred and sixty thousand ykas," Sofiya said. "I can't pay that much."

"Oh please," Lev said. "You'd probably spend that much on a party."

Anya laughed. "She'd probably spend that much on a *dress* for the party."

It was hard not to feel bitter towards the girl knowing she lived a gilded life, watching as her subjects starved to death on the streets below. It was hard not to feel as though the people of Sikveya were pawns in a long-forgotten game.

Anya reached across the table and plucked a bruised grape from the platter. The food and wine had been devoured quickly, though Anya had managed to pocket some bread for Daria.

"If you can't afford it, you can find someone else to help you," Vera snapped. She was in a fortunate position. She knew Sofiya needed something only Vera could find. She may kick and scream at first, but she had to give Vera what she wanted.

"Forty thousand each, your immunity, the doctor, my ring, and you don't go through my head," Sofiya confirmed.

Vera nodded and they shook hands across the table.

Sofiya glanced towards Lev and held out her hand.

"Milady," he said as he dropped the ring into her open

palm. "Although, there is one thing I would like to know."

"What?" Sofiya asked.

"How did you know we were all linked?"

In a quick movement, Sofiya flattened two scrunched up notes on the table. At first, Anya thought they were just scraps of paper, useless lint she kept at the bottom of her pocket. It wasn't until she looked closer that Anya saw the scribbly handwriting on the two notes, both identical. "You dropped this when you got off the train. Vera left the other note at the market stall. I figured you knew each other."

Vera reached across the table and snatched the two notes back. She stuffed them into the bodice of her dress and glared at Sofiya and then at Lev. "You need to be less reckless with these."

"It seems you do too, Vera," Lev replied. He was smiling softly as he always did, but there was a note of irritation in his voice.

Anya cleared her throat. "So, what are we looking for?"

"I don't know," Sofiya said quietly.

Lev laughed.

Vera rolled her eyes.

Anya sighed and said, "She's lying."

"Of course she's lying," Vera replied, draining the dregs of wine from the bottom of her cup. "And she better stop because it's pissing me off."

"I really don't know."

"And how exactly do you expect us to find something when we don't even know what it is?"

"All I know is that it's about the heir – that is to say, it's about me. That doesn't mean I know the secret, or that the secret is mine, and I am not about to air my dirty laundry to three strangers. You'll find a way to help me, or the deal is off."

Vera seemed to consider this for a moment, as though she really was about to call the deal off. She took a deep breath. Anya watched the girl steel herself. She had a way of setting her shoulders, of steadying herself before she took on a problem as though the weight of the issue was a tangible thing. "Lev, you said there were Pravinya officials talking about the secret?"

"Yes."

"So that's where we start."

Anya tilted her head to the side. "We break into their building?"

Vera nodded. "I'll look around. Someone must know something, even just to give us a lead. We need to figure out what the rumour is, and then we can narrow down who might have the secret." She got up from the table and pulled her scarf back over her face, veiling the bruise on the bridge of her nose. In one quick movement, Vera Datsyuk was gone, leaving the curtain to swing shut in her wake.

Lev plucked a cracker from the tray, Anya pretended to ignore the longing on his face, and Sofiya Meskov, Princess of Sikveya, threw her hands up in exasperation.

Part Two

The Outskirts of Life

11

SOFIYA

The next time Sofiya saw Vera, Anya, and Lev it was to meet with Aleks.

She had woken up that morning to find yet another note on her nightstand. She was uncomfortable with the fact that one of these three people had managed to get into her room not once, but twice. There were two ways they could have done it, and both felt impossible to Sofiya. The first was that they scaled the side of the palace and broke in through Sofiya's double locked balcony doors, and the second was that they had somehow managed to bypass guards, maids, roaming kitchen staff, various members of the royal circle, and Sofiya's family, and sneak up to Sofiya's room all without being noticed. She had realised then, as she'd scanned the note in the dim candlelight, that she was not safe in her own home. She was not safe with these people.

After the sun had gone down, she met them in an alleyway that had been described as 'three long steps past Second Bridge'. The instruction felt half-baked which gave Sofiya the distinct feeling Vera had written it.

Vera was leading them now with Lev at her side filling the silence with his stream of one-sided conversation. Sofiya watched as Vera turned to him and raised an eyebrow. He leaned closer to her and whispered something and in response Vera gave him a sharp jab in the side with her elbow and stormed ahead of the group.

Sofiya had ended up walking beside Anya.

She wasn't sure what to make of Anya. She'd spoken to Vera and even punched the girl, which seemed to solidify their mutual dislike of each other. Through Vera, Sofiya felt like she had a grasp on Lev, and he was the easiest to understand with his relentless loyalty and desperate need for money. But she did not know the girl standing beside her at all. Sofiya broke down the things she knew of Anya – the girl ran a stall on the blackmarket trading in magic, though she did not have any magical power of her own, she was an acrobat and a performer, and Anya was chatty, though not in the same way Lev was chatty. While Lev's verbal output was unfiltered, Anya seemed to be able to put a stopper on the information she leaked. There was something dark hiding behind Anya's face that appeared when she was nervous. She'd seen it when she first broke into the dressing room and again when Anya had asked for access to the palace doctor.

"Your friends broke into my room again," Sofiya said.

"No, they didn't," Anya replied, skipping gracefully over a dead rat.

"I found a note there. It wasn't Lev's writing."

"It wasn't Vera's, either."

"It must have been."

"Vera doesn't like to read and write in Sikveyan," Anya said. "You'll notice when things need to be in our language, Lev will write them for her. And if the handwriting wasn't Lev's, it must have been someone else's."

"Then how did you do it?"

"I'm an acrobat." Anya laughed softly.

"That's not an answer," Sofiya said.

"Well, that's all you're getting."

Anya stomped easily over one of the many makeshift bridges in Ivenko's Cauldron. Sofiya tried to follow suit and imitate her confidence, but she still found herself looking into the blackhole of a drain beneath her. She did not move with the same ease as Vera, Lev, or Anya. While they treated rats and cockroaches as welcome members of their city, Sofiya still flinched when they scurried over her feet. She also wasn't quite used to the washing lines – Vera didn't have to duck, though Anya and Lev did with a rehearsed grace – and Sofiya had almost hung herself on at least three in the last hour.

A hand grabbed Sofiya's arm as a voice shouted overhead. Sofiya turned to see Anya hauling her back a few paces. The girl pointed upwards to where a woman was preparing to tip a bucket from her window three stories above. As the liquid was poured out of the bucket, Sofiya jumped back, narrowly avoiding the splash of the water on the cobblestones. She squealed, her voice embarrassingly high pitched, and resisted the urge to vomit.

"Oh, relax," Anya said, pulling Sofiya forward. "We have plumbing. That's just washing up water."

Ahead, Vera and Lev stopped to wait for them. Lev was laughing as he always seemed to be, his shoulders shaking with each burst, and even Vera's face was contorted into something Sofiya might have been able to call amusement.

The further they ventured into the backstreets of the Cauldron, the closer the buildings got. The sun, which had been bright even beyond the smoke and soot of the city, was almost gone now, stuck somewhere above them beyond the sheets and canvas awnings, plunging them into a dreary darkness. Sofiya noticed that each house and shop front was more populated here, the people coughing and stumbling around in the dark, or leaning their cheeks on stone doorsteps. The thieves fell into single file, the alleyway not quite wide enough for two people to walk side by side.

Sofiya felt a jab between her shoulder blades as Anya urged her forward. "If you stop," the girl said, "they'll start grabbing you."

Sofiya picked up her pace, but she couldn't stop looking at the sickly faces, the darkness of the Cauldron, the squalor these people were forced to live in because of the monarchy, because of *her*. She felt sick to her stomach. She could feel her guilt like a tangible thing. Like blood in water, it mixed with her anger, a swirling mass of red in her mind. She chased the thought around – *this is my fault* – and each time it was met with the same furious determination. *I can change this. I* will *change this.*

It was an evil thing to do, but Sofiya had plotted a thousand ways to seize the throne. How could she convince her mother to give it up, to hand it all to Sofiya, to let her become the person she believed she could be? The door to politics had always been firmly shut in her face, but that didn't mean she wasn't born for it, that she couldn't learn.

She almost walked straight into Lev's back as they came to a sudden stop before a rotting wooden door. The house itself was two stories high and felt tiny in comparison to the buildings surrounding it. The whole thing was made of wood that seemed a light breeze away from caving in. Sofiya thought it must have been a makeshift home, built in the gaping mouth of a disused alleyway between two pre-existing stone buildings. It didn't look like it was supposed to be there.

Vera thumped her closed fist against the door. From somewhere further up the street, a scream echoed, bouncing off the stone. Sofiya's head shot towards it, but the others did not pay any attention to whoever was in distress. Sofiya saw the woman tugging at King Mikhail cloak, the baby screaming in her arms. She heard the gunshot.

Vera slammed her fist against the door again. "Aleks, open up!" She kicked the door once and it swung open.

Standing in the doorway and looking mildly annoyed was a man a little older than the rest of them. Sofiya assumed he was Aleks. He was well-built and had a head of curls that shone a deep copper in the candlelight coming from his entryway. The scowl on his face rivalled Vera's.

Vera just shoved her way past him and into the house.

Aleks stepped back and said sarcastically, "Please, do come in."

Lev strolled past, followed by Anya, and then Sofiya. As she passed him, something in his face went cold. Sofiya looked at him closer. He was taller than Sofiya was, but she could see his face and there was something familiar about it as though he'd worked at the palace for a short while. She fought to remember exactly who he was, but it was hopeless. With shame burning in her chest, she pushed past him.

The inside of the house was just as dire as the exterior. With bare walls, the main room consisted of a small kitchen unit, a single rusted hob, and a small round table in the centre. It was freezing inside the building, as though none of the winter air was kept out by the ramshackle walls. Sofiya's eyes drifted around the house to see bottles containing blue sparks on every available surface. The contents of the bottles seemed restless, swooping and swirling in the glass cages.

Aleks said nothing. There was something very quiet about him, something nervous and uncomfortable – his arms were crossed over his chest, his head tilted down slightly, and he seemed incapable of maintaining eye contact. "What do you want?"

"We've come here for your sparkling conversation," Anya said, throwing herself onto one of the chairs around the table.

Now they had stopped walking, the four people in that house seemed to pull their cloaks tighter around their bodies. She didn't trust or like these people, but she found she didn't like the thought of them huddled beneath blankets each night trying to keep warm. The image of Vera's face when Lev had brought them food flashed across Sofiya's mind. Her eyes had lit up for a moment and a smile had lifted her hollow cheeks. She was sure they'd feel patronised by her pity, but it wasn't just that feeling driving her; there was anger and guilt there, and perhaps a little fear too. These people were raised by the hand of desperation and their hunger had no end. Sofiya knew it was her family's fault and one day the Sikveya would rise up and take their revenge.

"You're going to help us," Vera said to Aleks. It was not a question and there was no uncertainty in her voice.

Sofiya couldn't help but wonder how well she knew this man, or if this was just how she spoke to everyone – friend, stranger, or enemy.

Aleks sighed.

Sofiya sympathised with him.

There was a clattering of metal on metal as Aleks put a beaten-up tea kettle on the stove. "What happened to your face?" He asked, gesturing to Vera's nose with a box of matches.

In the dim light of Aleks's house, the bruise shone a disturbing purplish black. It looked painful, but Vera had not said a word about it. The girl just shrugged and nodded at Sofiya.

Aleks smiled weakly and huffed a laugh. "Nice."

The kettle squealed and Aleks removed it from the stove and decanted the water into a teapot. Removing five cups from his cupboard, he set them on the table, pouring each of them a glass of tea. "What do you need?" He asked. "Pay for it and it's yours. I don't care."

Lev took a glass and wrapped his hands around it. "Insight to the government building," he said, taking a sip.

Worry creased Aleks' pale skin but he said nothing, raising a questioning eyebrow at them. "And what do you plan to do with that?"

"Invade. Gather intel. Who knows? Maybe I just want a tour," Vera snapped. "You said you don't care so stop asking questions."

Aleks turned towards Anya and held out his hand for the money.

"Why me?" Anya baulked.

"Because I know you're good for it and they're not." He nodded to Vera and Lev.

Sofiya spoke up then. "You give us everything we need for the next month, and I'll get you forty thousand ykas."

He watched her carefully, his eyes narrowing, the line of his mouth thinning, as if gauging whether she was lying or not. Sofiya tried to hold his gaze, but she looked away in shame. He knew her well enough to be cautious of her and she couldn't remember him at all. The fact burned a hole straight through her stomach. "Fine," he said at last. "But I want to be in on the plan. I want to know what I'm getting mixed up in."

"The princess is paying us a lot of money to be her friends," Lev said with a smile.

"What's her deal? What does she want with us? She'll have us executed."

"Firstly," Sofiya said, irritated now, "I *am* in the room, and you can talk to me directly. Secondly, I made a deal, and I won't go back on it." She could feel the tension aching in her throat.

Vera moved around the room, her fingers dancing across the bottles. "There's a secret. Sofiya wants it back," she said. "And it seems I've developed a patriotic streak."

"And I'm the long-lost prince," Aleks snorted.

Lev was up now. He seemed to be incapable of sitting still for longer than five-minute periods. He rocked back and forth on the balls of his feet, his eyes darting restlessly around the room. "Which one is ours, Aleks?"

Sofiya glanced at the bottles. The labels made no sense to her, but they must have meant something to Aleks because he quickly plucked a bottle from a shelf by the door and gestured for Vera to sit at the kitchen table.

The girl sat and brushed her hair back from her face. Sofiya watched as she set her jaw and her breathing turned shallow. For all her stealing and meddling in other people's minds, Vera clearly didn't like hers being altered. Aleks ignored her panic, popped the cork from the bottle and flexed his fingers. Vera squeezed her eyes shut and scrunched her hands into the fabric of her cloak as a string of blue light emerged from the bottle and wrapped itself around Aleks' fingers.

"Ready?" Aleks asked, curling his fingers.

Vera nodded sharply.

With what looked like minimal effort, Aleks pressed the blue threads into Vera's temple. The stolen memory seemed to dance across her skin for a moment before sinking into it, illuminating the veins. As Aleks pulled away, Vera took a sharp breath. She pressed her face to her palms and cradled her head in her hands. Sofiya knew the feeling; she had experienced having memories planted in her mind before and it was like making space for one more person in a crowded room. It felt like your whole mind had to be rearranged and things had to be shoved aside into dark corners to make room for that one new bit of information.

She'd always wanted to see Valhaarn City in the Republic of Falburen. She'd only ever seen it in paintings, and it was said to have the most breath-taking architecture. For her eighteenth birthday she'd treated herself to a trip down into the Cauldron to one of the houses that offered memories and dreams. They'd inserted a preloved memory of Valhaan

City into her mind and Sofiya saw it for herself as though she'd been there before. She saw the white stone bricks glinting gold in the dusk light, the windows, the metal spires darting straight into the sky and piercing the clouds up above. The city was clean, polished, so much more beautiful than the criminal lair she lived in. She felt drunk on the beauty of it all. She'd hoped having the memory might satiate that part of her that longed to go but it had only made the desire stronger.

Vera straightened her spine after a long moment of silence and rolled her shoulders.

"Do you feel enlightened?" Lev asked, offering her his hand. She took it and let him haul her to her feet.

"I feel like I've been hit in the head with a mallet."

"Well, it could be worse."

"How?"

"Could have been a sledgehammer."

Vera let go of Lev's hand and smoothed the wrinkled fabric of her cloak. Her hair fell back across her face, and she seemed to look like herself again, her anxiety and pain shoved back behind her usual miserable expression.

Sofiya cast a look around the room at their ramshackle crew. Vera and Lev were standing together silently, Anya was still sitting at the table fiddling with the discarded bottle, and Aleks was waiting by the now open door.

They took the cue.

Lev and Anya left first, now discussing something irrelevant. Vera was next, pulling her hood back up over her head as she went which left Sofiya, who hesitated for a moment and took one last look at his face before Aleks practically shoved her out the door.

"You're all welcome, by the way," Aleks called after them.

"Payment will be thank you enough," Vera replied. "Don't push it."

The door slammed shut behind them and a rattle of metal echoed through the street as the bolt slid home.

Sofiya trudged behind the group. They all had their hoods pulled up over their heads, the hems of their clothes dragging in the puddles of rainwater and other mysterious liquids which flooded the cobblestones.

Sofiya thought of Aleks, but when she tried to conjure his face in her mind, she couldn't do it. There was nothing there.

12

Aleks

Aleks kept a lot of secrets. The biggest one was Masha.

He reached into his kitchen cabinet and detached the false back. Behind it sat a roll of cash tied with string which he removed so he could flick through the notes.

Each week he came to this cupboard and counted out his earnings from stealing and selling memories on the market and each time he held tight to the image of Masha. The picture of the small girl with fiery red hair and a temper to match had started to blur at the edges. It was ironic, really; he could steal memories, but he was not able to hold onto his own. Whenever he closed his eyes, he tried to paint her there, to commit her to memory, but the knowledge that she was ageing and he was not there to see it never escaped him.

Aleks had last seen Masha three years ago when she had been a small baby in his arms, helplessly screaming as he'd held her tight. He remembered how empty his arms had felt as he handed her over to the family taking her out of the city, the quiet that had fallen over his life in her absence, how many hours he spent – was still spending – praying for safety so he could bring her home.

Masha would be walking now, talking, though he'd missed her first steps and her first words. His Masha, his daughter.

The ache pressed against his chest as he counted out the money and stuffed it into a crumpled envelope. It was the cost of her upkeep out in the country, to feed and clothe her, to send her to school when the time came. He was desperate to go out and visit her, but he knew it wasn't safe. There were people looking for him. If they followed him out there, they would both be killed just like Lina. Killed was too kind a term. They'd be murdered.

When he thought of Lina, her pale hair and the smile she gave him whenever he threw himself down in the kitchen chair with a heavy sigh, he could never keep back the hurt or the anger or the never-ending guilt. They'd been a matched set and without her he was filled with a bitter cold as though his soul was exposed to a constant breeze, never thawing.

They had met at the market. She was the daughter of an apothecary who ran a shop in the Veleer District, and who had just moved to Sikveya from The Republic of Falburen.

Once, when they had been wrapping themselves in layers of blankets and huddled by the fire to keep warm, Aleks had asked, "Why here? You could go to the Isles or Quipjin, somewhere warm."

"Why are you here, Aleks?" Lina had replied. "You could leave. You could go somewhere warm, but you haven't."

"I can hide here."

"Exactly," she'd replied, leaning forward to take the kettle off the fire.

It was true. It was easy to hide in Ytavosk, especially in Ivenko's Cauldron. There, it wasn't uncommon for documentation to be forged, or for people to pick up and drop names and identities like coins. There were plenty of shadows to hide in.

Why are you here? Aleks had been turning the question over in his mind ever since they'd caught and slaughtered Lina. The question had stopped being about why he'd come to the Cauldron in the first place but rather why he'd stayed. He didn't have an answer and every time the question coursed through his mind, he saw the pool of blood dyeing Lina's hair red and he heard their daughter crying in his arms.

Aleks shoved the memory away and focused on the present, on the envelope of money crushed between his fingers and the thought of Masha, who was still alive and who needed him.

Out in the street, the rain was slowly picking up. Aleks watched the chaos of clothing lines being reeled in, carts of stolen goods being wheeled back into houses, and men and women pulling their children off the streets to keep them from getting wet. It was one thing to be cold, it was another thing to be damp too. Aleks had no choice but to go out in the rain, though his body ached and his breath clouded in front of him.

He felt once for the money in his breast pocket, tucked his chin down, and ventured out into the Cauldron.

As much as he tried to keep his mind on the present,

he couldn't help but let it wander back to the thieves in his kitchen. To the girl with the copper hair. He'd recognised the Princess immediately and that same familiar feeling of fear and hatred bubbled up in his stomach, accompanied by Lina and her blood-soaked hair and her open eyes staring up at the ceiling.

He didn't know many of the details of Lina's death, only that her murder had been ordered by the Queen.

And then there Sofiya was, standing in his kitchen. Did she know? Was she aware of everything that had happened with Aleks and Lina? *No*, he thought. *If she had, she would have killed me too.*

Aleks paused and leaned against the cool bricks of the alleyway. He took a deep breath and closed his eyes, trying desperately to clear the memories of his wife and his daughter and the Princess from his mind. When he managed to open his eyes once more, he looked around the street and with his hands hidden by his cloak, reached out to the nearest mind.

When he found the world overwhelming, Aleks often resorted to using his power. It reminded him of his capabilities, it reminded him that he was not weak and useless in the face of tragedy, that he *could* fight back in some capacity. He'd always known he was dangerous. That was what had forced him into hiding in the first place.

His first victim was an elderly woman sitting on the front stoop of a tailor's shop. Her hair was short and tucked beneath a wide brimmed hat which hung over her eyes. Her skin was pale and hung in folds from her cheekbones. Aleks saw the breakdown of her mind, all the radiant strings tangled together, and reached for the blue ones. He saw her as a teenager lying in a meadow with a boy beside her. She reached for his hand, squeezed it tightly, and then he raised her palm to his lips. Aleks tugged at the string and the woman didn't so much as flinch.

Aleks was a talented magician; he knew his power was stronger than Vera's. Vera's magic was clumsy, and the strings snagged as she removed them, alerting the victim to her presence. She could steal the secret, the proof of the rumour, but not without a trace. Aleks could steal the memory like Vera could the secret, but he could also erase it from the victim's mind. Aleks had never met another magician that could work that particular miracle.

Removing memories was a dangerous task. While he *could* take it, that didn't mean it couldn't be sparked back to life. It didn't mean something couldn't jolt the memory back into existence or alert the victim to the hole in their mind.

He understood why people like him were a risk. He knew why they feared him and why they wanted him dead. He could erase their knowledge of experiences and events; he could alter the way they thought about or remembered something. He understood why people like Vera were dangerous to them too. A magician's loyalty couldn't be guaranteed, and they could not be fought with a bullet or a blade; the only defence was to instil fear in them, to force them into hiding.

Aleks pressed towards Second Bridge and the Veleer District. He always liked that part of the city. It bridged that gap between the chaos of Ivenko's Cauldron and the strait-laced propriety of Gambit Square. Things in the Veleer District were organised, the streets set out in neat, respected rows. It was dirty and the people there still went hungry, but it wasn't quite as feral as its neighbour.

The post office was a small building in the District crushed between a coffee shop and a doctor's office which had long since closed. The windows of the post office were now plastered with out-of-date newspapers and black paint which was chipped to reveal a small lamplight coming from within. Aleks pushed open the door and a bell rang above his head. Inside the post office, a woman with thick wire framed spectacles sat behind the counter reading the book open in her lap as she took a bite of an apple.

Aleks removed the envelope from his breast pocket and placed it on the counter. Wordlessly, Yelena put her apple onto her book and placed them both on the countertop beside Aleks's envelope of cash. She took it, flipped it over to show the address of the family Masha was staying with in Koverisha. She grunted under her breath and tucked the letter into one of the pigeonholes behind the desk.

"Three ykas, Aleks," Yelena said.

Aleks handed her the coins. "Is there any post for me?"

Yelena sighed like doing her job of serving perhaps three customers a day was too much of a tall order. Aleks waited patiently as she shuffled through a folder of post. She picked out a letter and handed it to him. Aleks tore it open and saw a charcoal drawing of two people, one taller and one shorter, with labels pointing to each person indicating 'Papa' and 'Masha'. Aleks folded the drawing back into the envelope and put it in his pocket where moments ago the money had been stored.

He imagined Masha sitting at the table, charcoal smeared across her cheeks, her eyebrows scrunched in concentration as one of her caretakers helped her write out their names. He struggled to see the three-year-old's face now.

"Thank you, Yelena," Aleks said, turning away from the counter. "See you next week."

Yelena did not reply and Aleks left the shop, the bell ringing above his head.

13

Anya

As Anya moved towards the train station, her dream played relentlessly in her mind. Each morning when she woke, she promised herself that she would make her sick hopes a reality, but she had to be patient if she wanted her twisted plan to work.

As she waited for the train, she thought of her little sister, of the blood on her chin, the tears she'd fought so hard to keep back as Anya had held a tissue to her face.

She felt that familiar anger bubbling to the surface, cold and calculated. That was what she needed, that fury to fuel the fire inside her.

Once Anya got to Gambit Square, the walk to Tvset Street was not too difficult. It was a busy time of day. Men and women roamed the street, paying little attention to Anya with her cap pulled low and her favourite green cloak hiding the loose threads of her dress. She felt out of place in that part of the city, as if at any moment someone might turn towards her and call for the law enforcement. She was too scruffy for Gambit Square. She looked like a thief.

When she arrived at Tvset Street, she lingered for a moment. She rubbed her hands together in an attempt to warm her frozen fingers. She caught herself and stopped – she didn't need to look any more villainous.

Number Twelve Tvset Street was a beautiful house. The exterior was painted a pastel yellow that glowed gold in the low evening light. Each window was decorated with a pretty flower box and lace curtain left open to reveal the rich interior. She wondered how her life might have turned out if the man inside had been better, if he had been true and honest. Would she have lived in a house like that, amongst the plush settees and crystal light shades? She knew it was pointless to waste her time thinking about a lost future, but she couldn't help it.

She stared at the short flight of stairs at the front of the house. They were lined with grey marble and had gold rails that glistened in the afternoon light.

Anya had cried on those steps more than once in those initial weeks after her mother's death.

The final time she'd been caught there, it had been raining.

She'd held Daria close with her cloak wrapped around them both to shelter them from the frosty rain. Daria squirmed in her arms, and she held the baby tighter as she slammed her hand against the door in a broken rhythm. The family maid answered and immediately slammed the door in Anya's face. Anya knocked again, her anger rising into her throat like an untamed beast. She hit her fist against the door until she felt the heat of bruises forming on her skin. Daria's scream split the night, slicing straight through the sound of rain on marble and the thump of Anya's fist against the solid oak.

Eventually a man opened the door and Anya faced him, her spine set, her head held high.

"You have to take her," Anya said, her voice cracking. Despite her best attempts at being grown up and responsible, despite that desperate need in her heart to take care of her little sister and to honour her mother in the only way she could, Anya knew deep down that she couldn't do it. She wasn't cut out for motherhood and no matter how hard she tried, she couldn't learn. She couldn't get Daria to sleep, she couldn't get her to eat, she couldn't get her to do anything but scream until Anya's head hurt and she was so *tired* of it all. "Please," Anya begged the man.

Kirill Katovich was tall with tanned skin and a sharp face. His greying hair was cut short and kept tidily combed over his head. He was always wearing a suit and he always walked with purpose. He stepped outside into the rain and shut the door behind him, doling out some notes from his wallet and holding them out to Anya. "You will leave now, and you will not come back here, do you understand me?"

Anya thrust the baby towards him, but Kirill only took a step back. "She's yours," Anya said. "She's not mine. I can't be responsible for her."

"Then hand her over to the orphanage. She is no daughter of mine."

For the second time that month, Anya's heart broke. She'd thought the worst of it was over once Daria had been born and her mother's cold, broken body had been taken away.

She'd lain awake at night as Daria screamed letting her tears drip over the bridge of her nose. *This is it*, she'd thought. *This is as bad as it's going to get. If you can get through this, then you will be okay.* But she was staring at her last hope and watching it wither and die. By avoiding Kirill, her mother's lover, Daria's father, the man who had made them promises of a beautiful life, she'd been living in blissful ignorance. She'd told herself that if she never knew the answer, she would never have to let go of that faith in goodness, in people doing the right thing. But there it was – the terrible, ugly truth – and Anya felt it right down to her bones. He wouldn't help her. He wouldn't take his daughter.

Anya opened her mouth, though she was not sure what she wanted to say. Did she want to scream? Or cry, or beg, or plead? Perhaps she just wanted to take the money he held out to her and stuff it down his throat. All she said was a soft, deflated, "Alright." She was not prideful. She took the money from him and tucked it into the bodice of her dress.

Kirill grunted and slipped back into the comfort of his beautiful life, ready to forget Iskra, Anya, and the baby he'd fathered.

Anya considered her options. She imagined giving Daria over to the orphanage. But she knew the orphanage was underfunded, that if she gave the girl to them, she'd be turned out onto the streets when she turned twelve and what would Anya do if she ever saw those grey eyes on the face of a beggar, on the face of someone dying in the streets of Ytavosk, cold and alone? Daria's father didn't want her, and her mother was dead. She had the offer from Lilja, the deal she'd cut with her to get childcare.

As she turned to head back down the stairs, her knees

gave out from under her. She sat on the bottom step and, clutching Daria close to her chest, cried until the rain stopped and the sun was starting to rise above the city.

She'd promised then that she'd get justice for the little girl, for her mother, for herself. Her promises would mean more than Kirill's and she'd find a way to make him suffer. That promise had been plaguing her ever since.

Now, Anya strolled around to the back of the house, to where a dog leapt against a fence in the backyard. She bent over the wall and scratched him beneath his chin and the dog sat down at her feet. "I'm sorry," she whispered. "I'm sorry you have such a terrible owner." The dog licked her hand and Anya pulled away, climbing over the low fence and into the garden.

She moved quickly towards the door to a conservatory attached to the back of the house. It was glass with a black slate roof and showed Anya the entire contents of the house, from the gold trinkets on the dining room mantel to the polished marble countertops in the kitchen. She tried the door. It was not locked. She laughed softly to herself and entered the house, treading mud across the tiles.

Anya wanted Kirill Katovich to know she had been there. She wanted him to be scared, to live in fear before her killing blow. She had been stalking him for years, showing up in the corners of his life like a spider, haunting him like a phantom. At first, she'd choreographed meetings that could be considered coincidental – seeing him at the grocery market in Gambit Square or strolling along the river on a summer's evening – but over time she had gathered more information, learnt the intricate details of his life, his schedule, all the little habits he'd fallen into. She started showing up at his offices, at his card games as a waitress, once she'd even paid the owner of his favourite club to let her dance on their stage on a night she knew Kirill would be in. He'd cheered for her until he'd seen her face and she'd watched the colour drain from his. That was the most satisfying of their meetings. Kirill was a friend of the royal family, but he wasn't as safe as they were. They could lock themselves away in their palace, safe with hordes of guards trained to sacrifice themselves for their country. Kirill had little more than a garden gate and his own ego to keep him safe. He was not very safe at all.

Anya ran her fingers along the marble counters, the wooden spindles of the bannister, the cool metal of the stove top. She heard it then – the voices of a man and a child. She followed the sound as it led her to the living room where she paused in the doorway. They had their backs to her. Kirill was sitting in an armchair with a small girl on his lap as she played with a stuffed bear. She couldn't have been more than four years old with the bear clenched in her chubby fists. He rocked her on his lap, back and forth, as Anya watched from the doorway. It was an anger she had never been able to alleviate, an anger for her mother, for her baby sister, that *they* had been abandoned, deprived of a life like that one.

The little girl stood from her father's lap and ran through an archway into the dining room, oblivious to Anya's presence. Anya took a knife from the sheath on her forearm and threw it. It landed in the back of the armchair, tearing a hole in the fabric and Kirill leaped up from where he was sitting with surprising speed, turning to face Anya who already had another knife in her hand.

"Go on," Anya said. "Call for help."

Kirill schooled his features, setting them in a condescending smile that would have infuriated Anya had she not been able to see the strain behind it. "A knife?" He asked. "Really, Anya? I know you can do better than that."

Anya threw the next blade and it cut his cheek before sticking into the wall behind him. She leaned her shoulder against the door frame. Kirill watched her, lingering in the middle of the living room with his hands outstretched as though he could stop Anya. He didn't reach up to touch his cheek, though there was blood oozing from the wound.

It felt strange to see his face this close, to be in the same room as the man who had been such a big part of her life when she had first moved to the city. She'd thought he'd loved her mother, that Iskra was more than a plaything.

"What do you want then?" He asked, his voice was strong, but his mask was melting like ice on a summer's day, revealing his panic. "Money?"

"I have money."

"A doctor?"

"I have arrangements for that too."

"Then what is it?" Kirill asked. The colour drained from his face.

There was nothing he could give her now to calm her down. There was nothing he could do to stop the incoming tide. It would swell, the wave would crash over him, and he would drown. "I don't really want anything from you," Anya replied, moving towards him. She pulled her knife out of the chair and the other from the wall. Kirill didn't move. "I just want you to know that I *can* get to you. I know where you are."

Anya wanted to drag out Kirill's suffering, to let him experience just a fraction of the fear she'd felt all those years ago. She wanted to isolate him, make him scared to leave his house. She wanted to see the age rise prematurely on his features and she wanted it to be because of *her*. She really was there for one reason: to make sure he knew she could get inside his house. That he was in imminent danger. By the look on his face – his eyebrows knitted together, his mouth set in a line – and the slight tremor in his hands, she guessed she'd done just that.

She sheathed her knives and picked some gold trinkets off the fireplace before returning to the entryway. "You might want to lock your doors."

The image of her mother shot into her mind then, dying in a puddle of her own blood as Anya cradled Daria, who was so small and helpless, in her arms. Across the other side of the city, Kirill had sat down to supper with his wife.

She turned her back on him and left through the front door. She didn't want to hurt him. Not yet. Over the years she had been creeping closer to him, edging around the outskirts of his life before moving in on him like a bird circling its prey.

Heading out into the evening light, Anya pulled her hood up over her head. She slammed Kirill's door shut behind her and lingered for a moment at the bottom of the porch steps. When she looked back, she saw Kirill's shadow peeking out from behind the now closed curtains, watching her go. He dropped the curtain and a moment later, she heard the click of a bolt sliding home.

She was so close now it made her fingers itch.

14

SOFIYA

Sofiya was very sure at that point that she did not like The Red Dumpling. She tried very hard not to be a snob or to let the part of her that had been raised on the finest meats and aged wine to show, but in moments like those, it was very difficult. The establishment smelt like stale food and lager that had been consumed and then regurgitated, and it was a kind of hot that felt heavy even after she'd removed her layers of clothing.

She was sitting alone at the back of the pub, nervously folding the edges of a menu. She wondered if she'd gotten the wrong time, or perhaps the wrong meeting place. She glanced at the watch strapped to her wrist.

Looking around the room it became clear just why the thieves had chosen it. Though the space was uncomfortably tight, and the men were too free with their hands, it was loud and full of people just as criminally inclined as they were.

Sofiya lifted her head as Anya stormed into the pub, shoving her way past a surly looking man to get to their table at the back of the room. Aleks trailed along behind her and through the gap they had made in the crowd, Sofiya could just about make out Lev talking to someone behind the bar. He smiled and leaned across the counter to retrieve a tray. A woman behind the bar filled five metal cups with lager and Lev kissed her on the cheek. The older woman blushed and swatted Lev away with her tea towel. He made his way towards them, expertly balancing the cups as he weaved in and out of the crowd. He placed the tray on the table and sat down beside Sofiya.

"Good evening," Lev said brightly, passing both Sofiya and Anya a cup each.

"Thank you," Sofiya muttered, though she wasn't sure she really trusted what an establishment like that one would put in an opaque cup.

Lev reached into his satchel and pulled out two sheets of paper. Sofiya recognised them – she had seen enough of them in her time spent listening to various advisors criticise the Pravinya. He flattened out the sheets of thick cream paper on the table along with a quill set and pushed them towards Anya. "I believe you're proving your worth today," he said.

Anya sighed and thumbed the papers absently. Both sheets were stamped with the symbol of the Pravinya – a swan with an arrow protruding from its neck – but one was filled in and signed in an extravagant script and the other remained blank. "Where did you get them?" Anya asked.

"A pickpocket never reveals his secrets," Lev replied.

"A guest in one of the parlours?"

He winked at her and said, "But a genius can guess them."

Anya shot him a smile so bright and conspicuous it almost made Sofiya want to be a part of their schemes, to be a part of this group that was banded together by treachery.

Vera arrived then and threw herself into the seat beside Anya. Lev stopped fiddling with a loose thread on his shirt-sleeve and sat up straighter like a flower at daybreak. Sofiya couldn't help but marvel at them for a moment. Vera was a shadow, a dark stain, and yet to him, she was sunlight. Vera didn't seem to notice; she was too busy removing her layers of clothing without nudging the bruise that had spread across her face. She bundled her scarf into her lap and said, "Shit, I need a drink."

"One step ahead of you," Lev replied, putting a metal cup in front of her.

Sofiya examined her crew briefly. She glanced at Vera, Lev, Anya, and Aleks. It felt like months ago that she'd ventured into the Cauldron and stumbled upon the band of thieves, though it had only been a couple of days. It showed in the way they danced around her, as though to them this was a simple routine, just means to an end. They didn't care that this meant the world to Sofiya. *And nor should they*, the voice said in the back of her head.

"Did you get the papers?" Vera asked.

Lev saluted briefly before nodding to the papers spread out in front of Anya. "She's got them."

"I'm assuming you and Lev are going?" Anya asked.

Sofiya supposed it would make sense. Vera could steal secrets and Lev could steal everything else. She still wished that she could get a chance to see the inside of the Halls of Pravinya, to see the party that rivalled her family, that wished them all dead.

Vera nodded.

Anya paused her brushstroke. "There's a coffee shop opposite. We'll wait there in case you need us. I'll cause a distraction to get you through security so they don't look too closely at the papers – there's only so much a forgery can do."

Sofiya watched the cogs clicking and whirring in Anya's mind. Her face grew serene when she was thinking, her mouth flattening, her eyes going from a whirlwind to a calm summer sea in a matter of moments.

Anya stretched her shoulders before picking up the quill and dipping it into the pot of ink Lev had put on the table. "Who are the lucky invitees?"

"Konstantin and Tatiana Rosovsky," Vera replied. "Living in the Veleer District. Moved to Ytavosk from Catalin three months ago."

"You're disguising as Sikveyan?" Sofiya asked, turning to Vera.

"Yes. Why?" Vera replied.

Sofiya shrugged. Visually, the girl could easily pass as Sikveyan. She had the same sharp features, the same starved look to her that Sofiya saw on the faces of all her subjects, but Vera's accent was clearly Lattierean. Her vowels were round at their edges and even the flow of the language was different like the rolling hills that formed the Isles. "Your accent might give you away."

Vera smiled then. She had a wicked smile. "My accent? What about it?" she asked, putting on a voice so convincingly Sikveyan – each word sharpened so severely they felt violent

– that Sofiya almost flinched when she switched back to her usual voice and said, "That's what I thought."

Sofiya was almost certain Vera's name was fake, but she was not sure where it had come from. Though the girl had the same harsh features and cruel nature that usually classified their people, she couldn't help but wonder who Vera had been before she stumbled onto the dockyard in Ytavosk. Had her skin been tanned from the sunlight? Had her heart been warm too? There was no way of knowing whether the girl had always been that sharp or whether something had made her so.

Sofiya nodded once and turned her attention back to curling up the edges of the menu.

Anya got to work on her forgery. Though she did the work, and as far as Sofiya could tell she did it well, it wasn't without a steady stream of complaints and curses. Sofiya watched her hands work, the tendons tightening and loosening as she gripped the quill and dipped it into the ink on the table. Her hands looked calloused and Sofiya presumed it was from years of working at the theatre pulling ropes and holding onto the bars of the trapeze. Her face was closed off in concentration and Sofiya couldn't help but watch her.

When Anya finished the document, she handed it back to Lev, who thanked her with a grin.

Vera wrapped her scarf around her neck and said, "Are we done here?"

"Is that it?" Sofiya replied. "Is that the plan?"

Lev shrugged and said, "Vera and I will go through our route later. Anya and Aleks know what they're doing. Follow their lead and you'll be fine."

Sofiya was fairly sure that it would *not* be fine, but when she looked into the faces of the crew, not one of them seemed all that concerned. She wondered how many times they had done that together – gotten a loose idea of a plot and botched it together as they went. The chaos of it brought a chill to Sofiya's spine. She knew that they had nothing to lose, that if anything went wrong, they could walk away with a minor loss and go back to normal. For Sofiya, the stakes were much higher. Her entire life would be ruined. She thought about the book beneath her floorboards, the glass vial she had crushed beneath her foot in the gardens to remove all evidence of it. If this went wrong for her, she would be executed.

Lev nodded to Vera. "Shall we?"

Vera clasped her cloak around her neck and left with no ceremony. Lev followed closely behind.

Sofiya glanced desperately towards Anya and Aleks, who looked about ready to disappear himself.

"We will meet at Hobbin's at dawn to scope the place out. Once Vera and Lev arrive, I'll go over and cause a slight disruption. We'll be fine."

"You don't have to tell me, Anya," Aleks said. "I've done this before."

"It was aimed at her," Anya said, nodding towards Sofiya. They shared a knowing smirk and Sofiya felt her pride sharpening at the edges.

Aleks flexed his fingers in his leather gloves and Anya checked the knives on her sleeves.

Sofiya wondered, not for the first time, just what she was in for.

15

Anya

Anya hadn't gone to the market that morning. She'd woken up to her sister coughing and when she'd gone into her room, Daria had spat up blood over her sheets. Anya had put Daria into her bed and spent the better part of the morning cleaning up blood from the tattered bed linen. By the time she had been ready to go to the market there had been no point in getting there only to close up an hour later.

Now, having tucked Daria back into bed, she pulled her cloak over her shoulders and left to meet Sofiya and Aleks.

She'd never had much reason to travel the Veleer District and her knowledge of that part of the city had holes in it. Before she'd left the house that afternoon, she'd pulled out a map, flattened it on the counter and traced her route three times until it was stuck firmly in her head. Now, she passed over Second Bridge and wormed her way through the cobbled streets until she came to Krata Plaza.

Krata Plaza was a collection of three white stone buildings overlooking a water fountain. The fountain was in the shape of Roman Krata, who was deemed to be the original politician in Sikveya. He had started the Pravinya, which at the time was a small band of men and women gathering in the kitchen of his house. The business had grown into a legitimate threat that the royals couldn't exterminate. They soon took over a huddle of disused factories which had been replaced with the new buildings and a narcissistic fountain.

Anya spared the Halls of the Pravinya no time and instead marched straight towards Hobbin's which was a small establishment that provided the members of the Pravinya their morning coffees. It was a shabby looking building with a chipped sign and low ceilings, but it had an excellent view of the plaza.

As she shoved the door open, a bell rang overhead. Its efforts to announce her entrance were futile against the babble of conversation and the clinking of metal spoons against teacups. It was busy and she only spotted Aleks and Sofiya by the glint of Sofiya's hair in the lamplight shining overhead.

"You're late," Aleks said bluntly.

"Good afternoon to you too," Anya muttered, pulling her hat from her head and tucking it into the pocket of her cloak. "Something overran at the market."

Aleks passed Anya a cup of something hot and she watched as the tendrils of steam floated up into the air. "Tea?" he asked, and she nodded.

She wrapped her hands around the cup, letting it warm her cold hands. The coffee shop wasn't as warm as the pub they'd been in the day before and she kept her coat on. Iskra used to tell her not to let the chill in, that the key to surviving the Sikveyan winters was to not get cold in the first place. Now Anya knew how ridiculous that rule was, but growing up her house had been a warm place. A fire always sat in the hearth and the heat from the stove always warmed the kitchen as her mother baked.

One day after her father had been particularly cruel, Iskra and Anya had holed up together in the kitchen baking all day. Anya had felt so warm and safe. They'd baked bread together and it was cooling on the stove top. It wasn't Anya's best work – she'd caught the top of the oven when she'd taken it out and it had a scorch mark on the crust. The bottom of the bread was burnt too but when she leaned in closer, it smelt wonderful. She was so proud of it. She had turned those few ingredients into something that could sustain her family.

Her father came in then and looked at them both. He swung the backdoor open and the cold air leaked into their lovely warm kitchen like a plague. His eyes were milky, and he stumbled with each step. Anya knew instantly that her father, like always, was drunk. It wasn't even midday.

Demek picked up the bread and turned his nose up at it. "It's burnt," he said bluntly. "You should feed it to the pigs."

Anya took a step forward, but her mother stood in her path and grabbed Anya's hand in hers, squeezing it tightly in warning. She heard her mother's voice then in her head, clear though she hadn't said anything at all. *Not here, Anya. Not now.* Anya squeezed her mother's hand to tell her that she'd heard her, and she saw the tight breath leave Iskra's body.

When Iskra brushed her hair over her shoulder, Anya could see a purple line of bruises like a collar around her mother's neck, a wound that she'd been given the day before. In a fit of rage, Demek had pinned Iskra to the wall. Her face had turned red and her eyes had bulged out of their sockets. Before she'd fully known what she'd been doing, Anya had grabbed the nearest thing to her – an old vase – and hit her father over the head with it. He'd stumbled back, raising his hands to his head and without another word, left the room like a spell had been broken.

In the kitchen, Anya cursed her father as he picked up the bread, the warmth now completely bled from the room, and threw it out of the door and into the animal pen. She had wished him dead numerous times throughout her childhood, but in that moment, with the memory of his hands around her mother's throat fresh in her mind, she knew she could actually do it. Before it had been a childish wish, a silly dream she held in her head for the rainy days, but as she watched her mother shiver and heard the pigs enjoying her lunch, she flexed her fingers and thought, *yes, I could kill you now. I could erase you from this earth.*

Her mother squeezed her hand again and drew her back to their dreary reality.

"We need him," she said after he'd left the room. "You know that."

Anya knew that. Without him, they'd have no money, no place to stay, nothing to sustain them. That was the gruesome reality of it. He was the mayor of Moskarisk, their small town in west Sikveya. He provided for them, but he could also exile them if he so pleased. It was more than that too – if Moskarisk's precious leader were to die, Iskra and Anya would be hunted and hanged.

"We could make it," Anya pleaded. "We could go to the city. We could hide there."

"Don't do anything reckless," her mother had said. "It's not worth it."

Of course, Anya hadn't taken that advice. Since they'd fled Moskarisk and come to Ytavosk, her life had become a string of reckless decisions and so had her mother's. And now she was partaking in the most ridiculous scheme for some money and a doctor. She could practically see her mother, her face distorted in fear.

Now, in the coffee shop as she watched the workers through the foggy glass, Anya shivered and pulled her cloak tighter around her body.

"What do we do now?" Sofiya asked.

Anya could see her patience wearing thin.

"Do we just wait for them to break in?"

As she said it, a woman behind them dressed in a fur coat and a hat to match took a startled breath and turned towards the thieves. She'd heard Sofiya. Aleks twitched his fingers once, a vial already open in his hand, and Anya watched as he guided the string of blue light into the glass and secured the stopper. It was really that simple for him to remove a memory, to alter the course of a life. It seemed like a small thing, to steal a memory, a secret, a thin thread of someone's existence, but the small things always banded together to create a big one – a memory could alter a life, a secret could alter history, a feeling could alter a heart. Though small on the surface, the mind played a much bigger part than they ever gave it credit for.

Aleks tucked the vial into his pocket and dropped his cloak back in place to cover it.

"You don't want it?" Sofiya asked, turning towards Anya.

Anya snorted. "No. What use is that to me?"

"To sell at the market."

"And incriminate myself? No, thank you," she replied. "Aleks can throw it in the river or something."

Sofiya took a sip of her tea and Anya took the seat beside her facing the window so she could see the rush of people around the Halls of the Pravinya manically going about their days. "How did you end up at the market anyway?" the Princess asked.

"What do you mean?"

Sofiya shrugged, her spine straightening as though she was preparing for an argument. "You aren't a thief."

"How do you know?" Anya replied with a sharp smile. "I could be searching through your mind right now." She lifted her hands and curled her fingers in her best imitation of Aleks and Vera.

"It's an asset. It would be useful for this job."

Anya tilted her head to the side. "Is it an asset?" she asked innocently. "Or is it something to be feared? Your family needs to get their story straight because if they found Vera or Aleks right now, they'd hang them."

Sofiya paused and took another sip of her tea. "It's difficult. We're vulnerable."

"They're people too," Anya replied, though she understood what Sofiya meant. Magic destroyed lives and no one was safe from it, particularly the leaders of their country, who had so far to fall. There was no way of hiding or putting any kind of defence up. They were all vulnerable.

After a while, Sofiya circled back around to their conversation. "So, how did you end up at the market?"

Anya tilted her head to the side and smiled. "I have a taste for crime."

"Be serious."

"No." She scoffed a laugh. "Just because we're helping you doesn't mean you're one of us. It doesn't mean we have to trust you."

Anya thought she might shut up, but Sofiya didn't back down. She almost respected her courage. Her eyebrows drew together, and her mouth straightened as she asked, "You see us as the enemy?"

"We thugs and thieves have a lot of enemies. You're one of them, yes."

"What about the Pravinya?"

"Is that what this is about?" Anya snapped then. "Do we have to pick a side? Both ends of the stick have shit on them, princess."

Anya turned away from the conversation and moved her attention to the customers sipping coffee. The truth was, she didn't know who she sided with. No party was better than the other – they were both corrupt systems, destined to bleed the country dry. She thought sometimes she would side with the Pravinya just for a change of pace, but she knew they could – and probably *would* – be worse. At least she knew the royal family were lazy and while they ruined the country with their neglect, they wouldn't go out of their way to make things harder. Well, Anya supposed, the whole family bar one.

Sofiya was growing restless beside Anya. "How can you just sit here and do nothing?"

"You tell me," Anya murmured. She frowned as she saw a flash of white hair in the distance. She saw Vera and Lev come into view. Vera barely met Lev's shoulder and Anya watched as she grabbed his arm in her stern manner and marched him towards the front entrance where the workers would get their papers checked. Vera turned to Lev and said something, her face sharp, and Lev turned away from her, lighting up with a bemused smile. "I'm not doing *nothing*," Anya said, pulling her cap from her pocket. She shoved it over her cropped hair and cast a grin at Sofiya. "Time to create some chaos."

Sofiya fixed her with a hard stare. "Don't do anything stupid."

Reaching into her pocket and feeling for the cloth banner, Anya shrugged and winked at Sofiya. "I can't make any promises."

16

Vera

Vera felt ridiculous in good quality clothing. There were only two other occasions for which she had been forced into wool and silk and other fabric that felt too expensive against her skin. The first time, she had been five and her father had dragged her to church with him. She'd complained and fidgeted the entire time and he'd given up trying to force religion upon her. The second time had been at her oldest sister's wedding. She'd been marring a wealthy man from their town. He'd insisted her sister paraded around the village with her entourage and at the back of the party stood Vera in a pink puffy dress. The thought of that dress still made her shudder now. There were two things she'd been made sure of that day – she would never wear tulle again and she would never marry.

Now, her outfit was considerably more toned down than her church best and the awful wedding outfit. Sofiya had bought her a pair of navy trousers, a ruffled silk blouse and a fitted waistcoat. It wasn't entirely different to the clothes she usually wore – trousers and loose shirts – but the fabric hung from her body in more tailored lines and with more grace than anything Vera had ever worn.

She looked at Lev. He was wearing his work uniform – black trousers, black shirt, and a black waistcoat – but Sofiya had insisted he pair it with a tailored coat rather than his usual cloak. They both had their hair brushed and tidied, and Anya had spent a considerable amount of time masking the worst of Vera's bruised face with various creams and powders she'd taken from one of the dressing tables at the theatre.

Vera and Lev had spent most of the night sitting together in the soft glow of the dying candlelight, using the stolen memory to draw up maps and plans of the building and where they needed to look. Lev's information had been frustratingly vague – his last name was Neska, and he had a moustache – which made it difficult for Vera to figure out where in the building his office might be or where they should begin their search. When Vera had asked what his job actually was, Lev had said, "To talk down to his inferiors and exert his power."

The sun had risen before they'd slept and Vera was desperate for a nap, but they shoved their way to Krata Plaza in the Veleer District and its glaringly white buildings.

Decorating the sides of the buildings were shrines to the Gods. Vera was not religious, but she had been in the city long enough to recognise the three most worshipped Gods in Sikveya: Henygast, the God of sight, Zura, the

Goddess of wealth, and Yarisich, the God of honour. The three figures looked similar, each one had long black hair and blacked out eyes, with strings of gold twined around their bodies. In the centre of their sternums sat different gems to distinguish them. Henygast was blue, Zura was green, and Yarisich was red. Each of their hands connected in the middle of their chests to form triangles around the gems. Vera had always found the major gods to be a poor representation of the country. The people were ignored, poor, and completely against any kind of law and order.

Vera patted her pocket to check for the identification sheets before grabbing Lev's arm and pulling him into the flow of the Pravinya going to work.

"I can walk on my own, you know," Lev grumbled, pulling his arm from Vera's grip and rubbing the skin she'd had hold of. "Gods, you've got some claws on you."

Vera didn't turn to him when she replied, "Stop complaining and look normal."

Lev let his arms rest at his side and put on his most passive face. It frightened Vera sometimes to see Lev look so serious. He had a way of removing all colour and life from his face – his smile dropped, his eyebrows flattened, and the light in his eyes dimmed. He tucked his hands into his pockets to stop them from fidgeting and strode towards the door to where the workers were funnelling into the main entrance.

The Halls of the Pravinya consisted of three buildings but there was one entrance in the centre where their identification sheets would be checked. Once they had gotten through security, Vera and Lev would be able to roam the halls f reely. Or as freely as two criminals with fake names could roam.

As they made their way towards the entrance, Vera spared a quick glance behind them to a coffee shop tucked between a bakery and a stationery shop across the street. In the window she saw Anya, Sofiya, and Aleks with their cups of tea. Vera signalled to Anya with a quick flick of her fingers and Anya stood, pulling her cap on. She said something to Sofiya and slipped out of the quaint building before getting lost in the crowd.

Vera found it hard to shed one stolen identity for another. She had taken on many identities throughout her life, but the one she liked most was Vera Datsyuk. She still remembered the original Vera-Ana Datsyuk, her short black hair and lean frame.

She had been on the boat for three days when the older woman had approached her. Vera was sitting on deck, her body curled up small to avoid touching any of the other passengers or drawing attention to herself. She hadn't known any Sikveyan, and the journey had been a confusing mixture of words she didn't understand and frustrated guards shoving her around.

Vera-Ana sat down beside her and said something, but she couldn't decipher the jagged letters or sharp accent. When the woman realised, she tried again, though her Lattierean wasn't perfect. "You do not understand?"

Vera shook her head and hugged her legs closer to her body.

The woman just smiled and said, "I can teach you."

Vera spent the next three days learning the basics of their language – the most common words and phrases, how to say *yes*, *no*, and *fuck off*. Once she was able to say those things, Vera-Ana moved onto single words. She made Vera go over and over each sound until it was comprehensible. The language felt odd on Vera's tongue, each sound felt cutting. Where Lattierean balanced soft round letters, Sikveyan threw out harsh ones.

"Kiviye," Vera-Ana said, her mouth accentuating each sound. *Knife.*

"Kiviye," Vera repeated.

The woman shook her head and Vera tried again, and again, and again, until she got it right and they moved onto a new word.

Once she was satisfied with Vera's progress, she held out her hand for Vera to shake. "Vera-Ana Datsyuk."

"Valerie Moreau," Vera replied, taking her hand.

"Why are you going to Ytavosk?" Vera-Ana replied, switching back to Lattierean.

"To hide."

The woman seemed to consider this and then said, "You need a different name."

Vera said nothing. She didn't like the thought of not being Valerie, of becoming someone her mother didn't know, of no longer being the girl her mother had died for, but deep down she knew that transition had already happened, that in her chest was a gaping wound that would only grow larger. She was not Valerie Moreau. She was a creature much darker, much more dangerous.

"You could try Melena? You look like a Melena," Vera-Ana had said, patting Vera's cheek lightly. "Or do you just look like my cousin Melena? I do not know. I think it is the hair – very pale."

Vera subconsciously tugged on her braids. She hadn't washed since boarding the boat and her hair was sticking to her head in greasy clumps. She thought the best way to stop it from matting would be to braid it back out of her face until she could wash and brush it. She was precious about her hair – her mother had always said it was her best feature, though Vera herself always thought her best feature was her nose.

"Melena it is then," Vera said, leaning her forearms on the railing of the ship. She watched the waves lap against the side of the boat. She didn't like looking out at the horizon, the endless ocean terrified her. Having been raised on the Isles, she could swim and was comfortable in the water, but only because she could always see the land. The islands were so close together, you could see the opposite shores even on a cloudy day, but on that ship, there was nothing but ice and water.

Vera turned back to Vera-Ana and said, "Tell me about Ytavosk."

The woman laughed softly and joined Vera at the railing. "Awful place. You will end up in Ivenko's Cauldron. You will need a knife – *kiviye* – do you have one?"

Vera shook her head. Her exit from the country had been quick and she had nothing but a few coppers and the clothes on her back.

Leaning down, Vera-Ana retrieved something from her boot. She was sly as she tucked a knife into Vera's sleeve, careful not to cut her.

"Thank you," Vera said in Lattierean.

"No," Vera-Ana replied. "Say it again."

"Dosta venost." *It is appreciated.*

"Good," she confirmed. "Get a job and find somewhere to live. Trust no one. If someone tries to grab you scream nonsense into their face and they will think you crazy and let you go."

Vera nodded and repositioned the knife so that the hilt poked out from the sleeve of her jacket. It was engraved with *V.D.*

On the eighth day of their trip, they ran out of drinking water. They'd had to let the anchor down to weather a storm and the journey was taking longer than expected. Vera-Ana went up to a guard and asked him what they intended to do. Vera only picked up small parts of the conversation – primarily the curses – and watched as the guard dragged the woman she had considered a friend below deck. Vera waited for them to re-emerge and when they didn't, she let herself fall asleep, her body tucked up beneath one of the ship's masts.

She did not see Vera-Ana the next day either and that was when panic started to seize her. She'd approached a few people to ask if they had seen the woman, but her Sikveyan was still poor, and they usually gave up trying to understand what she was asking and turned away before any information could be gathered.

Eventually she managed to find someone who would listen to her – a guard whose eyes lingered on the cinched waist of her coat. She did a very bad job of describing Vera-Ana and when she finished the man simply pointed to the ocean below and said, "Overboard."

Vera asked what he meant by that, her heart lodging in her throat.

"Thrown in the ocean. Dead. Not alive," he said.

Vera lashed out at the guard. For the first time, she truly *felt* the anger she had been suppressing since the gun had sounded on the harbour. It was eight days ago but Vera had changed. Her heart had rotted and so had her soul. She could feel a darkness creeping through her body. She had never been a nice person, she had never been sweet or kind or compassionate, but now a match had been taken to all the shreds of goodness inside her. Her mother had been shot, Vera-Ana had been killed too, her own godsdamned country had exiled her for a power she never chose to have, and which was never even strong enough to be worth the trouble.

She clawed at the guard's face with her nails and put all the curses Vera-Ana had taught her to good use. She screamed until her throat was raw and kicked until another guard – this one Lattierean in origin – dragged her away.

"You will go over too," the guard hissed, throwing Vera against the ship's railing.

Vera stayed where she was thrown, her fury burning her insides, turning the tissue of her body black and melting away the edges. It was then that she decided to adopt Vera-Ana Datsyuk's name.

She had taken on many names and identities since that day, switching them out like cheap theatre masks. She had been Sonia Tarera, Rebeka Galenko, Genevieve Laoux but it was always hard to leave Vera Datsyuk on the shelf. And now, she was Tatiana Rosovsky, wife and loyal partner to Konstantin, whom she had to practically run to keep up with.

They both seemed to blend in with the rest of the crowd. There were no gaudy colours of the Cauldron to be found as everyone seemed to be dressed in deep blues and black. She stayed close to Lev as the crowd slowed and thickened. She'd lost sight of Anya long ago, but she hoped the girl had managed to push through the crowd and get to the entryway before they did.

She felt Lev's hand wrap around hers, felt the coolness of the ring he wore on his index finger against her skin, and she held tight as he forced his way through, dragging her along with him.

When they emerged into the lobby, Vera's senses were assaulted by the echoing of voices and footsteps in the cavernous space. Though the memory had given her a good idea of what the building would like, she was still taken aback by its grandeur. The hall was decked out with black marble floors, dark oak walls, and a dome skylight set into the ceiling. Every bit of sound ricocheted through the room, whispers turning to shouts and bouncing off the tiles. Some part of her expected the Pravinya to still be living under cover, hiding in the cramped rooms of their houses, but there she was standing in their official base surrounded by people trying their hardest to bring down their country's monarchy.

Vera couldn't help but wonder what their thoughts were on magicians – they were probably still scared, still determined to exterminate people like her. The hatred would never cease, and she would spend her whole life in exile. She was sure of that. What was one governing force over another if she was still outcasted? At least they knew the monarchy were too lazy to really do anything about it. For now, at least she was safe – penniless and hungry, but safe.

Keeping close to one another, Vera and Lev let the crowd guide them towards the checkpoints and funnel them into one of four queues. She looped her arm through Lev's and moved closer to him.

"This is cosy, wife," he said softly, leaning closer so only she could hear him.

She pinched his arm hard and replied, "Shut up."

She felt his soft laugh more than she heard it, but she was glad to see the Lev she knew and tolerated slip out from beneath his stiff mask. He squeezed her arm back with considerably less force. Vera took a deep breath.

As they approached the front of the queue, Vera opened up their identification slips. On it were their names, country of origin, and a physical description.

Vera glanced around. "Where the fuck is Anya?" she hissed. The girl was nowhere to be seen and there was no distraction erupting from the back of the room. She tried to suppress her panic, but she could feel it sizzling in her chest and clogging her throat.

"She'll be here," Lev replied, though he was also starting to look nervous.

The concerned look on Lev's face frightened Vera. He was the solid presence in her life that balanced her out. He was sunny and chaotic and more than comfortable botching plans as they went. If Lev was worried, then there was good reason for her anxiety to spike too.

Then she heard a *bang* sound from somewhere in the cavernous room. It sounded like a heavy book being slammed onto a desk, except books didn't generally send up a wave of smoke.

Vera turned back to where she thought the noise was coming from – it was hard to tell in the echoing reception – and saw a girl in a red cap holding a banner above her head that read 'LONG LIVE THE SIKVEYAN THRONE'. Vera hadn't given Anya any instructions on the distraction, but she thought the choice to present as a royalist was interesting.

By the time they were handing over their papers, Anya was cutting through the crowds to evade capture, screaming bloody murder as she went. Vera almost laughed and when she glanced at Lev, she could tell he was hiding a smile too.

Vera gave the guard their papers, but he was too busy trying to track Anya. He read the papers briefly, glancing up and down once to confirm the basics of their descriptions. At that moment, Anya's path led her straight past their queue. She smiled quickly at Vera and Lev and knocked her shoulder into the guard holding their papers. The guard hastily dropped the papers and darted after Anya. Lev scooped them up off the floor and tucked them into his trouser pocket.

"Shall we, my love?" Lev held his arm out, but Vera shoved past him.

The Halls of the Pravinya were a confusing maze of meeting rooms and offices, each surface covered in polished marble and dark oak. There were numerous spiralling staircases and hordes of people buzzing around the place, high on their own self-importance. Even with her knowledge of the building, Vera felt overwhelmed. She tapped into the memory Aleks had given her, though she wasn't quite sure where to start. They had a last name but no job title and no idea of where his office might be based.

"I think we need to start at the top and work our way down," she said, guiding them both towards the nearest set of stairs.

"Why the top?" Lev asked, though he followed her all the same.

"The longer we're here, the more likely it is that we'll be caught. If we start at the top and work our way down, we'll be closer to an exit."

Lev nodded.

Vera knew that each of the three buildings had four floors. Generally, the top floor was reserved for those in the highest power roles – the politicians – the second floor was for those who discussed the smaller laws, the first floor was for administrative roles, and the ground floor was for security and dining. The system made little sense to Vera, who had spent so long in Ivenko's Cauldron. Generally, in the Cauldron, the lower floors were reserved for those who could pay the most money, the logic being that if the place caught fire, those in the upper floors would have no escape. As the buildings were packed together so tightly, fire was common in that part of Ytavosk as it spread with ease from building to building.

If Neska – whoever he was – had the means to hire out a private parlour in Gambit Square's most luxurious restaurant, then he had to be somewhat of a high-powered man.

They climbed the stairs as quickly as they could without drawing any attention to themselves. Being the one with the memory of the layout, Vera led the way. They caught glimpses of the other floors. The administrative floor was a collection of cramped desks and cranky sounding typewriters, the noise loud, the room stuffy. The second floor was slightly larger, and each desk was given a small booth and a shelving unit for filing. When they reached the top floor, it became very clear why it was used for the highest-ranking members of the Pravinya. The other floors had been stuffy, cramped, and overpopulated, but the top floor was bright and airy, contrasting everything else in that godsdamned city. There was a main office in the centre with desks scattered around and on the outside there were meeting rooms, each adorned with a small glass window, though most of the glass panes were covered with paper. Despite its openness, the upper floor of the building had a distinct air of secrecy.

The room was bustling with men in suits and women in the same wide legged trousers Vera was wearing, though the cluster of rooms did not feel as manic and busy as the lower floors.

Vera came to a halt at the top of the stairwell and felt Lev behind her waiting. "Well?" she asked.

"Well what?"

"Do you recognise anyone?"

"No." Lev tapped his fingers on the bannister. "What do we do now?"

Vera examined the room. She recognised it, but whoever this memory belonged to must not have spent much time up there. The memory had a hazy quality to it like a painting that had gotten wet; the edges of the image seemed to blur into a smudge of colour.

Vera reached towards the nearest desk and shuffled together two stacks of paper. She handed one to Lev and directed them towards the first office. It was occupied. Lev took a quick glance through the window and shook his head and they moved onto the next.

It took them little time to peer through the windows of each of the offices and realise that the man they were looking for was not there. They were about to move onto the next floor when they came across a small dark office tucked away, hidden by a wooden filing cabinet. Vera searched her memory but drew a blank. There was nothing there but a fuzzy image of a potted plant. She grabbed Lev's sleeve and directed him towards the office and when they peered through the small porthole of a window, they saw it was empty. Lev tried the door and it opened without issue.

The inside of the office was darker than the rest of the floor. It was windowless and looked more fitting to those in administration. In the corner was a dead plant, its brown leaves scattered over the floor. The desk, which sat in the centre of the room, was full of discarded papers and out of date letters, and in the back corner was a cupboard Vera assumed was for storage and other stationery.

They both began searching through the desk draws and the letters. There were hundreds, most of which were addressed to a 'Ms. Dukov' and had been cut open.

The first two drawers Vera tried were unlocked and contained only leaflets and Pravinya propaganda, but when she reached for the third drawer it wouldn't open. She tried again in the hopes that the drawer was just jammed. It didn't budge. Still crouched beside the desk, she reached for the letter opener Ms. Dukov kept in a pencil pot, vaguely aware of Lev stopping his search to join her at the mysteriously locked drawer. Lev would have made light work of the lock, but she didn't have his patience. Instead, she shoved the blade into the lock and twisted until the metal crunched and the lock snapped. The drawer swung open.

"Nicely done," Lev said sarcastically with a soft laugh.

"I learn from the best."

He reached around her and started rustling around in the drawer. She couldn't help but watch the way his hands moved – she'd always been fascinated by his movements. Even in the quiet of this room, with just the two of them and no one to hide from, Lev still moved like a thief as though it was innate. He plucked a letter out and turned it over. *Josef Neska*. The words were written on the letter in cursive script along with the address for the Halls of the Pravinya.

"So, this is his secretary's office," Vera said, picking up another letter. "Ms. Dukov."

"She's not very good at keeping things secure," Lev replied, slipping the letter opener back into the pencil pot on the secretary's desk.

"Our man has a private secretary who has a private office. He must be important."

"I think 'private' might be a bit of a stretch." Lev gestured to the unlocked drawers.

They heard footsteps coming towards the room.

"Shit," Lev hissed, jumping up and dragging Vera with him.

Vera kicked the drawer shut and shuffled the papers on the desk back into order. The footsteps were getting closer. There was no escape. The secretary would be coming through the only available exit at any second. She felt a hand on her arm and turned to see Lev gesturing silently to the storage cupboard. They just about managed to get in and shut the door as the secretary reached her office. The sound of her heels against the tiles slowed to a stop and there was a pause before she fully entered the room.

The cupboard was cramped, and Vera was practically pressed against Lev's chest. He had one hand still clutching Vera's arm and the other holding the door closed. She could feel him breathing steadily and tried to align each of her breaths with his to calm herself down.

Lev squeezed Vera's arm once and she looked up at him. *This is fun*, he mouthed. She stamped down on his toe and felt the soft rumble of his suppressed laugh.

Vera took a moment to look around the cupboard. It was barely big enough for the two of them but there was a simple stack of shelves to her left full of pots of pencils and wads of paper. On the door to her right was a small vent, though it was too high for her to look through. She tapped Lev's knee and pointed upwards to the vent. He nodded and crouched a little so she could stand on his thigh. She didn't have Anya's grace and her ascent was clumsy. As she pushed upward, she almost fell, and Lev caught her with a hand on her waist. He held her there for a moment until she steadied herself. Their mission would be over – as would their lives – if she fell through that door now.

Once she was sure she was steady, she peered through the slats in the vent. On the other side was a short woman with dark skin and long black braids pulled into a ribbon. She was thin, her navy blue dress hanging from her delicate frame. She was moving the papers around on her desk to make room for the cup of tea she was holding. As she settled herself into her chair, Vera reached towards her mind. She was steady and she kept her focus strong as she curled her fingers around the ball of tangled threads and began her search for secrets.

At the forefront of her mind were the little things – Dukov hadn't been wearing her engagement ring in her betrothed's disappearance – but as Vera dug deeper, she stumbled upon some things that were slightly more relevant to her cause. She saw where the key to the drawer was hidden on a chain around Dukov's neck. And then she saw the face of a man with a moustache. He was broad and his hair was grey. He wasn't a handsome man by Vera's standards, but he held his head high as if he were. She saw the man introduce himself as Josef Neska to Dukov, shaking her hand. She saw Dukov visiting his office and sitting in the chair opposite him. He was telling her about an undercover role he had been participating in. Then he slipped a note card across the table and Dukov picked it up wearily. Her nails were painted black, but the colour was chipping off. She turned the card over and on the back read *Grigory Petrolovich, Royal Advisor.*

Vera tried to tug at the thread, but she felt it stick and Dukov lifted her hand to her head, rubbing at her temple. She lowered her head slightly to lean on her hand but shot up again. She reached down towards the drawer to the broken lock. She opened the drawer and slammed it shut again.

Jumping down from her vantage point, Vera reached down towards her boot and pulled out a knife. Lev stood too and pulled a blade out from under his sleeve. He didn't ask her what she had found but stood at her side ready to fight.

They couldn't wait in the cupboard – they needed to strike first and catch Ms. Dukov by surprise. Vera kicked the door hard, and it fell open with a loud bang. She watched as Dukov grabbed the letter opener and lurched towards them. Vera struck out with her knife and caught the woman's arm. She was not a trained fighter, but she had spent enough time in the city to know how to make enough damage with a blade.

Dukov stumbled back and hit her hip against the desk.

Lev shoved Vera forward and together they ran.

17

Lev

"Next time, Vera," Lev said as they half walked and half ran through the building, "let Anya do the planning."

"Shut up," she replied in her usual inpatient tone.

The alarms hadn't yet been set off and they were still trying not to rouse suspicion. Their attempts were futile. As they breezed through the room, heads turned towards them, the workers of the Pravinya distracted by the two strangers who were now making a beeline for the stairs.

They'd just reached the top landing when a shrill alarm erupted overhead. Lev turned back for a moment to see Ms. Dukov talking to someone and pointing directly towards them. He felt Vera's hand on his shoulder as she shoved him towards the stairs, and they began their descent.

Once they reached the next floor, Vera grabbed Lev's arm and half led, half dragged him through the office.

"Be ready," Vera said.

Lev sighed and turned to her. Her instructions were always too short as though she assumed he just knew what she was talking about. "For what?" Lev replied. There were a hundred different outcomes for this scenario and most of them ended in capture. When Vera didn't respond Lev repeated, "For *what*?"

They shoved their way through the busy office, knocking papers over the floor in their haste. They approached a door with blacked out windows.

When they burst into the room, Vera's plan became a little clearer. In the centre of the room was a long table around which about a dozen workers were sitting. Behind the table was a row of wide windows looking out over the rooftop of the next building. That was her plan.

"Hello," Lev said cheerily, grabbing a spare chair and throwing it at the window.

That seemed to shock the workers into action. A man with long hair tied back in a bun lunged for Lev, who nodded to Vera once. Vera, narrowly avoiding another pair of hands, gracelessly threw herself through the window. Lev followed behind, though his exit was a little cleaner than hers as he grabbed the window frame and swung himself through the hole in the glass.

He crashed against the roof and just about managed to stop himself rolling to the edge. Gravel dug into his skin as he landed. Pulling himself to his feet, Lev grabbed Vera's arm and hauled her up too. She let him help her and he saw that she was bleeding.

"Let's go," she said, ignoring the blood staining her trouser leg. She shrugged him off and they took off running along the rooftops, their feet slipping on loose roof tiles.

Lev was used to the terrain, to the slanted roof tops, the chimneys, the threat of imminent death, but he knew Vera preferred not to see the city from this angle. She kept cutting glances to the cobbled street beneath them and each time she did, she would squeeze her eyes shut for a moment.

The cold Sikveyan breeze combed over their bodies and whipped their hair around their faces. He was glad he wasn't wearing a cloak – that high up in the skyline of the city, it would have been the thing that dragged him off the building's edge.

When Lev looked back, he saw that Vera was dragging behind. He slowed to let her catch up before he pulled her to a stop and made her lean against a crumbling chimney. A shot rang past his ear, and he ducked down behind the wall, tearing a strip of his shirt off. He hastily tied it around her thigh to staunch the bleeding before grabbing her hand. "Come on," he said as another gunshot pinged off the roof to his right.

His heart was racing and his palms were sweating, but in that moment of chaos, Lev felt truly alive.

Their footsteps fell in time, beating the same broken rhythm as they leapt over ledges and loose roof tiles. Lev squeezed Vera's hand harder and dragged her along as the sounds of gunfire dwindled out and they let themselves slow their pace.

He let go of her hand, ignoring the itch of regret in his chest.

Vera was struggling to walk, each step laboured, but she

held her head high as though she was not in pain at all. Lev reached for her again as her leg gave out beneath her. She shoved his hand away and crouched down to examine her wounded thigh. Lev knelt beside her and pulled back the strip of fabric. Again, she batted him away and untied the make-shift bandage.

"Let me help you, Vera," Lev said with a sigh.

She set her face, carving it out with sharp lines. Her anger was visible. "It's superficial," she said stubbornly.

It didn't look superficial, but Lev said nothing, just tied a fresh bit of cotton around the injury and helped Vera to her feet. He also said nothing when she held fast to his arm and leaned on him. If he'd offered his assistance, she would have denied it; he knew it was best to just let her take it. He didn't mind.

Eventually, they came to the edge of the terraced housing. They must have been close to the river now and Lev listened to the soft cries of seagulls and the shouts of the dockworkers.

Lev took one last look at the city below. He liked Ytavosk from this height. It felt so distant to him, as though the shapes and motions were an experiment he was watching from afar and not another challenge in the life he lived out each day.

He heard a soft yelp as Vera skirted inelegantly down the side of the wall, balancing precariously on window ledges. She clung desperately to the sharp ridges in the stones. He noticed she didn't look at her surroundings or at the ground as she made her descent and he couldn't help but laugh; fierce, blunt, unmovable Vera was scared of heights.

"What?" Vera snapped. There was a scuffle of feet against stone and when Lev looked over the edge, he saw Vera leaning against the opposite wall, looking up at him.

He moved closer to the edge of the roof.

"Don't do that," Vera said, taking a deep breath.

"Do what?" Lev asked with a grin as he traced the guttering of the roof, arms outstretched, teetering precariously close to the edge.

Vera closed her eyes and turned away. "Just climb down. I'm cold."

You're also bleeding out, Lev thought, but he knew better than to say that to her.

Lev bent down and gripped the edge of the roof with both hands, swinging his legs over the edge of the building and letting himself drop to the ground in one swift movement.

"How do you do that?" Vera asked in an irritated voice.

"I'm just great."

Lev had spent a long time trying to teach Vera to be swift when she scaled buildings or walls, but she was less sure of her surroundings than Lev was. Whenever she scaled a building, her movements were jagged and uncertain, as though she was waiting for the ground to move beneath her. Lev had grown up using the gaps in bricks as footholds and the ledges of windows as beams on which he could sit. Vera hadn't.

As they ventured back towards the boarding house, Vera gradually shifted her weight back to Lev's arm, her pace slowing. In that part of the city – the boundary between the Veleer District and Ivenko's Cauldron – the mood had shifted. Lev knew this was likely due to the disruption he and Vera had caused at the Halls of the Pravinya. The people were whispering to each other, their heads bent, their hands clutching at the gemstones they wore at their throats to honour their gods.

When he was five, Lev's mother had given him a red gemstone to represent Yarisich, the god of honour. As his mother tied the leather string around his neck, Lev looked up and asked, "Do you believe in the gods, mama?"

She leaned forward and tapped the red gemstone sitting at the base of Lev's throat. "I have different gods, Lev." Though she'd moved to live in Sikveya, Lev's mother had never lost the traces of her home in Quipjin. When he closed his eyes, he could still see the delicate paintings lining the mantlepiece with their white and pale pink blossoms, the gold tins full of engraved trinkets. He saw them in himself too, in his dark hair and sharp features.

"Do you believe in them?"

Mei smiled and rested her hands on his shoulder. He felt the cold press of her ring through his thin cotton shirt. "You don't have to believe in the Gods themselves to believe in what they represent," she'd said. "You can believe in sight, wealth, and honour without praying to their statues every day."

Now, Lev twisted the ring around his finger and blocked out the image of his dying mother pressing it into his palm as her laboured breaths echoed through the bedroom. He felt the gem still against his throat. *Honour*. He almost laughed. He'd promised himself that he would never be without it, but he'd grown desperate, and his needs had outweighed his conscience. Lev had considered himself good, but now, as he and Vera ran away from the chaos he'd willingly created, he wasn't so sure.

It took them an hour of walking with no respite to reach the boarding house. The Cauldron was blissfully uninterrupted by the break in at the Halls of the Pravinya and the streets were as raucous and messy as they always were.

As they approached the house and its moth-eaten curtains, Mrs Hanovich came running out of the door and down the steps fussing with her tea towel. When she saw them, she paused suddenly, catching herself on the railing of the crooked steps. "Oh!" she exclaimed, pressing her hand to her chest. "I thought Lev was hurt."

"No," Vera muttered through gritted teeth. "Just me. No need to worry."

As they passed Mrs Hanovich in the doorway, she reached out to take Vera's other arm. Vera shoved her off and instead clung to the bannister.

"I can carry you," Lev said with a sigh, looking up at the stairs they were about to climb.

"Don't even think about it," Vera said. "I'm fine."

As if trying to prove her point, Vera let go of Lev's arm and stumbled up the stairs. He kept a hand hovering behind her back, ready to catch her if she were to fall, but they made it to the top without any further injuries.

When they reached the landing, the door to Vera's room was already pushed open. Lev watched the tension rise in Vera's shoulders. She was defensive about her space; for someone who stole secrets, she kept a lot of her own. Vera shoved her door all the way open to reveal Anya, Sofiya, and Aleks standing in the centre of the room. They all looked incredibly uncomfortable in Vera's room and none of them were sitting. The room itself was a mirror of Lev's – a bed to the left beneath a window, a desk in the opposite corner, a chest at the foot of the bed, and three shelves beside the door. The difference between their living spaces was that Lev's room was constantly messy and Vera's was clean and clear of clutter. She'd taken Lev's advice all those years ago and regularly gotten rid of the things she stole; if she had kept them and she was found out, she'd be arrested and executed. If people found the trinkets he took from passersby, he'd get a slap on the wrist and a fine.

When Vera saw Aleks, her injury was forgotten. She threw herself across the room at him and shoved him against the wall, her forearm pressed to his throat. "What the hell was that?" Vera hissed.

"What?" Aleks replied, though his voice was hoarse. He reached up to her arm on his throat and tried to pry her off unsuccessfully.

"Oi," Anya called, attempting to push them apart. When Vera didn't let up, she sighed, threw her hands up in resignation and sat herself in Vera's desk chair.

Sofiya grabbed Vera by the arms and pulled her off of Aleks. "Sit down and talk like *civil* people."

"You lied to me. You knew that memory was faulty," Vera said as she pushed her hair back over her shoulder. The hair fanned across her forehead was sticking up at odd angles, revealing the sharpness of her cheeks and the fire in her eye. "I thought it was a storage cupboard and we went straight into a meeting room full of people."

"Wait," Lev said, resisting the urge to laugh. "That wasn't deliberate?"

She turned to face him. "Of course it wasn't fucking deliberate."

Aleks was standing still, nervously pressing his hands together. It wasn't fun to be on the receiving end of Vera's anger and Aleks wasn't holding up well. He stuttered when he spoke. "You know the risks, Vera."

Vera glared at him.

"I can't guarantee the memory will be true. I can give it to you as it's remembered, but it may be remembered wrong."

Magic was a complicated art. Lev wasn't sure if even Vera or Aleks fully understood the complexities of stealing from the mind. People's minds were irritatingly niche; they remembered things as they saw and experienced them.

Vera said nothing, though she was still heaving laboured breaths. She sat on the edge of her bed and tore away the leg of her trousers to reveal a brutal looking cut across her thigh. It was the first time either of them were seeing it properly and Lev was sure it was *not* superficial. Vera remained silent as she reached beneath her bed and pulled out a small wooden box. Inside was a needle, thread, some rubbing alcohol, and a spool of cotton to bandage a wound. Using the slightly cleaner part of the trouser leg, she blotted the worst of the blood and attacked the wound with rubbing alcohol. She didn't hiss at all, but Lev could see the pain on her face.

"What actually happened?" Anya asked, diffusing the silence that had settled amongst them. "Did you get any information?"

Lev quickly filled them in on what they'd discovered in the Pravinya headquarters and told them about their botched escape. He spared Vera a few glances as she stitched the hole in her leg and wrapped it in a fresh bandage – he'd have offered to help her, but needles made him queasy. After she was done, she undressed to her underwear, completely unbothered by her company, and threw on a pair of loose trousers and a white shirt that Lev recognised as his own.

"So, we know who we're looking for now?" Anya said as she fiddled with a scrap of paper Vera had left out.

"Grigory Petrolovich," Lev replied. He turned to Sofiya. "Do you know who that is?"

Sofiya had not spoken the entire time they had been back. When they all turned to her, she nodded, her face alarmed. "He's one of the most trusted royal advisors." She faced Vera, nodded to her leg and said, "Don't you need to see a proper doctor? It looks bad."

Vera watched Sofiya as she tugged at her clothes anxiously. "No, I don't. It's fine. You're changing the subject."

"We need a new plan," Anya said.

"The princess needs to weigh up what this is going to cost her," Vera muttered.

Sofiya sighed and pulled her cloak back on. "I think this conversation needs to happen over food."

18

SOFIYA

They found themselves in the same public house they'd been in before. There was straw lining the floors and the air was filled with the sickly scent of warm alcohol. Sofiya resisted the urge to gag. The others didn't respond to the squalor the same way Sofiya did, and it made her feel ashamed of the luxury in which she'd been raised.

Again, they took a booth at the back of the pub, deep in the shadows. She watched her company peel back their cloaks and slot themselves into the seats with ease.

Sofiya placed the menus on the table and said, "Order what you want."

They all stared at her for a long moment, none of them touching the menus. Anya eyed her sceptically.

"What's the catch?" she asked, reaching for a menu.

"There is no catch. It's on me. Get what you want or don't. I don't care."

She watched as the four street rats ordered an absurd amount of food which they all dug into immediately. There were various forms of potatoes – mashed, roasted, fried – an entire platter full of bread with a lumpy looking dip Sofiya didn't want to think too hard about, bowls of boiled vegetables, and tiny cakes with chocolate sauce in dishes. She was also concerned about the sheer volume of alcohol they'd added to the mix considering they were sitting down for a serious conversation that they all needed to remember in the morning.

Aleks was the first to speak. "So, you went in, found his assistant, and you discovered this man?"

Vera nodded and swallowed her mouthful. "His name is Josef Neska, but he goes by Grigory Petrolovich when he is spying on the royals. Sofiya knows him."

She knew him well. In fact, Grigory had been a big part of her life for as long as she could remember. He was close to her mother – there were rumours when her father was still alive that Grigory and the Queen were having an affair, but it remained a rumour. He was a trusted member of the royal court and even Sofiya, who was sceptical of everything that went on behind the palace walls, trusted the man. He came to her defence when he could and gave her reassuring nods whenever she spoke. She understood it now. Those looks weren't coming from someone who wanted to improve the pre-existing structure of their country, but from someone who wanted to demolish it all and start again.

She wondered what this man had on her. She couldn't help but wonder what he knew about her plans and intentions. Did he have the secret? Was he going to use it to tear the Meskovs apart and bring the Pravinya into power?

"So, what's next?" Anya asked, reaching across the table for an olive.

Aleks shrugged as though the matter were simple. "We go after him."

"I know that," Anya said with a sigh. "But *how*."

Vera rested her head on one hand as she swirled the drink with the other. "We've written off The Halls. Sofiya, do you know where he lives?"

Sofiya glared at them all. "We are not going to break into his house."

"Oh," Lev said sarcastically "It's *fine* to break into a government building but one man's house is too far?"

"Then it becomes personal," Sofiya said.

"This *is* personal." Vera popped a grape into her mouth.

Lev sighed. "You royals need to get your morals straight. It's very confusing."

Sofiya weighed up their options. They needed access to Grigory in a way that was public and could not be traced back to them. She had the perfect solution, but she knew she was going to regret suggesting it. She did it anyway. "They're throwing a ball a couple days' time."

Sofiya watched the idea ricochet around the table. Something dark passed across Aleks' face, a small flicker of a movement like a mask that slipped and was swiftly replaced. Anya straightened her spine as though she were about to walk onto a stage, Vera tilted her head to the side, and a small smile crept across Lev's features.

"Is that an invitation?" Lev asked.

Sofiya nodded once.

Anya looked up then and said, "You're really going to let us loose in the palace?"

"You will all be on your best behaviour." Sofiya gave a very pointed look at Vera and then at Lev.

"It would give us full access to the court," Aleks muttered, his hands fiddling in his lap.

"And to Grigory," Vera added. "We might even be able to find the actual secret."

"Exactly," agreed Sofiya. "And no one will be expecting anything bad to happen. Not at the ball, anyway." Lots of terrible things happened at the palace, but there were strict rules when it came to their balls. The ballroom was its own safe haven, encased by a hazy mist as the lights faded to a dim glow and the dancers shone in the shadows as if they themselves were alight.

"I know I'm not usually the voice of reason, but is this really a good idea?" Lev asked, his eyes skipping briefly to Vera and back again. Sofiya watched him as he tried to keep his posture casual, but there was something forced about his relaxed gait.

Vera ignored him. "I'm in."

Anya and Aleks both nodded too.

"Vera, if they find you there, they'll execute you." Lev fiddled anxiously with his glass. "You too, Aleks," he added, though the afterthought was obvious.

Vera scoffed bitterly and took another bite of bread. "I can do my job and I can do it well."

"That's not what I'm saying," Lev replied, and the calm left his body. His face tightened, sharpened, and the irritation shining there was startling on Lev's features. "You're walking into a room of people who fear you."

Her face was fierce, her voice cold. "It's my risk." She shrugged him off. "Let them kill me."

Lev sighed and rolled his eyes. "How outrageous of me to worry." He set his jaw and stared at his near empty drink. "You might not value your life that much, Vera, but I do."

Sofiya glanced up and caught Anya's eye. She assumed Anya was used to Lev and Vera bickering and when their eyes met Anya just rolled hers and went back to picking at the crumbs on the platter before her.

"It's my risk," Vera repeated and Sofiya didn't miss the slight tint rising on her pale cheeks or the way she refused to look at Lev as she swallowed hard.

In the awkward silence that descended over the table, Sofiya glanced back towards Anya. The girl was strung like a puppet with her spine so straight it was as though the top of her head was connected to a string. Her smile never quite seemed genuine. Sofiya was sure her cheeriness was a guise for something, though she didn't know what. There was a nervous energy to her, much like the one she often felt around Aleks, and when she didn't think anyone was watching, her expression dissolved into a frown.

"When is this party then?" Anya asked and Sofiya quickly looked away.

"It's not a party, it's a ball," Sofiya responded automatically.

"What's the difference?"

"A ball is political."

Anya scoffed. "And a party isn't? Surely, they are both just a room full of very important people drinking champagne and discussing all the nasty things that stain their country – so, *us*." She plucked a sad looking apple slice from a cheese board in the centre of the table.

Sofiya said nothing.

"Okay, great," Anya said with a smile, pressing her palms together as if she were praying. She rested the tops of her fingers against her forehead. "Will there be entertainment?"

"I can hire some," Sofiya said.

Anya smiled and glanced towards Lev. "That's us in. The acrobat and the waiter."

Lev tutted and lifted his glass to his lips. "So, I don't get a pretty costume?" It was as though nothing had happened between him and Vera.

"You're stuck with a waistcoat, I'm afraid."

He sighed. "Boring."

Sofiya cleared her throat and turned towards Vera and Aleks. "What about you two?"

"You mean the two magicians?" Aleks asked with an edge to his voice. She heard what he was really saying: *two criminals*.

Sofiya frowned.

"We'll need invites," Vera said bluntly. "Get Anya some paper and she can sort that."

When Sofiya looked at Anya she simply saluted and rolled her eyes, giving Sofiya a soft smile. It felt like a private moment, as though they had their own joke. She fought to quell the rough beat of her heart.

Vera cleared her throat. "If we're going to spend our evening listening to your people condemn us, you can at least buy us some nice clothes."

Sofiya rolled her eyes at her. "*Fine*."

She looked at her group of criminals – they were an unlikely set, but for the first time she was feeling hopeful. She turned to Anya once more, who was watching her with a soft, knowing smile.

"Don't underestimate us," she said.

Sofiya raised her eyebrow at her, feeling a smile curl her lips. "Never."

19

Vera

The group parted ways after they'd devised their plan and now Vera and Lev were the only two left in the dim light of the pub, finishing up the last scraps of food on the platters. Vera watched Lev for a long moment. His features seemed to sharpen in that light, the edges of his smile looked less welcoming and the brightness in his eyes was hidden by shadows. He swirled the last drops his drink around in the bottom of his cup and leaned his elbows on the table.

She would have stayed like that – the two of them in the warmth of the pub – forever if she could, but they both had tasks to accomplish before the ball and they were slowly running out of time.

Standing, Vera tucked her hair into her hood as she pulled it up over her head. Lev buttoned his cloak and together they emerged from the pub into the cold Sikveyan night. It was a matter of seconds before the warmth that had encased her faded away and was replaced by bitter air.

They crossed the street to the boarding house. It looked welcoming when it was cold outside. Through the thin mesh curtains, the fire glowed orange and yellow and though they both knew better, the place looked warm. It looked comfortable. The porch creaked beneath their feet as Lev held the door open for Vera, who ducked under his arm and headed straight for the stairs.

She stopped at the top of the landing. They were both cast in shadow but when her eyes adjusted, she could just about make out the lines of his face.

As Vera turned towards her own door, Lev asked, "Do you trust her?"

"Sofiya?" She paused, facing him once more.

Lev nodded and his hair glinted in the moonlight as it shone dimly through the hallway window.

She didn't want to admit it, but she was worried about the princess's motivations and Lev was right to be concerned. Sofiya knew what Vera could do and it was a power like hers that had created the mess in the first place. The princess had to be scared of Vera, of the destruction she could bring down on the family and why wouldn't she be? Vera was not loyal to the crown. In fact, she had spent the last six years ensuring she was only loyal to one person: herself. She would turn on the royal family if it suited her. It just so happened that it didn't.

"No," Vera replied sharply. "I don't think trust is a concept Sikveya is familiar with."

"Have you looked through–"

"No," Vera said. "You know I don't do that."

Vera remembered one night three years ago when the heat of the fire hadn't been enough, they'd turned to alcohol. Lev had found an unlabelled bottle of liquor in the cupboard beneath the kitchen sink, and they were sitting shoulder to shoulder in his room passing the bottle back and forth. It tasted like kerosene but the warmth that it hatched in their chests was addictive.

Lev leaned his head back against the wall and turned to face her. "Have you ever looked through my mind?"

"No," Vera replied.

"Why not? Aren't you curious?"

Vera looked back at him. They were close and she could see the rise and fall of his chest with each breath. "Magic needs boundaries, Lev," she replied. "People need them too."

"Where is the boundary, Vera?" Lev huffed a laugh. "Because you never turn down the tips I give you."

"My friends. The people I know personally." Though she knew that wasn't strictly true. Her brother would beg to differ.

Lev had laughed properly then, shaking his head and taking another swig from the bottle.

She could never admit it, but Vera wished she *could* go through Sofiya's mind. The thing stopping her was not her sense of boundaries or loyalty to the throne, it was the fact that her power was not strong enough to do it without Sofiya noticing. She'd rather Lev think it was a thread of goodness in her that stopped her from doing a terrible thing and not her lack of ability.

"What if she's got ulterior motives?" Lev asked now.

Vera shrugged and said, "She probably does. I want my money and immunity. What she does after that is not my problem."

"What are you going to do with it?" Lev asked. "The money, I mean."

"I don't know," Vera replied.

"You're lying. You frown when you lie."

Vera cut him a quick glance in the dark. At some point, he'd moved closer to her and was now leaning his shoulder against the wall by her bedroom door. "I frown all the time."

"It's different." He shook his head. "It's fine. You don't have to tell me anything."

His voice was genuine and when she looked at him, he only smiled softly at her in the same knowing way he always did. He knew that they ran in their own separate circles, and should they ever overlap, there would always be parts of their lives they would never share.

She paused, all too aware of Lev's presence. In the darkness she shifted so she could see the outline of his sharp features. Vera hesitated for a moment before she said quietly, "I'm going to go to Vor."

They were close enough now that even in the shadows, she could see his eyes soften and his eyebrows scrunch together as though he was trying to solve a difficult equation. "Why?" His voice was low.

"I want to learn to use my power properly. I think I can do it there." She didn't tell him about her mother's dying wish to take her to Vor or that she had sacrificed her life to get Vera to safety. She didn't tell him that each time she put herself in danger a sickening feeling pressed against her heart, like she was letting her mother down.

Lev nodded, though something dark shadowed his features. "You're leaving Sikveya?"

Her guilt surfaced. She'd spoken to Lev almost every day for six years. What would her life look like without him? Vera was sure it would be darker, that her days would feel longer. She wasn't quite sure what she felt for Lev but whatever it was, it had been built up, a slow dance growing to the beat of a song. It was an amalgamation of things – trust, friendship, loyalty – that had to develop over time. She could not trust anyone instantly, and she could not love instantly either. He was her friend and her closest one at that. Though she could admit to herself that she would miss him, when she itched to reach out to him, she clasped her hands to her chest.

"It was only ever meant to be temporary," she said into the still hallway.

With a melancholic smile Lev replied, "I think I've gotten used to having you around."

The truth was, she'd gotten used to having him around too. She was used to the way he clattered around his room, to the chaotic whirlwind that consumed such a large part of her life. She'd miss the evenings she spent with him playing cards by the fire. "I don't think I should settle for comfort," she said. "Not if I don't have to."

"Nor should you."

"It won't be easy," Vera said with as much courage as she could muster.

"To leave Sikveya?" Lev asked and Vera could see the hope creasing the corners of his soft smile.

"To leave you."

Lev opened his mouth to speak but closed it again. He glanced at the ground and his thick lashes fluttered against his pale skin. She could hear him breathing, she could see the rough rise and fall of his chest.

He flexed his hands at his side, and she wished, not for the first time, that she had the courage to reach out and take them. She didn't; she wasn't sure she ever would.

Desperate to fill the silence, Vera asked, "And you? What will you do?"

Opening his eyes, Lev plastered a smile onto his face. The change in him was frightening. "Oh, you know me, Vera. I'll be fine."

"That's not an answer."

"I'll eat like a king for a year and then I'll be right back where I started."

She knew he wasn't telling the truth; Lev smiled when he lied.

He was hiding something but if he respected her enough not to pry, then she wouldn't either. Despite that, Vera couldn't ignore the disappointment blooming in her chest, spreading through her body like blood on a white shirt. She knew they were walking on wires high above the ground, that their friendship was a choreographed dance, but she'd hoped he would give her something back in exchange for her admission. He didn't. Her defences rose.

"Fine, Lev," she said sharply. "Don't tell me."

Crossing her arms over her chest, Vera took a step back from Lev and moved towards her bedroom door. He stood up straight and watched her go. She didn't miss the look that passed across his face. Was it guilt? Or perhaps regret? He always said too much and she said too little. It seemed their roles had reversed.

Vera nodded once and left him on the landing. Her door clicked shut and a silence settled. She waited there, staring at the back of her closed door, her fingers skimming the rotting wood. She couldn't quite bring herself to disturb the stillness, though after a moment, it was broken by the familiar sound of Lev's footsteps as he walked away.

Part Three

The Unveiling of Secrets

20

Anya

Anya was just finishing up the last of the forgeries in the low light of the theatre when she heard a clattering sound and a loud bang. She lifted her head. The place had long since cleared out and the sun was starting to rise above the city, but she hadn't slept yet. She'd finished up her performance, forged her name onto Marina's list of performers attending the ball, and then set herself up at one of the tables in the main parlour to start on the invites for Camille Adrien and Ivan Novikov.

She looked up then as she heard footsteps scuffing the carpet. Since the princess had accosted her in the dressing room, Anya's guard had risen at work. She reached for the knife strapped to her thigh, horribly aware of how little clothing she was wearing. She had changed out of her costume and into her shirt which brushed the bare tops of her legs. She felt the weight of her knife in her hand and stood from the barstool she had been perched on.

A shadowed figure appeared, and Anya launched her knife at it. The figure ducked and the blade thudded into the wall.

They turned and pulled the knife out of the plaster, turning it over in their hands. "*Fucking hell*, Anya."

Anya recognised the voice instantly. "Why are you sneaking around?" she hissed.

Vera pulled her hood down to reveal her bruised face and her pale hair which glowed a softer yellow in the lamplight. "I tried the stage door. It was locked."

That was another thing she'd started doing since Sofiya's intrusion. She hadn't given much thought to the security of the dressing room. The girls came and went so frequently it often got left open or unlocked and, up until then, no one had ever tried to get in. In fact, most people didn't even know there was a thin sliver of an alleyway tucked between the two theatres.

"Why are you here?" Anya asked, moving back over to where she'd left the forgeries and her bottle of ink. When she realised how sharp she sounded she added, "In the nicest way possible."

Vera followed her, half turning her attention towards the rich cream papers on the desk. "Did Sofiya drop these to you?"

"I assume so," Anya replied. She'd not actually seen Sofiya. She had come back to her dressing room to see the sealed envelope tucked into the frame of her new mirror.

"Why are you here, Vera?" Anya repeated. "Shouldn't you and Lev be plotting?"

Something dark passed over Vera's face then and Anya knew she'd said the wrong thing. The shadow passed as Vera schooled her features into a look of hard passivity.

Vera leaned her elbows on the bar. "I need your help."

Anya let out a startled laugh. In the time she had known Vera, the girl had never once asked for her help. "Sorry," Anya said, unable to keep the amusement from her voice. "Can you repeat that?"

Shoving her hair over her shoulder and folding her arms across her chest, Vera frowned and said sharply, "Stop being a shit and help me. I don't know what to do with it."

"With what?"

Vera opened her mouth and closed it awkwardly. "My *hair*," she sputtered. "The dress is fine. Well, it's as fine as it's ever going to be. I don't know what to do with my hair."

Anya looked at Vera's hair. It was dry from the brutal winter and the ends were broken. She knew she could fix it. "Say please."

Vera sighed and rolled her eyes skyward. "*Please*," she hissed insincerely. She wouldn't keep eye contact and Anya almost felt sorry for her; she was clearly very far out of her depth.

"Of course." Anya smiled as she grabbed the forgeries and led Vera into the dressing room.

She turned up the lamplight, casting the room in a soft glow that made Vera's sickly pallor look a little less corpse-like. Anya pointed to the chair at her dressing table and Vera sat down. Anya caught her reflection in the mirror as she turned towards the girl and played absentmindedly with the long white strands of hair.

As she'd suspected, it was dry and felt crispy. She was certain Vera was concerned more with food and warmth than she was about the condition of her hair, but Anya couldn't help mourning it. She had always wondered what Vera's life had been like back on the Isles. Did her mother play with her hair? She struggled to imagine cold, sharp Vera in a scene so soft and maternal, and as she looked at the girl's reflection now, Anya could tell that it was taking everything in her not to pull away.

Anya's favourite part of the day was getting ready for an evening at the theatre. She loved painting her eyelids gold and donning her pink wig. She loved transforming herself into a person who had no responsibilities, who could fly across the stage and feel free for just a moment. She wished she'd kept her hair long in the braids her mother had given her when she was younger. She'd shaved her head when Daria had been born and sold her hair to buy a crib.

"What's the dress like?" Anya asked.

Vera frowned. "Awful."

"Brilliant," Anya replied sarcastically. "And the neckline?"

Vera gestured to her shoulders and mimed a slash straight across her collarbones and off her shoulders.

"Right." Anya grabbed the metal tongs from her neighbours dressing table and stuck them into the fire at the back of the room. "Move the chair over here."

Once they were heated, she took the tongs out of the fire and began setting Vera's hair into neat curls. She picked up a section of white-blonde hair and wrapped it around the iron until it smoked a little, then she unwound it and cradled it in her hands for a moment. As she moved up her head, she could tell Vera was growing restless.

"Did something happen?" Anya asked. "You seem more impatient than usual."

Vera continued to face forward when she said, "No."

Anya recalled the flash of darkness on her face when she'd mentioned Lev. She knew the topic was sensitive, but her curiosity got the better of her. "Did something happen with Lev?"

Vera's brow hardened and she took a deep breath. "I don't know what you're talking about. Nothing happened. Nothing *will* happen."

"Okay," Anya conceded, picking the tong back up. She guessed she wouldn't be gossiping with Vera any time soon. She was like a book with the pages glued shut – you couldn't pry it open without it tearing.

Anya picked up another section of Vera's hair and wrapped the lock around the metal tong. Vera jerked forwards and, surprised, Anya dropped the curl.

Vera cursed under her breath and pressed her palm to her head. "You burnt me," she snapped.

Anya sighed and picked the curl back up. "Behind every beautiful woman is a scorch mark on her scalp. Sit up. We're almost done."

Reluctantly, Vera sat up straighter and Anya went back to carefully curling each strand of her hair until her head was a mane of white curls. She pulled back various bits and twisted them into an elaborate style on the back of her head until half of her hair was piled onto the top of her head and the other half hung down her back.

"There's a headdress," Vera muttered sulkily.

"What's it like?" Anya asked.

"I look like a bird." Vera stood from the chair and examined the style in the mirror. She looped a curl around her finger. "I'm not going to wear it."

"I hate to be the bearer of bad news and you know I don't, under any circumstances, want you to be humiliated, Vera, but I think you're going to have to." Anya fought the laugh bubbling in her chest.

Vera glared daggers at her.

"Look, have you seen these people? You need to blend in." Anya joined Vera at the mirror and fluffed out her curls. "Does it cover your face?"

"No."

Anya hummed under her breath and started unearthing the makeup drawer of one of the other acrobats whose skin colour would match Vera's. "We need to cover your nose then."

"My nose is fine."

"That bruise looks awful, Vera. You look like a criminal. In fact, I actually think it looks worse than it did yesterday." Anya batted Vera's protective hands away and blotted the bruise with powder. At first it looked like it was going to cover, but when Vera turned towards the light, it still shimmered a grey blue. "It's not covering. Do you think we could start a new fashion trend?"

Vera pressed her fingers to her skin. "Bruise blush?"

Anya snorted a laugh and for the first time, she saw a small smile rise on Vera's mouth. She dabbed her face once more and said, "I think this is as good as it's going to get." She closed the case and handed it to Vera. "Top it up if you need to."

"Whose is this?"

"Ingrid's. Don't worry. She won't notice." Ingrid had gotten pregnant and hadn't been at work for over three weeks. When she'd first gone off sick, they'd sent her flowers but, as far as Anya was aware, they hadn't heard back from her.

Vera took the powder case and tucked it into the bodice of her dress.

Anya moved towards the stage door and unlocked it. "If you need to get in again, there's a spare key under the barrel next to the door."

Vera nodded stiffly and pulled on her cloak. Anya lifted the girl's hood carefully over the hairstyle to protect it from the misty rain that seemed to befall Ytavosk from autumn to spring.

"Take these. They're done." Anya handed the forged invites to Vera who lingered for a moment. "Stay safe."

"You too," Vera replied, her hand resting on the door.

In a blink the girl was gone, and the door clattered shut behind her. In her absence, Anya locked the door and took the tongs off the fire, placing them back on the right dressing table. She was fond of Vera, though if she was asked to explain why she was sure the words would get stuck on her tongue. Anya respected her grit and determination. She admired her selfishness; that was something Anya had never been. She often wondered how different things would be now if she'd never put her own life on hold for the sake of someone else's. Vera never did that. She served herself and she did it proudly. She thought the exception might be Lev but in the years of knowing them both, Anya had never seen any real evidence of that.

"I'll put myself first," Anya muttered to herself in a quiet promise before adding, "when the time is right."

Shoving Vera from her mind, Anya turned back to the dressing room. Now the invites were done and out of her possession, Anya finally had a chance to think about the day ahead of them. Her costume was bagged up and currently hanging on a clothing rail along with her wig. They were both labelled with her name as they sat huddled amongst the other performers' costumes. She reached up and curled her hands around the locket at her throat. It served as a reminder of her past, of everything that had happened to her and her mother, of all the scores that needed to be settled. She was supposed to take it off to perform, but Anya needed it.

As she fiddled with the pendant, she felt her skin start to itch. Her mother's face flashed into her mind. She saw her bruised eyes, the deep slashes across her back, Demek's hands at her throat as her mother refused to beg him or plead for herself. Then she heard the loud snap of her father's neck breaking as he tumbled down the stairs. She saw her mother in labour and was haunted nightly by the woman's screams and the shock as the blood pooled on the floorboards. Since then, she'd been consumed by Daria's pain and suffering, and her own too, which curdled in the deep crevices of her heart. When she reached for the locket, that is what she remembered – fury and suffering and all the things she'd promised to do in its wake.

Anya let the pendant fall to her chest with a thud before she turned towards her mirror. *I'll be selfish*, she thought. *The time is right.*

21

Vera

Vera felt ridiculous.

She watched herself shift in the mirror, the thick layers of her gown trailing along the plush carpet. Her fingers reached towards her skirt, anxiously straightening the folds of fabric.

Sofiya had sent her the address of the hotel and the name she was supposed to give to the receptionist. When Vera had arrived there that afternoon, she'd seen Aleks standing outside, the hood of his cloak pulled up over his head.

She'd taken a moment to look up at The Grand Belvar Hotel. She had been in rich places before and each time she felt like an intruder. She wasn't made to walk on pristine tile flooring or stand beneath chandeliers and each time she did, she felt as though she was going to slip or that the diamond monstrosity would come crashing down on her head. The Eva was bad enough, with its plush red curtains and excess of gold, but The Grand Belvar was something else entirely. The hotel stood alone, separate from the terraces on either side. The building itself was carved from thick black marble and shone in the afternoon light.

The Sikveyan aristocrats had a way of making money look tacky, but this building was different; it was the embodiment of true, old wealth.

She glanced back towards Aleks, who stood like a shadow blending into the dark walls of the hotel in his inky cloak. As she approached him, she pulled his hood down off his head to reveal his stern features and deep copper hair. He raised an eyebrow and swatted her hand away.

"You look like you're about to steal something," Vera had hissed, pushing past him and into the hotel lobby.

Now, she looked around the room. The walls were painted a deep forest green, and the upholstery was cream with green leaves and pink flowers embroidered in swirls across the fabric. In the gold mirror, she saw a girl with sallow cheeks and a fading bruise across her nose in a dress she hadn't yet laced up and a headdress to match. She hated the image staring back at her.

Vera had an older sister, Amandine, who had loved dressing up in their mother's clothes. When Vera had been small, Amandine had dressed her up like a doll, stringing pearls around her neck and pinning scarves around her body until Vera had cried in humiliation. One time their mother, Agathe, had caught Amandine pulling Vera's hair into a tight braid as fat tears rolled down her cheeks and she tried to push her older sister's hands away. Agathe had ushered Amandine out of the room and slowly removed the makeup and jewellery from Vera, hushing her as she'd cried. When Vera had closed her eyes, she'd felt her mother's soft hands against her cheeks, brushing her tears away and unwinding the jewels from her neck.

The vision of her sweet mother was always broken by the sound of the gunshot and the knowledge that Agathe's brutal death had been her fault.

Staring at the image reflected back at her now, she was taken back to being that child forced to play dress up. She looked out of place in the gown Sofiya had bought for her and she could feel her defences rising as they always did when she was embarrassed.

She pulled at the laces of the bodice and watched as it tightened over her ribs, cinching her waist.

The dress was the deep red of dried blood and fell off Vera's shoulders to reveal her sharp collarbones. It came with a string of rubies and a ridiculous head-dress that seemed to weigh more than Vera herself. The colour of the outfit was startling against her sickly pallor and pale hair. It was more flattering than anything Vera had ever worn, but she felt self-conscious standing there draped in rich fabrics that she never would have chosen for herself.

It was strange. Despite the luxury, the broad ceilings, the soft carpets squishing beneath her bare feet, Vera missed her torn cloak and the cold but comfortable rooms back at the boarding house. Perhaps it was the worry about the ball that made her long for familiarity. Perhaps she had just grown used to living in the shadows and taking what she needed but never what she wanted.

She tied the laces and straightened the headdress as she took a deep breath and shoved Amandine from her mind. She had never been unsure of herself, and she wouldn't start now.

She left her room and ventured down to the lobby to see Aleks pacing nervously back and forth across the entry parlour with such aggression Vera was surprised to see the carpet beneath his feet hadn't worn away.

"I'm starting to agree with Lev," he said as she approached him. "This is a terrible idea. They'll kill us."

"That's just great," Vera snapped sarcastically, turning towards him sharply. "Thank you, Aleks. Very helpful."

She didn't have the space in her mind for more doubt or anxiety. She'd been furious with Lev. In all the time she'd known him he'd never given her anything other than his support and relentless optimism. He'd always gone along with her plans and encouraged her thirst for thievery. That was the first time she'd seen him truly doubt her.

She couldn't keep the vision of him in the shadows from her mind. Embarrassment crept up her spine as she recalled telling him her plans to go to Vor and the way he had refused to be truthful with her.

Shoving the thought away, she grabbed Aleks by the shoulders to stop his pacing. "Get it together or stay behind," she said bluntly.

Aleks took a deep breath, nodded and shrugged Vera off, rubbing his arms where her hands had gripped him.

Taking a deep breath herself, Vera turned away from him. "At what point did I become your mother?"

"If that's your idea of mothering, I'm concerned for your future children."

"Then it's a good thing I don't want children, isn't it?"

Aleks shrugged and straightened the collar of his cloak. "You look nice, by the way."

"Fuck off, Aleks."

As they left the hotel, Vera was hit by a cool breeze. In the time since she'd entered the hotel, the temperature had dropped. She threw her cloak, which had been resting across her arm, around her shoulders and tied it at her throat, careful not to tangle the ribbon with the string of rubies. The cool wind bit at her arms and her face, threatening to knock the headdress off. She was grateful when the carriage arrived.

As it came into view, lit by the low light of the hotel, Vera almost laughed out loud. Emblazoned on the side of the carriage and the centres of the spoked wheels was the royal crest – the same cursive 'M' on Sofiya's signet ring.

A coachman jumped down from the seat above the carriage and smiled at them. His hair was radiant gold and the servant uniform looked wrong on him, as though he had been born for more than that role. He reached for Vera's hand, which she reluctantly outstretched, and helped her into the carriage. Aleks climbed in after her and in moments the carriage was moving, bouncing over the cobbled streets of Gambit Square.

She looked around the carriage. The inside was decorated with the royal colours, with purple velvet seats and gold curtains. The seats were plush and more comfortable than anything she had ever been privy to. She couldn't help but wonder which member of the royal entourage travelled in this carriage before her and how they would feel if they knew two magicians were now living a life of such luxury.

Vera ran through the plan Anya had laid out for them the night before as the candles on the pub table burned low. It was a chaotic plan, so outrageous that she was surprised Sofiya even agreed to it. It all felt too flimsy in Vera's head – she was to find a secret she didn't know in the mind of someone she had never met in a room full of people who would hang her if they found out what she was capable of. Lev was right to doubt the plan. He was right to doubt her.

No, she thought stubbornly, trying hard to give a louder voice to the part of her that knew she could do it. She tried to make peace with her power, its weakness, *her* weakness. She *was* capable, even with no training, but the longing for her secret city persisted.

The noise of Ytavosk was muffled by the walls of the carriage, but she could still hear the flower sellers' last calls of discounted bouquets, the soft thrum of the cable ferries pushing back and forth across the river, and the shouts coming up from the university rowing teams as they practised well into the night. The sounds from Gambit Square up to the Palace Quarter were considerably more wholesome than those Vera was exposed to in Ivenko's Cauldron.

She tried to imagine what her life might have been like if she had been born into nobility. Would she have been comfortable in rich clothing? Would the rubies have felt weightless around her neck? She remembered how far away it had all felt as she had stood on the window ledge, riffling through the threads of Karina Vitov's mind. Vera hadn't been able to shake the image of her dressed in green, draping strings of emeralds around her throat, her figure full from regular meals.

And what about her abilities – would she have given up magic if she hadn't been forced to claw her way through life? While she complained about the cold and the constant stiffness in her fingers, there was something wonderful about it all. She couldn't deny the power she felt every time her attention was drawn to the bundle of strings sparking in someone's head. She'd had so little power when as a child and she'd been forced to suppress that part of her that made her feel in control. Practising her magic was as close to freedom as she would ever get.

Karina was warm and fed, but her life was planned and rehearsed, her movements were scrutinised, and her mind was vulnerable to people like Vera and Aleks. Karina's one secret, her one deviation from the life she had been born for, had been sold on the market for less than a hot dinner. Vera's life was chaotic, but her magic made her free. She knew she'd never be able to let that go.

She cut a quick glance towards Aleks. His knee was shaking, and his fingers were picking at the stitching in the curtains. She couldn't help but wonder how much training he'd had growing up. He seemed more able than she was, the execution of his art felt seamless in comparison to Vera's fumbling. There was a surety to the way he moved when he used his magic. Jealousy burned in her chest.

Turning back towards the window, Vera watched the city pass by. She rarely had cause to be this close to the palace and to see it now felt like meeting a long-lost parent she'd grown to resent. She watched as the buildings became larger and the surrounding land became broader and less cramped. There were bigger gardens, bigger stables, the streets were lit by lanterns that didn't flicker and cut out, and the air felt cleaner. She thought that side of the city could be considered beautiful had those inhabiting it not been so rotten.

And there, in the distance, she saw it. The palace loomed up ahead. It was a stone building, glowing with golden light and surrounded by trees illuminated in the darkness. There were countless turrets, all breaking through the clouds and mist that seemed to float up from the river below like steam. Despite her hatred of the Meskovs and their laws, she could admit that it was a wonder.

The palace brought in a lot of tourism, but Vera had never ventured this far across the city to see it for herself. She had only caught glimpses of it on posters in shop windows or printed on the front of newspapers – it always made front page news. It was a thing of folklore with its cream walls, tall spires, and towers topped with round terracotta-red roofs.

The closer they got to the palace, the thicker the crowds grew. The streets were a mad array of colour and light. There were dancers at the edges of the widening thoroughfare twirling fire batons and women in their finest gowns were stopping to gawk at the flames as they reflected off their glimmering dresses. Vera caught sight of two women – one in black, the other in silver – as they stopped before a street magician. He was the ordinary kind who used distraction and false props instead of genuine magic. Perhaps it was her own history as a thief or the time she spent with Lev, but as Vera watched the magician take their hands, she saw him slip the wedding rings from their fingers. In a second, he closed his palms over the two bands and when he revealed them once more, they were linked. He hid them from view and when he opened his fingers like a clam revealing a pearl, the rings were separate again. He slipped the rings back onto the women's fingers as they shared a tender kiss.

Vera wondered if the rings he gave back were the real ones, or whether he had stolen the gold for himself as Lev would have.

The carriage drew to a stop and the young coachman appeared again to help them down.

Vera was grateful for the fresh air. She breathed it in large gulps, her lungs thanking her silently by letting the pressure release from her chest. She looked around. Revellers haunted the streets dressed in their finest clothes and calling to one another in their clipped accents. They marched past with the same steady flow as a river barrelling towards the sea.

When she turned to pair up with Aleks, he was already gone.

"You *shit*," she hissed under her breath.

"Pardon?" the coachman asked, turning towards Vera. He was clearly going for a look of concern, but she noticed the soft smirk rising on his mouth.

Vera ignored him, stepping into the horde pushing towards the palace. Aleks was supposed to stay with her and yet he was nowhere to be seen. *He better be dead*, she thought bitterly. *Dead or kidnapped.*

She moved with the crowd which guided her steadily up the cobbled slope, through the gates, and towards the palace entrance where she would be stopped to have her invitation checked. Vera tried desperately to remember Sofiya's instructions to keep her head high, her shoulders straight, and to behave like she had a right to be there.

"Because you *do* have a right to be there," Sofiya had said. "I invited you."

She had appreciated the sentiment of Sofiya's words, but she'd seen Anya ink the cards illegally in the theatre the night before, and they felt a little empty.

When she reached the front of the queue, Vera pulled out her invitation. The cream card was thick and smooth, and the calligraphy was impeccable. She silently thanked Anya as she handed the card over to a heavy-set man in dark clothes.

"Your name?" the guard asked.

"Camille Adrien," she said without covering her accent, once again shedding her skin to make room for a new persona.

The man looked her up and down and Vera resisted the urge to curl her body in on itself. She repeated Sofiya's instructions – *head up, shoulders straight, act as though you have a right to be there.* She held the man's gaze.

He checked the card again. "You're alone?"

Vera had known this might be a problem. That was why Aleks was supposed to stay at her side; it wasn't often that people attended balls alone.

She clutched her hands behind her back briefly, slipping her mother's ring onto her engagement finger. When she brought her hand back to the front, she held her ring up for the guard to see and giggled, brushing her hair over her shoulder with her other hand. She forced a smile and batted her eyelashes. "My fiancé is inside addressing some matters of business," she said, softening her voice. "It's a bit too complicated for the likes of me, so I said I'd meet him later on. That's not a problem, is it?"

The man softened then before this sweet, innocent, helpless girl. Vera took great pride in manipulating men. He let her pass.

She moved once more with the flow of the crowd through the palace entrance and up a flight of stairs. The palace was exactly what she'd imagined it would be – a series of long gilded rooms, each lined with portraits of long dead monarchs and paintings of the snowy Sikveyan mountains. The floors were made up of cream tiles and each window was shrouded in sheer drapes and purple velvet curtains that matched the interior of their carriage.

Vera began her assent up the staircase, though she managed to disappear at the top before she was announced. She skirted along the edge of the mezzanine, cutting a quick glance down at the ballroom below. She couldn't help her amazement as she looked around the room at the gold mirrors and the excessive crystal chandelier hanging precariously from the ceiling.

She was deprived of her moment to gawk when a hand reached out from behind a curtain and pulled her through into a small alcove. Her shoulder banged against the cold glass window and her ankle caught on a large plant pot.

"Sorry," Lev said, steadying her. "I thought you knew I was here."

"How would I know you were here? You were *hidden*."

They'd agreed to meet on the mezzanine, though she'd said nothing about hiding behind curtains or being particularly conspicuous about it. In fact, Sofiya had been right when she'd told them they wouldn't have to be quiet about it. There were no guards positioned up here – none that they could see – as if the royal family had no concerns beside the time their food would be served or whether their wine cellar could cope with the demand of a room full of raging drunkards.

Lev's eyes moved across her dress from the tight bodice to the aggressive flare of the skirt, but he said nothing, just leaned down to the window ledge and came back up with two filled champagne flutes. "I've never had champagne before," he said. "I'm worried I'm going to develop a taste for royal living and spend my whole life chasing the thrill."

"Then you'll have to find a way of charming Sofiya into marriage."

"Oh, please. Give me some credit. I've been scheming that since the beginning." Lev brushed back the curtain and led Vera towards the mezzanine balcony.

"How? I've only seen you be your irritating self."

"My *charming* self," Lev corrected. "You've just been exposed to it for too long. You've built up an immunity to it."

She was so glad that they could fall easily into their old ways. When she blinked, she saw the closed off look on his face, but now she rolled her eyes at him. "You're grating."

He laughed and leaned over the mezzanine railing. "Alright," he began, rubbing his palms together briefly before pointing towards a group of men standing together at the edge of the ballroom. "You see that man over there? Arms crossed with a woman in a silver gown? They both have grey hair."

Vera followed his gaze and said, "Silver rose in his lapel?"

"Yes."

"He's our man?"

"I think so."

Vera sighed. "You *think*? That's very reassuring."

Lev leaned closer. "Make your way towards him. I'll meet you there."

Vera nodded once before she turned her back on him.

"Oh, and Vera?" Lev asked, grabbing her arm, spinning her round to face him.

"What?"

Lev broke into a grin. "Have I told you how pretty you look tonight?"

She swatted his hand away. "Fuck off, Lev."

Vera turned away from Lev before he could see her smile and when she glanced back, he was gone.

She made her way back to the staircase and re-joined the flow of revellers making their way down to the ballroom. She had a good view from the top of the stairs but as she descended, Vera's vision became less clear, and the room became more stuffy. She noticed that it was organised in rings. On the outermost circle, the older revellers sat at round tables, their glasses resting beside discarded gloves. The middle circle looked to be full of men discussing matters of business, cutting their wives and mistresses from the conversations with turned backs. In the centre, an area was cleared beneath the chandelier where couples entered dance after dance, their bodies caught and multiplied in the mirrors around the room.

The closer Vera got to the chaos, the more the scene came to life before her. The men and women sitting at tables were leaning drunkenly on their hands, their voices blending into the sounds of violins and footsteps. The dancers weren't leaning on each other out of love or desire. They were too drunk to hold themselves upright. The only people in the room who seemed stable on their own feet were the men and women discussing business. The whole palace was corrupt, gorging themselves on extravagant foods and aged wine with little to no regard for those starving in the streets below. Vera had always been aware of the fact, but seeing it now, staring the problem in the eye, she couldn't help but feel that familiar rage burning a hole through her chest.

She was sure that if anyone had the secret, they would be in the palace. For the first time, she felt as though they were finally on the right track and her impatience was bubbling up from under her skin like a clogged drain in the Cauldron. She itched to move, to find the missing pieces, to take action, to do *something*.

But for now, she just had to wait.

22

SOFIYA

Sofiya tried to pay attention to the conversations happening inside the dressing room between her mother and her little sister, but all she could think about was the chaos ensuing in the ballroom below. She wasn't quite sure what had possessed her when she'd given out the invites and she was starting to regret her decision.

Sofiya stood before a gilded mirror pulling at the skirt of her gown, trying desperately to make the glittering fabric sit properly. Her mother had insisted she wear a dress of gold, though Sofiya had tried to push towards the green gown that made her copper hair glow. She'd lost the battle, of course, and now she was being tied into a gold monstrosity that hurt to look at.

"Suck in," her mother hissed, cutting off her conversation with Sofiya's sister, Olga.

Sofiya did not suck in, she stood naturally and let the dress hang as it did as her maid tied the gold ribbon in a bow at the small of her back and tucked the laces in. She still felt like she couldn't breathe, though she figured that had more to do with their flimsy plot than the tightness of her bodice.

Sofiya's mother ushered the maid away and took her place behind Sofiya. Ruslana combed her fingers through Sofiya's hair and pulled it back over her shoulder, beginning to twist and curl the sections into an elaborate updo. Sofiya looked up and met her mother's gaze in the mirror. Ruslana's eyes were bloodshot, her makeup was already starting to smudge, and she seemed unsteady on her feet.

Ruslana leaned closer to Sofiya. "Tonight is the night. You need to look your best."

"The night for what?" Sofiya asked tentatively.

"I have some people I'd like you to meet," Ruslana said. "You know your duties."

"Oh," Sofiya replied. "*That.*"

Sofiya knew she was foolish to think that just once she might be able to escape the slow suffocation that was her forced marriage to a man, but some part of her had hoped that just for one night she might be left alone, that she might not be subjected to that bespoke form of punishment. She wanted to give her full attention to the matter at hand – to the secret that would see her hanged – but now she had to divide her attention between that and batting off the sweaty hands of men three times her age.

Ruslana pressed her cold fingers to Sofiya's cheeks and pulled back the skin on her face. Sofiya stood still, her hands pinned to her sides as her mother primped and preened her into the princess everyone wanted to see. "You'll be a beautiful distraction, Sofiya. All of this will be forgotten," she said, her voice slow and calm, seemingly oblivious of the weight she was draping across Sofiya's shoulders.

All of this will be forgotten.

Sofiya was getting tired of her mother's cryptic comments. She wanted to hit her and demand to know what exactly she meant by 'this', but she knew her anger wouldn't help the cause, only hinder it. Instead, Sofiya smiled softly at her mother and slipped back into the part they wanted her to play: the docile princess, kind and accepting of her fate. Perhaps she wasn't so different from the other thieves. They all had parts to play, they all had scripts and roles to fall into and they did so seamlessly, switching out their names and personalities like cheap masks. She swore she could do that too.

"What will be forgotten?" Sofiya asked, flooding her voice with fake innocence.

Her mother's face dropped as she placed the tiara on the top of Sofiya's head, securing it at the back with a pin. She caught Sofiya's eyes in the mirror. "You look lovely, Sofiya. You'll receive a lot of attention tonight."

Sofiya wanted to scream.

She wondered, not for the first time, how much her mother really knew. Did she know what the secret was? Did she know just what Sofiya had done? Sofiya had never taken the botanicals book back to the library and it was still hidden safely beneath the floorboards in her room. What if they found it there? Then they wouldn't need to retrieve the secret to have some proof of what Sofiya had done and just how treasonous she had been. It was one thing to learn the basics of plants and poisons, it was another to use them to kill the King.

Sofiya had spent her life watching her country fall apart as her parents stood by and did nothing to save it. She'd grown tired of decay, of the guilt bubbling in her stomach each time she went into the city proper and saw the starved faces of the citizens below. She hadn't intended to kill the king so quickly; she'd meant to make his health decline gradually until he dropped dead of a mysterious illness, but she'd misjudged the power of her poison.

Her father had called her up to his rooms to speak with her and Sofiya obliged, taking up his tea tray as she did so. On the tray sat two glasses of tea in ceramic cups that rattled on their saucers as she made the ascent to his rooms at the top of the palace.

She knocked once on his door, and he let her in.

"Sit," Mikhail said sternly, gesturing to one of the plush purple armchairs set up by the window.

He must have moved them there. Sofiya was sure she hadn't seen them there before. She wondered whether he wanted her to have a clear view of the city as he lectured her.

"You know," Mikhail began, settling himself into the seat beside her. "You never did have the makings of a queen."

Sofiya bit down the hatred in the throat. "How so? You all seem to have an opinion on my capabilities, but no one wants to explain it to me."

"You weren't born for it. You're too abrasive, Sofiya, you wouldn't be a friend of the people."

And you are? she thought, but she knew not to rile him up even more. If her father so much as left the palace grounds he'd get a knife to the throat and a riot would break out across the country. The Meskovs were hated and Sofiya couldn't deny that their subjects had good reason to be angry. They were bled of their money while the royal family threw party after party and drank to excess instead of dealing with actual problems that arose throughout the city.

"You're hysterical, father, why don't you have some tea? To calm yourself." Sofiya felt the empty glass vial in the pocket of her dress.

She had been scheming for months, calculating each of her moves, perfecting her route to the throne. She would take out her father first and then turn on her mother, though she couldn't die in the same way. She would not be granted a slow death disguised as disease; a terrible accident would happen. She'd even planned her mourning period before she *reluctantly* accepted the role of queen.

"No, no, I'm fine." Her father waved her off.

"Why am I here?"

"We have someone for you to marry."

Sofiya had been successfully avoiding all topics surrounding marriage since she'd turned thirteen, but there she was, forced to confront it, nonetheless. "Their name?"

"Stanislav – you know him."

Sofiya did know him, though they were not yet friends. Stas had attended their parties since he was small. He was the son of a wealthy merchant and his first wife, Anatoly and Viktoria Vitov. When Stas' mother had died, Anatoly had remarried a woman barely older than his son and as far as Sofiya was aware, Stas had moved out of their family home in Gambit Square to his own flat.

"Why him?"

"He's from a respectable family."

That was true, but Sofiya knew that Stas himself was not respectable. "And you want me to marry him?"

"Yes."

"What if I don't want to?"

"Whether we think you're ready or not, you will be Queen of Sikveya. When you lead a country, what *you* want doesn't matter."

"Does that apply to you?"

Mikhail reached an unsteady hand towards the tea tray and Sofiya sucked in a breath. He didn't drink the tea, just held the cup in one hand as he settled his gaze on Sofiya. "Of course it does."

"Then you are incredibly naive."

"We do our best with the people we are given."

"You're ruining them."

"Look down at that city, Sofiya. Do you think it's worth saving?" His voice sharpened, a tone she so rarely heard from him.

Sofiya looked down at Ytavosk, to where the streets glowed golden in the evening light. She *did* think it was worth saving. She thought all the people down there had been driven to madness by their hunger and their desperation but that didn't make them bad people. Perhaps she only thought that because she was terrified of what it would mean for her if desperate people were condemned.

She recalled her first trip to the Cauldron. The woman who had begged for help and who had been shot for the trouble. They were never given the opportunity to be good, to be decent.

"Yes," she said honestly. "I do."

"Why?"

"Because they're *people. You* did this to them."

The next thought came as a chant, a secret incantation. *I can make it better. I will make it better.* Her childish longing for approval had long since dissipated, and in its place sat a vengeful fury that threatened to overtake her whenever she looked at her parents.

And then, in one moment, her prayers were answered, and she took one very large step towards the throne.

Her father raised his cup to his lips and took a swig of the tea. Sofiya expected him to cough a little, which he did. What she wasn't expecting was the excess of blood that sputtered from his lips or the pallor that quickly flooded his face. The King froze momentarily before dropping his cup and reaching up towards his throat. Before Sofiya knew it, he was on the floor and the life was bleeding from his skin, his eyes, the bulbous veins on the backs of his hands.

Mikhail opened his mouth to speak and Sofiya stood there, too shocked to move. She wasn't appalled by her actions – the time for feeling shame at the thought of murder had long since passed – but she hadn't expected it to happen so quickly. She let out a shrill and very artificial cry for help, though it wasn't loud enough for anyone to hear. She fell to her knees beside him and brushed his hair back from his face, waiting for that final breath.

"I'll be better," she whispered to her dying father. "I will be better than you."

Once Sofiya was sure he was dead, she screamed loud enough for the guards outside the door to hear her. They rushed in, the oak doors slamming against the walls, and Sofiya looked up at them. "Did you not hear me before?" she cried, dropping her father's hand so it fell across his chest.

She hoped they thought she'd been comforting him in his final moments and not checking for the last beat of his pulse. "I called and called, and no one came. He's *dead*."

She thought at that moment that had she not been a princess, she might have been an actress on a stage.

The guards pulled poor, helpless Sofiya to her feet and guided her out of the room and into the hallway. She cried and moaned in false pain until her mother and siblings arrived. Her mind was whirring with all the possibilities her future held now that she was one step closer to the throne. She had studied for this and was proud of everything she'd achieved. She was ready. She knew she was.

Now, years later, she stood before her mother, who was still very much alive and very much burdening Sofiya.

Her plan had been waylaid by the investigation into her father's death. The court had accused her, and she'd acted her way out of it. Sofiya had intended to kill her mother soon after her father's death, but she didn't want to arouse more suspicion.

She'd wondered if her mother would step into the role of queen with a little more enthusiasm after the untimely death of her husband, but Ruslana never had. And now her mother's sole task seemed to be a continuation of what her father had wanted – a series of extravagant parties and a husband for Sofiya.

Unexpectedly, she and Stas had formed an alliance. Something very solid had grown between them in the years since her father had tried to have them married. They believed in the same things, that was the foundation of their friendship. They had spent the years since those tedious afternoon teas wherein their parents had tried to force them together, saving each other gossip and dances. If it came down to it, she could marry Stas. If she needed a husband to get to the throne, to make people trust her, they would wed and have their own lives.

"Are you ready?" Olga's shrill voice pierced the silence and Sofiya startled back into the room.

Ruslana moved away from Sofiya, grabbing her glass from the vanity. She stumbled towards Olga, who squealed when her mother stepped on the hem of her silver ball gown.

"Is Miron coming?" Sofiya asked when her brother didn't appear.

"Oh," Ruslana said absently. "I'm not entirely sure where he is."

Sofiya resisted the urge to roll her eyes at her mother's complacency as she followed the Queen and her little sister out of the dressing room. She could make some pretty good guesses as to where Miron was and what he was up to. They headed towards the ballroom flanked on both sides by a set of guards loaded with weapons. She watched with embarrassment as Olga attempted to flirt with one of the guards before glancing up at the walls lined with portraits of all the kings and queens who'd come before her.

As she examined their faces, she wondered how she would feel once her portrait was up there with them. She wasn't sure of many things, but she was certain that there would be no pride in her heart when she saw her face amongst her ancestors. She would not look back on her predecessors and smile. When she became queen, she thought, she would take all the pictures down. She wanted to start again. She wanted to be different and create real change.

"Sofiya," Ruslana hissed from up ahead.

When Sofiya looked up, she saw that she had come to the entrance of the ball. She hated this part of the production.

Reluctantly, Sofiya pushed her shoulders back. She wanted to think about their plan, about the thieves hiding away in the ballroom below ready to create the utmost chaos, but all she could think of was herself. Of the men she was about to be paraded between, of the hands about to grab onto her hips and the watery stares of those already too drunk to stand as they made smarmy, poorly crafted jokes about her.

The doors opened and the orchestra inside the ballroom drew their song to a close.

"Her Royal Highness, Princess Olga Meskov." The announcer's voice echoed across the room, bouncing off the walls and the high-strung chandeliers.

Olga descended into the ballroom. Sofiya took a step forward but as she did so, Miron came skittering round the corner straightening his cravat and brushing his fingers through his dishevelled hair. He shoved in front of Sofiya and cleared his throat.

Miron straightened his spine and he transformed into the mischievous prince. "Announce me," he said sharply and the startled man standing at the entrance cleared his throat and glanced down the stairs to make sure Olga had made it to the bottom.

As Miron stepped forward, the announcer called, "His Royal Highness, Prince Miron Meskov."

It gave Sofiya a great amount of satisfaction to hear Miron's name be called. He sounded like a character in a children's story, though she doubted his actions and behaviour were all that appropriate for a younger audience.

Lastly, Sofiya took her place by the entrance and pulled her spine taut. She pushed down the fear rising in her chest and adjusted the thin straps of her dress so they sat smoothly over her freckled shoulders. She took a step towards the archway.

"Her Royal Highness, Princess Sofiya Meskov."

Sofiya stepped into the ballroom. Each step was careful and calculated. Luckily, there were no swans sauntering around ready for her to trip over this time and her descent down the stairs was as graceful as the room would expect from their heir. She looked around, desperate to locate the thieves she'd recklessly brought to the palace. In the corner of the room, she saw a girl with white blonde hair and a red headdress. Vera raised her eyebrow at Sofiya. By some miracle, the girl had managed to cover the harsh bruise that had spread across her face like a stain and make herself look somewhat presentable. Beside her stood a waiter with black hair and a smile that she recognised instantly. Of course, Lev would stick near Vera's side for as long as he possibly could. She could not locate Aleks and, in the centre of the room, a sheet of pink silk cascaded down from the ceiling, but Anya was nowhere to be seen.

Sofiya plastered a false smile onto her face and ran her hand along the bannister as she reached the final step. She was already too hot, too stressed, too sure that this whole plan was going to fall apart as quickly as it had been shoved together. Curling her fingers into fists and unfurling them once more, Sofiya fought to clear her mind. She took a deep breath.

She had to trust the thieves. She had to have faith in them.

23

Aleks

Aleks knew that breaking away from Vera would only create more problems for him. Not only would he have to find his own way into the palace, but he would also have to find her again in the hordes of wild revellers. He also knew that he couldn't enter through the palace gates – someone was sure to recognise his face when they were checking his papers and he hadn't spent so long under cover just to hand himself over.

Predictably, his mind wandered back to Lina as he pushed his way through the tide of people and towards the servants' entrance. She would have hated this crowd. He hated it too.

Luckily, Aleks knew the palace well. He knew each hidden entrance, he knew where every pathway led, and most importantly, he knew exactly where to hide when the slight feet of a maid crunched the grass. Aleks slipped expertly into a small sliver of space in the walls of the palace. Every couple of metres, one of those crevices appeared. They'd been designed for guards so they could stay undercover and protect the palace and those inside. Though the tradition had long since been forgotten, the holes remained and now Aleks squeezed inside, his shoulders brushing the pale stone on either side.

He heard the maid scuttle past muttering aggressively to herself about how cold she was and how she hadn't had a chance to eat since the night before. She sounded young and he doubted she'd know who he was, but he waited until he was sure she was gone before he emerged from the crack in the wall and continued towards the servants' entrance.

The formal entrance of the palace was absurd – a staircase gilded in gold and lined with hordes of flowers and gemstones – but the servants' entrance was little more than a cracked oak door that was often propped open by a tub of lard. As Aleks approached the door, he put his head down to avoid the hard stares of the tired waitstaff. He slumped his shoulders inward and tried to look like there was an almost unbearable weight hanging around his neck to mimic the other servants.

No one paid any attention to him as he slipped through the door and into the kitchen. It was a chaotic place to be and Aleks missed it – the fire was always lit and the room had a level of warmth to it that the rest of Sikveya lacked. It was homely and comforting. A chef bumped into Aleks and Aleks apologised solemnly, never once raising his head.

"Oi, you," someone barked. "Red hair."

Aleks nodded once to show he'd heard, and the chef said, "Pass the butter and a ladle."

Aleks did as he was told and then pushed towards the door that led to a dark set of stairs. He knew if he could just get to that staircase, he would be in the clear. The stairs were poorly lit, and, in the darkness, he would not be recognised. He recalled the first time he'd ever had to climb those stairs before he was used to their crookedness. He hadn't been able to see a thing and had tripped multiple times, bashing his shins on the cold stone. It had taken him a few trips to learn where he had to lift his foot slightly higher and which steps he needed to skip. Now it came back to him like a forgotten habit, a second nature, an old friend he hadn't realised he'd missed so sorely. It was a comfort to know that some things didn't change.

A firm hand gripped his forearm and pulled him to a stop. Startled, Aleks raised his head. He knew his mistake the second he saw the look of recognition rise across the older man's face. His eyes lit momentarily before his eyebrows scrunched together and his grip tightened.

Aleks opened his mouth to speak but the man spoke first. "It's *you.*"

Instinctively, Aleks curled his fingers and reached out towards the man's mind, catching hold of the nearest blue thread. He saw his face flash through the man's mind briefly before he pulled the thread, removing the memory and guiding it into a small vial he had tucked beneath his cloak. He had to move quickly before anyone else recognised him.

Panic surged through him, seizing his body and sending a cold sharpness straight to his chest. He clutched the bottle closely and darted towards the staircase.

He took the steps two at a time, skipping over the ones he knew were worn down to slopes, his hand running along the rail as he went. He embraced the darkness, letting it shield him and his identity. If he got caught now, it would all be over. He would be captured and murdered. He didn't know what would happen to Masha. He'd take the secret of her to his pyre but without his money, she would not be kept out in the country. She'd be kicked out onto the street, left to fend for herself. She'd die, cold and alone.

Aleks shoved his way through the door at the top of the stairs and stumbled into a hallway. From there he could hear the sounds of the ball echoing off the marble floors and high ceilings. He paused for a moment to gather his bearings before setting off towards the ballroom. He couldn't enter through the main entrance, so he slipped in through one of the side doors hidden by a sheet of purple velvet. He tried to catch his breath, but his heart was thumping heavily in his chest. He closed his eyes momentarily as the familiar sounds of music and laughter assaulted his scenes.

He'd once belonged in this scene. Long ago, he had been taught the dances, the etiquette, the correct way to congratulate a businessman on his most recent venture. He used to love the sound of violins; now they just made his shoulders tense. While he had once belonged there, he definitely didn't now. The songs had changed, the laughter had grown, and most importantly, he had seen the dark side of the royal family, the side that was a danger to him, that *would* kill him.

They'd exiled him. They'd murdered Lina.

Aleks looked around the ballroom, straightening his spine and searching for a shock of white hair and a blood red dress.

He needed to find Vera.

He needed to bring this all to an end.

24

Anya

Anya had no intention of following the plan.

And now she was desperately trying to breathe through the tightness of her costume.

Her head was starting to feel heavy, her eyes were unfocused, and there was a cold sweat beading on her spine. She tried to breathe through it, to focus on something that was less intimidating. She heard Lilja's voice then, both soft and gravelly, *three breaths, Anya, in and out. Just like that.* She felt like a traitor when she saw Lilja's face and not her own mother's.

She stared at herself in the mirror. Her makeup was pristine, her hair was concealed beneath the pink wig and her costume was free of wrinkles. In the dressing room, hordes of girls in different coloured outfits – blues, greens, purples – we're manically trying to get ready, pinning loose strands of hair, touching up their red lips. Anya watched them all as they smiled and laughed and tried to ignore the rapid voice in her head telling her that *something was wrong, everything is wrong, this whole plan was wrong and sure to get them killed.*

Anya knew she looked the part, she just had to figure out how to play it.

The room fell to an almost immediate hush and Anya turned to see Marina, their boss, sauntering into the room. The older woman was in a silver feathered dress. Her hair was pinned in her usual halo braid, her arms were decorated with intricate tattoos, and curving around each wrist was a metal cuff of leaves, silver to match the shimmer of her dress.

"Right, girls!" she called, a clipboard in one hand, a glass of champagne in the other. She began to list names alongside the roles they'd be taking that night. All around her, girls sighed and cheered and switched out their shoes. She struggled to hold onto any of Marina's words until she said, "Anya, silks in the main room."

A bit of the tension in Anya's chest was released. At least Marina hadn't noticed the forgery. She nodded once, sharply, and then Marina was ushering them out of the room.

Anya stole one last glance at herself in the mirror. She had on a short, floaty pink skirt that sat at the very tops of her thighs and a pink corseted bodice to match. It was tied with a gold cord at the back, tight enough to make the most of Anya's muscular body. Her skin had been coated in various oils to make it shine in the glittering ballroom light, and she'd taken the time to paint her eyelids and nails gold. She had always been beautiful, but she truly felt it when she was in costume.

One of the girls, Galina, grabbed Anya by the arm and dragged her out of the dressing room. They followed each other in one long line down the corridor and into the ballroom, deliberately accentuating the long lines of their arms and legs and necks. Each step was like a dance, a rhythm they'd all learnt at the theatre, and they moved as one beautiful, gilded unit.

As they passed various stations, the girls fell away from the line until it was just Anya strolling towards the string of pink silk in the centre of the ballroom.

She cast a glance around the ballroom once in search of her friends. She caught a glimpse of Vera as the girl circled the room like a snake about to strike. She was dressed in blood red with a headdress to match, the colour deep and stark against her skin and her pale hair. Vera hated waiting. She was always in motion, as if furiously pushing towards something they were not privy to. As Anya watched her walk alone around the outskirts of the ballroom, she could see the tension in the line of Vera's shoulders and the coarse look on her face, then in a blink, Vera was gone.

Anya turned towards the cascading silk, wrapping the smooth fabric around the palm of her hand and began levering herself up into the air, her feet and ankles tangling in the fabric. She glanced back down at the crowd, her view different from that height. She was above the heat and the sweat of the revellers, up in the air now watching them dance and trip over each other. Her eyes searched the room – she knew he had to be here. She'd seen a stack of envelopes sealed with the royal seal on his mantlepiece. He was a known reveller, a man with fewer morals than he had thin hairs on his head. He *had* to be there.

And then she saw him. Kirill was dressed in gaudy red velvet, with someone whom Anya assumed was not his wife draped over his arm. His mistress was dressed in a jarring shade of green. She watched Kirill and his mistress carefully as they began to dance, spinning each other round in circles, quickening with the swell of the music.

The rhythm made her heart beat faster until she felt sick. She tried to shove it all out of her mind, but the thoughts lingered, a thousand ways she could wind up dead rallying through her mind. She tried not to think about Daria at all or what would become of her should Anya perish that night.

Anya positioned herself on the silks and began her routine of twists and spins. The motion was as natural to her as walking and her mother's soothing voice echoed in the back of her mind. *You're a natural, Anya. Like a bird caught on the breeze.*

Back at home in Mosarisk, in the west of Sikveya, the winters had been less harsh. The earth had never turned to stone, snow only fell once or twice a year if they were unlucky, and she had been able to weather it. Even so, her father would rarely let them out of the house until the winter thawed and spring set in. Her mother, Iskra, would tell Anya that it was to protect them, to keep their little family safe. But Anya could see the bruises on her mother's cheek, the small cuts across her stomach, the way her mother tensed in her father's presence. They were not safe at all in that house.

The door had been firmly locked, their visits outside restricted to Anya's school timetable and her mother's job at the factory where she wore a scarf tied tight around her neck. Anya, therefore, became very familiar with their little house in that small town.

One day when Anya was little, she'd come home from school to find her mother eagerly waiting in the window of their living room. Iskra waved at Anya, a smile lighting her face briefly before she winced at the pain in one of her shoulders.

"Anya," her mother said, as Anya bolted the door shut behind her. "Follow me."

Her mother had gotten pregnant at sixteen and married her father, Demek, shortly after. Every now and again, that young girl reappeared, and Anya saw Iskra as more of an older sister than a mother. She was young, bright faced, made swift movements, and her excitement was relentless when she'd done something she thought would please Anya. Sparking a light in Anya's heart, Iskra took her hand and pulled her along the corridor and up the stairs.

When they reached the landing, there was a ladder hanging down from the attic.

Anya looked at her mother and Iskra nodded to the rickety ladder swinging from a hatch in the ceiling. "Up," her mother insisted, and Anya, wanting desperately to please her, took hold of the bottom rung and began climbing up into the roof of the house.

Anya pulled herself up into the small, dusty room. It was dark up there, with no light aside from the small gaslamp hanging at the top of the stairs below. The air was colder up there too. She almost felt as though she was outside and she was glad her mother hadn't given her time to take off her fur lined boots and coat. Anya heard Iskra behind her, dragging her bruised body over the threshold. She took out a metal hook and reached high above their heads, twisting what looked to be a small screw in the ceiling rafters. As she did, the whole room lit with a soft orange glow and Anya saw her mother had decorated the space with worn cushions, blankets, and even a stack of Anya's favourite books.

Anya stepped cautiously across the floorboards, careful to avoid the gaps between the wood for fear of falling through into one of the bedrooms below. Iskra pulled the ladder up into the room and closed the hatch, sealing them into the room.

"It's a secret," Iskra said, her voice soft. "Between you and me."

And it was the most precious secret Anya had ever been guardian of.

She turned her head to the ceiling, to where the rafters sat high above them. She had always loved climbing trees in the spring and summer, and missed the art sorely in the winter when they lost daylight and she was forced to stay within the tight confines of their house.

The room itself was cold, a bitter breeze slipping through the poorly sealed cracks in the roof tiles, but it *felt* warm.

She glanced at her mother, who was grinning back at her. "What do you think?" Iskra asked softly.

Her mother kept her voice low, as though worried her words would carry through the rest of the house and alert Demek of their secret hiding place.

Unsure how to respond, Anya ran to her mother and threw her arms around her waist. She held tight as her mother kissed the top of her head and said, "You can climb up here. You can go up into the rafters."

And Anya did. Each time her father would shout, and Anya's rage would threaten to overcome her, she would climb up into the attic, clawing her way up to the very top of the ceiling, as far away from his voice and her mother's shrieks as she could. Eventually, after the shouting had ceased and Demek had drunk too much to throw a straight punch, Iskra would join Anya up in the rafters.

One night, Iskra had climbed up onto the roof, pressing a cold cloth to her cheek. "Anya?" she whispered, looking up into the ceiling. She smiled when she saw Anya and Anya began her smooth descent. "You're a natural. Like a bird caught on the breeze."

Anya sat curled into her mother's side, smothered by the blistering silence until she worked up the courage to lean forward and press her fingers to her mother's broken skin.

"We can go," Anya said.

Iskra shook her head and replied softly, "We can't. You know that. But you're safe up here."

Of course, they had fled after one irreversible incident. Amid the howling of the rain and the wind whistling through their fragile windows, they'd packed their bags and left her father's body for the rats.

Eventually, they'd reached Ytavosk, battered by the journey, hungry from hours spent crouched in a cramped train car with no food and no water, and tired from long days of panicking. Anya and her mother had slept in the doorway of a disused shop towards the edge of the riverbank. They had no understanding of the city, no idea that they had found themselves in the worst part of Ytavosk: Ivenko's Cauldron.

As they lay in the cold, Anya longed for the comfort of their attic, for the rafters high up in the ceiling where the light's fingertips couldn't reach. She told her mother this, and Iskra kissed her head softly and said, "You will find another sanctuary."

The next day, Anya and Iskra went about finding jobs and a place to live. Her mother sold her wedding band for a week of accommodation in a rat-infested bed and breakfast, and Anya spent the day venturing in and out of coffee shops, public houses, and restaurants begging for work. The sun had gone down by the time she found herself on Tretr Lane. She had never seen something so bright and raucous. She resisted the urge to hold her hand over her face to stave off the glaring lights as they reflected off the glass windows and glittering costumes.

There was one building at the end of the street that stood apart from the others – there were no workers lingering on the streets handing out leaflets and coupons, there were no openings on the side of their buildings to reveal the show inside, just two aerial artists hanging from either side of the entrance way, spinning in slow circles as they contorted their bodies.

Anya pushed her way through the thick crowd of tourists and workers letting off steam after a hard day on the docks, towards the big green building she'd come to know as St. Polya's Theatre. By some miracle, they'd given Anya a job cleaning the stage after the evening shows. Her mother was waitressing in a public house in Ivenko's Cauldron, her hours long and gruelling, but eventually they'd saved up for deposit on a flat so they could move out of the bed and breakfast. Their rent was extortionate, but they made it work and Anya even found time after her shifts to stay and practice on the trapeze and the silks. She liked the trapeze the most. When she couldn't seem to catch her breath or shut off the worried voice in her head, the only thing that seemed to calm her was that feeling of flying as she spun through the air and caught the bar on the other side.

Each night she went home to her mother, who was already half-asleep on the mattress they shared, buried beneath all their blankets. Iskra would open one eye sleepily and ask how Anya's day had been and Anya would excitedly tell her about the magical woman who climbed silk, or the man who managed a cartwheel on the tightrope. Iskra would stroke her hair back and tell her how that would be her someday.

And it would.

She'd been working there for a year when the manager, Marina, hurried over to her as she was sweeping confetti off the stage.

"Put this on," Marina said, handing Anya a pink costume and wig.

"What?" Anya asked incredulously, her body frozen. "I don't–"

Marina thrust the costume into Anya's hand and forcefully turned her towards the dressing room. "I need you on stage in five minutes."

Anya, not quite believing what was happening, dug her heels in. "I don't know the routine."

"I don't care," Marina said sternly. "Anna has fallen and broken her ankle. Just do *something*."

Anya put the costume on and laced it up with shaking fingers. She was both terrified and excited, the feeling mixing in her stomach to make something acidic. One of the other girls in the dressing room helped Anya pin her wig in palace and straighten up the edges of her skirt and once she was dressed, she made her way backstage.

She knew where all the ropes and pulleys were from her evenings spent sweeping and scrubbing the floors, she also knew which ladder she was to climb, and which rung she was to throw herself at first. She tried to remind herself that this is what she was made for as the heat of the spotlights warmed her cheeks and made her palms sweat. She had taken a deep breath before launching herself off the platform as the orchestra hummed beneath her.

Now, as Anya hung over the crowd of people in the palace ballroom, her limbs tangled in the soft silk, she tried to recall her mother's words. *You're safe up here*. She tried to believe it, as she'd done each night in the theatre when the world felt too overwhelming, and her breaths kept coming in short, ragged bursts. *You're safe, you're safe, you're safe*. But hanging high above a room of people who would kill her if they found out what she was going to do, Anya did not feel safe at all.

She leaned back in the sling she'd made for her body and hung upside down. She felt the synthetic pink hair tickling her shoulders as her muscles strained. Tipping her head back, she looked for Lev, though he was indistinguishable amongst the men in tailored black jackets and other waitstaff in their white shirts and black waistcoats. He was supposed to be pointing out Grigory to her, but no matter how much she searched for him, he didn't appear. It wasn't unlike Lev to be late, but it was very inconvenient.

Anya searched for Vera instead, looking through the crowd of gold and silver to search for the girl in the blood red dress. She found Vera lingering by a purple velvet curtain, a drink raised to her mouth and a hand balled in the fabric of her skirt. She was staring straight across the other side of the ballroom and Anya followed her line of sight. It was there that she found Lev, hoisting a tray of glasses onto his flat palm before setting off into the crowd.

Lev looked up then, straight at Anya. His face didn't change but she saw in the slight widening of his eyes that he expected her to follow him. She spun in a soft circle, following Lev to where a man with a silver rose in his lapel stood, circled by his followers. Anya knew a man of power – whether that power be deserved or not – and Grigory Petrolovich was one of them. He stood tall, his spine elongated, his broad shoulders straight.

He paused every now and again between sentences and the men gave the appropriate response each time: a slap on the back, a loud laugh, a scornful shake of the head. He didn't just stand with the group, he conducted them.

Lev cut her another swift glance as if to say, *Got it?* and Anya nodded once.

Luckily, Grigory wasn't far off being directly beneath Anya, but she saw Vera cutting through the crowd like a stain on white fabric, moving towards the group of men. As she did so, she smoothed her features out. Anya was shocked and slightly fearful of the look that Vera managed to sculpt out of her face. Her lips curled in a pretty, silly smile, and her eyes flattened into a look of passivity Anya had never seen the girl wear before. When Vera actually *giggled* and tossed her hair over one shoulder Anya almost fell from her silks.

Vera marched unwaveringly through the crowd and straight into Grigory.

Anya knew the plan – she herself had designed most of it – and yet as Vera slammed her shoulder into Grigory's, her breath still caught in her throat, her body went cold, and the image of Vera murdered and strung up on the palace gates flashed across her mind.

Vera shoved the man a metre sideways so he was almost exactly beneath Anya, who was starting to lower herself on the silks.

Anya watched carefully as Vera rested her hand flirtatiously on Grigory's chest and apologised. Had Vera been on the outside watching herself bat her lashes, she would have vomited there and then, but her facade never once cracked, the mask of the pristine, immature girl never slipping.

"I'm *so* sorry," Vera said, brushing pretend lint from the man's lapels before picking up the hem of her dress and sauntering off into the crowd.

Anya watched her go, almost laughing at the way her smile slipped from her face as easily as butter in a hot pan and her eyes darkened like a storm rolling across the sea.

Lev reappeared then and gave Anya a very pointed look.

She looked back down at Grigory. He hadn't moved back to his group – they'd moved to him like water filling the cracks in the cobblestones and the circle now gathered beneath Anya. She took hold of the silk, twisting it once around her thigh, and lowered herself so she was resting just above the circle of men. They looked up at her in wonder as she elongated her limbs and pressed a beautiful smile onto her face. She tried her best to look ethereal to compliment the gold paint around her eyes and across the tops of her cheekbones.

Anya didn't miss the way their gazes lingered on the smooth skin of her thighs or the curves of her chest. She smiled sweetly and reached for Grigory's champagne, taking the flute from between his fingers and pressing it to her lips. He grinned at her hungrily and she tipped her head back to drain its contents before putting it back in his hand and pulling on the silks to ascend back up towards the chandelier once more. He shook his head at her and turned back to his colleagues, who were all elbowing and jostling each other.

Resisting the urge to roll her eyes, Anya continued with her dance, keeping one eye on the men and Lev as he moved towards them.

She wondered what these men thought she was doing. They acted like she was flirting with them because she *wanted* to and not because she was being paid to be there and keep people entertained. It was her job to flirt and look desirable, to look magnificent as she dangled high above their heads like a goddess dressed in pink silk. It was her job to steal that glass.

Lev appeared now, his tray balanced expertly on one hand. He lifted the glass nearest to him and handed it to Grigory, who snatched it and sneered, "I can get my own glass, thank you."

"Certainly," Lev said with a smile that one might think was polite. "Would you like to pick a different one?"

Grigory shook his head and turned back to his circle, cutting Lev off.

Anya caught Lev's eye briefly and he winked at her before merging with the crowd.

Anya glanced around the room once more, searching for that flash of red amongst the revellers. She finished her performance with a flourish as she fell to the ground, arms outstretched, and guests crashed into each other to get out of her way. She caught herself just in time, landing a foot above the crowd lingering beneath her. She let the silks go and stepped graciously onto solid ground. She left the silk there, dangling from the chandelier like a fall of pink water and made her way back through the crowd.

It was time to enact her second plan, the one Vera, Lev, Sofiya, and Aleks knew nothing of.

Anya made her way through the crowd, narrowly avoiding the hands of hungry men and women trying to claw at the thin scraps of her silk costume. At the edge of the room was a large set of glass doors leading to a balcony, which looked out over a dark garden. She pushed towards the veranda doors beside which a man was standing alone, a full glass in hand. Anya brushed past him, elbowing him hard enough that his drink spilled across his chest.

"*Oh*," Anya breathed, channelling her inner Vera to play the part of the ditzy, unserious girl. "I'm so sorry. Here, let me help you."

The man brushed her off but Anya persisted, grabbing his arm and blotting his shirt with a layer of her silk skirt.

"Come with me," she said, dragging him towards the balcony doors. "I'll help you get cleaned up."

Anya draped herself over the man's arm. It wasn't unusual for guests to want private time with the performers and the guards posted at the exit held the two glass doors open as Anya led the man through, still dabbing at the damp patch on his jacket.

As the doors slammed shut, the man brushed her off and moved to the edge of the balcony. Anya crossed her arms over her chest and stretched out the crick in her back as the stars shone above them.

He turned to her and said, "Well, Anya, do your worst."

Anya took a step towards Kirill and smiled.

25

Vera

The ball was now in full swing. Men and women were spinning in circles around the room, their smiles wide and drunk, their hair messy, their clothes falling from their bodies loosely. The whole palace had broken out in a mad fever. Queen Ruslana was drifting around the room with a glass in her hand. Vera watched as the Queen's subjects laughed behind her back and mimicked her as she stumbled around.

Vera had waited as Anya drained Grigory's glass and as Lev had swooped in to give him the drugged champagne. Anya was now gone, and she couldn't see Lev either. She looked around the ballroom in search of her friends and saw Sofiya in her mother's clutches. Lingering behind her was the blond man who had helped Vera into the carriage – he clearly knew Sofiya.

Grigory stood with his circle of men. A woman lingered behind him. She was around his age with greying hair and was dressed in a sparkling silver dress and matching gloves. The woman rolled her eyes to the ceiling as the men boomed with obnoxious laughter. Vera couldn't help but wonder how many times the woman had found herself in that position, standing on the outskirts of a conversation, ignored or disregarded. She was cut off like the head of a daffodil in the autumn.

Grigory was not touching his drink. Vera's impatience was growing; she felt it like a beast in her chest. Her body was starting to itch, her fingers longing to stretch out and grasp the strings of the older man's mind.

She cursed her power for the thousandth time. If it was stronger, she'd be able to do just that and he would never know. This whole thing would be over. They could grab the secret or *something* to help their mission and be on their merry way, but she couldn't without alerting him.

Be patient, she told herself. *This is so you can get stronger. You can go to Vor if you're patient and you get this job done without dying.*

The words were starting to become meaningless. The dream had always felt too unrealistic, too far out of reach.

"Oh, fuck it," Vera muttered, putting her glass down on the nearest table and storming towards the man and his wife.

Pushing her way through the crowds of warm bodies, she approached the older woman. Vera softened her face and readjusted the skirts of her dress. "My fiancé likes to discuss business at parties," she said. "Why are they so opposed to fun?" She raised her voice an octave in an attempt to sound more polite and approachable. Her smile strained the muscles in her cheeks.

The woman looked at her and blinked numbly as though in her boredom she'd forgotten the language. "Yes," she said, coming to her senses. "You're from the Isles?"

The woman's accent was so familiar that Vera almost cried. They both had accents of people who spoke a language they didn't have a full grasp on. She hadn't spoken Lattierean in a very long time; she hadn't realised how much she'd missed the lulls and flow of it. Sikveyan was a harsh language full of spiked edges and aggression. The language of the Isles was smoother, smokier.

Vera nodded and said in Lattierean, "But I have lived here for a while now."

She'd missed the comforts of her home. When she'd first arrived in Ytavosk, the city had been so startlingly new she had pushed aside everything she'd known to make room for it in her mind. She had been working so hard to learn the new place, she hadn't had the time to remember the old one. Now she did. She heard the soft curves of her language, her phrases, and suddenly she could smell the wildflowers in the meadow behind her home, she could see her mother hanging clothes outside to dry, and she could feel the sun warming her skin. Even the winters in the valleys were kinder, the snow on the mountaintops so beautiful it was easy to forget how harsh it could be.

The woman smiled at Vera as though she could sense her longing. "I haven't been back since my wedding."

"Do you miss it?" Vera asked. *Does that longing ever go away?*

"Dreadfully. The weather here does terrible things to my vanity."

Vera's heart sank heavily in her chest. She wanted to feel the sun on her skin. She wanted the ache in her bones to ease.

The woman sighed. "But business is here, isn't it?"

"Are you involved with business?" Vera asked. She tried to sound innocent but that was something she'd never been very good at.

The woman laughed bitterly. "I would be if they allowed it."

Vera leaned closer conspiratorially. "Have you heard what they've been saying?" She tried to sound like some silly, gossiping young girl, talking behind her betrothed's back and spreading rumours. Harmless things. "About the princess?"

"Their heir?" the woman questioned.

Vera nodded.

She shrugged. "Not specifically. But there is something there and it'll get out."

Vera's hope started to wither.

"I best get on," the woman said. "But you know what they say." Her eyes softened. "May your evening be remembered."

Despite her ever-growing disappointment, Vera couldn't help but smile. She hadn't heard that phrase since she'd moved to Sikveya. "For the night will soon be over," Vera responded, finishing the farewell of their home country.

"I love it when you speak Lattierean, my love."

Vera would have recognised his voice anywhere.

Lev appeared at her shoulder and passed her a champagne flute. He rested his hand on the small of Vera's back and when she turned to give him a hard glare, she saw that he had changed out of his waiter's uniform and was now wearing the dress coat of a guest.

She took a subtle step back and pressed her heel against Lev's toes lightly to say *she knows something. We have a lead.* Lev squeezed her elbow in acknowledgement.

The woman watched them both carefully.

"My fiancé," Vera clarified in Lattierean, letting herself lean slightly against Lev. She could feel the soft rise and fall of his chest. She fought to ignore it.

The woman tucked a curl behind her ear and glanced between the two of them as though she was trying to decipher the means of their arrangement – was Vera there out of choice or familial duty? "He seems like a fool."

Vera smiled. "You'd be correct."

The woman's mouth formed a soft, knowing smirk. "You're a fool for him too," she said. "I hope you'll be happier than me." She turned away from them, leaving Vera staring after her, startled, turning the woman's words over in her head.

You're a fool for him too.

Lev leaned over her shoulder and asked, "What does that phrase mean? I've heard it before. Something about the night."

Regretfully, Vera slipped back in Sikveyan, translating the phrase. She didn't like having to pause to think of words or the way people mocked her accent.

"May your evening be remembered, for your night will soon be over. Does that even make sense?"

"It doesn't translate well," Vera snapped.

"What does it mean?"

Vera thought for a moment. She wasn't quite sure what it meant. In the Isles, it was said without explanation, Lattiereans just *understood*. "Make the most of every moment. Moments weren't made to last," she said finally, and Lev responded with a soft *huh*.

"Did she have any information?" Lev asked.

"No, but I think our dear Grig does." Vera reached her fingers out towards Grigory's mind. She saw the threads, their colours sparking to life as though anticipating her touch, when Lev grabbed her hand and held her fingers closed in a fist.

"What are you doing?" he snapped.

"We need to act now. He isn't drinking. We needn't waste our time when–"

Lev half pulled Vera away from the man as he leaned closer. "We promised Sofiya that we wouldn't do anything reckless."

Vera sputtered a harsh laugh. "Since when were you a stickler for the rules?"

Something dark flashed across Lev's face. "Since when was your power strong enough to take a secret unnoticed?" The moment the words left his mouth, his eyes widened in regret.

Vera took a step back from him and shoved her own shock back down. "Nice to know you have a fucking spine, Lev, I was starting to worry," she spat, pulling her hands from his grip and shoving back towards Grigory. She was angry now. Downright furious and a little disappointed. He really didn't believe she could do it. She remembered what he'd said as they sat around the table in the pub. *You might not value your life that much, Vera, but I do.* He truly thought she was going to get caught and killed. Lev, who was always positive and smiling, didn't have any faith in her and it hurt a lot more than she thought it would.

Vera raised her hands and pushed her way through the crowd, circling Grigory like a viper. She heard Lev behind her hissing her name and apologising to guests as he followed her. She reached out towards Grigory's mind. She knew she was being reckless, and she knew she was so annoyed because Lev was right. Vera was not strong enough. She was so desperate to prove herself.

Vera wrapped her fingers around Grigory's mind and tugged at the gold strands. She saw the flash of a young boy with copper hair and a crown atop his head, but when she went to tug the thread, to bring the image into full view, Grigory pressed his hand to his temple and turned to look directly at Vera.

Vera stumbled backwards and Lev grabbed her shoulder to steady her. His hand slipped into hers and he pulled her towards the flow of dancing couples. They crashed into shoulders and knocked over those who had drunk too much.

He spun her to face him and pulled her body close. When he rested her hand on his shoulder and looped his arm around her waist, she realised just what he was doing, and her body went cold. They were dancing.

She felt his hand tighten on hers and she looked up at him, all too aware of how closely their bodies were pressed.

"So much for being discreet," he muttered, pulling her into the middle of the dance floor. He held her close, and she felt his chest against hers. Her breath hitched in her throat.

They were both terrible dancers. Neither Vera nor Lev were leading, but rather following the crowd, letting themselves be pushed back and forth by the tide of revellers. They were both desperately clinging to each other as they tried to keep up with the endless routine of steps and spins. They were always a second behind the other dancers.

"What are we doing?" Vera whispered irritably as she tripped on the hem of her dress.

"Trying to fucking hide," Lev replied. His voice sounded close to her ear and his breath tickled the hairs that had fallen loose from her updo.

"I didn't actually *take* anything."

"Oh well, that's reasonable," he said sarcastically. "Why don't you just go back and tell him that?"

Vera tightened her hand on Lev's shoulder. "We need to circle back around. There was something there–"

"Are you insane?"

She looked up at him as he looked down at her. They were nose to nose, and she could see the exact colour of his eyes, the smile lines around his mouth, the sharp cut of his jaw. She didn't respond; they both knew the answer. Yes, she was insane.

"Vera, no. We need to get out of here before he alerts someone and we find ourselves being hanged from the balcony," Lev said, his words coming out in a panicked rush. "Come to think of it, that would be quite a sight – the sun rising in the morning, reflecting off our corpses. I don't know about you, Vera, but I look fantastic in the pre-dawn light."

"Alright, Lev, I get it," she snapped. She was beginning to sweat and her dress suddenly felt too tight.

Delayed, they copied the twirl of the couple beside them. Lev spun Vera beneath his arm and pulled her close again. She crashed roughly into his chest and his hand gripped her waist. Her heart lurched into her throat as his fingers tangled in her corset strings.

Was he as aware of her as she was of him? Did he feel a tightness in his heart? Did the air catch in his lungs? She desperately wanted the feeling to go away.

He looked down at her and, for a moment, the chaos of the ballroom melted away, taking her anger and fear with it. It was just Lev. The image of him sleeping beside her echoed through her mind. For a week, he'd been avoiding the debt-collectors, hiding out in her room so they thought he was out of town. Each night she slept beside him and felt his warmth. It was comforting knowing he was there, that she could align her breathing with his when she couldn't quite seem to drift off to sleep.

Each morning she'd woken to his face mere inches from hers; his eyes had been closed, his hair had been scattered across his forehead, and for a moment in the quiet of the morning, she'd thought he might be the most beautiful person alive.

She could feel her mouth turning down into a frown now. She was too aware of her hand in his, the way their faces were too close together, the way she couldn't quite seem to control the heavy beat of her heart.

There was a very high chance she had just been caught, that she would be dead by morning, but all she could think was: *he has to feel it too*. It was a wild and desperate prayer that he should feel something towards his cold, calculative counterpart and her sharp tongue. She was the bitter frost that met him in the mornings, but when he leaned towards her, she thawed just a little. His eyes fluttered shut for a moment as though he couldn't quite believe she was there. Vera fought for breath.

She'd known him for so long and he had never been anything but trustworthy and loyal. They'd been running alongside each other since he'd first found her in that alleyway, dragging each other out of scrapes and near misses. The debt was constantly shifting between them, never truly being paid. She'd clung to him in her first weeks in the city and he had never complained. She didn't need him anymore, not really, but she liked having him around.

"Vera, I–"

He was cut off by the blare of a gunshot cracking through the room. It was like lightning. She heard the bullet ping and the sound of glass shattering as a mirror crashed to the floor. Vera instinctively shoved Lev behind her. Then, through the now panicked crowd, she saw Aleks holding a gun and pointing it straight at her. She hesitated a moment, not quite sure what to make of the situation.

What was he doing? His eyes were wide, and his hair was dishevelled. He looked as though he regretted what he was doing but couldn't quite seem to stop.

Vera had one rule, one boundary: she never looked through the minds of the people she knew, the people she considered to be her friends. But when Aleks raised the gun again, she knew she could make an exception. Aleks pulled the trigger, but the gun did not fire. He tried again and, taking advantage of the delay, Vera curled her fingers and reached out towards Aleks' mind.

She saw flashes of his life – a small girl with strawberry coloured hair nestled in his arms, a handful of conversations with a blonde woman, and then there, an image of Aleks as a boy wearing a crown.

She felt her pulse raise as she fought to maintain control of her power.

He couldn't have been older than fifteen as he stood in the court before King Mikhail, Queen Ruslana, a young Sofiya, and her two siblings. He pressed his palm to Sofiya's cheek.

Her eyes were filled with frightened tears.

"Where will you go?" she asked, her voice small. She was not yet the fighter Vera knew.

"It's okay, sister, I'll be safe," Aleks said, and Vera's heart stopped.

Sister. Aleks was a Meskov.

Vera fought to put the pieces of the puzzle together, but her mind was whirring too loudly. All Sofiya had known was that the secret was about the heir, but it was not about her; she was not the heir to the Meskov throne, *Aleks* was. Vera had no memory of an older prince, though that wasn't surprising as she hadn't taken a huge amount of interest in the Royal Family at all. Did Lev remember? Or Anya? Or had the memory been so neglected that soon the whole country just forgot the boy's existence?

Pressing a pistol into Sofiya's hands, Aleks said quietly, "Keep it safe for me." In any other world, the sight of the firearm in such tiny hands would have been absurd, but the measure was necessary in theirs and Sofiya cradled the gun's pearl handle lovingly as though the need for such violence was still a novelty to her.

Aleks turned back to the Queen and drew himself up straighter.

Queen Ruslana faced him. She was at war with herself; there was something fearful and yet sad hidden beneath her eyes and when she raised her head to face her son, tears shone on her cheeks.

The King cleared his throat. His face was closed off and emotionless when he said sternly, "Do it now."

Aleks nodded and raised his hands. He closed his eyes and a single tear trickled down his cheek. A blue glow illuminated the chamber. It was a power unlike any Vera had seen – stronger, sharper as he pulled strings from multiple minds at once. They did not tangle, and the edges did not fray. Vera struggled with one thread, but Aleks pulled the memory of his existence from every mind in that room except his own and his parents'. He slipped the memory into a bottle and passed it to his mother for safekeeping. She took it and locked it in a small velvet lined box.

She'd known Aleks was strong, that his magic was seamless, and she had spent long hours shoving down her jealousy, but she did not know the extent of his ability. Not only could he steal memories, but he could completely remove them. It was a unique form of thievery. He left no trace behind. She understood it now – he was a true danger to the royal family. He had the power to alter history, to select what was remembered and what wasn't.

I'm the long-lost prince. That was Aleks' joke. One Vera had heard him make so many times. Vera knew now that he hadn't been joking and she almost laughed at the absurdity of it all.

"*Vera*," a voice called. "Come on, we have to go."

Vera reached out to grab the secret, but her fingers slipped. She hated her power. She hated her poor grip on it. She hated herself for trying and failing every damn time. She reached out again, and a frustrated shriek slipped out of her mouth. Just when she thought she had it, she was shoved to the side and her body hit the floor with a hard thud.

"Fucking hell!" she yelled as she skittered across the polished ballroom tiles. Gathering her breath and shoving her hair out of her face, she pulled her body upright. Her arm hung limply at her side, aching terribly, and her heart was racing.

Lev hissed as he appeared at her side. He gripped her mobile arm tightly and dragged her to her feet. He had one hand pressed to his stomach and the other slipped into Vera's as panicked guests shoved and trampled them.

The ballroom had descended into chaos. A woman screamed as she gathered her skirts and darted for the exit and Vera caught a glimmer of a knife on the floor. It was covered in blood. She held tight to Lev's hand. They had to get out before they closed the gates. Already, the guards were grabbing people to keep them within the ballroom.

Vera shoved her way through the crowd, dragging Lev along behind her. She felt bodies crash into her and curse her as she wormed her way through, sending shocks of pain to her shoulder. They managed to get outside the palace without being dragged back in by the guards and Vera took off towards the gates with Lev in tow.

The night was alive with screams, each one bouncing off the river and the cobbled streets, echoing through the Palace Quarter as Vera and Lev took off into the night.

They'd just managed to cross the bridge and find shelter in a neat side street in Gambit Square when Lev's pace started to slow.

Vera turned towards him and saw that he was leaning against the wall, one hand pressed to his stomach, the other resting against the bricks of a closed-up jewellery shop. A lamp flickered overhead, and Vera saw that his waistcoat was sodden and his hand was stained red. She grabbed him just as he fell against the wall. Lev had the audacity to laugh.

She supported his weight as best as she could with one working arm and helped him to the floor. He collapsed in a heap on the stones and took a deep breath.

"It's alright," he said, though his voice was thin and wispy; he barely had the energy to speak. "I'll be alright in a minute." He took a sharp breath.

It wasn't alright. She tore the hem of her dress with her teeth and nudged Lev's hand out of the way, pressing the silk to the wound in his abdomen. *The knife*, she thought then, remembering the blood-soaked blade on the ballroom floor. Aleks had shot at them and when he'd run out of bullets, he must have thrown the knife. Lev had shoved her to the floor to save her from it.

She bit back the panicked tears rising in her throat and held the fabric to the wound. Lev's eyes fluttered shut. Vera's hands were shaking.

Vera reached out and patted his cheek once. "Lev, we have to go. We need to get you somewhere safe. Get up."

Lev nodded once, his eyes still shut. She stroked her thumb across his skin, leaning closer so they were nose to nose. He had broken out in a feverish sweat. "Move," she insisted, though it sounded more like a plea. Her voice cracked when she said, "I can't carry you." Even if her arm hadn't been completely useless, she wouldn't have been able to carry him. She wanted to scream.

She'd never felt so helpless.

"Stay with me," she said softly. "Lev, please." She felt something begin to fracture in her chest, sending splinters straight into her lungs. It hurt.

His hand came to rest over hers as she pressed the fabric to his bloody wound. "You never say please," he mused. "Why start now?" He huffed another laugh and his eyes flickered open for a moment.

She pressed the fabric harder against his stomach and he hissed softly. "Stay, you sorry prick," she commanded. "You're going to stay with me."

Lev smiled absently as Vera struggled to breathe, and then his hand, which had been wrapped around hers, fell away.

26

Anya

"Do you remember my mother, Kirill?"

The man had his back to the wall of the balcony. The night air breezed through the wisps of hair on his head, ruffling the salt and pepper strands. It was cold on the balcony, but Anya's brutal anger warmed her through as she faced Kirill with a new kind of fury. She had been moving towards this moment for the last eight years, prowling the outskirts of his life, drawing closer and closer like a beast with its prey. She was done waiting.

Kirill smiled and she resisted the urge to send a knife straight through his throat there and then. "Of course I do. Iskra was a beautiful woman. She would have made a lovely wife."

Anya bit back the hot ball burning in the base of her throat. "She was never given the chance," Anya said. "She was never loved as a wife."

Demek had never loved her, and Kirill had certainly never intended to marry her. At the time they'd met, he was already engaged to the daughter of a nobleman.

"Did you love her?" Anya asked, though she already knew the answer. Like her father, Anya wasn't sure Kirill was capable of any such emotion.

"I was infatuated by her."

"You saw her as a game, didn't you?"

Kirill laughed and pushed his body up off the wall with the sole of his foot. He oozed an arrogance, a confidence that she couldn't wait to strip him of. "And you're seeing this as a game, Anya, dear. What do you want? Money? A good job? Let's get this over with."

Anya shrugged, relaxed, though she was far from it. From him, there was only one thing she wanted, and it was not money or a job. "If you insist. I wanted to ask a few questions first."

In a moment, Kirill had reached to a sheath at his waist and removed a gun. It was a small thing, though Anya figured it packed enough power to kill her. The man's shoulders relaxed as he pointed the gun at Anya. "Go ahead. There's nothing you can do to me."

Anya stepped into the line of fire. In the last week alone, she'd found herself at the barrel of a gun more than she had in her entire life. What was it with royalty and their acquaintances owning pretty guns? She felt the cold steel of the knife hidden in the folds of her costume and wondered when the classic blade had gone out of fashion. "If you say so," she replied, lifting her fingers to the locket at her throat.

"Try something and I'll shoot."

"Do you know what the problem is with men like you, Kirill?" Anya asked as a breeze passed over them. She felt the pink silk of her skirt shift around her thighs, and she straightened her spine. She cut a quick glance to the gold and purple railings. The grounds below were black, lit only by the soft glow of scattered lanterns.

"We have a lot of money, and the thugs and thieves of this city don't like it."

Anya pouted. "I mean, that's definitely one of the issues, but not the one I was thinking of. Would you like another go?"

"Enlighten me."

Anya took a step towards Kirill. Her heeled boots clicked against the tiles. "You never falter," she said, frowning. "You will never fall. It makes revenge very difficult. I could take everything from you, and you'd find a way back from it. You would change your name or move to another city, but you will *always* return. You're like an untreated infection. It looks like it's starting to clear up, but it just keeps coming back."

Kirill held the gun higher and drew himself taller, bristling with pride. "That's true power."

"Was it power that made you think you could play with my mother? Was it power that made you think you could leave her pregnant and afraid?"

Kirill frowned then and Anya was surprised to see remorse behind his cold, dark eyes. "You know, I was never proud of what I did to your mother."

The slight glimpse of guilt was not good enough. "Then why did you do it? You abandoned your daughter."

"I am not proud, but she is no daughter of mine. And your mother meant nothing to me."

Anya took another step closer to the barrel of the gun and raised her chin stubbornly. She wondered how far she could push it – at what point would this man pull the trigger? Not ten feet away stood a set of glass doors. Would he be brave enough to murder her when there were so many potential witnesses? She was just a performer. She was from the Cauldron, she knew they saw her as a dispensable girl, a girl who would not be missed. She could die, he could hide her body, and she would be forgotten. It wouldn't be long before Daria died too without Anya there to look after her. It frightened her how quickly the life she'd scraped together could fall apart, but she refused to move out of range of the gun. She refused to be a coward.

She tilted her head to the side. "Why didn't you kill us? Erase us?"

"I'm no murderer."

Anya nodded to the gun. "I beg to differ. You killed my mother."

"It's not my fault that she was naive. She should have known that I could not give her the life she wanted."

Iskra was responsible for a lot of things and Anya was too, but she was not responsible for the blatant abuse she'd suffered. It was not her fault that men couldn't be decent. Anya's anger flared. Red flickered across her vision and for a moment she swore she'd lose control.

She fought to keep her voice level as she said, "She was desperate. She wanted a better life, and she thought you would give her that. You made promises to her and then you broke them."

Kirill sighed. "I'm getting bored of this conversation, Anya."

Her mother meant so little to him that talk of her couldn't even keep Kirill's attention.

Kirill cocked the gun with a polished click and Anya pulled the locket from her throat and clutched it in the sweaty palm of her hand.

"Shall I begin?" Anya asked. "You told me to do my worst. Did you mean it?"

Kirill fired the gun, but Anya smacked it from his hands and the bullet shot off into the dark of the night. She didn't miss a beat. She snapped the pendant clean in half and from it a bright red thread burst to life. She tensed her hands, letting the string curl around her thin fingers before shooting the pain straight into Kirill's chest.

Anya hadn't used her magic like this since her father had died. Each time he'd hurt her mother and Anya had been tasked with cleaning her mother's wounds, she had collected Iskra's pain and kept it safe in the confines of the locket until the time was right. She had never been a strong enough magician to remove the pain completely, but she could steal the essence of it, and from that she was able to forge her own kind of weapon.

Her father had just been fired. He'd spent all day in the pub in town, drinking away his sorrows and the last of their savings. He'd come home that night with dilated pupils and an anger that couldn't be satiated with curses and the slamming of doors.

"Stay here," Iskra said, planting Anya in her bedroom and pulling the door shut.

Anya stayed where her mother had left her in the dark confines of her bedroom. There was no light, and she was too aware of the loudness of each breath as it echoed around the room.

The silence was broken by her mother's scream and the sound of her father climbing the stairs. She pressed herself into the corner of the room as her mother screamed again and she heard her follow Demek up the stairs, her footsteps lighter than his.

"Leave her alone," her mother shrieked, her voice raw as she begged her husband. "Do it to me, not her!" Iskra begged.

But the door still opened.

Her father didn't know Anya could steal pain.

Anya wrapped her fingers around the locket at her throat, unclasping the pendant and letting the years of pain her mother had suffered spark to life in a startlingly bright shade of red. The moment she saw her father, she projected each cut, the impact of each punch, each kick, each pinch into his body. He let out a feral cry and took a step backwards. She couldn't seem to reel it in. She couldn't seem to stop. All the years of fear and anger she'd suffered bubbled to the surface, materialising like a wild beast beside her.

"*Anya*," her mother gasped. "Anya. No. No, Anya–"

But Anya wasn't listening. She couldn't seem to process what her mother was saying. All she could see was her father's mouth gaping open in a startled oh and the way life seemed to drain from his skin. He took another step back, his body teetering on the top of the wooden staircase momentarily before he lost his footing and his body hit each stair with a thump.

It was almost comical seeing his body hit the wood, hearing the rhythmic *thump, thump, thump* until he landed at the bottom and the rhythmic beat was replaced by a sickening crack as his head hit the ground hard and his neck snapped. Anya watched, startled as thick red blood oozed from her father's skull and trickled down between the cracks in the floorboards.

Anya looked at her mother, who had stepped out of the way to let Demek tumble past her on the steps. Her mother gaped at her, tears filling her eyes. She raised a shaky hand to her mouth and looked down at her dying husband. Anya looked at her open palms half expecting them to be covered in blood, but there was nothing there, just the soft skin and bony knuckles of a body that she hadn't quite grown into yet.

She didn't have time to think about what she'd done. Her mother had grabbed her, told her to pack her bags, and they had fled that night.

Now, Anya threw every ounce of anger and hatred into harming Kirill. He could not falter and he could not fall, but he wasn't immortal. He could be killed. After the incident with her father, Anya had promised herself that she would not use her power again, that it was dangerous and uncontrollable. She'd decided she would not use it at all. But now she understood it. It was dangerous and uncontrollable, but there was a strength behind it that she hadn't seen before. It allowed her to exact her revenge.

Anya would never use her power as frivolously as Vera used hers; it would not be her means of survival, but she would not ignore it entirely. She squeezed her fingers together and laughed bitterly as Kirill's body curled in on itself.

When her mother had been dying, Anya had laid beside her, smoothing her hair back and comforting her as she'd writhed in pain. She had hated herself then; she could not take her mother's pain away. The best she had been able to do was bottle the emotion up and save it for this scheme. The pain would not kill Kirill, but it would make him suffer like he'd made Iskra suffer eight years ago.

Kirill had promised Iskra a beautiful life. He'd laid beside her each night, and he had disappeared each morning. When things had gotten too real, too irreversible, he had left and never come back.

He could move on, but Anya couldn't.

Anya felt her mother's suffering as she delivered it to Kirill's body. She remembered her mother as she'd gone into labour, as she'd given birth to Daria, as she'd held her in her arms knowing she would not live to see the little girl grow, as she'd bled out on the kitchen floor. She felt it all over again.

Anya had spent eight years trying to block out the memory, to put that tragic part of her past into a locked box in the back of her mind. She'd thought about asking Aleks to remove the memory, but she didn't want to lose the one thing that drove her.

Kirill was panting now, bent over at his waist and all but vomiting. Vile gagging sounds left his mouth and Anya almost laughed at how small and pathetic he looked.

She let her hands hang at her sides, trying to steady her heavy breaths. Her heart was racing uncontrollably, and she wanted to scream violently, but she couldn't for fear of alerting the party on the other side of the palace walls. "You aren't so smug anymore," Anya said, pressing her sweaty hands to her bare thighs. "*That's* power."

Kirill choked back a sob as he leaned one hand against the wall. "Is it over?"

Anya huffed out a laugh and said, "Wouldn't that be lovely?"

"You're going to kill me!" Kirill cried. "You're going to kill me." His breaths were still coming in ragged bursts and his speech was suffering for it.

Anya remembered how her mother had told her about Kirill. Iskra had been so happy, so sure that they'd been about to fall on something great.

"He's a good man, Anya," she'd whispered. "I've finally found a good man who will take us far away from here."

And now Iskra was as far away as she could possibly get and she'd left Anya behind.

"Beg for your life," Anya said flatly, though she'd already removed the knife from where she'd concealed it in the back of her corset beneath the ribbon ties.

"What?" Kirill quivered.

"*Beg.*"

Kirill drew himself up so he could look Anya in the eye. His face was creased in pain. His eyebrows were scrunched together, his mouth was set in a taut line, and his nostrils were flared. "*Please*. I have children, I–"

"How many?"

"Anya–"

"How many children do you have?"

"Three. *Three*. I'll take the girl, she'll be mine."

Anya smiled then. Did he think she was the same scared girl he'd left on his doorstep all those years ago? She almost pitied the man then as he stood there with his bitter heart and soulless body. Her life had been hard, and she had suffered, but at least she wasn't some cold shell of a human being.

She would rather love and risk losing it then never feel anything at all.

Anya ran the blunt edge of the knife over her fingers and the blade caught in the light coming from the ballroom. She saw herself reflected in the polished metal. Her wig was askew, her corset was pushed to the side, and her eyes were wild with a kind of fury Anya rarely let herself feel. "Not good enough," she said at last and took one more look at Kirill before she slashed the knife over his throat.

She watched with grim satisfaction as blood cascaded in thick waves down his chest turning his white shirt red. Anya caught his body as it fell, the blood seeping into her bodice and dripping onto her silk skirt. She lowered him to the floor as blood gurgled in his throat and he gave one last cough of life before he went completely limp.

Standing over Kirill, Anya admired her work. She felt oddly empty now it was all over. She bent down and picked up the two halves of her mother's locket from where she'd dropped them on the bricks. As she straightened, she heard the glass doors open and clatter shut. Her heart leapt in her throat and she stood frozen with her back to the intruder.

Someone behind her swore violently and Anya recognised the crisp Sikveyan accent.

She turned to see Sofiya, her dress and hair glinting in the candlelight.

Sofiya looked down at the body and to the blood that covered Anya's clothes, arms, and chest. "What the *fuck* have you done?"

27

SOFIYA

Sofiya couldn't seem to wrap her head around the image before her. Kirill Katovich, one of her mother's friends, was lying dead on the stones with his throat cut and Anya was standing smiling over his body. She'd been watching Anya for a while, though she did not think the girl would kill him. She'd seen the bright red light through the window of the palace. She now knew what Anya was capable of. She was a magician. It was another line on the list of lies the thieves had been feeding her since she'd entered the Cauldron.

"What the *fuck* have you done?" Sofiya bit out.

Anya pinched something in her fingertips and Sofiya felt a flare of fear rush through her body. Anya was capable of hurting her like that, of leaving her body on the cold stones like she had with Kirill's, but Anya only fixed her with a hard glare.

"We need to go," Sofiya said. She reached out and grabbed Anya's arm.

"Where?" Anya replied, though her voice was so soft Sofiya almost missed it.

Sofiya looked at Anya. Her face looked grey with shock, she was covered in blood, and her hands were shaking. "Are you hurt? Did he hurt you?"

"Not recently."

"*Shit*," Sofiya hissed under her breath, towing Anya towards the doors. "This whole night has been a disaster. I shouldn't have brought you all here."

"It's a little late for that, isn't it?" Anya replied.

Sofiya bit back another curse.

Given the choice, Sofiya would not have taken a blood-soaked Anya through the ballroom, but there was no other way off the balcony. She hoped that the chaos that had broken out in the palace would cover them, and Anya's bloody costume would melt away amongst the screams and shouts of the guests.

The second they entered the ballroom, the sound of fleeing revellers replaced the odd tranquillity that had befallen the space on the balcony. Sofiya guided Anya towards a set of purple velvet curtains at the back of the room. She knew there was a servants' corridor there to allow waiters to bring food and take away empty plates.

She shoved the curtain aside and pushed Anya into the corridor. "Walk," she commanded, and Anya seemed to come back to life then, the shock of what she'd done wearing off. She began to march down the corridor with such frightening speed Sofiya had to almost run to catch up.

The light in the servants' corridor was better than most. Every couple of metres a wall sconce holding a candle cast a soft glow over the wood panels and eventually, they broke out into one of the palace halls. Sofiya moved in front of Anya then and led the way through the palace. Anya may have known the city, but this was Sofiya's domain, and while there were no makeshift bridges and strung washing lines, the palace had its own dance.

Sofiya took hold of Anya's wrist and guided her through the labyrinthine corridors, taking sharp turn after sharp turn to avoid the staff. "How did you find your way to my room when you delivered that note?" The question had been plaguing Sofiya.

Anya was walking beside Sofiya now and she leaned in close as she said, "Natural instinct."

Sofiya felt a blush warm her cheeks. "Really?"

Anya snorted. "No. We have a map."

She cut Anya a begrudgingly amused glance.

As they rounded the corner, a maid scurrying along with a plate of hot towels appeared. They caught sight of each other at the same time and as Anya turned the corner, Sofiya panicked, grabbed her, and pressed her against the palace wall. She leaned closer to Anya and planted her hands on either side of her waist to hide the blood soaking her costume. She leaned her face closer to Anya, feeling the girl's breath against her skin.

She heard the maid give a startled laugh. Sofiya knew this would be primary gossip but for a moment, all she could think about was how close Anya was and how she smelled faintly like the coal smoke and soap. Sofiya's eyes flickered shut for a moment. She resisted the urge to move closer.

Anya huffed a startled breath and said, "*Oh.*"

Sofiya looked at the girl. Her eyes were wide and at some point, she'd finger combed out some of the knots in her wig. Sofiya almost laughed at her vanity, but she knew she would do the same. She swallowed hard. "Is she gone?" Sofiya asked, breathless.

Anya peeked over Sofiya's shoulder and nodded.

Sofiya wasn't used to doing things awkwardly. She was generally self-assured, stable enough to do the things she wanted to do and not feel odd about it, but when she stepped away from Anya, she felt, well, *awkward.*

Straightening out her costume, Anya cleared her throat and Sofiya came back to herself. They were in the palace where there had been gunshots and currently Stas was waiting for them in the courtyard. They'd close the gates soon; they needed to move.

Without a word, Sofiya turned on her heel and continued to march down the corridor. Anya followed and she could hear her delicate footsteps on the tiled flooring behind her.

"What in Henygast is going on?" Anya hissed, coming up on Sofiya's left.

"Just then? We were almost caught." *And I almost kissed you*, she thought, though she knew she ought not say it. "Prior to that? A gun was fired, Lev, Vera, and Aleks all disappeared, and you *killed* someone."

Anya scoffed, "And what were you doing?"

"Trying to follow through on the plan *you* outlined for us." Sofiya shoved open one of the servants' doors at the side of the palace and they broke out into the night air. The courtyard was full of fleeing aristocrats in their horse drawn carts. Most were leaving by foot, running down the palace steps and out of the gates, though some were waiting for their transport. Sofiya looked for Stas, her eyes darting desperately between the carriages until she saw a glint of golden hair and he waved to her subtly.

"Come on," Sofya said, grabbing Anya's arm and pulling her towards Stas' carriage.

The stones crunched beneath their feet and as they approached, Stas hopped down from the carriage and opened the door. He helped Sofiya in first and she slipped onto the bench.

Anya followed but she stopped short when she saw the man sitting opposite Sofiya before she burst out with a startled laugh. "You got him?" she queried, shaking her head in disbelief. Her shocked smile turned to a more frantic look and her eyes widened. Her voice tightened with panic. "You fucking *stole* him?"

Sofiya was very aware of the absurdity of their situation. She and Stas had managed to steal Grigory Petrolovich as they had planned to. They'd kept him in a side room off the main ballroom. They'd waited for the others to show up and when they hadn't and they'd instead been blessed with a gunshot, Sofiya had sent Stas to the carriage with Grigory while she'd gone to locate the others.

Now she was livid. She'd had no help from any of them and Anya had the audacity to criticise her decision. She hadn't been able to find Vera, Lev, or Aleks. The three of them seemed to have vanished into thin air. She'd been about to give up her search for

Anya when she'd seen the bright red light coming from outside the balcony doors.

Sofiya looked at Grigory now. "Yes," she said sharply. "With no help from you."

Anya rested her head in her hands and muttered something into her palms. "You kidnapped him?"

"And you killed a person," Sofiya replied, her voice rising. "At least this was the plan!"

"This wasn't the plan," Anya hissed. "This was *not* the plan."

Sofiya sighed.

"What are we going to do with him?"

"Interrogate him."

"And then just give him back? I don't think he'll appreciate that."

Sofiya rolled her eyes and Anya continued to stare at her. "We'll get Aleks to remove the memory. He's drugged. We'll blind fold him and he'll never know it was us."

"I don't mean to rush anyone, but we really do need to get going," Stas said as he stood behind Anya, who was still only half inside the carriage.

Sofiya leaned out of the door and pulled Anya all the way in. Anya slumped down on the bench beside her. She heard Stas' feet stomp against the wood of the driver's cabin. She thumped her fist against the roof three times and wheels began to crunch across the gravel driveway.

28

Anya

Anya couldn't breathe.

She sat staring out of the window as the streets of Gambit Square flew past and tried desperately to regulate her breathing. Her palms were sweating, and her skin felt too tight over her bones. She would keep her panic under control; she would not let it get the better of her. It was an awful task. She leaned her forehead against the gloriously cool windowpane and sucked air into her lungs, though it felt thick and unpalatable.

She tried not to think about the blood staining her clothes. The situation had been satisfying at the time, but now the adrenaline had worn off and she was burdened with the gravity of it. She had killed a man. Not only that, but she'd killed a member of the court. In front of the princess. In front of the *heir to the throne*. She wanted to throw up. She cursed under her breath and wrung her hands. And there it was, the swell of emotion rising in her throat, choking her. Overtaken by dizziness, Anya closed her eyes for a moment. When she opened them, the situation only worsened in her head.

They were just approaching the square when Anya realised just how much more terrible the night could get. She bolted upright in her seat and said, "Stop." When the carriage rattled on, she hit her fist against the roof and shouted, "Stop. *Stop*!"

The carriage slowed but hadn't halted completely when Anya jumped down and stumbled as she fought to keep her footing. She half clung to the door frame as her feet skittered out from beneath her, scratching against loose stones. It was then that Vera looked up.

Vera was crouched in the shadows, out of view of the fleeing aristocrats, with one hand pressed to Lev's abdomen and the other hanging limply at her side. Anya could hear her panicked sobs over the chaos. She'd torn her dress and her hair was falling in bloody clumps around her face. Anya hadn't given much thought to Vera and Lev's survival. She was sure that they were scrappy enough to claw their way out of the palace and they had been, but the sight she saw before them made her blood run cold.

Sofiya unhooked the lantern from the ceiling of the carriage and leapt out after Anya, who was already halfway to Vera. It was only when she and Sofiya drew closer, and the light of the lantern hit their huddled bodies that Anya realised Vera was covered in Lev's blood. It matched Vera's dress almost exactly and the light cast eerie shadows across the scene, making the blood on Vera's hands look as black as tar.

"I can't carry him," she said as Anya approached, looking up at her with wide, panicked eyes.

Anya stood there for a moment, too startled to move. She looked from Vera to Lev. There was something hideous about bright, smiling Lev bleeding out on the pretty cobbled streets of Gambit Square.

Vera choked out a sob. "Fucking *help me*."

Sofiya was the first to act. She turned back to the carriage. "Stas!"

Stas leapt down from his seat and hurried towards them.

It was then that Anya jerked into motion. Fighting her way back to her body, she helped Vera stand, careful not to jolt the arm hanging limply at the girl's side. Vera cradled her elbow against her body and watched with wide eyes as Stas and Sofiya looped their hands under Lev's arms and hauled him to his feet. He made a soft noise, a quiet cry of pain and Anya felt her own fear flare to life. Vera flinched.

It was all too much. Anya focused on Vera, on Lev, on anything but the tightness in her chest. It felt like a clawed talon had pierced her lungs and she was trying to breathe through her panic. The air was wheezing out of the holes in her organs. She wanted to sit and close her eyes and never open them again.

Anya kept one hand on Vera's shoulder as she guided her to the carriage. Sofiya and Stas helped Lev, lowering him carefully onto the bench opposite Grigory. The movement was awkward as they banged their own limbs in an effort to not to hurt Lev any more. Vera sat beside Lev, propping his body up with her own and Sofiya hopped in beside Grigory.

They were supposed to make their way back to the boarding house. If by some miracle Aleks was still alive, that was where he'd meet them. But it was too far away, right across the other side of Ivenko's Cauldron and she knew Lev needed help now. Anya slammed the door shut and said through the open window, "We can go to my place. I don't live far from here."

"You live in Gambit Square?" Sofiya asked.

Anya rolled her eyes. "I said not far." She cast one last concerned look at Vera and Lev and hopped up onto the driver's bench beside Stas.

When Anya climbed up onto the driver's seat and sat beside him, he pulled his midnight blue cloak off his shoulders and draped it around Anya's.

"You look like you need it more than I do," he said.

Did she look as awful as she felt? She was still wearing her wig, her bodice was covered in blood, and at some point throughout the evening, she'd smeared the kohl and gold glitter around her eyes.

Anya glanced up at the golden man beside her. His hair was the colour of honey and curled around his ears, and his face was sharp, but when he smiled at her, his jaw softened. She pulled the cloak tightly around herself and said, "Take a right here."

She guided him through Gambit Square to the outskirts of Ivenko's Cauldron. She lived in a disused factory along the river's edge. The factory had been converted into flats long before Anya had ever made it to the city. They were ridden with rats and other creatures she didn't like to think too much about, and they flooded during storms when the river would come up over its banks, but it was a shelter.

When they drew close to the river, Anya told Stas to stop. "This is as close as you'll get or you'll get stuck." The walkway between the river and the factory was too narrow for the cart.

She glanced at the factory. It still had advertisements plastered on the side of the building for expensive soaps imported from the Isles of Lattiere and various types of boot polish designed specifically for authentic Vorian leather.

She had wanted to keep her home separate from the other thieves. Lev was the only one who had ever visited her there. She'd wanted to keep the mess away from her little sister, her innocent Daria, but she'd brought the bloody battle straight to the front door like river water in a winter storm. The stiff waves were sure to rot the wood.

When Anya looked at the shabby, rundown buildings, the chipped cobblestones, the darkness from lack of lamplight, she felt shame prickle in her gut. She was sure this place was nicer than the house Vera and Lev resided in, but it was still a slum. She was bringing a princess and the princess's aristocrat friend to see it. That part of the Ytavosk was not as dark as the depths of the Cauldron; the glass here was often shattered but it was not found buried in skin. Still, it looked like a wasteland.

Anya unlocked her flat door as she heard a scuffing noise behind her. She turned to see Sofiya and Stas helping Lev out of the carriage.

As Vera clambered out after them, still cradling her arm, she hesitated. "What about him?" She gestured to the slumped figure of Grigory Petrolovich.

"Leave him. He's…" Stas trailed off. "Had a lot to drink."

Vera nodded once and Anya turned back to her flat door.

She pushed it open tentatively. "Daria?"

There was no reply.

"Daria," she said again. "It's only me. We have company."

Anya heard two small feet scuffling along the floorboards. Stas and Sofiya lingered awkwardly in the doorway to the flat as Anya went in and crouched before the small girl. She tried as best as she could to block Daria's vision so she wouldn't see Lev's lifeless body. "It's fine. They're our friends." 'Friends' felt like a bit of a stretch. "Stay in your room. Don't come out until I say so."

Despite Anya's efforts, Daria poked her head up so she could look over Anya's shoulder. "Is he okay?" The girl was completely undisturbed by the blood, though Anya guessed she'd grown accustomed to it. She coughed and vomited it up most nights.

Anya's nerves were frayed and her mean, older sister instincts got the better of her when she snapped, "Does he look okay, Daria?"

The little girl's face hardened, and Anya felt terrible instantly. She let out a resigned sigh and combed her sister's hair back with her fingertips. "Please, just go back to bed. I'll tell you when you can come out."

Daria reached out her scrawny hand and wrapped it around Anya's wrist, squeezed once, and then turned to go back to her room. Her room was the box at the end of their short hallway. It was barely big enough for a bed and had nothing else in it.

When she heard the door click shut, she gestured for Stas and Sofiya to follow her and guided them into her bedroom. The sheets weren't made, her clothes weren't stored away, and the curtains weren't drawn. In short, the place was a mess. Moonlight hit the windows and cascaded across the floorboards, illuminating them with a milk-coloured sheen. Anya lit the candles beside the bed as Stas and Sofiya carefully placed Lev onto the mattress. Vera lingered beside the doorway, still holding her arm to her chest, and taking long, laboured breaths.

"We need a needle, some thread, some bandages, and something to sterilise the wound," Sofiya said, turning to Anya. "We need to call for a doctor."

"No," Vera said from her spot by the doorframe. She was cradling her bloody hands to her body as though they were burnt. She looked very small.

"He needs proper medical attention," Sofiya replied. "And by the looks of things, you do too."

"He won't be able to afford it. None of us can," Anya snapped. She thought about her bargain for Daria. If she could afford a doctor, one who would actually help, she wouldn't have fallen into this plan in the first place. Doctors in the Cauldron were scarce, and even then, all they usually did was pull teeth or tell patients they were about to die before they charged extortionate amounts of money for the trouble of coming out.

"I'll sort it." Sofiya looked between Anya and Vera, as if waiting for one of them to challenge her. "I'll call for a doctor. We just need to keep the wound bandaged up for now to stop the bleeding."

Anya heard a scuffle of feet and when she turned, Vera was gone.

Anya crouched down beside her bed to reach for the small medical tin she had stashed there. It was a little blue box containing a needle and thread, a pair of blunt scissors, bandages, and some rubbing alcohol to sterilise the wound.

Anya grabbed a cloth from the chair by the window and doused it in the rubbing alcohol. When she pressed it to Lev's abdomen, he barely moved, though it must have stung. His eyes were half closed and Anya had to wonder how conscious he was. She was just glad he was breathing. Once she'd cleaned the wound, Sofiya hoisted Lev's body up and Anya got to wrapping the bandages around his middle. The work was messy and awkward but soon they had him laid back down on the bed resting and Anya wiped her hands on the cloth she'd used to clean the wound.

She felt sick. Her head was spinning. "I'm just going to get some air," she said, turning towards the bedroom door.

Sofiya nodded.

The bathroom door was off its hinges and, as she left her bedroom, she saw a small light illuminating the crack in the door. Through it, she could see Vera sitting on the edge of the bath, her face scrunched up tight, her lips pressed together in an attempt to keep the sobs in. She cradled her arm against her chest, her face was tear-stained, and her shoulders shook.

Anya took a step towards the door, scared to alert Vera of her presence. She didn't like seeing her so distressed. As long as she'd known Vera, she'd only ever known her as the cold, calculative girl who could cut a person down with one sharp glare. For once, her guard was down; it was a terrifying sight.

A fool could see Lev's fondness of her, but it was more difficult to see the dangerous things that lurked in Vera's heart. She was unpredictable in her alliances, but seeing her there with her hair scraped back and her watery eyes, Anya was certain of her feelings.

At the very least, Vera worried for him, and that meant a lot.

Anya knocked on the bathroom door, careful not to jolt it all the way off its hinges. Vera's head shot up and she rushed to wipe the tears from her cheeks.

"What do you want?" Vera snapped. Anya could hear the heavy weight of tears in her voice; she could practically see her defences rising, though they seemed to be made of something brittle.

"Do you want me to put your shoulder back in place?" Anya asked. At the theatre, performers were always falling and dislocating various joints. They were all pretty well versed in shoving shoulders back into their sockets.

Vera stood from the edge of the bath as Anya edged into the room. The girl's hands were shaking, and her hair was sticking up at odd angles around her face. Anya helped her shrug off the dropped sleeve of her dress. Vera braced herself as Anya took hold of her shoulders and slammed her palm against the one that hung loosely at Vera's side. It cracked sickeningly but the only response Vera gave was to scrunch up her makeup-smeared face.

Anya helped Vera rotate her shoulder twice until the movement came back to it. Vera would still be stiff, but she could at least use her hand now.

The first thing she did was turn the tap on. She didn't wait for the coppery water to clear before she started scrubbing at her hands. The flakes of Lev's blood came away, though Vera did not stop until her hands were red raw.

She didn't look up when she said bluntly, "You can go now."

"Do you want help taking your hair out?" Anya asked, looking at the ratty mess atop Vera's head.

"No."

"Okay," Anya said. She glanced back at Vera once more to see that she was still attacking her hands. The image haunted Anya as she left the room.

29

Vera

The doctor left as the sun rose slowly over the dockyard. Vera watched from the grimy kitchen window as the pink morning light danced across the river. The water was rough; the moored boats crashed against each other and the men and women patrolling the water's edge were leaning into the strong wind. She stood there for a long moment, not quite ready to face everything that had happened the night before. It felt like a blur to her, like a hazy film had already settled over it all.

She recalled her conversation in Lattierean, the feeling of Lev holding her close as they did a poor job at imitating the practised dancers around them, Aleks, his secret, the gunshot, the knife, Lev's blood on her hands, and his smile. Always his smile.

She knew she should be thinking about their job – she knew the secret, she knew what Aleks was and what Sofiya wasn't – but each time she tried to weigh up the new information, she found her mind drifting back to the boy in the next room lying alone and hurt on that bed.

"Is your friend okay?"

Vera turned to see Anya's little sister appear in the kitchen doorway. She was clutching a rag in her hand and had a threadbare blanket thrown over her shoulders.

When Vera didn't answer, Daria spoke again. "How was he hurt?"

Vera wanted to snap at the girl for asking so many questions, but her eyes were wide, and her head was tilted to the side in curiosity. Even Vera wasn't cruel enough to shut her down so quickly. "He was stabbed."

"What did he do?"

"He didn't do anything."

"So why was he stabbed?"

Even a girl that young knew the language of violence. It was a conversation, a battle with two sides to it. Things didn't happen for no reason in the Cauldron.

"To save me," Vera said. She hadn't said that aloud. She'd barely even let herself think about his act of self-sacrifice. There she was again on that ballroom floor, his face tilted towards hers, so close she could see the flash of gold in his eyes and the soft glint of his hair.

Daria broke out into a harsh cough and held the rag to her mouth.

"Can I get you anything to help?" Vera asked. "Water?'

Daria nodded and Vera turned to take a glass off the draining board. She filled it halfway and, crouching down, handed it to the girl. The glass looked too big in her tiny, skeletal hands. She took a tentative sip. "What did you do? For someone to want to stab you?"

Vera sputtered a bitter laugh. "Exist." She wasn't sure what exactly Aleks was plotting, she just knew she was a threat to it.

"You sell to Anya. You have power."

Vera could have sworn she had not been that annoyingly inquisitive as a child.

When Vera didn't answer, Daria asked, "Does he love you?"

Her heart stuttered in her chest like a snagged thread. Lev loved everyone. It was in his nature to love and to be loved, to be loyal to those he chose to be loyal too, and to do it all with a smile on his face. But she'd learnt quickly that he couldn't be honest with her. She'd opened her heart a little to him, she'd told him her plans, her dreams, and he hadn't responded in kind. How many of his true feelings were hidden behind that smile?

"He must love you if he was willing to die for you," Daria said casually.

"Well," Vera said, her skin prickling with embarrassment. "Hopefully he won't die. Though I bet he'll never stop going on about the gnarly scar." Vera didn't wait for Daria to respond before she left the kitchen, leaving the girl with her bloody rag standing in the archway.

She made her way back along the corridor to Anya's bedroom. The room was quiet and when she poked her head around the bedroom door, she saw Lev with his head propped up on a pillow and a ragged blanket pulled up to his waist. The wound was clean now and a bandage had been tied around his middle. In the corner of the room sat a bucket of pink water, a stained cloth, and what remained of his shirt.

Vera edged around the doorway and sat beside Lev, careful not to jostle him. She brushed her fingers across his skin, pushing back the strands of hair on his forehead.

She recalled a conversation they'd had before. He'd needed a secret and she'd found it for him, though she couldn't remember what it had been. He'd come to thank her one night after his shift, long after her candle had burnt out.

He'd knocked on her door. She'd answered. And for a long moment, she just stood there, looking at him in the dim light of the hallway.

"Thank you for helping me," Lev said suddenly, his voice too loud in the quiet house. "I appreciate you."

Vera replied stubbornly, "I'm not helping you. It's a favour. You're indebted to me."

She had very strict rules on helping people. She *never* helped people.

Lev laughed softly. "What do you want then? In return?"

Vera had thought about it for a moment. *What did she want?*

She asked herself that now in Anya's flat as she watched the rise and fall of his chest, his skin pale in the early morning light. *I want you to be selfish, Lev. I want you to stop existing for other people and I want you to stay alive.*

"You're ridiculous, you know," she whispered to him. "If you'd have died, I would have crawled down to hell just to tell you that."

"Not to bring me back?" Lev's eyes flickered open, and Vera almost sobbed at the sound of his voice. He sounded weak, almost delirious, but he was there. He'd stayed with her just as she'd told him to.

"No," she replied, keeping her voice low in the quiet of the room. She leaned against the headboard and drew her knees up to her chest, her limbs tangling in the torn fabric of her blood-stained dress. "If you're stupid enough to die in the first place, then coming back is your problem. I'd just want to say that to you so you can rot with it fresh in your mind."

Lev huffed a laugh and immediately cringed in pain. "So long as I'd get to hear your voice one last time."

She bit back the lump in her throat, feeling the ache of tears press against her skull. She pinched her mouth closed until she was sure she could speak without her voice wavering. "Stop being nice. You almost died." She couldn't ignore the rapid beat of her heart or the comfort she felt sitting there beside him, sure that he was okay. She hadn't realised how cold she'd felt until his light was back. She never wanted to be without it again. "Why did you do it?" she whispered.

She looked down at Lev and saw something snag in his face, as though he was considering his next words carefully and couldn't seem to decide on them. "You're my friend, Vera."

She was his friend – she knew that – and he was hers too, her closest one at that, but she was selfish through and through. That trait would never leave her; she wasn't sure she could ever be anything but self-serving. "I wouldn't sacrifice myself for you." The words were bitter on her tongue, but they were true. She hated that part of herself, but she had to acknowledge it.

"I know that. I've always known that," Lev said, his voice patient, resigned, as though he knew but didn't mind. The darkness inside her would not seep into him. "That doesn't change anything."

"It should."

Lev released a soft, tired sigh.

It felt like they were somewhere else, in their own tired, hazy universe. Vera wasn't sure she was entirely in control of her body when she brushed her thumb across his cheek and Lev's eyes fluttered shut once more. He was right – he did look lovely in the predawn light. "Go to sleep," she whispered.

He nodded once and held his hand out to her, palm to the ceiling. She stared at it for a moment before closing her fingers around his. He squeezed once and she let herself breathe. For a moment, she could pretend that it was just the two of them, that they didn't have ulterior motives, secrets, plans that sent them in opposite directions. For a moment, she could pretend that there was nothing else to it, just hands held across a fragile space.

30

Anya

Anya, Sofiya, and Stas watched the deflated body of Grigory Petrolovich.

They'd tied him up to one of the kitchen chairs with ropes and various scarfs that Anya had around the house. His head had fallen forward and was resting against his broad chest and his arms looked like they were about to be ripped out of their sockets.

"This is starting to get a bit creepy," Stas murmured, as the minutes ticked by and they continued to stare. "What do we do with him?"

Anya crossed her arms over her chest. She'd changed out of her costume and left the bloody rags in the corner of Daria's bedroom with the rest of the laundry. She was now in a loose pair of trousers and a long white shirt. She glanced at the others. Sofiya was still in her gold ballgown, though she'd let her hair down and the copper strands fell in spiral curls down her back. Anya tried not to look at the freckles dusting her shoulders or the way her eyelashes hit her cheeks when she blinked tiredly. Stas had discarded his jacket and waistcoat and had rolled up his sleeves.

"Wake him up?" Sofiya suggested, brushing her hair back behind her ears.

Anya grabbed a tea towel from the kitchen counter. "We need to blindfold him first." She tied the damp scrap of fabric over his eyes.

"We need Vera ready. She'll be able to find something," Sofiya said.

Stas glanced at Sofiya and Anya quizzically. "The angry blonde?"

"The angry blonde," Sofiya confirmed.

Anya nodded and said, "I'll go get her." She wrung her hands together. "I think she's with Lev."

Anya left the kitchen and wandered down the hallway towards the room Lev and Vera were both in. She'd seen Vera sneak into the room shortly after the doctor had left, though she hadn't said anything more to any of them.

Anya caught sight of herself in a fractured mirror on the wall. She thought she'd been doing a good job of deep breathing and not looking as panicked as she felt, but when she saw the image reflected back at her she realised she looked awful. She paused for a moment, her heart still racing, her palms still sweating aggressively and watched herself. Her chest rose. *See*, she thought, breathing in and out rhythmically, *you're doing it. You're breathing. It's not so hard*. But just as she thought she was calming down, she heard the other voice, its bitter cadence echoing through her head. *I've been found out. I have the power to cause such intense pain and it is right at my fingertips. And Sofiya knows. She's going to have me hanged.* She wasn't even bothered by the death of Kirill – he was the least of her concerns – he was dead, and she had done exactly as she had needed to do. She was not worried about that, she was satisfied. She thought about little Daria. What would happen if Anya was no longer around? She knew what would happen – Daria would not get the help she needed and she would die too.

Oh gods, she thought desperately, looking away from the mirror. She usually took such pride in her appearance, and she couldn't stand to look at the anxious wreck in the mirror.

The tremor returned to her hands, her heart, her knees. She needed to sit down. She needed to get her shit together, get Vera, and get that terrible night over with.

As she turned into her room, she stopped short.

The sunlight was starting to stream through the curtainless windows, casting beams of orange across the floorboards and the bed to where Vera and Lev slept. Something twinged in Anya's heart. Lev was on his back, one hand over his chest and the other clutched firmly in Vera's. Vera was curled up on top of the covers beside him. She was lying on her side, one hand holding Lev's and the other clutching his forearm. Lev's head was turned towards Vera in his sleep. She was in just her white underclothes. Beside the bed, the dress pooled like blood.

Anya crept into the room, careful to avoid the floorboards she knew would creak. Retrieving a blanket from where it was tossed over the end of her bed, she draped it across Vera's sleeping body. The girl stirred and, for a moment, Anya thought she was going to wake up. To wake Vera would be to wake an ill-tempered dog. She looked peaceful when she slept, but Anya didn't want to risk the bite. Her eyes stayed closed and she settled.

Taking a step back, Anya cut them one more glance before going back into the kitchen where Sofiya and Stas were waiting.

"She's asleep," Anya said. "I think we should let her rest."

Sofiya let out a frustrated sigh but nodded. "What about Aleks?"

Anya had barely given a thought to Aleks but now she did, his disappearance was added to her list of things to worry about. He was one of them. He was promised just as much as they all were. He could be dead; in fact, if he hadn't shown up by now, that chance was very high.

"We were supposed to gather at the boarding house," Anya said. The boarding house was generally the safest place for them to stay. It was full of unsavoury people doing unsavoury things, and a couple more would make very little difference. Besides, Mrs Hanovich guarded the place; Anya had only met the woman on a few occasions, but she was terrified of her.

"Okay," Sofiya said, adjusting the straps of her dress.

Anya averted her gaze.

"I'll swing by on my way back to the palace and see if he's there."

"You're going back to the palace?" Anya asked, trying to sound casual. What she really wanted to add was: *are you insane?*

Sofiya nodded. "I need to find out what they know."

"We have one of their advisors captive. Their *princess* stole him. Are you trying to get yourself killed?"

"They have no reason to believe it was me. Or any of us. I'll go back and I'll assess the situation." Sofiya held her chin high, prideful to the very end. "Stas, you don't have to stay here–"

"I'll stay. I'll be here with old Grig." He smiled but even Anya could see the tension behind it.

"You don't–"

"Sof," Stas said firmly. "If I didn't want to be here, I wouldn't be here. You pulled me into a room where you'd stored an unconscious body. It was very obvious that what you were trying to do wasn't quite up to the standards of a princess. I know what I'm in for. I'll stay."

Sofiya took a deep breath and steadied her shoulders. "If you're staying, you might want to abandon the carriage somewhere. It looks a bit out of place in this part of the city." She looked at Anya and added, "I mean no offence."

Anya settled her with a glare. "Offence."

In a moment Sofiya was gone, the door to Anya's flat slamming shut behind her.

Anya turned to Stas who smiled apologetically. "It's a lovely place you've got here," he said.

Anya frowned and gave him her best glare too. "Go sort the carriage out."

Stas nodded and jumped to his feet quickly. "Of course." He too slammed the door shut behind him and Anya could have sworn the whole building shook.

Crouching down and closing her eyes tightly, Anya took a deep breath. Her chest hurt. She hugged her knees. She felt like a child when her worry started to overtake her. Where was the voice of reason? Where was that logical part of her brain when her breaths grew ragged, and her mind ran wild?

She remembered what her mother used to tell her as she smoothed Anya's hair and rocked her back and forth in her lap. "Imagine the water," she'd say. "How it washes up and down the beach. Look at all those things on the beach, all of your problems like pebbles scattered amongst the sand. The wave comes up, it wraps its fingers around the pebbles, and it drags them out to sea. Do you notice? They're gone."

It had always made Anya feel better, watching her worries wash away. Now, she listed them all, placed them delicately amongst the sand. Daria, the blood smeared around her mouth, the money, magic, the body she'd left at the palace, Lev and the wound in his abdomen, Sofiya and the prospect of being hanged. She imagined the wave drawing closer to the shore, washing up over the sand, rising higher and higher until all the stones were covered, except this time, the water kept rising. It was choking her. It was happening. She watched the wave grow higher until it hit her hard. The water knocked her back, filled her eyes, her nose, clogged her throat and filled her lungs.

Breathe, Anya, it's not difficult. You do it all the time.

But she couldn't. It wasn't that easy.

The water dragged her down beneath its current, drowning her in its depths.

31

Lev

Lev often dreamed of Vera.

So much of his time was taken up by her bitterness and inevitably his dreams wandered back to the night they'd met. To the girl in the street with her eye torn out of its socket. She had seemed so scared of the world she'd tumbled into.

Lev didn't know how she'd ended up there, just that when he had gone to take out the bins, he'd found her curled up in the damp alleyway behind The Red Dumpling.

At first, he had thought she was dead. She was not moving and there was blood smeared across her face, pooling on the ground where she had collapsed. He threw the full bag into the bin and, when she still didn't move, he crouched down beside her to see if she had a money pouch or some jewellery he could take. He wasn't proud of it, but he was desperate.

Honour, Lev, his mother had once said, tapping her broken nail against the red stone hanging from his neck. *They can take everything from you, but they cannot take your honour.*

She had been wrong. Since the death of his mother, the city seemed to be determined to strip Lev of everything including his honour. He'd tried so hard to hold onto it, to the sweet sound of his mother's voice as she'd taught him kindness and patience. He tried to see the good in the ugly, but it was a futile mission. It was a lesson Ytavosk had slowly untaught him: decency had no place in the city.

"Where's honour going to get me, Mama?" he muttered to no one but himself and the body sprawled out on the ground. "And what's she going to do? She's dead."

He crouched down beside her. Having grown up in the city, he was used to seeing such disturbing things. The alleyways were full of people with terrible illnesses, coughing and spluttering as they propped themselves up against the walls of apothecaries and banks. He'd once had to step over a man who had choked on his own vomit, his eyes open, staring up at the sky as bile leaked down his cheeks and pooled around his ears. But as he looked at the girl something pinched his heart. She looked to be around his age – perhaps fifteen? – and it alarmed him to know that he was teetering on that same knife's edge between poor and homeless. When he saw bodies of people older, he could give them a false history to make himself feel better about it, but looking down at the young girl, it all felt too real.

As he reached towards her, her hand shot out and she swiped at him with a small blade. Stumbling back, Lev just about dodged the hit, but a sharp pain ricocheted up his wrists as he broke his fall.

"*Fuck*," he cursed under his breath as the girl crawled to her knees.

He shuffled backwards until his back was against the wall and when he looked up, he was face to face with her. She had one hand pressed over her eye and her blonde hair was matted with thick red blood. Her skin looked transparent, stretched thin over her sharp bones and her dress hung loosely from her frame. She held the knife out, her mouth pulled in a grimace, her hands shaking slightly. Lev couldn't tell if they were shaking from fear, anger, or starvation.

He held his hand out. He wasn't sure if the movement was an attempt at calming her or to defend himself. "It's alright," he said. "It's alright. I'm not going to hurt you."

"That's what the other man said," she hissed. Her Sikveyan was poor, the syllables strained as though her mouth didn't know how to shape each sound.

Lev looked at her. He'd been about to rob her corpse. "You'll die out here," Lev said. He couldn't ignore the guilt that coursed through his veins.

The girl was breathing deeply like a wounded animal. Her lungs were wheezing with each inhale and exhale, rattling like a bag of broken bones. She tried to get to her feet, but her legs gave way and she collapsed in a heap on the floor. He watched her for a moment, unsure whether she was still alive. He'd heard the phrase *dropped dead* many times in his life. His grandmother had 'dropped dead', Mrs Hanovich's husband had 'dropped dead' and when he imagined the phrase as an action, he always thought it was exaggerated. He thought that by 'dropped dead' what they really meant was that they'd grown ill and died relatively quickly. He never thought it was literal, but she really had just dropped to the floor in a heap.

He took a deep breath and edged closer to her.

Keep your honour safe, Lev. The voice came unbidden, familiar yet so far away it made his chest ache. *They can't take it from you.*

He swore then that he would prove the voice right. He would be like his mother and keep his goodness whichever way he could. And he could start that night.

Wiping his hands on his striped apron, Lev moved towards the girl's broken body. When he reached down to check her pulse, her skin was ice cold and though it was there, it was slow and unsteady. He scooped her up into his arms, tucking her knife into his pocket. She was frighteningly light. Her skirts were dirty and now that she was no longer covering it, he saw her eye was a gaping bloody hole in her face. It looked infected and, given the layer of grime that covered the city, he wouldn't be shocked if it was.

I should kill her, he thought. It would be the kindest thing to do. Could he? Though he'd seen plenty of murdered bodies in the streets, he wasn't sure he could ever take out a knife and kill someone himself.

He took her back across the street to the boarding house, nudging the door open with his hip to keep him from jostling her body or dropping her. Mrs. Hanovich was standing behind the counter digging dirt out from under her nails with a letter opener.

"What have you got there, boy?" she asked, putting the letter opener onto the front desk with a clang.

Lev stared at her blankly for a moment, not quite sure what to say. "I found her in the street. She's hurt. Can you send for a doctor?"

"You have the money for that?"

In truth, he probably couldn't afford it. He was paying for his father's care, his place in the boarding house, and his own survival. Despite working in the pub and pickpocketing, he still barely scraped by each day. He went to bed most nights balancing on the edge of starvation and he woke most mornings weakened by the cold.

Mrs. Hanovich came out from behind the desk and moved towards Lev and the girl. When she saw the girl's face she hissed and cringed away. "Looks nasty, Lev. I'd put her back outside and pretend I never saw her."

As if in response to her bluntness, Lev held the girl a little tighter, his defences rising. "I can't do that," he said, and he knew it was true. He was so relieved he almost cried – he was not a bad person, he *could* do the right thing. He saw his mother smile and felt he'd been redeemed ever so slightly.

Mrs. Hanovich shrugged her shoulders and said, "You're nursing a bird that's fallen from its nest. Don't be surprised when it dies."

Lev took the girl upstairs and placed her carefully onto his bed. He wasn't quite sure what to do next as she lay bleeding onto his pillow. He put her knife on the set of drawers beside the bed.

Eventually, the doctor arrived, removed what remained of her eye, did his best to clean and bandage the wound, and drained what little money Lev had managed to save.

He let her sleep in his room for five days while he slept on the small sofa in the reception room downstairs. He didn't mind it. With the fire blazing in the hearth and the thick curtains hanging from the windows, the reception was warmer than his bedroom.

Lev had been working a shift in the pub across the street when the girl finally emerged from the bedroom.

There was always a lull in the late afternoon after the workers on their lunch breaks had wandered back down to the docks but before they finished for the day and came to drink away the blistering cold.

Hearing the door open and slam in the almost deserted room, Lev turned towards it and saw the girl with an eye patch secured on her face. She must have found the bathroom and washed because her hair was hanging in wet clumps and was no longer stained red. She didn't look quite so terrified standing there in the dim light; something angry had settled across her features. The old cloak he'd thrown over his bed to use as a blanket was draped over her shoulders. She looked more like a phantom than a girl.

Lev smiled at her. She frowned at him.

Dropping his empty tray onto the bar, he moved towards her. She didn't flinch, but she crossed her arms over her chest defensively. She still looked sickly, her skin too tight, her knuckles bulging out of her flesh, but she didn't look on the brink of death anymore. He wasn't sure he'd seen or heard her move at all since he'd taken her in.

"Do you want something to eat?" he asked. He almost touched her arm but caught himself. He didn't want to scare her.

She looked at him blankly before she nodded and took a seat in a booth at the back of the room. She seemed to be drawn to the shadows.

Lev made his way to the kitchen where he scavenged for food. He stole scraps, small chunks of bread and cheese that would go unnoticed. He put them on a plate and took them back out to her. When he placed the small feast in front of her, she looked up at him. Something flickered across her face and pursed her lips.

She slid some money across the table.

"Oh," Lev said, pushing it back towards her. He was surprised she had any money at all. "You don't need to pay me. It's on the house."

The girl pushed the money towards him again. "It's your money."

"Really," he insisted. "You don't have to."

She settled him with a hard glare. "Listen to what I'm saying, idiot. You need a better hiding place. The top drawer of your dresser is too obvious."

Lev gaped at her. She'd taken his money. It didn't amount to much after he'd paid for the doctor and somehow scraped the bill for his father's care, but it was his. At first, he was irritated but he knew desperation and she was desperate. "Oh," Lev conceded, taking the cash and tucking it into his apron pocket.

He watched her eat the bread and cheese and drink the water he'd put beside the plate. She picked at the food as though she'd gone without it for so long, she couldn't remember what to do with it. She said nothing to him as she filled her empty stomach and sipped her drink. When she was done, she stood without ceremony and left the pub, leaving Lev with an empty plate and a memory of her he wasn't sure was real.

That night, he'd been heading back to his room when he stopped short in the corridor. She was there again, locking the door beside his, a satchel thrown over her shoulder. She no longer wore the eyepatch. Instead, a glass eye shone a darker shade of brown.

"What are you doing here?" he asked.

She shrugged. "There was a vacancy."

As far as Lev knew, his neighbour Ori had never shown any intention of leaving. Though he rarely saw the man, he was sure he was comfortable in the boarding house and was unlikely to have fallen into some unexpected fortune.

"I'm Vera," she said, holding her hand out. There was blood crusted under her nails.

Taking her bony hand, he replied, "Lev."

Vera had been existing alongside him ever since.

Now, from somewhere outside of his hazy exhaustion, he heard his own name echo.

"Lev." It was the same voice, though this time he recognised it. "Are you awake?" Vera asked, her voice low.

Lev muttered, "I am now. Are you alright?"

She hissed a sharp laugh. "Am *I* alright?"

He forced his eyes open to see Vera leaning over him, her long hair tickling his face. She glowed in the sun, the orange and yellow beams of light softening her edges, casting shadows over her skin. He was sure he wasn't imagining the press of her hand in his or the warmth radiating from the bed beside him.

"I need to go," she whispered, her face so close to his he could feel her breath on his skin.

"Where?"

Vera hesitated. "I need to figure something out."

"Will you come back?"

"As soon as I can."

He nodded. There was a pause – he fought to keep his eyes

open, and she didn't move. He committed her to memory, tracing the sharp edges of her cheeks, the bruise across her now slightly crooked nose, the soft fall of her white-blonde hair. He watched her swallow as she leaned closer. Then she pressed a kiss against his mouth. He thought he must be dreaming, but when she pulled away, he was sure the sudden cold left in her wake was real, that she was real, the kiss was real. She squeezed his hand once before she dropped it. She was slowly carving out his heart with a serrated knife. He let her.

The mattress shifted as she climbed off the bed. Shadows flickered across his vision as she cut through the room. He wanted to be stronger, and he wanted to stay awake. He wanted to tell her to stay with him in that room beneath the sun, to lay back down and sleep beside him for one more hour. But Lev was exhausted, and he knew deep down no amount of pleading would make her stay. She was nothing if not stubborn and she would do exactly what she'd set out to do.

Locking away the memory of her kiss, he fell back into a fitful sleep and let her go.

32

SOFIYA

A terrifying hush had fallen over the city. It was the kind of quiet that settled in your bones and made your heart race.

Sofiya had swung by the boarding house but there was no sign of Aleks. She'd even attempted a brief conversation with Mrs Hanovich, but the woman had only grunted at her in return and claimed she'd never heard of him. Now, the streets between the train station and the palace were deserted with no sign of the disastrous ball that had taken place the night before. Usually at that time of day, as the winter sun was starting to set, the streets of Gambit Square were bustling with evening shoppers and couples on their way out for dinner by the water's edge. Now, it was silent.

Sofiya always loved Gambit Square, but it was even more beautiful in the afternoon light, the orange glow echoing across the pale stones and reflecting off the gilded buildings. She wanted to walk the main streets to see the stalls of brightly coloured flowers and pastries, but she knew they would not be there. The ball had scared the citizens of Gambit Square into hiding. After all, the palace ballroom was supposed to be a safe space where troubles could be forgotten. Money was supposed to keep the demons at bay; Sofiya had invited them into the room and let them loose. She'd caused the chaos.

Traipsing around the city in her torn ball gown, Sofiya should have felt ashamed. She didn't. Her mind was consumed by her determination. She needed to speak with her mother. She needed to get a grasp on the situation and take her next steps.

Inevitably, her mind wandered back to her band of thieves holed up in Anya's home. Lev wounded, Vera refusing to leave his side, and Anya trying to keep them all together. She wasn't sure where Aleks was, but she wanted to know. He was a valuable member of their team and, whilst she wanted to keep their circle small, she had to admit that they needed him.

Her mind led her back to the sight of Anya, the relentless anger that had dominated her features as she'd curled her fingers. She heard Kirill's cry of pain. She saw the satisfaction flood Anya's body, and something spark to life as her mouth spread into a grim smile. Though they had been raised in different worlds, she and Anya weren't so different.

Sofiya wasn't sure of much, but she was sure Anya was a threat. She was terrified of what she saw when she looked at the girl; when she looked at Anya, Sofiya saw her own fury reflected back like light hitting the water's surface. Perhaps that was what drew Sofiya to her. She tried not to think about that moment in the corridor. She'd been so close to Anya. She had felt the warmth of her soft sigh on her skin.

As she drew nearer to the palace, the guards grew more vigilant. They'd always been stricter around that part of the city. After her father's death, Sofiya had attended the meeting that saw her mother post guards on the outskirts of the palace. She'd sat straight in her chair and nodded solemnly as they'd grieved her father and insisted that more protection of the beloved royal family be put in place. There had been another vial of poison in her pocket, and she still hadn't returned the book to the library. They'd been scared of the monsters crawling around Ivenko's Cauldron; they didn't know it was Sofiya who had the King's blood on her hands.

Sofiya stepped out of the shadows of the side street and into the broad light of the strip leading up to the palace.

"You!" a guard called, raising his sword.

A pistol clicked as another guard shouted, "Stop!"

Someone grabbed Sofiya's arm and locked it behind her back. She was unarmed but that didn't stop them. Sofiya whirled around as best as she could with her arm trapped and faced the two guards. The one holding her let go immediately and they both fell into pathetic bows at Sofiya's feet.

As one of the guards rose and let his gun fall to his side, the second muttered, "Princess."

"Yes," Sofiya said sternly. "*Princess*. Touch me again and I will have you executed."

"My most sincere apologies," the man with the sword said.

Sofiya was sure his apology was anything but sincere. She was the heir and yet they did not deem her fit for politics. They did not know what she was plotting. They didn't know that Queen Ruslana, who they believed to be fit for rule, was a crumbling mockery of leadership. Sofiya did not need their sincerity. She did not want it.

Sofiya righted her posture and mustered up her most authoritative voice. "What's going on soldier?" She cast a glance at the thick crowds of guards.

One of the guards cleared his throat. "A member of the court has gone missing. We are looking for him."

"Who?" Sofiya queried as though she hadn't bashed him over the head with a lamp and stuffed him into a carriage not twenty-four hours ago.

When they did not reply, she pressed, "*Who?*"

"I am not at liberty to tell you."

"One day, I will be your queen and you will be at my mercy. Think about that for a moment, won't you?" She didn't like abusing her power to get her answers and one day she hoped people would respect her enough to answer immediately, but for now she would do what she must.

"Grigory Petrolovich."

Sofiya pretended to consider what the guards had told her. "Let me know once he is safely returned." She marched onward to the palace, stopping briefly to nod at the men outside the palace gates. They let her pass with no question and once she was out of their sight and safely on palace grounds, she broke into a run. She needed to speak with her mother, but first, she needed to make herself presentable.

She managed to get to her rooms unseen and when she turned to the mirror, she looked wrecked. Her hair had long since fallen out of its elegant updo and her dress, which had once shone gold, looked dull against her tired skin. She could not change her dress without the help of a maid, so she settled for straightening it and retying the sash to hide the worst of Lev's blood. She scrubbed the blood from beneath her nails and pulled on some gloves to cover the bruises on her arms from her battle with Grigory.

She examined her work in the mirror. She still looked worn and weathered but she hoped she looked like she had consumed too much alcohol and not like she had been dragging two bodies across the city. She wished she had a chance to nap before her confrontation with her mother, but she had to make do with splashing some cold water on her face and faking a smile.

Taking a deep breath, Sofiya straightened her shoulders and emerged from her rooms. Her trip through the palace was smooth. With a few strategic sharp turns, she managed to avoid the workers scuttling around the palace readying it for dinner and when she arrived at her mother's room, the guards let her in with no fuss.

Fools, she thought. *I'm the monster.*

Her mother did not miss a beat. "Did you have a good night?"

Sofiya tried to calculate how much her mother knew. She was never sure if Ruslana truly was absent from politics or whether it was a facade. She played along with the charade.

"Yes, it was lovely," she said with a smile before adding, "until it wasn't, of course." *Because I stole a man and I've been spending a little too much time with some of the most unsavoury char-*

acters this city has to offer. "I heard about Grigory. We will do all we can to get him back. He's a very valuable member of the court."

Ruslana cleared her throat. "He will be sorely missed until his return."

Give me something, Sofiya thought. *What do you know?* Her mother must have known of Grigory's betrayal. For all her faults, of which she had many, she was neither stupid nor naive.

Ruslana gave nothing away. She was sitting at her vanity, her hair freshly pinned, her face freshly painted. She raised an eyebrow at Sofiya in the mirror and she felt like a child again crushed beneath the weight of her mother's stare. "You didn't spend the night here."

Sofiya met her mother's eyes. "No, I didn't." Was her exhaustion that obvious?

"Where were you?"

"I spent the night with Stanislav." Stas' full name felt strange on her tongue, but she knew to Ruslana she should not refer to him so familiarly. "When the… commotion erupted, I left with him. That's what you wanted, wasn't it?"

Her mother said nothing for a moment. Satisfaction sat heavily in Sofiya's chest. That *was* what her mother had wanted a long time ago, before things had started to fall apart. She'd wanted Sofiya to marry Stas and have an heir. She just hadn't been sure as to why Ruslana was pushing it so hard.

Sofiya had to admit it was a fine solution to the issue of marriage and heirs. She'd be happy enough with Stas. They would be committed to each other as friends, companions, colleagues running a country together, but not as husband and wife.

Her mother lifted her chin stubbornly. "Good. I'm glad you're taking my advice."

Sofiya smiled. "Always."

"Where did you stay?" Ruslana asked sharply.

Sofiya needed to shut the conversation down. "His flat in Gambit Square. Would you like to know what we did, too? I can go into detail." Sofiya knew that kind of talk made Ruslana uncomfortable. "He's very good with his hands–"

"That's enough, Sofiya," her mother snapped, her cheeks turning a shade of pink so vivid it was visible even beneath her layers of powder. "And where is he now?"

"Obtaining a ring I hope," Sofiya said. She could practically see Stas lounging on one of Anya's kitchen chairs watching over the unconscious body of Grigory.

"There was another incident also," Ruslana began.

Sofiya's stomach dropped, and her entire body went cold.

Her mother looked exhausted when she said, "Kirill Katovich was found last night with his throat slit."

The image reappeared. Anya, her fingers curled, her gaze fierce and steady as the red threads tangled around Kirill's pain-stricken body and brought him to his knees.

"What happened?" Sofiya asked carefully.

Ruslana shook her head. "We aren't sure yet. We have increased security, and we will find out who killed him. You do not need to be afraid."

I know who killed him, you fool, Sofiya thought bitterly. And another thought followed, one which surprised her. *I am not afraid.*

"You are not stupid, Sofiya." That was about as close to a compliment as her mother was able to give. "Our position is fragile."

She wanted to ask her mother just why *she* thought that was. They had a pretence of perfection, as though they truly believed they were safe up in their palace as the country rotted beneath them. She'd never heard her mother admit to their weakness before. Of course, Sofiya knew why. Their country hated them, they were sure to revolt, there was an entire community of powerful magicians fuelled by anger and resentment, and the royal family ignored it all. She knew better than to say any of it, but she thought it nonetheless.

"You are not to do anything reckless," she said. "You will stay in the palace until the creases have been ironed out."

It clicked then. Ruslana was scared. She had not felt that vulnerable since the death of Mikhail and there it was, all that fear bubbling back up to the surface. Someone had broken into the palace and abducted one of her closest confidants and she was powerless to stop it.

She got a great amount of satisfaction knowing that her mother was warding herself against a danger that was now to be locked up in the palace.

Sofiya knew better than to argue with the Queen. "Of course." She smiled at her mother who settled her with a dull stare. "I need to bathe," Sofiya said by way of excusing herself.

Ruslana nodded once and Sofiya left her room. In the corridor, she maintained her composure with difficulty, but she could not let her guard down when there were soldiers and maids patrolling every inch of the palace. They were her mother's eyes, and they would feed back every bit of Sofiya's reaction to their queen. It wasn't until she was safely in the confines of her bedroom that she let herself fall apart.

She racked her brain to recount all the things her mother did and didn't know. She knew there was a secret that had been stolen; she didn't know Sofiya was trying to get it back. She also didn't know just what Sofiya was plotting and how she intended to become queen.

Sofiya threw open the glass doors leading to her balcony. In her teenage years, she had spent her time sneaking out of this room and into the garden below. Though it had been a while since she'd made that descent, she hadn't forgotten how. Clinging to the balcony railing, she hoisted herself over the bannister and began to lower herself down the wall. She jammed her feet and hands into the crevices of the stone wall as she descended into the garden.

She didn't want to sit in her rooms and wait for the storm to pass. She couldn't sit stationary and let it all resolve itself. She needed to finish what she'd started.

33

Vera

Vera had stolen a dress from Anya's wardrobe. It was too big on her, and she had to cinch the bodice in as tight as it would go. The hem dragged along the floor and had already soaked up a bucket's worth of rainwater as she traipsed through the city, venturing further into the Cauldron. She had Lev's old cloak thrown around her shoulders. She'd intended to replace it all those years ago, but she'd never had the spare money. Eventually the fabric had softened to her narrow shoulders, and it had become too comfortable to part with.

She'd only spent two days away from Ivenko's Cauldron, but it already felt unfamiliar to her. It was as though the edges had shifted and were now almost unrecognisable. Vera knew the city moved quickly, it shifted and changed as gangs fought and prosperous families fell, but she hadn't expected the change to be quite so drastic. She wanted to go to Vor, but she could help but wonder what Ytavosk would look like if she ever came back. Would it welcome her, or would she have to carve herself a new space?

She was burdened by a more pressing fear. Would Lev remember her, or would his feelings shift like the city?

She couldn't help but recall the warmth of him when she'd woken at his side with her cheek resting against his shoulder and his hand still clasped in hers. She'd watched him for a long moment, remembering the curve of his jaw and the exact fall of his lashes against his skin. She wouldn't forget the press of her lips against his, his short exhale of breath, the faint flutter of a moth's wings in her stomach. She wasn't sure what that feeling was, and she didn't know what had made her do it – perhaps the thought that he wouldn't remember or the fear she'd felt when she thought she'd lost him.

She pressed her eyes shut and allowed herself one more moment of quiet before she committed to facing the other pressing matter.

She needed to find Aleks.

Aleks lived in the worst part of the Cauldron amongst the dead and dying. As you ventured through the winding streets, the walls grew narrower and if you didn't move fast enough the diseased residents would reach out and grab clothing and limbs like branches snagging threads. Even Vera didn't venture that deeply into the Cauldron. She had never been sure as to why Aleks lived there, but she understood now. He was hiding; no one expected a prince to be rotting away in the gutters of the city he was supposed to rule.

She wasn't sure what to make of the answers she'd gotten.

Vera drew to a stop outside the ramshackle building Aleks called a home. She almost laughed at how absurd it was that the boy who had eaten with hand-polished cutlery in the fine palace dining room was now living in a building that looked to be one gust of wind away from collapse. Did he want to go back after they'd exiled him? She couldn't help but wonder if he dreamed of his life in the palace as he lay freezing beneath a threadbare blanket. Aleks' family had been cruel to him, but a winter in the city could be just as brutal. Had she ever experienced it, Vera didn't think she could ever give up that kind of comfortable wealth.

Thumping her fist hard against the door, she shouted, "Aleks!" She knew she should be more stealthy about it – Lev would have scaled the building, climbed through the window and ambushed Aleks and Anya would have charmed him into complacecy – but she was tired and she wanted an explanation. When Aleks didn't answer, she hit out again, this time kicking the door in tandem with her hands. "Open the fucking door!" The little patience she had was fraying.

There was a scuffle from within like the sound of a bucket being kicked across the floor. Vera threw her weight against the door and the ache of her relocated shoulder ricocheted through her body. The door was surprisingly sturdy for something that was rotting and looked like it had woodworm. She heard more crashes from within and she kicked the door as hard as she could. It gave way and Vera stumbled through the open doorway, catching herself on the small three-legged table beside the door.

The house fell silent. She adjusted the too-long skirts of her dress, pulled the hem out from under her feet and called, "Let's talk, Aleks." Her voice echoed through the house.

Overhead, the floorboards creaked. Vera made for the stairs, her pace slow and steady as she listened for signs of him. She wasn't surprised that he'd come back here; she knew what it was like to have nowhere else to go and it was easy to feel safe in the most dangerous places. As she reached the bottom step, she prepared herself for the fight. She slipped a blade out from her sleeve, feeling the cold steel against the inside of her wrist. She ascended the stairs cautiously. She knew he was here somewhere, and he was hiding from her; she had enough information to get him killed and he didn't know she'd kept it to herself.

Vera stepped out onto the upstairs landing. She'd been readying herself for Aleks' attack but when it came it still knocked the air from her lungs. Aleks threw himself against her, knocking her to the ground and slamming her head against the bannister. She swiped out with her knife, catching his cheek before he pinned her hands either side of her head. Vera kicked up with her knee and slammed it into his abdomen and when he didn't waver, she turned her face to the side and sunk her teeth into his forearm.

Instinctively, Aleks let her go to wrap his hand around the two rows of teeth marks now pulsing an angry red on his skin. "Are you fucking feral?" he shouted, startled, his brows scrunching together in pain.

Vera took the opportunity to shove herself to her feet and grab her blade from where it had skittered across the floor.

"Why? Because I wasn't raised in a palace?" she hissed, sending a swift kick to Aleks' side for good measure.

From where he was crouched on his knees, Aleks looked up at her then and the image he'd been portraying to them all those years fell away. He'd been quiet, like a storm on the horizon, a dark and angry mist that made no sound and caused no real harm. But now that storm had reached them and there he stood on the shoreline with fury in his eyes.

Now she had reason to draw lines between the two, Vera could see the resemblance between Aleks and Sofiya. Though Sofiya's was a couple of shades brighter, she and Aleks had the same copper hair, the same splatter of freckles across their noses, but the similarities ran deeper than that. They held their heads with the same groomed authority.

Aleks levelled his shoulders and fixed his gaze on the shattered window at the top of the stairs. "What do you know?"

Vera flexed her fingers and echoed his words back to him. "The long-lost prince." She had a plan. Her fingers curled at her sides.

Aleks sputtered a sarcastic laugh. "I wasn't lost," he said. "I was forced to leave."

Shrugging her shoulders she replied, "Your words, Aleks. Is that even your name?" She needed to keep him talking but she needed to keep her focus too as she reached out slowly towards his mind. "I'm assuming you changed it?"

Aleks shook his head, his deep copper hair shifting like flames. "Kiska."

Vera reached out towards his mind, feeling for the gold stings that he'd kept so expertly all these years. "How did you erase yourself from the collective memory of an entire country?"

It seemed like a weight was slowly lifting off Aleks' shoulders, as though he had carried the burden of his existence alone for so long it had started to push him into the ground, but now he could share it. He didn't know that Vera was inside his mind. "I didn't. I took the memory from the people who knew me best and slowly I became little more than a fable. People are easily forgotten. Even royalty."

"You took the memory from Sofiya? Your sister?"

"Yes."

A headache was beginning at the base of Vera's skull as she focused on the theft. She flicked through the threads of Aleks' mind. She saw the little girl again, the blonde woman, all the things she'd seen the first time around, small moments from his life that he kept not-so-safely contained in the darkest crevices of his mind. And then there it was again. Aleks in the throne room, the blue spark as he erased himself from history. Vera wrapped her fingers around the thread and slowly reached for the bottle she'd put in the pocket of Anya's dress. Aleks didn't seem to register what Vera was doing – she still had the element of surprise on her side. She took a deep breath and pulled at the secret. It was like pulling a tooth.

Aleks' eyes widened then as she snatched the secret away. His hand flew to his temple. Again, her power had failed her.

She'd just put the gold thread in the bottle and replaced the stopper when Aleks launched to his feet.

"What are you doing?" he demanded, his voice low and lethal. His nostrils flared and his eyes grew wild.

"I don't care that you were the prince," Vera snapped. "I don't care about *your* life; I care about mine. I need that money." She clutched the bottle in her hands and made a break for the stairs. As she did, Aleks hooked his foot around her ankle and sent her tumbling down. She felt the impact of each crooked step and landed with a thump at the bottom, knocking over a coat rack. Aleks was on top of her in a moment. She reached for her blade and lurched at him, swiping aimlessly at his face.

"You don't care, Vera?" he sneered. "Would you care if you had a rope around your neck?"

Vera said nothing as he pinned her to the floor once more. This time he held her hands away from her body and kept his own limbs far enough away that she couldn't bite him again.

Aleks leaned closer to her, his mouth grimacing as he said, "You think you're above it, but you'll get caught. This is your problem too."

Vera shook her hair out of her face as best as she could and met Aleks' eyes. "I'll get my money and then I'll be gone. I'm not tied to them like you are."

"They'll wonder how my dear sister got that secret back," he said. "We could be of use to them if they let us. We're powerful. We're *useful.* But they have to pretend that we are monsters in need of extermination. They may not remember me, but I remember them. I know them. They're terrified of people like us. Do you really think they won't start questioning Sofiya's loyalty? She will sell you out in a heartbeat and you will be strung up by morning."

"You're not above murdering me, Aleks," Vera hissed. "You're no better than they are."

"That was for a greater good." Aleks jabbed his elbow into Vera's stomach. "Give me the secret."

Vera laughed aloud then, the loud, brash noise echoing in the silence of the hallway. "Why the fuck would I do that?

You tried to kill me, and you almost killed Lev. Revenge is a sweet thing, you know."

"You should care more."

"Why? *I'm* fine. What more should I be caring about?"

Aleks face darkened. "I knew a thief of secrets. They left her bleeding on the kitchen floor. I found my daughter playing in her blood like it was rainwater."

Vera said harshly, "Poor you. You're never going to make me a defender of the people, Aleks, you may as well stop trying."

Aleks hit her around her face. She felt blood flood her mouth, sour and metallic, and the bruise that his sister had left a week before started to ache all over again. Vera spat the blood straight into his face, but he didn't reach up to wipe it. "You must want something," Aleks said, reaching up to brush his fingers over her temple.

Vera tried to shove him away, but he held her firmly against the floor. She couldn't feel the soft tug as he perused her memory. His abilities were worlds better than hers – stronger, smoother – he was everything she wanted to be and wasn't. Even through her fear, she felt the jealousy rise to the surface.

Then Aleks smiled. "You were exiled, too, Vera."

She pushed against him, trying desperately to get out of his grip, but she couldn't. She wanted to cry in frustration. "I left."

"They forced you to leave." Aleks pressed his forearm across her throat. "You wanted to go to Vor. How did you end up here?" He paused. "Ah. Well, your mother tried her best, didn't she? She paid the price for your existence."

Vera's mother had been the only person who had tried to protect her when the others all threw her to the wolves.

Some nights she still woke in a cold sweat, and she swore she could feel the bullet as it wedged itself into her mother's skull. There was truth in what Aleks was saying and Vera knew that. Her anger at the unfairness of their world burnt through her like a wildfire, an uncontrollable force, but there was nothing she could do about it. Hopelessness was worse than anger. Since her mother had told her about the city in Vor, it had consumed her every thought; if she couldn't be safe in the Isles or in Sikveya, she would find safety elsewhere. It was not up to her to change the mindset of entire populations and she wouldn't waste her life trying.

That's what Aleks wanted – he wanted to fix his nation.

"So, what's the solution, Aleks?" she jeered.

"There's only one. We get the Meskovs off the throne and get the Pravinya into power. They'll change things. I've seen their manifesto. They can change things for people like us."

Vera laughed then, though the sound was strained as Aleks' arm tightened on her neck. "They won't. We're a threat. You can't change everything just because the power has shifted."

"You won't change anything if you don't try," Aleks said, his voice growing desperate, snapping like twigs underfoot. "*Please*. Give me the secret."

His arm relaxed for a moment and Vera took the opportunity to shove Aleks off her. The second she was free, she scuttled away from him, as far as she could get. She pressed her back to the wall and held her knife out.

She needed a minute to think. She understood the desperation. She understood his desire to be free, but she wanted no part in the war he was waging. "If you want to fight your family, Aleks, on your head be it. I don't want to be a part of it."

"You want to go to Vor." It wasn't a question. He'd seen the memory of her mother's promises in her head. "I'll give you the money to go. You give me the secret and I will get you to Vor." There was something manic in his face, widening his eyes and tightening his mouth.

She'd been wanting to hear those words since she'd woken in Lev's bed with a missing eye and an ache set so deeply in her she could taste it. She'd been fighting the city for almost seven years, and she hadn't moved at all. The money she'd get from Sofiya would be a big step forward, but it wouldn't be enough to make the trip and live comfortably once she'd got there.

Inevitably, she thought about Lev. She'd finally have to snap the fraying tie that connected them. If she left, she knew the chances of her seeing him again were slim; she wouldn't come back to that soot-stained city and though she didn't know what, something was keeping him in Ytavosk.

She squeezed her eyes shut and her mother stared back at her.

"I'll make sure you're safe, Valerie," Agathe had whispered to her. "Or I will die trying. You just have to hide a little longer."

Vera tried to harden herself to the cruel reality of their world, but all she wanted was sanctuary, somewhere she could train, for her heart to stop feeling so heavy. She wanted to be stronger. She *would* be stronger. If she didn't go now, she would spend her whole life wishing she had. Lev could give her comfort, he could give her warmth, but he couldn't ever give her safety and she would only bring darkness to his life.

Squeezing the glass bottle tightly once, she opened her palm. Aleks didn't hesitate. He snatched up the bottle as it glowed a bright gold. Vera watched car fully as he stood and marched into the kitchen. He dug around in the cupboards for a moment and when he came back, he held out a ball of cash to her.

In a low, dangerous voice, he said, "If you ever come back to Sikveya, I will kill you. You go to Vor, and you stay there, understand?"

"I don't fear death, Aleks, and I don't fear you."

"You will not come back here."

"I won't," Vera promised, and the relief that flooded her stomach and washed away all the guilt that had been building there told her one thing: her promise was true.

Vera adjusted the strings of her cloak. She held out her hand to Aleks. He caught her hand and shook it once before letting it go.

She knew she'd betrayed the others, that they needed her to complete the job. She hated how easy it had been for her to make that decision and that nothing had managed to outweigh the prospect of Vor.

With a deep breath, Vera left.

34

Anya

Anya pressed her spine against the kitchen counter and drew her knees up to her chest. She focused on the cold cabinet seeping through the thin cotton of her shirt and the feel of the hard tiles against her feet. She could ground herself if she just tried hard enough, she could focus on solid things and bring herself back from whatever hell she'd been thrown into. She pressed her hands against her eyes, digging her knuckles into the sockets. She gasped for breath.

It's alright, she told herself, but again the other voice was louder, and she had no control over it. *They're going to kill you, Daria will be out on the streets, she'll be dead within a week and then what was it all for?*

What was it all for? It was a question she found herself asking each day when she woke to Daria with blood crusted on her chin, to frozen water pipes, to that same feeling of bitterness she couldn't seem to escape. What was it all for? She survived just to keep surviving in a world that never seemed to get any better. She'd finally wrapped her hands around an opportunity to make a difference and she was in it for the money and a doctor, for her own selfish reasons.

She'd revealed her power, she'd murdered a member of the royal court, and had been caught by the Princess of Sikveya. She wouldn't be surviving much longer.

Her chest was too tight, and her head was aching. She needed air but each time she tried to breathe, something lodged in her throat like a stone, and she felt it rattling, refusing to let any air in. *I'm going to die*, she thought. *This is it. I'm going to die.* She let out a choked sob, careful to muffle it with the back of her hand. She could at least die quietly.

Perhaps I'll see my mother again, she thought nonsensically – wasn't that what she'd wished for all those years ago in the small hours as she'd comforted her sister? She'd wanted so badly for them both to fall into an endless sleep. She didn't wish that anymore, but she couldn't seem to tell her body that and it was insistent on dragging her into a miserable death.

"Anya?"

Anya squeezed her eyes shut and pressed her hands to her stomach. "Go away," she gasped. Her heart was racing, her whole body was shivering, and there were blackspots growing across her vision like a plague.

She heard hesitant feet scuff the tiles. Then someone sat beside her, far enough away that she didn't feel trapped but close enough that she knew they were there. She just about managed to open her eyes to see Lev sitting beside her. He was shirtless and had one hand pressed against the bloody bandage on his stomach and the other clinging to the cabinet as he lowered himself carefully to the floor.

A sob broke out from within her chest, loud, untamed. He reached out to her and squeezed her knee softly. "Breath in time with me," he said calmly, exaggerating each breath.

Anya watched him for a moment, her eyes filled with tears, her chest still unbearably tight. "I can't," she choked. "I'm going to die." She couldn't quite seem to articulate the feeling, but it felt like death; from the outside, Lev must have thought her mad.

He helped her sit up as he shook his head and took her hand in his. "You're not going to die." He took another deep breath. "Copy me."

She tried to mimic him, watching the rise and fall of his bare chest and the soft movement of his shoulders with each inhale and exhale.

"You've got it," he assured her. "Close your eyes. Focus on all the good things in your life."

There weren't many good things in Anya's life. The good things were the ones that gave her the most anxiety – she couldn't bear to lose them – but she did as he instructed, closing her eyes and visualising all the things she loved most: Daria smiling after she'd done something mischievous, her mother, the space she'd carved out for them back in Moskarisk, how she'd felt when Kirill was brought to his knees. Lev was there and she was so grateful for his friendship. Vera and Aleks appeared too, standing in the corners of her mind. She was surprised when the memory of Sofiya's hands on her hips resurfaced. She finally managed to fill her lungs with air though her head hurt profusely, and her hands were still struck with a tremor.

"See," Lev said. "You're not going to die. We're alright."

She squeezed Lev's hand once, but she couldn't bring herself to face him. Instead, she fixed her gaze on the kitchen window, still gasping for breath. The sun had gone down and the only light coming through the grimy glass came from the ships sailing up and down the river. She watched each beam force its way through the soot and cast light across the kitchen tiles.

"Thank you," Anya whispered.

"You're the most sane of all of us," Lev said. "We have to keep you."

"I'm not sane," Anya said, unable to keep back the tide of tears that had been threatening her since they'd begun this mess. The dam burst and Lev awkwardly pulled her into his side.

Lev was right – the group had descended into complete madness. Sofiya was flustered, Lev was the human embodiment of chaos, something had snapped inside Vera, Aleks was missing, and Stas, whoever he was, didn't seem at all alarmed by any of it. Anya had just killed a person. A person she had been stalking for the better part of eight years. And the worst part was that, while she'd felt guilty about a lot of the things she'd done during that time, stalking him and plotting his murder was not one of them. What did that make her? She was a monster, she was a criminal, she was just so *desperate*.

She'd have laughed had her heart not been beating quite so aggressively. Anya wiped her eyes. *Right,* she told herself firmly. *You've cried about it now. Get up and keep going.* She took a steadying breath. She had a fight to win and a sister to keep alive. It was strange how she always found clarity in her most jagged moments.

She closed her eyes and heard Lilja's voice. *Three deep breaths.* Three deep breaths made the world seem a lot less dire.

She turned to Lev. "You won't tell anyone, will you?" She didn't want them to know that she was falling apart.

Lev seemed to consider this for a moment. "It's not something to be ashamed of."

She nodded. She did know that, but she wasn't sure she believed it. She felt that shame like it was its own entity hanging heavily around her neck. "I know. But…" Anya trailed off.

"I won't tell anyone," Lev assured her, squeezing her hand lightly.

Not for the first time, Anya considered how odd Lev and Vera's relationship was; she was the thief of secrets, and he was the keeper of them.

Anya pulled herself to her feet and straightened out her shirt, tucking it into the waistband of her trousers. She nodded to herself, steeling her nerves. She looked down at Lev.

"You're going to have to help me up, Anya," he said with a soft, pained laugh. "I think I've pulled some stitches."

Anya reached down and hooked him under one arm. Using the counter, she managed to get him standing and Anya nodded at the bloody bandages. Her heart was still racing, and her head still felt fuzzy, but the thought of having something to do grounded her. "Come on," Anya said. "I'll help you change them."

35

Sofiya

Sofiya's feet hurt.

She'd escaped the palace through the gardens and walked from the grounds, through Gambit Square, and all the way to the Cauldron. It was no minor trek, and the balls of her feet were starting to blister in the gold heels she hadn't thought to change. The ballgown weighed her down and though she'd long since let her hair down, her scalp was starting to itch as sweat beaded on her skin.

Shifting the basket of pastries she'd stolen from the palace kitchen on her way out, Sofiya picked up her pace. She was tracing the edge of the river on her way back to Anya's home and there were already dockworkers beginning their shifts in the early morning light. She wasn't sure where the time had gone. When she'd arrived at the palace it had been the evening and now it must have gone well past midnight. If they intended on returning Grigory, they needed to start interrogating him; he'd been kept unconscious for a whole day.

Eventually she drew to a stop at Anya's door. She knocked her elbow against the wood and heard the snapping of multiple keys and bolts. The door swung open and Stas let her in. He had gotten rid of the carriage.

Inside the flat, she saw Anya sitting at the crooked dining table, one leg propped up on the chair beside her as she dropped a bloodied rag into a pail. Lev sat on the other side of Anya, a fresh bandage covering his waist.

"You're supposed to be resting," Sofiya said sternly and in that moment, she felt like one of her childhood governesses with their hair scraped back and permanent frown lines buried in their skin. "You've moved."

Lev smiled at her, stood, and stretched out his slender limbs. "People do tend to do that," he said. "You know, *move*. I don't know what happened. One minute I was lying there in absolute agony and the next I was compelled by an invisible hand to stand and dance–"

"I'm glad to see you're better," Sofiya said, waving him off. She put the basket of pastries on the table.

"Is that because you care about your band of street rats, Princess?" Lev grinned at her.

Sofiya ignored his attempt at humour. "No. I'm just glad you didn't die at my party. My family would have had *more* blood on their ballroom floor. They already have enough of that, don't they, Anya?" she said sharply. She handed Lev and Anya pastries.

Lev smelt the pastry and laughed softly under his breath. "This is fancy."

"You keep rich company," Stas said, pulling out a chair beside Lev and taking a pastry from the basket.

"We're dining like kings and queens."

Stas snorted. "More like princes and princesses."

Lev took a bite of his pastry and turned back to Sofiya. "I feel like I've missed something."

Sofiya crossed her arms over her chest. She was still reeling. "Only a bit of casual murder."

Of all the things she thought Lev would do, shrugging flippantly wasn't one of them. "Well," he said. "Anya's sensible. I'm sure she had her reasons."

Sofiya snapped, "Oh, that's okay then." She turned to Anya, who was barely picking at the golden pastry in her hands. "Do you not understand the gravity of killing a member of the court? You're a *murderer*."

Really, she didn't have much of a right to her anger. After all, she had killed the King. That was considerably worse than a family friend – she had committed outright treason. The point was that at least Sofiya had been subtle about it. Perhaps it wasn't just about the murder; perhaps she was angry at her direct disregard of the plan or the fact they'd all left her to deal with Grigory alone. Or perhaps it was the thought of the power that coursed through the other girl's veins.

"What, and you're not?" Anya spat.

Sofiya took a deep, steadying breath. Surely Anya didn't know just what Sofiya had done all those years ago? She guessed it was a possibility that Vera had gone through her mind, dug around until she found Sofiya's darkest secrets and had planned to use them as collateral.

"You sit up there in your palace, and you let us rot," Anya said, standing from her chair so sharply that the legs ground loudly against the floor. As she rose, Sofiya could see the Anya that had killed Kirill. There was something dangerous in her face, untamed. "We can't afford food, we're freezing, we're dying in the streets while you piss money on a party your guests won't even remember in the morning. My sister is dying, and no one is helping us. You would be celebrated if you executed Aleks, Vera, and me. You're a murderer, too, *Princess*. At least I had a motive." She pressed her hands to her chest like she was choking.

Lev's gaze flickered between them. "I have definitely missed something."

Sofiya transitioned her posture into a fighter's stance. "I'm trying to–"

"You're not *trying* to do anything," Anya scoffed, cutting her off. "You sit up there crying in your tower and you do *nothing*. You have power and you don't use it."

Sofiya's fury rose in her like a beast thrashing against her vital organs. She felt it, a tangible thing, and she wondered whether Anya would feel it too if she reached out. She didn't understand the boundaries of Anya's power and perhaps the other girl didn't either. Could she take her anger? Would Sofiya know? "You think I can go into that room and just demand things?"

She had tried that. Before she had ever learned to have tact, she had gone into that room with a list of demands. She had been so sure they would listen to their heir, their soon-to-be queen, but they hadn't. Soon she'd learned to play their game, to listen to them and coddle their egos, embed her ideas and pat the old men on the back when *they* put them forth. The changes she had managed to make had been few and far between – she'd managed to raise the age of factory workers in an attempt to stop child labour and keep them in school for longer, and she had managed to lift the restrictions on ships to bring in more trade – but she knew it wasn't enough. "They don't listen to me. They won't give me anything. I'm supposed to be queen but every day I move further and further away from it."

And now she'd left the palace altogether.

"They won't give you the crown," Anya said, an odd calm settling over her. "So, *take* it."

Sofiya had tried that. And she had almost been caught.

"Sorry," Lev interjected. "Can we back up a little, please? As you may or may not have noticed, I was unconscious for quite a pivotal part of this plot, and I'm lost."

"Anya can steal emotions and she killed a member of the royal court," Stas said bluntly. "In her defence, he was a vile man."

Lev nodded, though he couldn't quite keep the surprise off his face. He didn't know Anya was a thief either. Did Vera? "Thank you," he said. "I don't think we've met. I'm Lev."

"Stas." Stas shook Lev's hand.

Sofiya ignored them. Her mind was whirring. She'd left the palace. She had to find this secret and then what? Crawl back with it and hand it over? *Take it.*

Sofiya turned back to Anya. "And how do you propose I do that?" she snapped, breathing heavily. Really, she already knew how. She would go back as the Queen, or she would not go back at all. If the secret was what she thought it was, she would find it, she would bring it back and she would follow through with her plan. She would kill her mother and take the crown.

Anya didn't get a chance to respond.

They all jumped as a knock sounded at the door. Lev leapt up out of his seat and lunged for the scissors Anya had used to cut the bandages, Anya slipped a knife out of her sleeve, and Sofiya pulled out her pistol. Only Stas was without a weapon. Sofiya stepped in front of him defensively.

Another fist thumped against the door and then a voice shouted over the rain, "It's me. Let me in."

36

Lev

"*Aleks?*" Anya dropped her knife onto the table and made for the door, unbolting it quickly and letting in a rain soaked Aleks. He looked like a cat that had been pulled out of a gutter.

Glancing briefly towards Lev, Aleks took off his cloak and threw it over the back of a kitchen chair.

Anya crossed her arms over her chest like an agitated mother and said, "Where have you been?" She showed no signs that she had been in a heated argument with Sofiya only moments before.

"I've been laying low. They followed me out," Aleks replied. "Do you have water?"

Anya picked a glass off the draining board and ran the tap, waiting for a moment for the water to run clear.

Aleks accepted the glass of water and turned to Lev. “What happened to you?”

“I got stabbed,” he said, looking down at his stomach, to where a bandage was wrapped around his waist. He hadn’t put his shirt back on. “Someone threw a knife at Vera – they must know what she can do – and I… well…” Lev gestured to the wound.

“Did you see who it was?”

“No,” he admitted. All he saw was the knife heading straight towards Vera; whoever had thrown it had perfect aim. They’d been dancing – or their best imitation of dancing – and in the moment the world had fallen away, leaving just the two of them. After the gunshot, she’d gone into a trance, her hand raised mid-air, fingers curling like talons. He’d tried to make out who she was reaching towards, but he couldn’t and then the knife was cutting through the crowd. It had embedded itself in his abdomen as he’d thrown her to the floor. She’d cursed him and if he hadn’t been in so much pain and had they not been facing capture, he might have laughed. “I didn’t.”

Sofiya dusted pastry crumbs off her fingers and said, “Where’s Vera?”

“Last I saw, she was with you, Lev. Did she say where she was going?” Anya asked.

Lev could feel the heat rising to his cheeks. He *had* been the last one to see her. Vera had kissed, him and he’d been replaying that moment since he’d regained consciousness, unsure whether it had been a dream or if she really had pressed her lips softly to his. He still wasn’t sure, though he’d felt her hair tickling his skin and the warmth of her hand in his – if the memory wasn’t real then he had a worryingly vivid imagination. "She just said she had to go."

Aleks cleared his throat, his eyes shifting uncomfortably around the room. "I saw her at the boarding house. She was packing a case."

Lev's heart sank hard in his chest.

"She's leaving the city," Anya said flatly.

Sofiya frowned and swore under her breath. "She's just cut her losses and run?"

Lev knew exactly where she would be going, though he wasn't sure where she'd found the money. He still recalled the unfamiliar softness resting over her features as she'd admitted to him that she wanted to go to Vor. And she had done exactly as she'd intended. He wasn't sure why he was surprised; Vera had always been selfish, and she had never tried to be anything else. *I wouldn't sacrifice myself for you.* That was what she had said to him, and he'd believed her, and yet disappointment was simmering in the deepest crevices of his heart.

He desperately wanted to be the exception.

If they had any chance of getting the secret back, they needed Vera. They could find another thief, but they would not be able to trust them. *Well*, he thought bitterly, *Vera can't be trusted either*. She had kept her promises to herself but not the ones she'd made to the crew.

Lev had once believed that he would always love her, that she could do the most terrible things and the fire burning in his heart would not be put out. He wasn't sure that was true anymore. She'd betrayed Anya, Sofiya, and Aleks. She'd betrayed *him*.

He couldn't meet the others' eyes, though he could feel them looking at him. He swallowed the lump in his throat and pushed aside the memory of Vera from the night before. She'd kissed him because she'd known she would not stay, that she would not see him again. The likelihood of her ever coming back to the Ytavosk was slim.

Anya threw herself into a chair with a sigh. "So, what do we do now?"

Sofiya looked at her. "We wake Grigory up."

"And do what?" Stas asked. At some point he'd become a part of the operation and they had all just accepted it.

"Get some information out of him." Sofiya turned her attention to Aleks. "You can see his memories. We have Anya–"

"No," Anya said sharply. "I'm retired. I don't–"

Stas huffed a laugh. "A good bit of old-fashioned torture. Nice."

"I don't do that. I don't just *torture* people."

"Well, you do," Sofiya said, her face darkening and twisting into something dangerous. It seemed she was stepping into Vera's shoes. "Do you want your money and your doctor?"

Anya's mouth drew into a sharp line and her jaw set when she said tightly, "Yes."

"Then you use all of your resources."

"And then when we're done you can convict me of murder and going against the laws of nature." Standing from the chair, Anya drew closer to Sofiya, who also refused to back down. "You can hang me and use it as a way back into your family's good favour," she spat.

As if on cue, Daria coughed in the other room. The fit was excruciatingly long. They all stood there listening until the coughs ended and Anya moved away from Sofiya, grabbing a glass of water and a wet cloth and disappearing down the hall.

Lev looked up then and met Sofiya's gaze. "I'm sorry Vera left."

"Her actions are not your actions, Lev," Sofiya replied, her face softening in pity.

"No," he said. "I know." He had always felt the need to clean up her messes and apologise to the people she shoved out of her way.

Sofiya turned to Stas. "Wake him up."

Stas nodded once and moved towards Grigory, who was still sitting motionless in the corner of the room. At some point, someone had thrown a ragged blanket over his shoulders, though it had slipped down and was now hanging over just one arm like a cape.

Stas took a bottle that had been resting beside Grigory on the window ledge. He dumped the contents of the bottle onto a rag and held it under the older man's nose.

With a gasp, Grigory woke and said nonsensically, "Don't kill me. I'll tell you anything – just *please* don't kill me."

Stas snorted. "Well, this should be easy."

"Where am I? Don't hurt me. Where am I?" the man stuttered, blinking rapidly.

His complete lack of dignity was embarrassing to watch. Lev resisted the urge to laugh. This aristocrat was quivering before them. Lev knew he wouldn't do much damage to the man, but he supposed the others might.

Sofiya and Stas shared a quick glance and Lev remembered then that while to him Grigory Petrolovich was a stranger, to them he was a friend, a confidant. Neither of them seemed inclined to talk to the man or even to look at his wretched form. He looked completely dishevelled. His shirt was crinkled and bloodstained, his hair, or what was left of it, was sticking up at odd angles. He didn't look like he was born to nobility. He looked like a scared old man who had been stripped of all his integrity. Had Lev not been preoccupied by so many other things, he might have found it in his heart to feel sympathy for him.

Anya re-emerged then and threw a rag into the bucket she'd dropped Lev's bandages into. She joined them silently as they faced the royal advisor.

"Okay," Sofiya said, stepping forward. She took a deep breath. "Let's find out what he knows."

Epilogue

Aleks

Aleks was exhausted.

He had come so close to being found out. He was an heir in exile, he was a magician who had the power to steal a collective memory. He still remembered Vera's face when he'd offered her freedom in exchange for the secret. Now it was safely back in his possession. The rest of the crew had no idea who he really was and what he intended to do.

He looked around the now almost empty room. The pastries had been discarded on the rickety dining table and the curtains had been drawn closed over the grimy windows.

They'd questioned Grigory Petrolovich until the sun had started to rise. Watching him had been painful; he'd squirmed and fidgeted in the chair, and every other sentence out of his mouth had been *please don't kill me.* At one point he'd even cried. Anya had not used her power, though the longer the investigation went on, the more her hands seemed to fidget at her sides as though she wanted to put an end to Grigory's pathetic quivering.

Fed up with the lack of cooperation, they'd gagged him again, tightened his blindfold, and gone their separate ways. Anya had gone to tend to her sister, Sofiya and Stas had gone into Anya's bedroom, and Lev had left the house without a word.

Only Aleks had stayed.

Now, he pulled up a chair and took a seat opposite Grigory. He pulled down the man's blindfold in one swift motion and the man's eyes widened. He started to groan through the gag.

Aleks shushed him. "Shut up," he said sharply. "Shut up or I won't help you."

Grigory fell silent, though his eyes remained wide, and his brows still knotted together, creasing his forehead. His hair was falling in his face and sweat beaded on his skin.

"We want the same things, you and I," Aleks said as he took the bottle out of his pocket and balanced it on his knee. The gold thread bounced around in its glass cage, glowing softly in the darkness of the room. "We both want the Mescovs off the throne."

His plan all along had been to destroy the dynasty. He didn't care to rule; he wanted to create a better world for people like him, who had a different, more magical kind of power at their disposal. He'd tried to explain that to Vera, but the girl in all her selfishness had not wanted to listen. He wasn't surprised. He knew her well and he had seen inside her head; he'd used her worst traits to his advantage. She'd left it all behind so easily – the plan, the money, the crew – she had turned her back on all of it the second Aleks had offered her the freedom she craved.

Aleks watched as Grigory leaned forward in his chair to get a better view of the secret in its bottle like a moth drawn to a flame. He made a noise, though it was muffled by the rag slicing across his mouth, and bit down on the fabric in frustration.

"Don't try to speak," Aleks said. "Just nod. We want the same things, yes?" *To bring the Meskovs to their knees. To create a better world. To make room for magic.*

He was a highly respected member of the Pravinya and Aleks had poured over their manifesto. He'd seen countless promises to help those like Aleks and Vera. It was true – a statement on paper did not mean much, but it was a start, and it was more than the Meskovs had ever offered. Words on paper became rules to abide by, they became laws that could be enforced.

Grigory nodded once.

Aleks smiled and curled his fingers around the secret. "Then I think we can come to some kind of agreement."

Acknowledgements

This is one of the most absurd things I have ever done.

I have always wanted to get a book out into the world, but I never once thought I would actually have the courage to do it. I never thought I was smart enough or bold enough to ever attempt to write a fantasy book, let alone publish it. But here it is. The story that has been in my heart for five years. Put onto paper. *Finally*. I started properly writing this book on and off (emphasis on off) about three years ago. It was only in the summer of 2023 that I decided to take it more seriously and only in the November that I decided to actually publish it. I am so incredibly happy that I did.

For my dad: I don't even know where to start with my thank yous, so I will begin with the person who always encouraged my writing, though he didn't get the chance to see it. This book is for my dad. Though I only got sixteen years with him, I know I am so lucky to have had a dad as great as him. He is no longer here. but I can still hear his voice in the back of my head telling me that *someone* has to make it whenever I start to lose faith. The road may not always be clear cut or easy, but when I hear that voice, I know I can make it. I really fucking miss you, dad.

For my mum: I would also like to thank you, mum, firstly for donating your flared jeans to me and secondly, for being a great mum (but most importantly: the jeans). Without the power of those jeans, I would never have been able to gather the courage to shove this book out into the world. Never again will I underestimate the power of a well fitting pair of jeans. Seriously, though, mum – I love you. You have been such a strong figure in my life. You always balanced me out when I was being a bitch and you have always supported me, no matter how strange or questionable my actions have been. When dad died, you became both of my parents and nothing I ever say or do will ever be enough of a thank you.

For Will: You have been so endlessly supportive of this whole process and I am so grateful for that. Lives changed when you said on the phone 'are you busy? Come over and we can chat about this in person.' That 'chat' turned into a four hour discussion of how I should end this book. One might even say you wrote the ending. Love you, bro. Thank you.

For Joe: I feel like I should acknowledge you too but idk you didn't really do anything. Just kidding. Thank you (and will) for bullying me into becoming the person I am today. I am all the louder and stranger for it.

For myself: It might be a bit unbecoming, but I'd also like to thank myself for pushing through the self-doubt, the overwhelming sense of worthlessness, and the incessant need to apologise for the things I'm proud of – you did it!

For Jodie: This whole process gave me some (painful) uni flashbacks. Suddenly, it was 3am and I was back in the 'office', riddled with anxiety, and listening to Michelle Featherstone on repeat as Freya came to check on us and offer to make us some chicken nuggets. Thank you for all your help. I don't tell you this often, so you know I really do mean it: I love ya, mate. *Cough* beer *Cough* bro *Cough* football.

For Freya: Thank you for hyping me up. Your gentle parenting really does go a long way and I am so glad you're my friend. Thank you for all the "it'll be alright, mate" and the "cracking stuff" comments. Love you, Big F.

For Carrie: Thank you for for just getting me. There is nothing greater in life than that one person who not only supports you, but who truly understands you. You are that person. Thank you.

For Marie, Lauren, and Courtney: Thank you Marie for being my favourite mean Leo, and Lauren for being the nice one to counteract it. Courtney, as promised, my very big thank you for the 320 messages sent back and forth in an effort to pin down a book title, a pen name, and release date. I love you all so much. You guys have been so supportive of this project. Thank you for hyping me up when I needed it the most.

For Jo: You're considered to be a true legend in our family, and for good reason. Thank you for all your support over the years. I promise I'll name a character after you in book two.

And finally, thank you to everyone who has supported me throughout this process. Thank you for taking the time to read this book in all its chaos and thank you for joining me on this journey. For every reader, for every message on social media, and for every kind word or bit of encouragement – thank you. I can never tell you how much it means to me.

About the Author

Elizabeth Rose Archer was born and raised in Hampshire, United Kingdom, where she lives with her family and her beloved dog, Bo. Fostering her passion for all things literary, she graduated from Cardiff University in 2022 with a degree in English Literature. Though she spends her time trying new hobbies, her affinity for fiction has stayed with her. Since graduating, she has funnelled her love for magic and morally grey characters into her debut fantasy novel Twisted Thieves.

Instagram: @whenelizabethreads
TikTok: Elizabethrosearcher
www.elizabethrosearcher.com

Printed in Great Britain
by Amazon

37504175R00212